MAIDEN OF HONOR
A Maiden Harlow Mystery – Book 4
Camille Sharp

CONTENTS

1. Chapter 1 — 1

2. Chapter 2 — 17

3. Chapter 3 — 29

4. Chapter 4 — 43

5. Chapter 5 — 56

6. Chapter 6 — 70

7. Chapter 7 — 80

8. Chapter 8 — 96

9. Chapter 9 — 113

10. Chapter 10 — 119

11. Chapter 11 — 135

12. Chapter 12 — 153

13. Chapter 13 — 160

14. Chapter 14 — 177

15. Chapter 15 — 193

16. Chapter 16 — 203

17. Chapter 17 — 217

18. Chapter 18 — 232

19. Chapter 19   244

20. Chapter 20   255

21. Chapter 21   266

22. Chapter 22   280

23. Chapter 23   290

24. Chapter 24   313

25. Chapter 25   325

26. Chapter 26   339

27. Chapter 27   356

28. Chapter 28   366

Join the fun!   370

Thank You!   371

Also by Camille Sharp   372

About Camille Sharp   373

CHAPTER ONE

"I can't believe the weddin' is almost here!" Bella twittered happily. "It's like a dream!"

Maiden Harlow smiled at her aunt's enthusiasm. Despite having been down the aisle several times already, Bella was still approaching her latest marriage with the exuberance of a first-time bride.

"And I can't believe you're gonna wear white," Gloria chortled at her older sister.

"Shut your mouth, brat!" Bella laughed and waved a pudgy hand at her. "Fresh marriage, fresh start. That's how it works."

Maiden didn't dare voice her opinion on that. Bella's string of soured relationships was a tangle that even the woman herself couldn't fully explain. But now wasn't the time for regrets; there was a wedding on the horizon and they were all determined to keep the mood cheerful. Even the notoriously fickle weather seemed to be on Bella's side.

It was early autumn in Golden Glen, Michigan. The temperature was crisp and the sky was blue and bright. Maiden was sitting at the long kitchen table in her family's apartment sipping coffee while her mother, Gloria, and her Aunt Bella poured over a dizzying array of bridal magazines.

It was a quiet Monday morning at Harlow House, the inn her family had owned since she was in her early teens. They were nearly fully booked and all the guests had arrived. There would be the inevitable calls for assistance and the odd complaint, but nothing too momentous.

This meant that the women could focus on the finishing touches to Bella's upcoming wedding while Alfie, Maiden's father, could hide downstairs and run the reception desk singlehanded.

Alfie had volunteered to man the desk quite a bit since Bella breezed back into town. It wasn't that they didn't get along, but he found her better in small doses. Particularly as her excitement over her fast-approaching nuptials kept building.

Maiden glanced over at her gorgeously boisterous aunt and smiled fondly. She and Bella had always been close. Bella had no children of her own, despite the numerous marriages that had left her older, wiser and richer. She had grown quite attached to her sister's two children.

Maiden picked up one of the dozens of catalogues that were strewn across the table and turned to a section of bridesmaids' dresses.

They hadn't been officially asked yet, but it stood to reason that she and her sister would be part of the ceremony. As she flicked through the pages she saw that a few dresses had already been circled.

Maiden's heart sank and she suppressed a groan. They were awful. Every dress that had been marked was flouncy, poofy and in shades of lime and tangerine. She loved Bella enough to wear almost anything but, if these were the choices, that love was going to be seriously put to the test.

"Okay, we're ready!" Vonny emerged from her bedroom with a dramatic sigh. "Let's do this!"

Maiden glanced over at her sister and smiled. Rowdy and Ruffian, the kittens that were gifted to them from Vonny's boyfriend, Tony, scampered ahead and darted under the table. Within seconds Maiden felt Ruffian scaling her jeans, hooking his little claws in like a mountaineer, before emerging on her lap. She hoped the tiny black kitten would eventually learn that he could easily jump up instead, and save her the nicks and scratches on her shins.

Vonny plonked down in a chair across from Maiden and looked at the assortment of fabric swatches, candles, magazines and catalogues. Never one to bother with subtlety, Von glanced at Bella hopefully.

"So, what's my dress gonna look like?" she asked eagerly.

"Is this *your* weddin'?" Bella teased. "Why am I doin' all the work then?"

"Fine, have it your way, I'll just sit in the audience and throw rotten fruit," Von sniffed.

Maiden gave her a speaking look and discreetly slid the marked catalogue over. Vonny glanced down at it and made the same face she had when she accidently swallowed a horsefly. Something between disbelieving fear and vomitus disgust.

"Actually, I'm happy to be a spectator." She poked out her tongue as if the hideous dresses were stuck to it. "I'll have a better view of the ceremony."

"Don't be silly, honeypot!" Bella laughed. "You don't think I'd get married right here with my sweetest little baby nieces and not have them in my weddin'? I was gonna ask you today anyhow."

"Cool." Vonny smiled weakly as she picked up Rowdy and cuddled her. "Thanks."

"Now, Maiden." Bella turned to her and clasped her hands together in a business-like manner. "I want you to be my maid of honor."

"Oh, that's wonderful!" Maiden said happily. "Thank you, Aunt Bella."

Maiden's eyes flitted from Bella to Vonny and back again. She wet her lips and suppressed a sigh, bracing for the inevitable sulk.

Maiden had always been closer to Bella than Vonny had, but she knew that wouldn't stop her sister from feeling that she ought to have been chosen because she was the oldest. Vonny's chestnut brows were just beginning to furrow when Bella shifted her crystal blue eyes to her.

"And Vonny, I want *you* to walk down the aisle with Tony," she said firmly.

"Tony?" Vonny stared at her.

"Yes, I've spoken with Elvan and he's one groomsman short. His son Bradley is the best man, so he'll be standin' there with him any-way," she explained. "But I need two boys to balance out my two bridesmaids. Tony's the closest I got to a son and you two will look so sweet together. I didn't think you'd mind."

"Of course I don't." Von's cheeks were slightly pink but she looked incredibly happy. "Thank you, Aunt Bella."

Maiden was relieved that her sister's grumbles had been stopped in their tracks but felt a glimmer of her own annoyance when her mother chimed in.

"And Maiden doesn't have a man, so it don't matter if she walks alone." Gloria said.

Always nice when we can work that in to the conversation, Maiden thought dryly.

"Elvan doesn't have any other family?" she asked, more to change the subject than out of any real curiosity.

"He has a nephew, Pierce. I like him," Bella murmured and then pursed her lips irately. "But Elvan's mother is a spiteful old hag; she insists that one of the boys sit with her through the ceremony. Pierce very kindly threw himself on that grenade for us."

"Is she really that bad?" Maiden smiled at the mental image her aunt had inspired.

"If anything she's worse!" Bella groused. "Gail Hedgewick has nev-er had a kind word to say to me or about me. But I really don't care.

After the weddin' we can settle in *my* house and not have to see the old bat at all."

"Elvan lives with his mommy?" Vonny smirked.

"So does Tony," Maiden reminded her.

"That's different." Vonny gave her a look. "She's got a separate apartment, and she's old and can't drive."

"She ain't *that* old, little girl," Gloria gave her a teasingly warning look, she and Amelia Ferris were only a few years apart.

"Anyway," Bella said loudly, calling the attention back to her. "Elvan lives in the family estate. It's different with old families like theirs; they got history and pedigree."

"And money," Maiden said wryly.

"Plenty of it, baby." Bella winked but then waved it away. "But that ain't the point. Elvan and I go way back. I didn't know it at the time, but he's been in love with me since high school. He's already promised me that he won't let his mother interfere."

"'Interfere'?" Maiden frowned uneasily at her. "Are things that bad? She wouldn't really try to talk him out of marrying you, would she?"

"I wouldn't put it past her for a second!" Bella exclaimed angrily. "From what I've heard, she's done it before. Hateful old wad of gristle! But Elvan loves me; he won't listen to her."

"What's her problem?" Vonny asked, not bothering with delicacy. "Does she think you're after his money?"

"Oh, who knows?" Bella rolled her eyes. "Put it this way, I wouldn't dare turn my back on Gail Hedgewick, she'd sink a knife in it the first chance she got!"

Maiden tried not to scowl as she took that in. The thought of someone being so hostile to Aunt Bella was hard to imagine and deeply upsetting. She looked at her beloved aunt; beneath the anger she could see shadows of pain in her bright blue eyes. Maiden could only hope that Elvan really did love her.

"We'll have to keep an eye on her then. Hey, speaking of Maiden not having a man," Vonny quickly shifted the conversation back to something she found more palatable. "What's Elvan's son like?"

Maiden shut her eyes briefly. Bella scoffed and then shuddered as she held up a hand in Vonny's direction.

"No, baby. Absolutely not," she said seriously. "Don't even joke about that spoiled brat."

"Is he that bad?" Vonny looked intrigued now.

"He's bad enough to have gone through a string of women that were too open-minded for their own good." Bella shook her head. "Like a child with a toy, he either gets tired of them or his granny takes them away. Pathetic."

"She couldn't actually make him break up with anyone, could she?" Maiden asked.

"She holds the purse strings, baby," Bella sighed.

"Is that what she'll hold against Elvan then?" she tried not to let her concern show through.

"I have no idea, but it don't matter," Bella shrugged. "He don't need her permission for nothin', even if she does think she's the dog's danglers."

"That's...um, yeah. But *Elvan* is definitely nice, right?" Maiden was starting to feel her confidence bleed away as she learned more about Aunt Bella's prospective in-laws.

"Of course," Bella gave her a teasing look, "you think I'd marry a man that didn't treat me well?"

Maiden, Vonny and Gloria all slid their eyes away uncomfortably. Bella planted her fists on her full hips.

"Hush up," she said.

***

After lunch the ladies all piled into Vonny's car and headed for the bridal boutique Bella had chosen. It was two towns away but apparently the nicest in the entire state, according to Aunt Bella. Maiden spent the relatively long drive staring out the window and thinking about her sister's playful remarks.

While it was true that she didn't happen to have a man in her life at the moment, she was convinced that she'd come painfully close a couple of times. The head of the local police department, Captain David McAlister, had a habit of flirting and teasing enough to make her think he was interested, but so far he'd always backed off again.

Despite that, she had started to hope that things were progressing at last. Only a couple of weeks ago, during a particularly personal murder case, she felt like they'd started growing much closer. But when the case was resolved, a couple of days quickly became a couple of weeks without so much as a word from him.

It was silly to cultivate any further interest there, logically she could see that, but she was strongly drawn to him. He was smart and sexy and they got along so well. She honestly didn't know what kept holding him back but, whatever it was, it sure did the trick every time.

Even her mother had finally stopped mentioning him, the sly winks and nudges had disappeared. No more constantly asking if he'd called or stopped by to see her. All of Gloria's joyful enthusiasm had moved on to other pursuits, namely Bella's wedding.

That was a good thing. It's what Maiden wanted, peace and quiet and respite from the teasing. And yet, as much as she'd always complained about others' stubborn insistence that McAlister liked her, Maiden now found the resulting silence kind of depressing.

The flirty repartee she'd enjoyed with the handsome cop had been a bit of meaningless diversion and everyone accepted that now. If she was honest with herself, it was an unflattering letdown.

You need to move on, Maiden, she thought bracingly. *You might never even see the guy again. You gave him every chance and plenty of encouragement; he didn't want you bad enough to pursue it. Let it go and stop thinking about him.*

Maiden was relieved for the distraction when they pulled up outside of a very fancy looking boutique called *Happily Ever After*. Her eyes rounded in wonder and she very nearly whistled as she admired the lavish storefront.

Large, gleaming windows were framed by stone columns. Above these were relief carvings of doves, roses and beautiful women draped in robes. The window displays were equally impressive. Mannequin brides were swathed in silken gowns with ornate tiaras fastened to their perfectly styled wigs.

"Oh wow!" Vonny whispered as she climbed out of the car and shut her door. "This place is incredible!"

"I know!" Bella clapped her hands together lightly and looked like she wanted to bounce up and down. "I found it online and knew this was the perfect place to get you girls your dresses."

"What? *Our* dresses?" Maiden gaped at her. "I thought we were here for you."

"I got my dress ages ago, honeypot." Bella gave her a smiling look. "The weddin' is in two weeks, you thought I'd wait until now to get somethin' as critical as my dress?"

"Oh. Well, no, of course not." Maiden couldn't help feeling a bit foolish at her naïve assumption. Now that she really thought about it, it was ridiculous.

"Come on, babies!" Bella tittered. "Let's hurry, I can't wait for you to see 'em!"

"You chose our dresses already?" Von slid her sister a wary look as they followed Bella and Gloria into the remarkable shop.

"Once again," Bella glanced back with a patient expression, "the weddin' is in *two weeks*. Have you girls never had anything to do with plannin' somethin' like this?"

They both shook their heads. Maiden and Vonny had never been terribly popular and most of their friends were male. These sorts of excursions were unknown territory for them both.

Neither of them had ever been asked to be a bridesmaid before, and they had no real grasp of what they were supposed to do with the privilege. Maiden started to worry that she was going to be a terrible maid of honor; she hadn't even met the groom yet. Her mother seemed to pick up on her worries.

"Well, it's a good thing we're here with you girls!" Gloria laughed and motioned for them to follow. "Don't you worry, babies. You just let Mama and Aunt Bella guide you on the way."

The younger women smiled humbly and obediently. The instant the older pair looked away, Vonny grasped her sister's arm and leaned in with a foreboding scowl.

"This is gonna suck like a straw!" she hissed. "Those daffy old birds are gonna dress us up in more frills than a rack of lamb!"

"Dour, but probably accurate," Maiden sighed and shuffled onward to accept the inevitable.

The inside of the boutique was tastefully elegant. Maiden was sure that the façade was designed to lull unsuspecting women into thinking they were safe before they were ambushed and punched in the face with some neon taffeta horror show.

Bella was prancing around, stopping occasionally to admire the dresses on display. When she stopped and gasped at a floor-length beaded evening gown trimmed with flamingo pink feathers, Maiden felt her shoulders droop.

"Von," she whispered desperately. "Kill me now!"

"Forget it," her sister scoffed. "You're not leaving me to deal with this on my own. At least we'll look stupid together."

They watched as Gloria corralled her distracted sibling and pointed to the far side of the large room. There were several dressing rooms with garlands of fake flowers over each door. To the side was a small platform placed in front of a full-length trifold mirror.

As they approached, a saleswoman appeared and greeted them with a smile. She was a tall, gaunt woman wearing a finely tailored suit. Her darkly blond hair was arranged in an understated French twist and a pair of bifocals were perched on the end of her long nose.

"Ms. Fontaine." She stepped forward and shook Bella's hand warmly. "You've brought your nieces, excellent. As you know, there isn't much time left if any alterations are needed."

"I know it, Laura." Bella raised her hands in a conceding gesture. "Let's get straight down to business then."

"I'll just bring the dresses out," Laura murmured and slipped off through a side door.

Maiden and Vonny stood side by side as they waited for the unveiling. As a few moments ticked by Maiden felt her apprehension grow. She saw Vonny glance over at her and smirk.

"Hoop skirts," Vonny whispered her guess from the corner of her mouth.

"Feather boas," Maiden replied in kind.

"Parasols," Vonny giggled.

"Bonnets." Maiden grinned.

Laura returned with a polite smile and an air of happy anticipation. She, at least, was pleased about whatever sequin-encrusted circus costume she was about to present. She was carrying a garment bag that was far too small to hold anything Aunt Bella would have chosen.

It must be the wrong bag, Maiden mused to herself. *Or the first piece of whatever it is. I really hope there aren't tassels.*

Laura pulled over a rolling garment rack and hung the bag on it. She glanced at Bella and waited for the lady to nod enthusiastically before turning back to her task. She carefully unzipped and removed the bag with a pleased flourish.

Maiden's mouth dropped open and her eyebrows leapt towards the ceiling when she saw what Bella had picked. It was nothing close to what she'd braced herself for.

The dress was shorter than she'd expected; it would barely brush her knees. It was floaty, filmy and blood red.

"Is that what you're wearing on the honeymoon?" Maiden asked tightly.

Bella and Gloria burst into giggles and Laura chuckled quietly down at her shoes. Bella sauntered over and started heaping on the southern charm.

"Don't you be silly, sweet baby." She smiled fondly and gave her niece's shoulders a gentle squeeze. "That's your dress, my little honeypot. Ain't it great? You're both gonna look so beautiful!"

Maiden turned back to the dress, staring at the thin straps and draped neckline, and started shaking her head in silent refusal. Vonny squeaked with delight and skipped towards the dresses eagerly. She grasped hers and held it up against her slender frame.

"I absolutely love it, Aunt Bella!" She twirled around and admired herself in the mirror. A mischievous gleam lit her pale blue eyes as she nodded towards her little sister. "Maiden's gonna look like a hooker, though."

"Hush up!" Gloria and Bella both snapped at her.

"She's right, I'm not wearing that thing!" Maiden folded her arms over her full bust and shook her head more vehemently. "It's ridiculous!"

***

As Gloria swooped in to reassure her youngest daughter, a grimly serious Bella took Vonny aside. Von was smiling happily; she knew she hadn't helped but she still felt quite pleased with herself. Bella's left eyebrow rose to an angle that always heralded open war.

"Now you listen to me, girlie. I don't want you discouragin' Maiden from wearin' this dress," she said quietly. "I'm not jokin'."

"Can't I speak up for my sister?" Vonny tried to look innocently hurt, briefly forgetting that she was confronting the master of the art.

"I'll tell you what *I* can do. I can make *you* maid of honor instead, then you can stand up with Elvan's son for the whole ceremony," Bella whispered sweetly. "And little Maiden can walk down the aisle with Tony. And, of course, there's the bridal dance. Wouldn't that be nice?"

"You wouldn't." Vonny shook her head slightly.

"For giggles." Bella's eyes narrowed. "Now, I've put a lot of thought and all of my tender little heart into this weddin', Vonny. *Don't mess with nothin'!*"

Vonny pressed her lips together as she weighed up her options, but it was an easy decision. She looked at the dress and then at her sister and then back to Bella's slightly scary smile. She swallowed hard and grasped the flimsy garment a little tighter.

"Actually Maiden, I think this will look great on you!" She turned and beamed at her. "Both of us together, it's perfect, we'll be like twins! It's great!"

Vonny glanced at her aunt hopefully. Bella was smiling happily and actually rubbing her hands together like a cartoon villainess. Vonny felt every bit as terrible as she knew she ought to but ignored it and grabbed Maiden's dress from the rail.

"Come on," she said too cheerfully as she thrust it at her and waved her towards the change rooms. "Let's try these beauties on!"

***

"No way!" Maiden said stubbornly as she stepped out of the dressing room.

Gloria, Bella and the saleswoman all started gushing at the sight of her. She was inundated with insistent compliments and vehement assurances that she certainly did *not* look like a complete tart.

She glanced at Vonny who was admiring herself in the nearest mirror. Her big sister looked adorable in the flirty little dress. Feeling her gaze on her, Von finally glanced over and stilled when she saw Maiden. There was an undeniable look of surprise in her eyes along with a very obvious dose of guilt.

"It looks fine, Mae," she lied quietly and turned back to her own reflection. "No one will even think twice about it...it's classy."

Maiden's eyes widened incredulously at that blatant fib but, before she could respond or protest, she found herself prodded onto the pedestal in front of the triad of mirrors. With an uncomfortable grumble, she stood there and studied the dress from every angle.

Maiden silently admitted that it was rather pretty, but she never wore dresses like this, not ever. She turned enough to look at her full bottom where it was caressed by the dreamy fabric. A hint of panic seized her and she started shaking her head again.

"I can't walk around in a crowded room in this!" she said in an exasperated huff. "It looks like lingerie!"

"Nonsense, angel." Gloria smiled lightly and waved that away. "Modesty is one thing, but don't turn into some frigid old prude."

"I wonder if Dad would agree with that suggestion," Maiden grumbled as she adjusted the neckline to better cover her cleavage.

"This has nothin' to do with Alfie," Bella said. "And I don't want either of you tellin' anyone about your dresses. *All* our gowns are going to be a surprise; I want maximum impact."

"Then *you* wear this stupid thing." Maiden gave her an angry look. "I can't think why you both would want me to wear something this showy at a wedding! That's tacky, isn't it?"

"Not if you're in the bridal party." Bella dismissed her concern despite past instances of criticizing other women—at length—for wearing a sexy dress to someone else's wedding. "These are the dresses I've chosen; that's all there is to it."

"Well, I'm sorry, but the answer is no," Maiden said firmly. "I'm not going to wear something this provocative at my aunt's wedding. What would people think of me?"

"What would they think? They'd think that you were a sweet, unselfish girl who loves her poor auntie," Gloria said in a softly startled voice, as though she couldn't fathom her daughter's concerns. "I don't know what's got into you, angel. Talkin' so mean to Bella like that."

Laura was watching the drama unfold with quiet interest. She'd no doubt heard some arguments over the course of her career but probably nothing quite like this. She merely suppressed a smile and hurried to bring a chair over when Bella pressed a hand to her ample bosom and swayed slightly on her feet.

"Here you are, Ms. Fontaine," the lady said kindly and then withdrew a few paces.

"Thank you, dear. I just don't know what to do now." Bella drew a tissue from her perfumed cleavage. "I have this image in my mind of what I want this weddin' to be...but I guess I'm askin' too much."

"Too much?" Gloria tsked and shook her head. "I wouldn't have thought so, especially with how close you two have always been. Goodness...to just refuse outright like that."

"I spent hours lookin' through dresses, hopin' for the perfect one." Bella dabbed at her eyes, she'd actually dredged up a few tears. "Red is Elvan's favorite color. I saw that dress and it just looked like an absolute dream."

"Honestly, angel," Gloria said as she turned to Maiden. "All you have to do is wear a dress, maybe one you don't particularly like, but just for one single day and then it's done."

Maiden shut her eyes briefly. Despite knowing that it was a manipulative trick, she started to feel badly. Maybe she was being too sensitive. For whatever reason, the sassy little dress was important to Aunt Bella, and it *was* only for one day.

"The weddin' is in two weeks." Bella gazed forlornly down at the toes of her shiny patent-leather pumps. "I don't think I could find another dress for you girls by then...not the right one. I can't bear to think of my sweet girls bein' at my weddin' and I still have to walk down the aisle all alone..."

Bella sniffled and then started to cry, gently and softly. Maiden felt even more conspicuous now. She was standing there dressed like something from a burlesque act and now she'd just reduced her favorite aunt to tears right before her wedding. She sighed and shifted awkwardly.

"I do like the color," she allowed reluctantly.

"It looks so perfect on you," Bella managed to whisper.

"I love it, Aunt Bella. *I'm* happy to wear it," Vonny chimed in, which earned her a dirty look from Maiden.

Bella just closed her eyes and sniffled. Gloria shook her head sadly and gave her shoulders a comforting pat. Maiden quickly decided she'd rather feel uncomfortable for a day than deal with the crying and the drama for two weeks.

"Look, fine." Maiden rolled her eyes and rested her hands on her hips. "I'll wear it, okay?"

"Only if you're sure." Bella's eyes glistened with tears as she gazed up at her. "Are you sure, my little honeypot?"

"I said I'd wear it," Maiden muttered. "I'm not going to beg for the privilege."

"Oh, thank you, sugar! I was so sure you'd never *really* break my poor heart like that." Bella smiled happily and dabbed at her eyes one last time before stuffing her tissue back into the abyss. "Now then, on to the shoes!"

CHAPTER TWO

David was sitting at his desk reviewing some reports when he heard a knock on his door.

"Come in," he said and glanced up to see his receptionist walk in with a knowing smile and a stack of letters clutched in her hands. "Hey, Nancy. What's up?"

She fixed sparkling eyes on him and tried not to grin; he sat back a bit and studied her watchfully. Nancy was a quiet and very level-headed person; she never sparkled.

"Just bringing you the mail, sir," Nancy said as she set the letters right under his nose.

He gave her a questioning look and then glanced down. She'd set a large pink envelope on the very top of the pile. He wrinkled his nose as a heavy waft of perfume floated up at him.

"What's this?" he asked as he picked it up gingerly and looked it over like it might explode.

"It looks like an invitation," Nancy murmured and made no move to leave. "And I think I recognize the scent. Honeysuckle. A favorite in the south, I believe."

"I take it you looked at the return address?" he asked dryly, noting the personalized silver label that said *Harlow House.*

"I may have glanced at it," she admitted calmly. "I also had a brief chat with Mr. Ferris when he delivered it."

The local postman, Tony Ferris, was certainly a fixture in the community. David had learned a bit more about him when he was compelled to arrest him a few weeks ago. Tony seemed like a genuinely nice guy, it hadn't taken long to dismiss him as a suspect. But he was also a renowned local gossip. In this instance, the mention of his name gave David pause.

"What's going on, Nancy?" he asked patiently.

"Just the dutiful delivery of mail to its rightful recipient," she said innocently, and without budging. "Don't let me distract you, sir."

David gave her a wry smile but obligingly opened the envelope and pulled out a stiff white card. As he did so, a scattering of confetti in the shape of flowers and hearts spilled over the top of his desk. He sighed at the mess but then opened the card and arched a brow.

Join our celebration!
You are cordially invited to share in the blissful union
of
Annabella-Rose Fontaine
&
Elvan Abraham Hedgewick

"Who're they?" Nancy shook her head uncertainly, not even trying to pretend she wasn't reading over his shoulder.

"You mean Tony didn't explain the whole thing to you already?" he asked with a smile.

"No, he was in a hurry," she almost sighed. "He said it was an invitation, a big one, and then he left...so, who are they?"

"No idea who the guy is, but Bella Fontaine," he glanced up at her, "is Maiden Harlow's aunt."

"Really?" Nancy looked intrigued and deeply pleased. "That's very interesting."

"Even more interesting is the note at the bottom." He smiled faintly as he read it aloud. *"Dear Captain McAlister, we'd be just so very <u>thrilled</u> if you could come along as an honored guest and friend of the family. Love and hugs, Gloria Harlow and Bella Fontaine."*

"That's perfect! When is it?" Nancy asked happily.

"In two weeks." He pulled a face. "That's pretty short notice."

"But you'll go." She stared at his teasingly defiant expression. "Captain, you *have* to go!"

"It says 'formal attire'," he gave a long-suffering sigh. "I don't have time to get a tux."

"You don't wear a tux unless you're in the wedding!" Nancy said with a tinge of disgust. "Do you have a dark suit? That's clean?"

"Yes, I do," he chuckled down at the invite and Gloria's flouncy handwriting. "You realize this is some sort of a trap, right?"

"And what's the bait likely to be, sir?" she asked dryly as she looked him in the eye.

David held her gaze for a moment, he then thought about Harlow being forced into a ridiculously frilly bridesmaid's dress and grinned. That alone would be worth sitting through a wedding for people he didn't even know.

He lowered his gaze back to the invitation and let his thoughts linger on Harlow for a moment. He hadn't seen her lately, not since the grisly business surrounding her high school reunion.

It wasn't a deliberate distance, but a lot of follow-up had gone into the messy case. It had been time consuming, and he was conscious of not burdening her with reminders of what she'd been through.

He also hadn't forgotten that one of the last times they'd spoken alone together she'd let him off a hook he'd been more than happy to stay on. He'd kept telling himself that he didn't have time for a relationship until he'd settled in more and got a handle on the running of the station. That was quickly ceasing to be a satisfying excuse. His feelings for her were a bit complicated, but they weren't going away.

He hadn't seen her in weeks and he missed her, he'd never experienced that before. He'd started trying to think up an excuse to see her again and finally decided that he'd just call her and hope she hadn't written him off completely.

This invitation was a timely and promising sign, or a complete debacle in the making. He didn't really care which one it was at this point, he was just grateful for the opportunity to see her again.

"You have to go, Captain." Nancy repeated adamantly, pulling his attention back to the present.

"Why?" He smiled at her. "You're getting pretty worked up over a stranger's wedding."

"Because something's up," she mused, rubbing her chin thoughtfully, "and I want to know what it is."

He pretended to mull it over, partly to tease Nancy a little and partly to avoid looking too eager. He had made up his mind to go the instant he'd realized what the invitation was, but Nancy didn't need to know that. No one needed to know that.

He'd overheard enough whispered conversations in the office across the hall to be sure that his chemistry with Harlow hadn't gone unnoticed. No one dared to pry by asking him personally, but the main question that was debated was why he hadn't asked her out, and he was running out of answers to that question.

"Do you want me to arrange to have your suit cleaned, sir?" Nancy persisted politely enough.

"It's clean!" He couldn't help laughing at her stern expression. "If I promise to go will you stop glowering at me like that?"

"Of course, sir." She shrugged and strolled towards the door. "It's good of you to make the sacrifice. I'm sure you're not fussed whether you ever see Miss Harlow again or not; hopefully you won't be too bored."

"Don't let the door hit you on the way out," he replied with a smirk.

***

It was two days before the wedding when Elvan Hedgewick arrived in Golden Glen. His bright red, blatantly expensive, European sportscar pulled up outside Harlow House late Thursday afternoon. Maiden watched from her balcony as he climbed out followed a moment later by another, much younger, man.

She looked them over curiously. Elvan was fairly short and rather pudgy. He wasn't quite what Maiden had imagined from the dreamy way Bella smiled whenever she talked about him, or from the tall and dashing type that the lady usually went for.

His hair was brown and wavy but graying at the temples and thinning on top. He had a thick, well-groomed beard that was also flecked with distinguished threads of silver. He was impeccably dressed but what struck her the most was his kindly face. His dark eyes were soft and he seemed to have a hint of a perpetual smile hovering around his mouth, ready to break loose at a moment's notice.

She shifted her study to the younger man. It had to be his son, Bradley, the one Aunt Bella seemed to deeply dislike. He was a bit taller and a bit slimmer than his father, but he definitely looked like he was trying too hard. His shiny suit, cowboy boots and massive belt buckle were ostentatious enough, and then he sat a massive Stetson on his head.

She knew exactly what her father would think when he saw him, she just hoped he wouldn't say it out loud. *You're a sorry excuse for a cowboy, pal.*

Bradley gave the front of the inn a quick, assessing look and didn't appear to be impressed with any of it. But a big, cheesy grin softened his features as soon as his father turned to him. She couldn't hear what Bradley said but his enthusiasm was obvious, and obviously fake.

She recalled Bella's reaction when Vonny asked about him and felt her own opinion start to form. It wasn't fair, she hadn't even spoken to him yet, but he really did look like a bit of a tool.

"Be nice, Maiden," she whispered to herself. "It's only for a week-end, you can be polite for Aunt Bella's sake...at least he's not wearing spurs."

She gave them a few minutes to make their way upstairs. When she heard an explosion of boisterous southern accents drift down the hallway and through her closed door, she knew she needed to go and be sociable.

She walked out into the living area and found Bella and Elvan standing side-by-side with their arms around each other while Bradley shifted his weight from one foot to the other and shoved his hands deep in his pockets.

Her own parents were politely chatting with Elvan and tried to include Bradley, but he just smiled wanly and offered monosyllabic replies. Until he glanced over and saw Maiden approaching.

His eyes rounded slightly and he immediately stopped fidgeting. His hands slid from his pockets to politely remove his enormous hat.

"Maiden!" Bella said happily when she also spotted her. "Come and meet your future uncle!"

Maiden smiled nicely and held out her hand only to have Elvan wave it away and hug her instead. He patted her back and then released her gently as he slipped his arm back around Bella.

"Pleased to meet you, sweetheart." Elvan's voice was soft and kind. "My Bella's told me so much about you."

"Hey, don't I get a hug too?" Bradley pretended to sulk and held his arms out towards Maiden.

"Of course you do!" Alfie stepped in smoothly and wrapped his arms around him. "Welcome to the family, young man!"

Maiden looked away to hide her smile, she'd never been more grateful for her father's protective streak, or his sense of humor. She heard Bella snort and strove to continue the conversation quickly as her father set a red-faced Bradley away from him again.

"How was your trip here?" she asked as she made a point of looking only at Elvan.

"It was good, thank you, darlin'," Elvan smiled again. "I flew in not long ago and Bradley very kindly met me with the car. He's got a bit more time on his hands to indulge in a road trip than I have."

Elvan chortled pleasantly but she noticed Bradley shoot him a sharp look. The scowl disappeared almost instantly to be replaced by a placid smile.

Maiden found the exchange interesting. Elvan hadn't appeared to have meant any offence but Bradley clearly took some anyway.

"It was a long drive," Bradley smiled slowly. "Takes a certain amount of stamina."

Oh, this is getting a bit catty, Maiden cleared her throat discreetly and glanced away. Her eyes met with Aunt Bella's, the older woman set her teeth and shook her head in disgust.

"Yes, son," Elvan laughed and clapped him firmly on the shoulder. "You gotta work with what you have, don't you? That sure is the truth. You, uh...didn't have any troubles along the way, did you?"

"No," Bradley eyed him uncertainly. "Like what?"

"Nothin', son," Elvan said after the slightest pause, he smiled and patted his shoulder again before releasing him. "I just noticed lately that—oh, nothin', it's fine. I've had a long day, I guess. I'm just a little tired."

"Well, you're both here now, that's the important thing," Bella interrupted loudly before Bradley could venture a comment. "Let's relax for the afternoon and then all go out to dinner tonight, shall we?"

"That sounds wonderful, sugar." Elvan smiled fondly but then pulled an apologetic face. "I just need to go and make sure Mama's settled in first."

"Ah, of course," Bella said with less enthusiasm.

"Your mother's in town already?" Maiden asked, folding her arms over her chest to discourage Bradley from staring at it.

"Yes, she was on the same flight as me." Elvan looked a shade embarrassed. "She went straight to her hotel to rest after the journey. When she's tired she can be a bit...cranky."

"Now don't you let that worry you, Daddy." Bradley was suddenly far more vocal and concerned with the situation than he looked to be before. "She'll perk up by Saturday, you'll see."

"Yes, I expect she will." Elvan nodded and visibly rallied. "Anyway, Bradley and I will quickly check on her and then go and get changed. We've rented a house just a couple streets over. We won't be long."

"Is Mrs. Hedgewick staying with you?" Gloria asked.

"No, she likes her own space," Elvan murmured. "But she has her nurse with her, she's quite used to having things as she likes them."

Bella glanced away in an attempt to hide her unimpressed eyeroll but Maiden saw it. Elvan did too and looked briefly uncomfortable, but he found another smile when his bride-to-be looked at him.

Maiden quietly wondered why none of them were staying at the inn, closer to Bella. The attic suites were vacant at the moment, except for the largest one, which Bella had all to herself. She didn't ask, of course, it really wasn't any of her business. She also suspected that it might be because Aunt Bella hated Bradley.

She stood back as Bella escorted the men out of the apartment. Bradley turned and waved to them as they went, Maiden inclined her head politely but didn't wave back.

When they were alone, she turned to her parents and lifted her brows questioningly. Gloria shook her head and Alfie grumbled under his breath.

"Well, I see why Bella don't like that boy," Gloria sighed. "He's not exactly personable until it suits him."

"Until it suits him to leer at my daughter," Alfie said flatly. "These young punks have no manners!"

"Elvan seems nice, though." Maiden said, trying to be positive.

"He is, he's very nice." Gloria nodded. "I don't honestly remember too much about him from our school days, but I do recall that he was always real attentive to Bella."

"She really didn't know he had a crush on her?" Maiden asked curiously.

"Not according to her." Gloria shrugged. "But Bella chased a different boy every week in those days; nothin' serious came of any of it until she met her first husband. He was a tall drink of water, handsome too. Swept her right off her feet."

"But not for very long," Alfie reminded her. "I don't know how Elvan thinks he's going to fare any better than the rest did."

"Don't you talk about her like that, Alfred Harlow!" Gloria fisted her hands on her hips. "You know darn well that most of them breakups weren't her fault!"

***

Dinner that night was a mixed bag, as far as Maiden was concerned at least. They had a large table at the most expensive steak house in town, with Elvan insisting on footing the bill.

Tony and Vonny joined them, after Vonny had managed to get out of the earlier introductions by hiding the instant she saw Bradley in his over-sized hat. Tony was as nice and likeable as ever. He and Elvan got along well from the moment they met, with Elvan saying more than once that he was quite pleased to have the kind young man as one of his groomsmen.

Bradley sulked for a while when his attempts to sit next to Maiden were thwarted by Bella and Alfie insisting that she sit between them. He still tried to get her attention, however, and dropped a few mentions of his college days and things he learned at medical school. He smiled and shrugged with feigned modesty as he talked fondly of his alma mater.

Maiden wasn't sure if he was a doctor or some sort of specialist but she didn't want to encourage him by asking for any details. Instead, she stayed tucked next to her father and chatted with him for most of the night, doing her best not to laugh at his whispered observations of a few of their fellow diners.

She occasionally turned to listen to Elvan and Bella as they cuddled up and reminisced about their school days. The soft-spoken man's affection for Bella was palpable and very sweet. He spent most of the night gazing at her and smiled whenever she looked his way.

Maiden couldn't help feeling happy for them and started to hope that this was finally Bella's dream match, the man that she'd spend the rest of her life with. As pleased as she was for them, she also started wondering if she'd ever find that kind of love. So far she hadn't even come close.

The few guys she'd dated had all turned out to be selfish and pushy. None of them had really cared about what she wanted or even bothered to get to know her. She'd ended up dumping them all after only a handful of dates.

Her thoughts again drifted to Captain McAlister. He knew something of what she was capable of, whether he wanted to or not. She wasn't a vain person, but she knew she was smart and she didn't try to hide it. She hoped that wasn't what kept him from pursuing the interest she knew darn well was there.

But something about him made her believe that he wasn't like that. He wasn't the kind of guy that would bring her flowers and then get caught laughing with his friends as they tried to guess her bra size.

That last grim thought brought her mind back to Bradley. He was staring again and it was getting increasingly annoying. She deliberately held the drink menu in front of her and glared as he finally looked away.

She groused under her breath but her attention was caught when she saw Elvan turn and look behind him sharply. He frowned slightly and surveyed the room cautiously; he looked uncertain, maybe even a little worried. Maiden followed his gaze but didn't see anything that looked sinister.

There were a lot of people there that evening, every table was occupied by groups of various sizes. Maiden noticed a few people look their way and then turn back to their conversations. She slid her gaze back to Elvan.

He slowly turned back to their table and rubbed his hands as if they were cold. For a brief moment he looked frightened, but then Bella said something and he was immediately all smiles again.

Maiden drew her brows together slightly. She recalled him asking Bradley if he'd had any trouble on his way to Golden Glen. She hadn't thought too much about it at the time but, now that she did, she found it kind of weird. It had been a vague and uneasy question. She risked looking at Bradley and received a smarmy smile for her trouble.

She was suddenly really looking forward to Sunday morning. By then the wedding would be over and all the Hedgewicks would be on their way out of town.

CHAPTER THREE

The following day was a busy one. By this time all the Harlows were ready to get on with the festivities, for various reasons. Alfie was getting annoyed over all the fussy last-minute details, and even Gloria was growing more excitable as the wedding drew closer. She and Bella exchanged a lot of giggly whispers and smiling looks.

The wedding rehearsal was the last hurdle to be cleared before the event itself. That meant she would finally get a look at the illustrious venue that Bella had fallen in love with.

Maiden rode with Vonny and Tony to the large and stately Riley Manor. It sat in the furthest reaches of the northernmost part of town and was shrouded on three sides by thick forests. As they drove through the old wrought iron gates they all looked around in silent wonder.

The front lawn sprawled out to either side of a long driveway. It looked recently mowed and the massive trees that dotted the landscape were still clutching most of their vibrantly jewel-toned leaves.

Tony was driving, which was a good thing since Maiden and Vonny were pressed against the windows staring at the breathtaking old house as it came into view. It showed its age, certainly, but Riley Manor was still deeply impressive.

The exterior was made from hewn stone, it had a beautiful terrace and an elaborate portico framed the large front door. Dozens of windows glinted down at them in the fading sunlight.

Maiden wondered how much better it had looked in its early days, back when the Rileys still lived there. Apparently the patriarch of the family, Jackson Riley, was a successful businessman. One of many casualties of the stock market crash of 1929, he was rumored to have committed suicide after losing his entire fortune.

If he'd left any family behind, they'd either died without progeny or gave up on trying to maintain the place. The incredible house now belonged to some sort of trust. Maiden had heard of a few ambitious individuals who had attempted to refurbish it over the years, but no one stuck with it. The manor had changed hands several times and slowly sank further into disrepair.

She wasn't sure how Aunt Bella came to know about it, much less be so determined to have her wedding there. Most of her and Elvan's friends lived in a coastal town in Florida called Seashell Cove. But Bella insisted that she wanted to be married in Riley Manor and, having now seen how besotted Elvan was with her, Maiden couldn't imagine him refusing her anything.

As they pulled in closer, they saw three other cars parked in front of the house. Apart from Alfie's station wagon and Elvan's red Mercedes, there was a blue rental car that Maiden hadn't seen before. Tony parked his own small, reasonably-priced sedan a little further from Elvan's sportscar than was probably necessary and they all climbed out.

"This place is incredible!" Vonny exclaimed as she looked around. "I can't believe we live twenty minutes away from something like this and have never checked it out."

"It's not like it's open to the public," Tony pointed out. "It is amazing though. It looks like the backdrop to some old-fashioned movie."

"Yeah, it really does. It also looks like we're the last ones to arrive," Maiden said as she started up the front steps. "Let's see what the inside is like."

They walked through the elegant front door and into a spacious foyer. The floors were made of hardwood that had been meticulously laid in a herringbone pattern, it was scuffed and could do with refinishing but the incredible workmanship still shone through.

The walls were quite faded and hung with large portraits and landscapes. A few cracks, and possibly a bit of mold, peeking out from the edges of the paintings suggested that the large frames had been strategically placed to hide the worst of the flaws. Maiden smiled faintly and glanced up with a hint of child-like awe at the intricate crystal chandelier that glinted down at them.

Her attention next went to the left where a large room was already set up for the ceremony. There were two banks of chairs all facing towards a dais decorated with vases of blood red roses. A long red carpet had been laid down the aisle and red bows were tied on every chair.

Aunt Bella might have been serious about Elvan loving red, Maiden thought to herself. She'd assumed it was just another ploy to get her to wear that tacky dress.

She scowled as she thought about it, and she wasn't looking forward to the bridal dance with Bradley at all. She reminded herself that she would be wearing some pretty serious stilettos, she could always step on his foot if need be. She smiled and returned to her admiring study.

Directly across from the front doors was a wide, elegant staircase that led to the second floor before turning to continue up to the third. The banister was decorated with flowers, ribbons and countless yards of scarlet tulle.

A few pieces of quite nice furniture were dotted around, and ivory candles were scattered across every table. It was beautiful and atmospheric despite the patches of cracked plaster and peeling wallpaper.

"What an incredible place to get married," Maiden said dreamily as she turned in a slow circle.

"You'd need to at least have a boyfriend first," Vonny laughed.

"There's always a catch." Maiden snapped her fingers and then stepped further into the foyer. "So, where is everyone? We should probably get on with the rehearsal before it gets any later."

"They have to be here somewhere." Tony said before grasping Vonny's hand. He led her down a long hallway next to the room set up for the wedding.

They looked pretty cozy together so Maiden decided to leave them alone and checked out the remaining options. There was a door to her right; she walked over and peered inside. It was a decent-sized room filled with moldering cardboard boxes, a couple of couches covered in sheets and a large deer head hanging on the wall.

Fighting the feeling that the unfortunate animal was staring at her, Maiden quickly noted that no one else was in the room and shut the door again. She walked on and glanced down one of the four hallways that branched out from the foyer.

The first, which stretched out beside the deer-head room, was comparatively short and led to a handful of doors. She assumed that their party would be somewhere more central.

The next two hallways sat on either side of the magnificent staircase. The last was the one Tony and Vonny walked through. Maiden decided to continue on straight ahead, to the right of the stairs.

She wandered down the hall, glancing into the rooms that she passed. There was a huge central room that sat behind the staircase. She glanced at the vintage furniture and smiled when she saw a beautiful stone fireplace. Another door on the opposite side of the room opened into the other hall.

There was no sign of anyone inside this room either, but it looked to have been refurbished enough to render it useable for guests. The whole place looked like it could do with a more thorough clean. Maiden wondered how long it would take to clean a place this size; it was a chilling thought that she quickly dismissed.

She glanced across the hall into some sort of fancy lounge, complete with a bar. It was a tempting distraction but she made herself keep moving.

The hallway was long and almost completely unlit. The only relief from the oppressive, slightly musty gloom was the faint glow of a few weak sconces and a small pool of light coming from under a door that sat directly in front of her.

Drawn to it like a wandering moth, Maiden pushed the door open and found the kitchen. Like the rest of the house, it was huge and a bit chilly. But unlike what she'd seen thus far, there was a flutter of activity here. She stepped just inside and quickly spotted Kylie, their chef at Harlow House.

Kylie's pristine and glowing chef's whites put the overhead lights to shame. Her blonde hair was pulled back in a tightly bound utilitarian bun. Her clear eyes shifted around the room, silently scrutinizing every detail.

The woman was incredibly talented but so shy and socially awkward that she struggled to make friends and sometimes even to converse. But at the moment she was unrecognizable. Maiden had never seen her so confident and in control as she issued instructions to half a dozen teenaged minions.

"The cake will arrive tomorrow at 10 am, it needs to go into the dessert fridge *immediately*," she said sternly. "Who's job is it to look after the desserts?"

"Mine, Ms. Abrams." A red-headed girl with pigtails held up her hand.

"Good...Goldie, is it?" Kylie asked after looking at the clipboard she was holding.

"Yes, ma'am." The girl nodded bravely, she looked like she was about nineteen.

"And do you realize that the wedding cake is the highlight of the reception?" she asked calmly. "People will walk away and forget if the canapes were late or the soup needed more salt, but if the cake is ruined in any way, that's a story that will be told every time the marriage is discussed. Do you understand?"

"Y-yes, Ms. Abrams." Goldie swallowed hard but stood tall. "You can count on me, ma'am."

"I certainly hope so." Kylie glanced back at her notes and went on to terrorize the poor unfortunate fool that was tasked with preparing the salads.

Maiden stared at the unexpectedly formidable chef for a moment before shaking her head and stepping out again. She didn't want to undermine her rarely flexed authority by questioning it in front of her workers. She knew that Kylie had been classically trained; maybe she felt more in her element in a high-pressure atmosphere.

She slipped out of the kitchen and looked down another long corridor that stretched deeper into the house. The place was massive, yet it seemed to rely on only the dim wall sconces to light the way. Maiden was considering pulling out her phone and using the flashlight when a nearby movement caught her eye.

Even in the anemic light she spotted someone tucked behind a corner. It must have been where the hallway on the other side of the staircase intersected. Maiden froze but quickly realized that the person wasn't looking her way. As her eyes adjusted a bit more to the dim light, she was able to see her more clearly.

It was a woman in a nurse's uniform. She had short, darkly brown hair and was quite petite in stature. Until she turned her head enough to reveal her profile, Maiden almost mistook her for a child. Her skillfully painted eyes were definitely those of a grown woman and they were fixed on the partially open door that sat diagonally across from her. She was leaning forward, straining to hear whatever was happening in the room.

Maiden faltered, she really wasn't sure what to do in that circumstance. She recalled Elvan mentioning that his mother had a nurse, it seemed reasonable to assume that this was her. Less clear was why she was eavesdropping, or on whom.

Before she could decide whether to say something or not, the woman glanced back at her without warning. Her eyes widened and she immediately stood up straight, plastering an unconvincing smile on her face.

"Hello there. I was just looking for Mrs. Hedgewick," she said in a discreetly lowered tone. "Excuse me."

The nurse turned and hurried down the hall she'd been hiding in without another word. Maiden walked over and peered after her but the lady had already ducked out of sight.

Maiden found the encounter uncomfortable, and yet also felt an impolite urge to take up where the nurse had left off. She didn't consider herself overly nosy by nature, but she was curious about what the nurse had been listening to.

Deciding to justify it as looking out for Aunt Bella's interests, Maiden crept closer to the partly opened door and peered cautiously inside. She caught a glimpse of tables and chairs, it had to be the dining room. As she edged further into the doorway, she heard voices.

Whoever was talking was obviously in the midst of an argument and she really didn't want to interrupt. As Maiden dithered about whether to walk past quickly or go back the way she came, she couldn't help overhearing a bit.

"I'm tired of you ignorin' me, Elvan."

It was a voice she hadn't heard before but it sounded like an elderly woman, she wondered if it was Gail Hedgewick. Elvan soon confirmed her suspicion.

"Now, Mama, I didn't ever ignore you," he said patiently. "I just don't happen to agree with you on everything. We used to be able to talk together without you gettin' angry and sayin' nasty things. What's happened to that?"

"You know damn well what happened!" she snapped. "Bella Fontaine happened! I can't believe you'd make the same idiotic mistake again! I warned you about Ree and you ignored me, now I'm warnin' you about this Fontaine woman and you *still* ignore me!"

"Mama, you don't even know her," he said with a sigh that suggested they'd trod this ground before. "She's not like Ree was, not one single bit! Just spend a little time with her and you'll see that for yourself."

"I've heard enough to make up my mind about that woman," Gail huffed.

"Heard from who?" Elvan sounded skeptical.

"Never mind," she said darkly. "Mark my words, son, I won't stand for this sort of defiance. Don't test me; you won't like what happens."

"Mama, honestly," Elvan said wearily. "We aren't a mafia family and it's the night before my weddin', can we please be civil at least? I wouldn't put *you* through this sort of grief."

Maiden fought a strong urge to seethe; she quickly decided that she'd heard enough. This Gail Hedgewick sounded just as nasty as Aunt Bella had said, and clearly her concern that Gail would try to talk her son out of the marriage was well founded.

Gail's feelings on the matter were her own choice, but Maiden didn't want the argument to escalate and ruin the evening. She took a few steps down the hall and then walked back towards the dining room, deliberately letting her footsteps ring out loudly against the hardwood. She stepped through the doorway and pretended to look surprised.

"Oh, hello," she smiled sweetly at them as she approached. "I wondered where everyone was."

"Well, we're here, obviously, but I couldn't vouch for anyone else," Gail said crisply.

She was a small, frail-looking creature. Thin, with stooped shoulders and short, pure white hair combed back in a stylish quaff. She looked like she might be in her late eighties, her skin was crepey and sallow and her pale eyes squinted at her.

She was sitting in a chair, clutching the handle of a cane, while Elvan stood nearby. He looked a shade relieved at the interruption and gave Maiden a tiny smile.

"Well hello, little Maiden," he said kindly and gestured towards the sour-faced woman beside him. "Let me introduce my mama, Gail Hedgewick."

"Nice to meet you, Mrs. Hedgewick." Maiden resisted the urge to curtsy.

"You're some relation of Bella Fontaine's?" Gail exuded sheer disdain as she looked her over.

"That's absolutely right," Maiden replied as she squared her shoulders proudly, not appreciating the woman's unfounded dislike of one of her favorite people. "I'm her niece."

"Mm." She pushed to her feet and flicked her son a displeased look. "I'm tired, I'm goin' back to my hotel."

"You won't even stay for the rehearsal?" Elvan failed to hide the hurt in his voice.

"I've made my standpoint very clear," was her only reply as she waved him away and limped past.

Maiden followed her through the doorway and watched her make her way down the hall until the nurse quickly appeared and took her arm gently. The younger lady glanced furtively at Maiden before darting her gaze away and gently urging Gail along to the foyer beyond.

"That's Agnes Gray."

Maiden jumped slightly and glanced over to find Elvan standing right beside her; she hadn't heard a single step as he walked closer.

"Is she your mother's nurse?" Maiden pushed past her surprise to politely inquire.

"Yes, she's been lookin' after Mama for the last couple of years." Elvan nodded.

"She certainly doesn't like Aunt Bella." Maiden gave him a searching look. "Your mother, I mean."

"I know it sounds that way, darlin'." He winced apologetically. "And I'm so sorry she was rude to you, but the situation ain't really as bad as she makes it seem."

"Are you sure about that?" Maiden asked dubiously. Gail had seemed pretty adamant.

"Yes, Maiden, I'm sure," he said kindly. "Please understand that Mama's 89 years old. Mentally, she isn't what she used to be."

"You think she hates Aunt Bella because of senility?" She pulled an unconvinced face.

"In a roundabout way, yes." He nodded and folded his arms loosely. "Mama's reached the point where she's mixin' the past with the present. My first wife was a living nightmare; she tore the whole family apart and Mama never did fully recover from it. Now that she's not so sharp anymore, she's confusin' my sweet Bella with my first wife, Ree."

"Oh, that's really sad," Maiden said quietly. "Actually it's awful, for everyone."

"I know that, honey. I promise that I'm doin' my best," he said and ran a hand over his thinning hair. "Mama's at the stage in her decline where she's become hostile, her doctor told me that's sometimes the way these things go. I'm doin' all I can to shield Bella from the tirades."

"That can't be easy on you." Maiden frowned gently at him, suddenly feeling more sympathy for the soft-spoken man.

"To be honest, it's not. But the situation is what it is." He shrugged. "Mama can't really help it, you know. The lady she used to be would be appalled at how she acts now...we just have to try and be understandin'."

"Yeah, I suppose so," Maiden said quietly and looked him in the eye. "Is, um, is everything else okay, Elvan? I noticed that you looked a little worried at the restaurant last night."

"Oh," he was clearly taken aback by that. "I'm sorry, honey, I didn't mean to be that indiscreet. I hope I didn't scare you."

"No, not really," she frowned at the word 'scare'. "But you looked like something was wrong...so, is something wrong?"

"Not really, no." He tried to wave it away but it wasn't convincing. He met her doubtful gaze and sighed. "Well, to be honest, I'm a bit on edge. Not just because of Mama fallin' apart, although that doesn't help. Some odd things have been happenin' lately, that's all."

"What kind of things?" Maiden blinked at him.

"Kinda near-misses," he rubbed the back of his neck. "Probably just accidents but, well, it keeps happenin'. I slipped on the stairs the other week and found a puddle of floor cleaner had been left there. I also nearly got cracked on the head by a flower pot that fell off an upstairs balcony. Like I said, probably accidents."

"Did anyone else see what happened?" Maiden tried not to let her newly born concerns show through.

"No, Bradley was upstairs at the time and he didn't see anything," Elvan sighed again. "He said it would've just been the wind that knocked it loose. And he's probably right...but there have also been a few times where I would've sworn someone was followin' me."

"Really? Did you tell the police?" Maiden pressed a hand to her chest.

"Tell them what?" he pulled a face. "That some silly old fool is gettin' paranoid and jumpin' at shadows? They'd laugh me right out of the station, and I wouldn't blame them one bit."

"They might hear you out. Especially if you have some reason to think someone might want to hurt you," Maiden said tactfully, trying not to sound like she was suspicious of anyone in particular. "You never know."

"If it happens again, I'll think about it, fair enough?" Elvan offered and smiled brightly at her when she just nodded. "Now then, you stop makin' that sad face right this instant! Let's go find everybody else and get on with the rehearsal. The sooner this night is over, the sooner I get to marry my sweet Bella."

Maiden returned the smile and gestured for him to proceed. As she fell in step beside him she couldn't help wondering how difficult it must be for Elvan; seeing his mother deteriorate right in front of him would be heartbreaking.

She also wondered what the relationship was going to be like for Aunt Bella. It would be hard to walk into a marriage knowing your husband's mother hated you.

They made their way down the hallway and back into the foyer. Everyone had now gathered and seemed ready to get down to business.

Bella was chatting happily with Gloria and Vonny while Tony was standing off to the side with Alfie. Judging by Tony's barely contained amusement, Maiden guessed that her father was sharing more observations of his in-laws, both current and prospective.

Maiden glanced away before she got the giggles, spotted Bradley in his giant hat, and nearly lost it anyway. The day had been too long and the last few minutes too strange for her to dredge up much good grace. Aunt Bella's loud voice was a welcome distraction.

"All right, let's get this show on the road!" she said cheerfully and gestured towards the far end of the aisle. "Elvan, if you and Bradley could take your places please, sweetie."

As Elvan and Bradley headed down the long aisle Bella turned to Maiden and Vonny. She pointed past them to the room on the right of the front door. The one with the disembodied deer head.

"You girls will wait in there and then walk down," she gently nudged them towards the door. "Vonny first and then Maiden."

They did as they were told and things finally got underway. The rehearsal went smoothly enough. Maiden assumed it did at least, she had no experience to draw on and therefore just walked at the pace she was told to and stood on a spot near the alter that was marked with a piece of masking tape.

Vonny and Tony had gone first and giggled the whole time. Maiden smiled at them and deliberately avoided letting Bradley catch her eye as she walked alone down the long red carpet. He took her hand and tried to rub it with his thumb as he escorted her to her place. She pulled it away swiftly and looked resolutely towards the open doors as Bella made her entrance.

Maiden stood in her place and practiced the smile she would have to force once she was poured into her awful bridesmaid's dress. Bella sashayed and batted her eyes, making everyone chuckle as she laid it on deliberately thick.

Bella was just reaching out to take Elvan's hand when Maiden started to feel strangely uncomfortable. Maybe it was the worrying conversation with Elvan playing on her mind, but she got goosebumps on her arms.

Her gaze slid to the row of large windows on the left side of the room. They had been cleaned and, although the curtains showed some age, they were beautifully arched at the top and offered an attractive view of the front yard.

Well, they probably did in the daytime. The sun had lowered enough to make it hard to see much outside. Maiden looked anyway but couldn't see anything, or anyone. And yet, she knew with frightening certainty that someone was out there, and they were watching them.

Chapter Four

The following day the sun was shining, birds were singing and the sky was gloriously blue. The weather was reasonably mild and nearly every bit of available parking at Riley Manor was taken. It looked to be a very good start to Bella Fontaine's big day.

David, who'd been obliged to park a fair way out, walked up the long drive and took a moment to examine the incredible house. He was still relatively new to the area and didn't know too much about its landmarks, he'd certainly had no idea that there was a place like this in their backyard.

He left off his admiring study and headed for the front door, glancing at a big sign that was decorated with red ribbons and clusters of balloons.

Fontaine & Hedgewick Wedding.

He glanced at his watch. The ceremony was supposed to start at 3 pm, that was a little over ten minutes away. He had deliberately come close to the start time to avoid needless mingling.

He wasn't anti-social, but he didn't trust Gloria Harlow enough to give her any extra opportunity to create mischief. If he was honest with himself, however, he was very curious to know what the woman was up to. It was possible that she was just genuinely grateful for the part he'd played in saving Maiden's life a few weeks ago, but he doubted that.

He entered the foyer and was again struck by the grandeur of the old house. It had certainly been rendered useable; it was all a bit faded and aged but the history was there to be seen and made for a remarkable wedding venue.

The place was very elegant, it was also packed. The guests were predominantly of mature years and unabashedly wealthy. They wandered around in lavish, expensive clothes as they mingled, chattered and laughed while teenagers with trays full of food and glasses of punch waded around them.

It was all very classy but a bit snooty and stuffy; not the sort of party he expected from the warm and hospitable Harlow family. Of course, he didn't know Bella Fontaine at all. He was pretty sure he'd never actually met her.

She'd been on hand that night a few weeks ago when he'd driven Harlow home after she came way too damn close to getting killed. Bella had panicked and circled along with Gloria but he hadn't paid much attention to her. If they spoke at all it would have only been when he told them both to quiet down and get out of Harlow's face.

He'd been more polite than that, but he hadn't been in any condition to be friendly. The decidedly personal invitation to Bella's wedding was growing increasingly interesting.

He glanced over and smiled faintly when Gloria Harlow trundled towards him with Alfie in tow. She was dressed in a bright pink silk dress with an impressively ornate hat perched on her blonde curls.

She looked delighted to see him and surprised him a little when she stepped closer and hugged him. He hid his reaction smoothly and just kept smiling.

"Captain McAlister! I'm so glad you could join us!" she said happily as she pulled back and looked him over. "You gorgeous man! Don't you clean up nice!"

"Thanks, Mrs. Harlow." He inclined his head a fraction. "You're looking lovely as always. It was kind of you to include me. I was a bit surprised, actually."

Behind Gloria's shoulder Alfie rolled his eyes and shook his head. Gloria gushed and twittered for a few more minutes before pointing out where she wanted him to sit for the ceremony, she then waggled her fingers at him and pranced off to continue playing hostess.

When he was left with just Alfie, David slid him a curious look. Alfie was...an unusual man. He was an interesting blend of amusingly acerbic wit and eccentric oddity. Today was no exception. The man was dressed in a tux but his vest was buttoned crooked and his left trouser leg was tucked into his sock. A pair of glasses sat nestled, and probably long forgotten, in his bushy, heavily graying hair.

"How's your day been, Mr. Harlow?" he asked.

"Very long and ear-splittingly loud, thanks to Bella's horde of southerners. Flitting around all over the place fussing about nothing and talking *incessantly*. If I manage to get bitten by a dog, that'll round things out nicely," Alfie grumbled dryly. "You know, I deliberately moved Gloria this far north to try and avoid this kind of turkey-circus. A whole day wasted!"

"That's a bit harsh," David said. "Look on the bright side, they'll clear out after this, right?"

"Yes, that's true," Alfie conceded. "And it'll keep Bella too busy to visit for a while...I suppose I can stomach it since the payoff will be worthwhile. And stop smirking at me, young man, we'll see how you feel after a day spent with these kooks."

"You're not really selling me on it." He kept smirking. "Where's Harlow?"

"I wonder which one you mean," Alfie said sarcastically but then relented and smiled faintly. "Traditionally you don't get a peek at the female portion of the bridal party until it's too late to get away. In any case, my little Maiden is smart, she's probably climbed out a window and made her own escape by now. Goodness knows what sort of frilly, antebellum sack they'll have forced her into."

David tried not to laugh too hard but it was a struggle, he genuinely liked Alfie. He glanced at his watch again and tried to be positive as he turned back to the older man.

"Well, it's almost 3 o'clock," David said. "You could probably start drinking if it'll cheer you up."

"I started an hour ago," he replied as he arched a thick brow and sipped from the mug he was holding. "But don't tell Gloria, she thinks it's coffee."

Alfie gave him a wink and wandered off into a side room. David was smiling and shaking his head slightly when Tony approached him.

"Captain McAlister!" He smiled and held out his hand in greeting. "I didn't know if you were coming or not, it's great to see you!"

"Yeah, I was kind of surprised I was invited too," he admitted as he shook his hand.

"I never said I was surprised," Tony pointed out mildly.

"That's true, you didn't." He glanced away and cleared his throat. "So, how's the family doing? Are they coping with all the excitement?"

"Yeah, *coping* is about right," Tony said as he glanced briefly heavenward. "I'm glad the big day is finally here, put it that way."

"Sounds interesting. So, what's the groom like?" he asked curiously.

"Elvan's really nice. I like him a lot," Tony said but then pulled an unimpressed face. "His family though...not so good."

"Really? What's wrong with them?" He shook his head question-ingly, falling quickly into the old habit of gathering information.

"His mom is completely and deliberately rude. We met her last night as she was leaving and she looked through me and Von like we weren't even there." Tony didn't seem too choked up about it, but then his expression turned angry. "And then there's his son, Bradley. I don't like the way he stares at Maiden. It's too much and I know it bothers her. If he makes her uncomfortable again today I'm gonna say something about it."

Before David could even try to form a reply to that unwelcome bit of information everyone's attention was called to the center of the foyer.

Gloria had reappeared and clasped her hands together daintily as she let rip with her bold but sugary southern tones.

"Everyone take your seats, please!" She was easily heard above the countless other conversations in the room. "The ceremony is about to begin!"

A rush of excited chatter rippled through the group as everyone went to sit as requested. As he waded through the sea of fancy suits and large hats and made his way to his seat, David noticed a small, older woman shuffling grimly to the front of the room.

She was dressed in a somber black dress and wore a small hat with a black veil that half covered her face. Her stooped shoulders were tense and her hand gripped the top of her cane so hard that it shook.

As he looked closer he couldn't help noticing that she wore three diamond rings on her left hand. They looked like engagement rings. They were all large and, judging by the whiff of old money that perme-ated the room, probably real. David frowned curiously at the unusual sight.

A slightly doughy, middle-aged man that had to be the groom stepped away from the altar long enough to try and take her gently by the arm. The old woman said something that caused him to back off abruptly; the man shut his eyes and shook his head sadly before going back to his place at the top of the aisle.

The younger man that stood beside him gave Elvan's shoulder a comforting pat. David assumed it was the son that Tony didn't like. One look at his smarmy, fake smile and David started to dislike him as well. He decided to ignore him and obligingly took up his seat amidst the other guests.

His eyes strayed to the strange woman again. Another youngish man was settling in beside her. He looked pleasant enough, but the moment his gaze strayed to her left hand his expression hardened. He leaned closer and muttered something. The old lady sneered; whatever she said in reply made him grit his teeth and turn sharply away from her.

David wondered what that angry exchange was about, but then the music started. He, along with all the other guests, turned to look at the back of the room. Tony was standing patiently at the end of the aisle.

A door across the foyer opened and Vonny emerged holding a bouquet of pink roses. He saw Tony blink and then smile widely when he saw her. As she entered the main room David had to admit she did look quite lovely.

Her little red dress was nothing like the big, ruffly ballgown he'd been expecting. It was very pretty, although a bit flimsy on her slender frame. Vonny wore a gentle smile as she made her way towards the aisle and cradled her bouquet like it was a baby.

She and Tony exchanged a quick, sweetly happy look as she took his arm at the last row of seats and walked beside him to the front of the room. She stood to the left while Tony took up his spot on the right, next to the best man.

It distantly occurred to David that Harlow probably would have squeezed into the same little dress. He glanced back to the door but he stopped thinking very deeply about anything when she stepped out.

He knew he was staring and was reasonably sure his mouth had fallen open as well. Harlow stood in the doorway for a heartbeat before releasing a soft, resigned little sigh and then started the long walk.

He'd taken note of her curvy figure many times before, he was trained to notice physical characteristics, and he was only flesh and blood. He still dreamed about her sometimes, fairly often actually. But this was different and it was incredibly blatant.

He felt his pulse kick up and absently loosened his tie as she drew steadily closer. He heard a few people whisper indistinctly and chuckle slyly while a few others tsked and murmured to each other. David barely noticed and really didn't care. Yes, the dress was sexy and showy and questionable at a wedding to put it nicely, but it was amazing.

Slim straps threatened to be unequal to the task of keeping her figure contained, while the loosely draped neckline would probably test his moral fortitude all evening. The fabric was some fascinating concoction that hugged her waist and then drifted over sweetly curved hips down to legs that seemed miles long. He felt himself smile at the sight of matching red stiletto heels with a tuft of marabou feathers on each vamp.

Harlow floated along at a pace that would have been carefully practiced. She dutifully performed her role but he could see in her tight smile, and her steadfast refusal to look at anyone in the audience, that she wasn't happy to be put on display so obviously. He agreed with that sentiment, but made the best of the situation.

David felt his last niggling fears dwindling away with each step she took, and the view once she'd passed him didn't hurt either. He sighed to himself and shook his head. He knew he shouldn't let himself get caught up in the occasion, especially since it felt like a total setup. But as he looked at her now he couldn't think of a single good reason not to throw himself headlong into the trap.

His gaze shifted to Gloria, he took only the briefest note of Alfie's horrified reaction to Harlow's dress. Gloria was watching her youngest daughter with a pleased smile. Without warning she glanced directly at him and arched a finely plucked brow. Her expression said it all. *That's what you'll lose if you keep wastin' time.*

Message received, ma'am, David thought wryly.

He knew himself and he was sure that once he started anything with Harlow, he'd move fast. That was one of the reasons he'd forced himself to hold back, to try to slow down and get to know her better. But now he felt the shift in his attitude. He was starting to assure himself that he'd waited long enough, he knew her well enough, it was time to make something happen.

For the sake of maintaining some dignity, however, he tore his gaze from Harlow and looked at the rest of the party. He couldn't help noticing the best man who stood there leering at her as she approached. David saw Tony glare at him and felt his own mood darken as the man all but licked his lips as he stepped forward to escort her to her place beside Vonny.

David noticed that she placed her hand very lightly on his and pulled it away as soon as politeness allowed. Once the man had resumed his place next to Elvan the music picked up in a more solemn and momentous tune. Everyone looked to the grand staircase as Bella appeared and made her way gracefully down.

Despite several previous marriages, Bella had chosen a volumi-nous ballgown in virginal white. The crowd obligingly smiled and whispered to each other about how lovely everything was. If anyone thought that it was all a bit over the top, they kept it to themselves. Bella swept past majestically, basking in the attention.

The bride and groom took their places, Elvan's eyes were soft and misty as he stared at Bella, it was sweet actually. David glanced at the old lady in black and found her glowering at the happy couple. He shook his head at her and then allowed himself to look at Harlow again.

He watched as she swept her big green eyes over the crowd, but they widened when they settled on him and her mouth fell slightly open. He met her startled gaze and smiled broadly.

So, they didn't tell you they invited me, he thought to himself. *I won-der if you're happy to see me.* He watched as Harlow started putting the pieces together, she slid narrowed eyes to her mother before looking back at him. She shook her head minutely and turned back to the ceremony as a genuine smile finally curved her deeply red lips.

David was still grinning when he was distracted by a movement at the groom's elbow. He glanced at the younger man stationed beside him and saw the unmistakable look of surprise on his face.

The man, Bradley, if he recalled correctly, was looking into the audience. David followed his gaze to a woman sitting in a middle row on the other side of the room. She looked to be in her mid-twenties, was slim with long brown hair and had big soulful eyes that reminded him of a bashful doe. She was sitting next to an older woman who had an appearance he could only describe as striking.

He saw enough of a resemblance to assume it might be her mother. The lady was incredibly polished with dark hair that was accented by a thick streak of silver that ran back from her right temple. Her nose and jaw were very strong but still feminine and her dark eyes looked shrewd. She looked like the sort of woman you didn't want to mess with.

Both of them were watching the ceremony with shuttered expressions, but when the younger woman shifted her gaze to Bradley, the effect was immediate. Her lovely eyes narrowed and she set her teeth. David was struck by the venom in her countenance and glanced at Bradley to gauge his reaction.

Far from being alarmed or even mildly concerned, Bradley looked pleased. He actually looked snidely amused as he quirked a brow and turned back to the ceremony.

***

Maiden was still trying to overcome the shock of seeing Captain McAlister sitting in the audience. Suddenly Gloria and Bella's insistence on her dress made perfect sense. She should have known that they wouldn't have given up so easily. Their conspicuous silence on the subject of the handsome captain had been a trick to stop her from guessing what they were up to.

She became acutely aware of how strappy the dress was, as well as the draft of cool air that was drifting over her bared skin. Her cheeks tinted pink and she had to fight hard not to look at him again.

Don't squirm. Don't fidget, she silently ordered herself. *I can't believe they invited him without telling me, and he actually came, and I'm dressed like a tart. There's just no way I could climb out the window without someone noticing...still tempted to try.*

Maiden scanned the family rows instead. Her father was visibly fuming about something and muttering under his breath to Gloria, who kept smiling as she ignored him completely. Maiden decided to ignore them both and shifted her attention to the row in front of them.

Suppressing the urge to toss her bouquet onto the woman's head, Maiden noticed that Gail Hedgewick had come to her own son's wedding dressed for a funeral. Talk about tacky.

But at least she didn't turn up in a trashy red dress. Maiden felt an inappropriate giggle well up and pretended to gently smell her roses to hide it. She saw McAlister smile at her from the corner of her eye and silently cursed her lack of subtlety.

She dared to look at Gail again. Her face was thunderous, the harsh anger carved the lines that mapped her face even deeper into her fragile skin. The sheer contempt made her look so withered and hateful.

Maiden then noticed the hand that gripped her walking stick. She blinked and started to frown before recalling that she was thoroughly on display. She cleared her expression but still took note of the three diamond rings that were stacked snugly on Gail's gnarled finger. The stones glinted brightly in the softly lit room.

She next looked at the man sitting beside Gail. It had to have been Pierce, the self-sacrificing nephew that Bella had told her about. He looked to be in his early thirties, close to Bradley's age. He was watching Bella and Elvan with a faint, pleased smile on his cleanshaven face.

He looked sincerely happy as he watched the proceedings. Maiden appreciated the genuineness of his expression. She decided to follow his example and actually pay attention to the wedding.

The celebrant related a few anecdotes about how the couple had met years ago, but then lost touch only to find each other again. Apparently Elvan had learned that they had mutual friends and was quick to reestablish contact. He asked her on their first date that same day. The crowd cooed and awed appreciatively.

When it came time for the vows, Elvan went first and repeated the words warmly and firmly, clutching Bella's hand the whole time.

The bride smiled sweetly at him and held his gaze as she recited her vows next. She'd nearly finished and Elvan was gazing at her with such unquestioning love, but then Gail clambered to her feet.

She cried out loudly and clutched at her chest. Beside her, Pierce looked startled and possibly annoyed, but he dutifully stood and put an arm around her frail shoulders.

"What's wrong with you, Granny?" he tried to keep his voice discreetly lowered. "Sit back down!"

"It's my heart!" she gasped loudly and fearfully. "Someone help me! Please!"

Bella watched Gail coldly through half-lowered lids while Elvan and Bradley moved in to assist. Whispers ran through the crowd and Maiden and Vonny edged closer as the frail woman was gently urged to sit again.

Maiden was surprised to hear a couple of quickly muffled titters from the audience. She looked over to see a pair of glossy socialites watching Gail with looks of undisguised contempt. They looked like they might have been mother and daughter, they were both polished and confident. Maiden couldn't help wondering at the evident animosity in both their gazes as they watched Gail sway in her seat and fan herself with her feeble hands.

Moments ticked by awkwardly; Maiden noticed that Gail's dedicated, and doubtless well paid, nurse was nowhere to be seen. Finally, Elvan murmured something to Bradley and Pierce. The younger men nodded and helped Gail limp pitifully from the room.

Maiden watched the spectacle in silent horror. If it was a real attack, it was dreadful. If it was fake, it was simply appalling. She already had her suspicions about which one she believed it was.

Elvan took a deep breath, his expression was flustered but determined. He resumed his place next to Bella and nodded to the celebrant.

"Carry on," he said firmly, grasping his bride's hand once again.

That stoic command sent more startled whispers through the crowd but no one dared to argue. Maiden released a startled breath and eased back to her spot, gently tugging Vonny along with her.

Bella raised her chin to a defiant angle as she finished her vows in a steady voice. She and Elvan then shared their first married kiss. The applause was supportive but a bit subdued.

Regardless, Bella continued to hold her head up high and smiled brightly as she and Elvan were introduced as Mr. and Mrs. Hedgewick. Maiden watched them walk triumphantly down the aisle as she and Vonny quietly followed.

CHAPTER FIVE

"That evil old hag!" Bella said through clenched teeth, clutching her champagne flute as though it were Gail Hedgewick's throat. "How dare she try to upstage me at my own weddin'! I wish the nasty old prune had stayed in Florida."

"I'll say." Gloria rolled her eyes. "Who the heck wears a black dress to a weddin'?"

They'd taken every quiet moment to grumble ever since the ceremony, pausing only to thank well-wishers and occasionally offer tight-lipped reassurances that Mrs. Hedgewick was just fine now.

"Where's Elvan?" Gloria demanded, sounding entirely unimpressed. "Shouldn't the groom be with you at your own reception?"

"He's checkin' on her royal highness," Bella muttered, taking a hearty swig of champagne. "But he'd better get his butt back here soon or he'll be bunkin' in with her tonight. I swear this is the worst weddin' I've ever been to!"

"You've had more than your share," Gloria sniggered, digging her in the ribs with her elbow. "Well, come on. We don't have to let this party fizzle out, your *charming* mother-in-law is safely tucked upstairs in bed, so let's have some fun!"

***

David was standing near the doorway of the large dining room that had been decked out for the reception. He'd been talking to Tony when loud music suddenly filled the room.

Laughter and a few cheers rang out as the guests cleared the dance-floor for Bella and Gloria. The pair strutted out and started doing the hustle, and they were surprisingly good. They bounced, strutted and jiggled perfectly in time to the music.

Tony grinned as he watched his mother, Amelia, swagger out to join them. Draped in vibrant tangerine chiffon, she clapped her hands and snapped her fingers as she slid in step beside the bride.

"Sorry, Captain." Tony shook his head as he started past. "I gotta get in on this. Excuse me."

David smiled as more guests joined in and the atmosphere finally started to feel like a celebration. He wasn't much of a dancer, so he decided to leave them to it before he got dragged in. He also hadn't seen Harlow since the ceremony, and she was the reason he came.

He slipped out of the room and into the foyer. He looked around but didn't see her, she seemed to have vanished after the bizarre ceremony. As much as he wanted to find her straight away, his more responsible side nagged at him. Something in this whole strange business wasn't right and, despite being off duty, he couldn't make himself ignore it.

He stood for a moment as he debated what he wanted to do, he then nodded as he came to a decision and headed for the remarkable old staircase.

Some gut instinct told him he ought to check on Mrs. Hedgewick; he'd quickly been informed of the identity of the brazenly disruptive lady. He wasn't entirely sure what was bothering him. Maybe it was because she'd acted like she'd had a heart attack but had refused to see a doctor. Or so he'd been told.

Distrust was a hazard of his profession and he wasn't immune. He just needed to assure himself that she was okay, then he could go and find Harlow with a clear conscience and get on with the things he'd much rather be doing.

He had stepped in earlier and helped to find a suitable guest room, unfortunately it was on the third floor. But he and the two men that escorted her from the ceremony, who turned out to be the lady's grandsons, had helped to carry her up. She'd protested the fuss a little bit but then collapsed against them.

The bedrooms seemed to be mostly on the third floor; the lower levels were either for more public use or were still closed up. David reached the top of the stairs and walked along the hallway to the left until he came to the first door. He knocked gently and waited.

It wasn't long before a young woman in a nurse's uniform opened the door and peered out at him. She smiled as she pushed the door wide and absently straightened her skirt.

"Can I help you?" she asked quietly, running a smoothing hand over her bobbed, glossy brown hair.

"I wanted to see how Mrs. Hedgewick is doing," he replied in a similar tone. "Is she asleep?"

"No, she isn't." The lady's voice resounded strong and loud from the bed. "Come on in, sonny."

David smiled faintly and walked inside the dimly lit room. Gail Hedgewick looked even smaller now, tucked into the overstuffed bed, she had sunk down into soft cotton sheets and was covered in thick quilts. Her eyes were slightly cloudy from the years they'd seen but they still appeared shrewd and intelligent.

"Are you feeling any better?" he asked kindly.

"No, not really," she grumbled. "I'm *told* that the ceremony went on without me."

"It did. Don't tell me you're sorry you missed it?" he said dryly. "You certainly didn't seem to be enjoying yourself."

She stilled at that, but then a begrudging smile slipped into view. She smoothed her wrinkled hands over the quilt, her skin looked fragile and papery.

"You're very observant," she informed him as she gazed down at the trio of rings she wore.

"I tend to be," he said modestly.

"We met earlier, but we weren't introduced," she said, eyeing him calmly.

"David McAlister," he obligingly replied.

"Are you a friend of Bella Fontaine's?" Her eyes narrowed a fraction.

"I don't actually know the lady," he admitted with a shrug. "I'm more acquainted with the Harlows."

"Just as bad," Gail muttered quietly.

"Do you want a doctor now?" David decided to address the concern that had brought him up there in the first place. "I was told you refused one earlier."

"And I refuse again," she said simply as she admired the back of her left hand.

"Do you always wear three engagement rings?" he asked mildly.

"No, young man." She smirked. "But this was a special occasion, deservin' of special measures."

"I assume that statement makes sense to you, Mrs. Hedgewick," he said and decided to poke his nose in a little. "You don't seem fond of your new daughter-in-law."

"That son of mine has never presented me with anything I could be *fond* of," Gail replied tartly.

"Bella seems nice," he offered casually.

"She's a snake, Mr. McAlister," she narrowed her eyes at him. "A parasite. She's managed to insinuate herself back into Elvan's life and he's fallen for her every trick."

"Has he?" David deliberately sounded skeptical.

"Did you know he hadn't even spoken to her in decades? Not since she married some other fool straight out of high school," Gail harumphed. "Suddenly she turns up again, with a half-dozen ex-husbands behind her, and the next thing we know they're engaged!"

"According to what I heard, Elvan sought her out," he rubbed his chin thoughtfully.

"A ruse!" she scoffed. "That woman will have made sure she was thrown into his path. Elvan's turned into a sentimental fool. He's paranoid too, always lookin' over his shoulder and accusin' people of things. I do believe he's come unhinged; today is certainly proof of that."

"That's...an interesting theory, Mrs. Hedgewick," he said politely and took a subtle step backwards. "Well, if you're sure you don't want any medical attention, I'd better get back to the reception."

"Yes, you do that. I'm sure you'll all enjoy yourselves," she said with a hint of bitterness. "I'll rest for tonight. I have a *lot* to do tomorrow."

"I'll leave you to it then," David said simply.

He nodded to the stoic woman and then to the smiling nurse before excusing himself and walking out. The door closed softly behind him and he stood there for a thoughtful moment listening to the muffled voices of the two women on the other side of it.

The cop in him found the situation strange and wanted to start asking more questions. The normal guy in him recalled that he was there as a guest and had no real reason to start snooping around in someone else's dirty laundry. He'd already asked more than he really needed to.

David shook his head at himself and headed back downstairs. He'd barely reached the foyer when he heard Gloria's clarion tones announce that dinner was about to be served. Realizing that a private chat with Harlow would have to wait a bit longer, he sighed and followed the throng of other guests.

Tony had mentioned earlier that Kylie, the chef at Harlow House, had planned the menu. David hadn't actually ever eaten at the inn, despite being compelled to visit numerous times, but he'd heard good things about the food.

He entered the dining room, again marveled at the sheer size of the manor, and glanced at the seating chart just inside the door. He quirked a brow when he saw that he was seated next to Alfie and Gloria. That seemed an interesting choice considering he wasn't family, but he certainly wasn't going to argue. Alfie was great fun.

He found his place card and inclined his head politely to the others seated at the table. These were Alfie, Gloria, Amelia Ferris and Pierce Hedgewick. When they all fell into conversation, David glanced around the rest of the room.

There were dozens of large round tables set up and they were all full. He wasn't sure how many of the happy couple's friends had traveled up from Florida, but it didn't look like many people had declined to attend.

He again spotted the two women that had been glaring at Bradley through the ceremony. They both seemed a bit calmer now as they sipped champagne and murmured to the others at their table.

The bridal party sat at a long rectangular table at the rear of the room. They were gently bathed in the warm glow of tiny lights tucked in garlands of fake roses and ivy. Bella had cheered up noticeably, as had Elvan. The pair smiled, kissed and whispered happily to each other.

David finally saw Harlow as she slipped into the room and approached the table, he smiled reflexively; she looked better every time he looked at her. Bradley spotted her too and started to stand, but Tony was already on his feet and pulling her chair out for her before the other man got very far.

Bradley scowled at the interference but backed off when Tony gave him a look of stone-cold dislike. Harlow smiled at her friend as she settled in next to Bella. David recalled Harlow telling him that Tony had always looked out for her when they were kids; that feeling of responsibility clearly hadn't faded.

Dinner was served and everyone busied themselves eating and chatting. The food was excellent, but David's attention kept drifting back to the bridal table. He frowned pensively at the happy couple.

Bella was radiating joy, and probably a bit of satisfaction that Gail's stunt had failed. But Elvan looked a little subdued whenever he wasn't talking directly to his new bride. He glanced around at the door and the windows behind them a few times. While he didn't necessarily look worried, he was definitely watchful.

Bella turned and whispered something in his ear and any trace of concern was instantly banished. David wondered at the man but then shifted his gaze to the others. Vonny spent much of her time passing notes to Tony while Harlow picked at her plate and deliberately looked away every time Bradley tried to get her attention.

Alfie also noticed Bradley's persistent efforts and nudged his wife with his elbow. Fortunately, he kept his voice reasonably low, considering that Bradley's cousin was seated on the other side of the table.

"That idiot is staring at Maiden again," Alfie grumbled. "Look at him!"

"Ignore him, it don't matter," Gloria waved it away. "She don't like him, nothin's gonna happen."

"Of course she doesn't like him! That moronic turkey?! My little Maiden wouldn't waste the energy to spit on him. But she still has to put up with his nonsense, thanks to you and that sister of yours," he muttered indignantly. "*Why* did you put her in that awful dress?"

"Oh, I put her in it, did I?" Gloria gave him a tolerant look, clearly trying to sidestep the suggestion. "I dressed her up like she was a baby and sent her toddlin' on her way? Are you drunk?"

David pinched the bridge of his nose and tried not to laugh out loud.

"No, I am not drunk, unfortunately." Alfie gave her an irate look. "But I don't appreciate you sneaking around behind my back and dressing my daughters up like streetwalkers!"

"What a horrible thing to say!" Gloria gasped and pressed a hand to her bosom. "Those girls are ladies, through and through!"

"*I* know that, you dizzy blonde." Alfie glowered and nodded towards the bridal table. "But that idiot doesn't! You *know* what Maiden looks like, but you still threw that useless scrap of fabric at her and say she's covered! What the hell were you thinking!?"

"It was Bella's choice, not mine!" Gloria unceremoniously threw her sister to the dogs.

"Oh, sure it was," Alfie said. "You two and your bright ideas."

David pushed his plate away, there was no way he could swallow another bite without choking. He understood Alfie's point of view, but he was still entirely sold on Gloria's choice. The fact that they were fussing over a grown woman like she was a teenager made it even more ridiculous.

"Vonny looks fine!" she said as though the defense had just occurred to her, or could in any way make the dress more suitable for anyone else.

"Vonny has Tony, who happens to be a gentleman. This has nothing to do with her." He rolled his eyes and then glared at his wife. "You know what you've done and I know why you've done it! Just leave the girl alone!"

"Maiden loved that dress!" Gloria insisted, but her eye gave a betraying twitch as she met Alfie's steely gaze. "Well...she didn't hate it...entirely. She looks good, dammit! Grow up!"

"That's it, Gloria. You can't be trusted. The next time you go dress shopping I'm going with you!" he muttered, but the blood drained from his face when he realized what he'd committed himself to. "*Oh lord no!* That's even worse! Look, no more dresses! They have plenty already!"

At that point David had to get up and discreetly walk away for a few minutes.

***

The reception had only been going for a couple of hours but Maiden was already wishing it was over. Dinner had been wonderful, Kylie's skill was undeniable, and then there were the bridal dances.

She'd spent the longest four and a half minutes of her life keeping Bradley rigidly at arm's length as he kept trying to force her closer. A tight-lipped reminder that she wasn't afraid to let her knee do the talking finally seemed to get through to him. He spent the rest of the dance chit-chatting about nothing in particular.

The instant the music stopped, Maiden walked away and was pleased to see Tony and Von nearby. Tony put his arm around Von and gestured for Maiden to walk ahead of them with a kind smile. Maiden was happy to let herself be escorted peacefully back to the table.

As she walked past, she noticed the same young woman she'd seen smirking in the audience when Gail nearly collapsed. She was sitting at one of the guest tables sipping champagne and muttering irately to the woman next to her. Maiden followed her gaze to Bradley, who appeared to be trying to get a disinterested Pierce to step outside with him.

When Maiden turned back to the ladies at the table, she found them both looking right at her. They smiled instantly, clearly knowing they'd been caught, and the younger woman nodded politely before glancing away.

Maiden sighed, it was too much to hope, of course, that no one had noticed the awkward and fumbling dance. She tried not to feel embarrassed as she walked resolutely back to her seat and sank down into it.

Those uncomfortable realizations made her think of McAlister. Her eyes widened and she immediately looked at his table. She'd noticed earlier, with a twinge of mortification, that he'd been seated with the extended family. She could only hope and pray that her mother wasn't laying it on too thick.

At the moment, McAlister was in the midst of a conversation with Amelia. Whatever they were discussing, it was making him laugh.

Maiden tried not to smile too obviously when she saw the dimple flash in his left cheek. It was nice to see him happy and relaxed.

A little time passed and Maiden spent it covertly studying him while also managing to chat with Vonny.

"When are they gonna cut the cake?" Von leaned close enough to whisper. "This is taking forever!"

"You want Aunt Bella to rush through her wedding reception because you're bored?" Maiden slid her a wry look. "Way to think of others."

"I'm not bored. I want cake," Vonny corrected as her eyes shifted to the towering confection that dominated the dessert table. "Do you think the little bride and groom statues are edible?"

"Please don't start eating the decorations," Maiden giggled as discreetly as she could, but the effort to keep quiet only made her laugh harder. "Have you tasted the candles yet?"

"I don't recommend them," Von snorted, "'vanilla spice' is grossly misleading."

They were both laughing when the music started up again and couples started filling the dance floor. Maiden's attention went to the large doorway when she saw one of few people present that she recognized.

It was Pierce Hedgewick. He was stalking back inside holding the arm of the slender dark-haired woman she'd noticed earlier. The look on Pierce's face was one of irritation, but the lady with him was harder to read. She looked upset, but it wasn't immediately obvious if she was hurt, disappointed or angry.

Maiden watched them murmur a few words and then part ways, each returning to their own tables. Maiden wondered who that woman was and why she was at the wedding; she didn't seem to like Elvan's family very much. A moment later Bradley walked in. He glanced at his cousin and scowled before being distracted by some of the other guests. His annoyed expression evaporated as he turned on his version of charm.

It was all very strange. There was an unmistakable tension there between the three of them but she wasn't sure what it meant. It was none of her business, of course, but she couldn't help feeling curious.

"Don't look now," Von interrupted her thoughts as she nudged her with her elbow and grinned down into her glass, "Captain McCutie is checking you out. *Again.*"

It was as good as an order to look at him immediately. That was the effect, at least. Maiden shifted her eyes over in time for them to lock with McAlister's. She pulled in an indiscreet breath and heard Vonny snigger.

"Yeah, play it cool, Mae," she chuckled. "Are you gonna faint if he asks you to dance?"

"Feel free to shut up," Maiden said under her breath even as she kept her expression carefully composed. Her nerves started to fail her when he maintained eye contact and smiled warmly at her. "He's not looking away. Von! He's not looking away! I don't know what to do!"

"This is even better than cake!" Vonny chortled gleefully. "You're absolutely hopeless!"

"You weren't any smoother with Tony," Maiden grumbled even as she smiled shyly at the gorgeous cop.

"I got him, didn't I?" Vonny said confidently as she sipped her champagne and did her best to affect a casually sophisticated pose. "Can't argue with results."

"Took you twenty years, though," Maiden felt herself relax when McAlister finally, and very slowly, turned to listen to Pierce as the man started talking to him.

"All part of the master plan," Vonny said smugly. "You want quantity or quality?"

"You're ridiculous," Maiden gave her a fondly smiling look.

"Sometimes," she admitted with a shrug.

Ten minutes later the bride and groom were ushered over to cut the cake. Maiden and Vonny stood dutifully nearby and applauded as Bella and Elvan fed each other. Maiden subtly grasped Von by the arm and held her still so she wouldn't swoop in before the photos were finished.

The instant the photographers walked away, Vonny was beside Aunt Bella and flashing her a big, hopeful smile. As Bella laughed and started to slice another piece, Maiden couldn't help overhearing a few of the people around her.

"Nice to see Elvan looking so happy," a man standing behind her whispered to someone.

"Yes, I'm glad he didn't let that damn woman spoil everything," his companion replied just as quietly. "It's about time she was put out to pasture, she's a menace."

Maiden couldn't exactly argue with that but she was glad she wasn't a part of the conversation either. Gail's stunt had certainly been mean, hateful really. Her thoughts drifted back to the conversation she'd overheard between her and Elvan the night before.

Apart from silently admitting that she eavesdropped a lot, she recalled that Gail's words had been phrased as a threat. Maiden wondered if the fake heart attack was the full extent of the unkind woman's plans.

In any case, Gail didn't seem to have won any fans with her performance. Maiden glanced over her shoulder to try and see who had been voicing their grievances but the people behind her had merged into a larger group. She couldn't be sure who she'd heard.

As everyone selected their desserts and returned to their seats, Bradley stood up and made a lengthy speech. He went on for several minutes about his dear sweet daddy and his lovely new bride. Maiden could see that Bella wasn't impressed in the slightest but she kept smiling politely.

After that Elvan said a few words, thanking all their friends that had travelled so far to share their special day. He then gazed at Bella and told her how happy she'd made him and how complete he felt now that they were married. It was sweet and so genuine that Maiden felt a little awkward watching them. He kept his sentiments brief, however, and then handed back to Bradley to read out the messages from friends that couldn't attend.

Then there was more dancing. Music filled the room and dozens of couples took to the dance floor. Maiden danced with Elvan, her father and then Tony. She'd been gathering up all the poise she could muster in expectation of a dance with a certain police captain. But more than an hour passed and the reception started to sputter out.

It was understandable. Most of the guests had likely arrived in town that same day and evidently weren't interested in dancing all night. Evidently Captain McAlister was even less interested. Every time she looked at him he was talking to someone, or he'd slipped out of the room for a few minutes. He never got anywhere near her or the dancefloor.

Finally, she decided she'd waited around long enough. He'd had yet another chance and he still hadn't taken it. She ducked out quietly and went in search of solitude...and hopefully a drink.

Chapter Six

David scanned the large, slowly emptying room. It was about 9:30 and the caterers were packing up. Gloria and Alfie had evidently made up; they were smiling and chatting warmly to each other at a corner table.

The older guests were congratulating the newlyweds and saying their goodnights. Vonny was slow dancing with Tony despite no music playing and Bradley looked to be in the midst of a whispered argument with his cousin.

David had spoken briefly with Pierce Hedgewick earlier in the evening and found him to be nice enough. He obviously had money but he wasn't obnoxious about it. He had no idea what the two men were discussing but Bradley looked indignant and Pierce looked ready to throttle him.

Their family conflicts weren't his concern, he had other, more pressing matters on his mind. As he looked around he saw no sign of Harlow anywhere.

He'd been hoping to get some time alone with her all evening and he knew he was running out of opportunities.

He slipped out of the dining room and looked around. He'd gathered that the handful of rooms that had been refurbished, apart from a few guestrooms upstairs, were all on the ground floor. Heading down the numerous hallways that snaked around back on each other, he passed one room after another without spotting her.

He found himself back in the foyer and heard conversations drifting from the room where the ceremony had been held. He took a subtle look inside but he still couldn't find her. For a moment he worried that she'd left, but then he recalled Alfie grousing about missing his own bed as they were all staying at the manor for the night. Harlow had to still be there somewhere.

David glanced at the remarkable staircase. It was elegantly stylish and tastefully decked out in red ribbons and clusters of flowers. He edged closer and tried to see up into the shadows above.

He knew Gail Hedgewick was tucked away on the third floor, he had no desire to chat to her again, but he hadn't given the second floor much of a look as he'd passed it. It was certainly worth a try now.

David climbed the stairs quietly and was greeted by stale, slightly musty air as he stepped out onto the second-floor landing. A long passageway stretched out to the left but it was too dark to see how extensive it was or how many rooms were tucked away in the shadows.

There were no lights on and he didn't really want to announce his presence by trying any switches. It wasn't necessary anyway, he was soon rewarded by the sight of soft light spilling from under a doorway to his right. He walked over and gave the knob a careful twist. The door glided open easily and with only the faintest creak of the hinges. He peered inside and did his best to hide a wide grin.

***

Maiden didn't regret abandoning the reception for an instant. She was content that she'd done everything that had been asked of her. She wore the infamous dress, smiled in every photo and even danced with the obnoxiously smarmy best man. She'd paid her dues; she was done.

After glancing around to make sure no one would see her, she dashed upstairs into the darkness that enveloped the second floor. The first door she tried was unlocked. She felt around the wall inside the door until she found a light switch and smiled delightedly when the room lit up to reveal a rather snazzy bar.

It was all a bit faded and probably needed a few repairs but it appeared clean enough to suggest that it had been used relatively recently. Above all, no one else was there and the lights worked. It was perfect.

The walls were dark purple and the windows were hung with heavy black curtains. The ceiling was dotted with miniature crystal chandeliers and several art-deco wall sconces provided a soft, atmospheric glow.

There was a long bar made from polished oak with stained glass inlays. A dozen tufted barstools were lined up across the front and each one held out the sweet, seductive promise of giving her aching feet a much-needed rest. The wall behind the bar was filled with glasses and countless glistening bottles; her eyes grew wide and her heart grew happy.

Maiden was trying not to feel too disappointed that Captain McAlister hadn't asked her to dance or even tried to talk to her all evening. They exchanged a lot of looks and smiles, but it was getting late and the party was essentially over. It was turning into another big fat could've been.

With a rueful shake of her head she turned her attention to the fabulous bar. She couldn't be bothered to walk all the way around, it was huge and she'd been wearing her ridiculous feathered stilettos all day. As there was no one there to see her, she climbed up onto one of the padded stools and stretched over. She couldn't quite reach so she climbed higher and knelt on the polished bar top, grabbing the first bottle of wine she could wrap her fingers around.

Maiden was still poised, half climbed over the bar when she heard the door open and looked over sharply. She was relieved that it wasn't Bradley that quietly entered and shut the door behind him, but was still unnerved to see Captain McAlister stride towards her instead.

She pressed her lips together briefly. She set the bottle aside and climbed down as demurely as she could, aware that being caught with her bottom in the air reaching for a bottle of wine wasn't the best look she could go for.

If McAlister thought it odd or unladylike he didn't mention it. She cleared her throat and looked him over as discreetly as she could; she'd never seen him so dressed up before. She sighed very softly and perched on the stool behind her.

His dark blue suit looked great on him. He had undone his tie, she assumed he must hate the things, and opened the top two buttons of his shirt. She dragged her gaze from the glimpse of his dark chest hair that peeked out from behind the crisp fabric and looked into eyes the color of molten chocolate.

"Hey," she said softly.

"I wondered where you'd run off to," he chuckled. "Weren't you enjoying the party?"

"Oh, it's not so bad." She smiled at herself for getting caught sneaking away. "I just needed a break."

"And a drink?" he asked with a smile.

"You've spent an entire evening with Aunt Bella and her friends," Maiden said teasingly. "How much were *you* enjoying it?"

"Enough to wander off too," he admitted as he came and stood beside her. "I checked on Mrs. Hedgewick earlier, by the way, she was resting comfortably. I thought you'd like to know."

"That's good news, thank you, Captain." She shifted, conscious of how the strap of her dress kept threatening to slip off her shoulder, she subtly pushed it back into place.

"I'm off duty," he mentioned as he reached over the bar, far more easily than she had, and pulled out two glasses. "You can call me David."

"Oh, right." Her eyes widened briefly; he'd never suggested that she use his first name before. Her stomach fluttered. "Thanks...David."

He nodded as he opened the bottle she'd dug out. Maiden watched him fill the glasses and thanked him quietly when he handed her one. He settled onto the stool next to hers and considered her over the rim of his glass.

"You look very...um." Words failed him as he ran his gaze over her and then cleared his throat quietly. "Yeah. I like the dress."

"It wasn't my idea," she said quickly and tried not to squirm as she took a large sip of wine.

"Yes, I managed to piece that much together." He grinned briefly at the faint blush that she felt stain her cheeks. "You should wear red more often."

She was feeling too embarrassed and on display to say much in reply. She smiled a little and toyed with the stem of her glass. He was acting differently tonight; he wasn't being subtle and he seemed fine with that. Something was *very* different. Her heart started beating a little faster as David shifted closer and set his glass down on the bar.

"So, you didn't seem too thrilled with the leering idiot that stood up with you for the ceremony," he sounded casual despite his ungenerous description.

"Oh, yeah. That's Bradley Hedgewick." She wrinkled her nose down at her glass. "He's Elvan's son."

"And what's his story?" He sounded more like Captain McAlister when he asked that question but he was still looking at her with a smile that would melt solid ice.

"I don't really know much about him. I only met him the day before yesterday," she admitted as she sipped her wine. "He said he's a doctor, or something medical, but I think he's a sleaze, to be honest."

"Yeah, that's a pretty safe bet," David laughed quietly and also took another drink. "I knew you were clever."

"Well, what about you?" Two sips of wine evidently made her quite brave. "I noticed you didn't bring a date."

"Did you?" He smiled again.

"I'm clever, don't forget," she replied pertly.

"The ceremony was interesting," he shifted the subject. "I was a little surprised that they continued on after Mrs. Hedgewick's episode."

"Oh, that was nothing. She just doesn't like Aunt Bella," Maiden said as she swiveled absently on the stool. "I'm glad they did go through with it, we've gone to too much trouble to have it fall apart over one little spat."

"You don't think she was actually ill?" He gave her a quietly curious look.

"It can be very hard to tell if an old southern woman is actually ill, Captain," she said with an air of authority.

"David," he reminded her and topped up their glasses. He gave her a teasing look as he set the bottle aside. "You aren't planning to turn into a southern drama queen, are you?"

"No, never, I'm half Yankee," she assured him. "My father's blood will protect me...I'll just be eccentric instead."

David laughed at that. It was a genuine laugh that showed the dimple in his left cheek and made the corners of his eyes crinkle. The deep, joyful sound made her feel happy, she looked him over subtly.

"So...when did Mom invite you?" she asked, not doubting for a moment that her mother had been behind the scheme.

"Two weeks ago." He still looked amused. "You really didn't know about it?"

"No, I fought against wearing this dress as it was." She smiled ruefully. "She wouldn't risk...well...no, I didn't know about it."

"What's there to fight about? It's a great dress. You look sexy." He visibly caught himself and smiled sheepishly as he stared resolutely at the other side of the room. "I mean it's a lovely dress. You look very nice."

"Smooth as silk, David," she laughed softly down into her glass.

"I have my moments," he conceded with a chuckle. "That wasn't one of them."

"Well, if we're counting on *my* small talk, we're in trouble," she said but tried anyway. "Do you have any family?"

"Yeah, I have my parents. Two sisters and a brother." He nodded. "I'm the oldest of the kids."

"Wow." Maiden stared at him. "I have my hands full with just Von."

"I moved away, easy fix for a big family," he said with a smile. "They're good people. Mostly anyway. Life just happened to have brought me here."

"Do you miss them?" she asked.

"Not at the moment," he replied.

"Good." She ran her fingertip around the rim of her glass and searched for something else to say. "So...did you enjoy the ceremony?"

"Parts of it." He slid her a playful look.

"Really?" She smiled skeptically. "Which part was your favorite?"

"Every part of you is sexy, Harlow." He shrugged. "I don't think I could choose a favorite."

She stared at him but David didn't look away, he didn't make excuses or try to take anything back. He actually shifted closer and turned to face her more fully.

Okay, we're done being subtle, apparently. I don't know where this version of you came from, Captain, but I wish you'd brought him out sooner. She felt herself smile a little wider.

"What about you?" he asked gently. "It's been a busy few weeks. You've...been okay?"

She recalled that they hadn't seen each other since the business with her high school reunion; he looked quietly watchful as he waited for her to answer. She didn't want to talk about that case, and she didn't want to wander too far from the flirty exchange he'd started.

"Yeah, I'm all right," she assured him. "And you?"

"It's been busy, but no one's found any bodies for a few days, so I can't complain," he laughed softly and shook his head at himself. "My small talk also sucks, by the way."

"Oh, I don't know, you managed to casually work corpses into the conversation. Fortunately, you've found the right woman." She shut her eyes briefly when she realized what she said. "For that kind of topic, I mean...Seriously, you really do make me say stupid things."

"I know." He smiled at her. "It's pretty cute. Are you this articulate with anyone but me?"

She wasn't, it was only with him, so she tried for a nonchalant shrug. She instantly regretted it, however, when his eyes dipped lower of their own accord.

"Are you...um, are you warm enough in that?" His dark brows lifted in polite inquiry, but his eyes took their own sweet time to join them.

"Of course I am. 'Why, it's an indoor ceremony, honey!'" she mimicked her mother's heavy accent perfectly. "'It'll be plenty warm!'"

David laughed even as he stood and slipped out of his coat. Maiden was smirking but held her breath when he reached his arms around her and draped the warm garment around her bare shoulders. When she did breathe again her senses were filled with his spicy cologne, she knew she had absolutely no chance.

If you walk away from this again, she warned silently as his eyes locked with hers, *I swear I'll bounce my wineglass off your head.*

He didn't walk away. He didn't even shift back a single step. David still grasped the lapels of his jacket, pinning her gently in place. Maiden's eyes gleamed in the soft light from the old sconces as she watched him and waited. There was now no doubt in her mind that this man was about to kiss her, and she wanted him to.

After holding her gaze for a moment, possibly giving her a chance to speak up, David lowered his head and touched his lips to hers. They were soft and warm; she instinctively slid closer to him and rested a hand against his chest.

Apparently deciding that lack of warmth was no longer a concern, David slid his arms around her, letting his coat fall forgotten around her hips. Maiden closed her eyes and leaned into him. She felt one of his large hands splay across her back while the other gently cradled the back of her head, she grasped either side of his loose necktie and pulled him closer.

She had to reassure herself that this was actually happening. After months of teasing and flirting and wondering, he had finally made a move, and it was absolute bliss. For a precious moment she curled up against him and forgot about everything else.

He drew his thumb across her cheek and pressed her closer with the hand on her back as he kissed her more deeply. She slid her hands up over his broad shoulders, nestling against him, and felt his warmth seep through the thin fabric of her dress.

She had just reached up and touched his hair when he lifted his head slightly. He ran his fingertips along her bare arm, smiling when he felt goosebumps on her soft skin.

"Are you busy tomorrow night?" His deep voice sounded a little extra deep now.

"Don't think so," she replied as she touched his clean-shaven jaw.

"Dinner?" He kissed her again before she could answer.

"Sounds nice," she murmured against his mouth.

She sank her fingers into his thick hair; he slid his hands around her waist and sighed contentedly. She smiled as she felt his thumbs draw circles on her ribs. In that indescribably happy moment, they were the only two people in the world.

The moment was shattered, however, when a terrified scream pierced the air. They broke the kiss and both turned sharply to the door as another anguished howl drifted from upstairs.

"What the—" David carefully released her before running to the door and flinging it open. Maiden slid off the stool and followed as fast as she could in the towering stilettos.

David was in the hallway and looking up the grand staircase when Elvan half ran towards him, nearly toppling over more than once.

"Careful!" He frowned as he grabbed the older man's arm to steady him. "What's going on? What's happened?"

"It's Mama!" Elvan was shaking and his pale face was coated in sweat. "She's dead! *She's been murdered!*"

CHAPTER SEVEN

"**J**ust stay downstairs and wait with the others!" David said loudly and sternly, thoroughly back in cop-mode now. "I'm calling for backup!"

He had already gone to Gail's room to confirm Elvan's panicked announcement. He'd then headed straight downstairs and ordered the remaining guests to stay put.

Maiden, who'd been listening to all of it from the doorway of the old bar, backed into the room as he charged in. He ran over and grabbed his coat from where they'd left it on the barstool. As he pulled his phone out of the inside pocket he looked at her and shook his head ruefully.

"I'm sorry about this," he said genuinely and then stalked off to a more discreet corner muttering under his breath as he waited for someone to pick up. "I can't get a single night off in this lunatic town!"

Maiden could sympathize, she'd been having a much better time than she'd ever expected until Elvan started screaming. She dried her damp palms on her uselessly flimsy dress and tried to listen to what David was saying.

She blinked when she thought of him as David and not Captain McAlister, she supposed that's what being inside a man's jacket with him will do. The memory brought a telling heat to her cheeks but she was called jarringly back to the present when she heard him say 'suffocation' and 'Doc Jenkins'.

Doctor Ben Jenkins was a surprisingly genial coroner, a man she'd met in his official capacity more times than most civilians. As for suffocation, her thoughts went to poor, cranky old Mrs. Hedgewick and she felt a bit queasy. A moment later David finished his call and quickly walked back to her.

"All right, that's the wedding well and truly over with," he said grimly as he slipped his jacket back on. "The whole team will be here in fifteen minutes. I'll have to keep an eye on everyone and make sure nobody tries to leave."

"Wait!" She grabbed his arm as he moved past, he turned back to her uncertainly as she reached into his top pocket and pulled out his crisp white handkerchief. She wiped it over his lips and held it up for him to see. "There'll be enough questions asked without added clues."

He looked at the smear of her crimson red lipstick and grinned. There was no time to linger, unfortunately, but he gave her a wink as he reclaimed his handkerchief and tucked it back where she found it.

Maiden watched him walk swiftly through the door, by appearances in complete and utter control of the situation. She released a shaky breath and hugged herself as she considered the possibility of another murderer in their midst; she wasn't feeling so confident herself.

***

Maiden hadn't left the upstairs bar, but she'd crept out into the hall and leaned into the banister as she tried to hear everything that was happening downstairs. Her clandestine nosiness was balanced by the background terror of a killer that could be hiding anywhere. Time passed quickly as she alternated between listening to David warn everyone to stay put while also keeping an ear out for any lunatics that might be skulking around on the floor above her.

It wasn't long before she saw the distinctive bright lights of police cars flashing across the foyer. David must have opened the front door. She watched as dozens of officers rushed inside the antiquated mansion.

She half listened to David as he gave a brief rundown of the situation and instructed them to question every guest and search every room. As he took care of the routine police procedures, her mind wandered to the events of the afternoon and evening.

Gail's attempt to spoil her own son's wedding really was shocking. Maiden couldn't imagine ever doing anything so brazenly selfish. No one had been impressed by the stunt, she recalled the reactions of some of the guests, the sentiments weren't generous towards the brassy woman. And now Gail was dead, apparently smothered to death.

How awful, how horribly awful for the whole Hedgewick family. A family that now included Aunt Bella. A part of Maiden felt badly for not being with her, but she was hardly alone and was probably too busy helping Elvan to notice where anyone else was.

As for Maiden, she was too on edge to deal with the other guests or half of the local police department just yet. And she certainly had an alibi for this murder.

She walked back into the room and sat down at the bar with a troubled frown. Through the half open door she saw a glimpse of David and Dr. Jenkins, their cheerful coroner, as they headed up to the third floor. Maiden tried not to be grossed out by the thought of forensics and impending autopsies.

She listened to the din that floated up the staircase from the ground floor. Lots of brisk footsteps and authoritative voices slicing through the air. She could only imagine how exhausted and stunned the remaining guests must be. Some had already left, of course. She wondered if the killer had managed to slip out already.

Time ticked by. She was vaguely aware of David walking past again and peeking in on her briefly. By the time she'd looked over he was already walking away again.

She glanced at an ornate silver clock that hung on the wall and noticed that it was caked in dust and stuck at half past 2. A bit of guesswork suggested that it was actually closer to 11 pm. It had been a massive day, however, and that made it feel much later.

Maiden had barely had the chance to prop her sore feet up on the neighboring stool when the door opened wide and a slew of policemen poured in like a trail of ants. She immediately lowered her feet and smoothed her filmy skirt down to cover as much of her legs as possible.

Several officers glanced over and spotted her; a few looked her over and smirked while one or two even let out low whistles. Maiden shifted uncomfortably, it got even worse when she saw Officer Sarah-Jane Parker walk in.

Officer Parker was the newest member of the Golden Glen police department and had intensely disliked Maiden from the moment they met. Maiden still wasn't sure what she'd done to offend the feisty officer.

True to form, Parker glared at her openly the instant she saw her. She whipped her notebook out of her pocket and started scribbling angrily.

Maiden could only imagine what she was writing to justify her irritated expression; wearing a sexy dress was hardly illegal. And yet, when Parker had finished her note, she met Maiden's gaze with a smug smile that she punctuated by closing her pen with a loud click. Maiden raised her chin a fraction and did her best to look calm and innocent.

Yeah right, Maiden, you look perfectly innocent. She glanced away and rolled her eyes at herself. *I should've grabbed my jacket, but it's upstairs in the room next to the crime scene...it probably wouldn't be discreet to ask David if I could put his coat back on either. Don't laugh, don't laugh, don't laugh.*

She distracted herself from her threatening giggles by indulging in another internal grumble at her meddling family. She was more annoyed than shocked by the lengths her mother and aunt had gone to. Although, they couldn't have foreseen her ending up flaunting herself in front of almost every cop in town. David had been their only true target, the rest were just collateral damage. And, even at that, their scheme hadn't exactly failed.

As if to punish her further, Maiden shifted and caught a whiff of David's cologne where it still clung to her bared shoulders. It smelled *really* nice. Her pathetically wandering thoughts were interrupted a moment later when David returned to the room along with Dr. Jenkins.

The doctor was resplendent in full hazmat once again. He walked towards the bar and away from the other officers, his expression was serious as he talked quietly with David. When they drew closer, however, he looked over and noticed her sitting there. His face lit up with a pleased and friendly smile.

"Oh wow! Va-va-voom, Miss Harlow!" He gave her an approving waggle of his eyebrows, ignored the quiet chuckles his blurted statement gave rise to, and was instantly all business once again. "Have a look at this, David."

Maiden said absolutely nothing while he and David sank into a quiet and intense discussion as they perused the piece of paper that the doctor was showing him, possibly some sort of preliminary report. From the corner of her eye she saw Parker motioning to get her attention.

When she looked at her, Officer Parker beckoned her over with a furious expression and pointed emphatically to the floor in front of her. Not about to be ordered to stand before her like a naughty child, Maiden pretended not to have seen her and turned back to the two men at the bar.

Maiden stubbornly reminded herself that *she'd* found the jazzy little bar, not any of them. They'd barged in and she wasn't going to volunteer to be tossed out. She crossed her legs casually, immediately realized it was a mistake, and attempted to push her skirt a little further down her thighs without betraying her discomfort.

By the time David and the doctor had finished conferring, Parker was tapping her foot irately and Maiden was contemplating diving behind the bar and hiding there until morning. Dr. Jenkins glanced back and waved to her before walking out; Maiden smiled at the pleasant man as he disappeared through the door.

She turned back to David as he ran his hands over his hair with a sigh. It was brief and the only sign of frustration or weariness that he allowed himself to show. Maiden wondered how much he had to keep bottled up to maintain the confidence and loyalty of his squad.

"All right." He turned to address his officers, either forgetting or not caring that she was there to hear it. "You've got your orders. I need everyone downstairs to give a full account of their movements for the evening. Also, the hotels and home addresses for the out-of-town guests. Get those statements signed and turned in to me ASAP. We also have to track down the guests that had already left. Let's move."

Most of the officers started to disperse but Parker, clearly still incensed by Maiden's snub, folded her arms over her chest and lifted her chin a fraction.

"And what about Miss Harlow?" she demanded loudly, giving Maiden a cold look. "Shall I question her, sir?"

"No. That's not necessary." David cleared his throat and focused very deliberately on his notes.

"'Not necessary'?" Parker's irritation was clearly strong enough to overcome her common sense. "But she's a suspect, sir! Again! I'm aware that she spends a *lot* of time hanging around the station but surely she still has to account for her whereabouts like everyone else!"

The room fell awkwardly silent. Maiden was both annoyed by the unfriendly woman's bossiness and a tiny bit pleased by the way David instantly tensed. The other officers edged away and waited to see how the captain would respond; they didn't have to wait long.

David slowly raised his eyes to lock coolly on the mouthy young officer. Parker's quietly embarrassed expression suggested that she realized she'd crossed a line. To her credit, she didn't try to argue or make excuses, she stood still and waited stoically to accept the consequences.

"Listen close, Parker. I know you've been out of training for about a week and you have a lot to learn. Here's a good opportunity; rookies don't tell a superior officer how to conduct an investigation. *Ever!*" he said in a coldly steady voice. "You will do as you're instructed and interview the people you are told to interview. Is that understood?"

"Yes, Captain." She'd reddened slightly, but doubtless knew that she'd invited the rebuke by being publicly insubordinate.

"Fine," he murmured and nodded in Maiden's direction as he continued. "As for Miss Harlow, in this instance I happen to know exactly where the lady was and precisely what she was doing at the time of the murder, so there's no cause for concern there."

Parker's blush deepened at the implication. The other officers in the room exchanged looks and slid their gazes to Maiden, whose quietly pleased expression had been replaced by a slightly incredulous glare.

Maiden draped her hands on her hips, only to be reminded of the slinky dress she'd been tricked into wearing. She exhaled her breath in a slow hiss and looked around for her glass of wine.

Parker inclined her head stiffly when David dismissed her and the others and stalked out without raising her eyes to anyone. The other officers filed out with only a little sniggering and a few knowing looks exchanged.

David waited until they were alone before turning to Maiden. She was still perched on the stool, leaning casually back against the bar, watching him coolly as she sipped her wine. He made a visible effort not to chuckle but wasn't entirely successful as he came and stood beside her again.

"There you go," he smiled at her, "I rescued you from the fire-breathing Sarah-Jane and kept you neatly out of another tangle."

"Oh yes. I won't be given a second thought now, thanks a lot," she drawled sardonically. "If I'd known you were going to throw me to the dogs like that I wouldn't have warned you to wipe away my lipstick."

"Yes, you would've; you're such a sweetheart." His smile widened.

"Yeah, that's me all right." She arched a brow as he leaned a bit closer. "Have fun trying to get that shade of red out of a white hand-kerchief, by the way."

"I don't plan on washing it. I like it the way it is," he said warmly as he reached out and ran his thumb just under the curve of her bottom lip. "You're a bit smudged yourself, by the way."

Maiden held his gaze and felt herself start to smile. Her lipstick was perfect, she'd checked that very carefully already and made the necessary repairs.

"Making excuses to touch me again?" she asked. "And right after blabbing my personal business. Gutsy."

"That's gratitude," he protested with an incredibly transparent look of hurt. He picked up one of her dark curls that had come loose and fallen over her shoulder. "I was trying to protect your honor."

"You just told your whole squad that we made out!" she reminded him in a grumpy whisper, gesturing towards the door with her wineglass before setting it aside.

"Nah, the whole squad isn't here yet." He waved it away and just barely managed not to laugh. "Anyway, I only stated a fact. I can't help it if they jump to conclusions."

Maiden tried and failed to stop smiling at him. She was surprised that he was slipping back into his more flirtatious behavior so readily. Of course, she was also surprised that he essentially told all his colleagues that something had happened in the first place.

"Have you done something with the real Captain McAlister?" she asked as she grasped his loosened tie and gently urged him to stand a little closer.

"I *had* tried to put him away for the evening," he said quietly. "I don't get to be just David very often."

"That's a shame," Maiden replied. "I really like him."

"I'm glad to hear it." He looked pleased and touched his fingertips to her cheek. "And what about Captain McAlister?"

"I like him too," she murmured warmly, resting her hand on his chest. "He's kind of a tease, but he's hot."

"You're incredible, Harlow," he whispered with a smile and shook his head slightly.

"Thanks." She held his gaze until they both started to smirk. "We really don't have time for this, do we?"

"Not tonight, no." He shut his eyes briefly and let his fingers trail down her throat before resting his hand at his side. "And I can't fully explain to you how deeply I regret that."

"I think I can imagine," she assured him dryly and forced herself to broach the most obvious issue. "So...you do realize that a lot of your prime suspects in this murder are going to be members of my family?"

"Yeah, I'm a reasonably good policeman," he said mildly and sat beside her.

"I'm not criticizing. You just don't seem worried about it." She couldn't help laughing softly.

"Well, I'm confident that *you* didn't do it, so that's my biggest potential conflict avoided," he replied as he let his gaze wander over her a bit, his thoughts weren't far from the matter at hand though. "Bella did seem ill-disposed towards Mrs. Hedgewick."

"I'd say it was mutual." Maiden acknowledged.

"What about the rest of the family?" he asked with a resigned sigh. "Did you notice much friction there?"

"Yes, to be honest." She pulled a face as she thought it over. "I did detect some animosity coming from Bradley. But there was more outright hostility between Elvan and Mrs. Hedgewick than anyone else."

"Except Bella," he said impassively.

"Ugh!" She favored him with a teasing scowl. "And you go straight back to the obnoxious cop."

"Thanks a lot." He didn't sound deeply stung. "The obnoxious cop was hot a few minutes ago."

"Yeah, he was. He was managing to keep me warm even in this ridiculous little dress," she replied, a bit surprised at her own playfulness.

David closed his eyes briefly and exhaled slowly in an obvious effort to regain his professional calm. She could see that he was finally sobering; when he looked at her again his expression was more serious.

"Maiden, please listen to me." He had never addressed her by her first name before and it got her full attention. "I have to remain impartial in this investigation."

"Yeah, granted. So...does that mean you can flirt but I can't?" she asked.

"No, of course not," he conceded.

"Do you want me to stop flirting?" She shook her head uncertainly.

"No," he said quickly and then ran a hand through his hair. "This is getting complicated."

"I'm glad you finally noticed," she chuckled. "So, what happens now?"

"I don't know." He rubbed his eyes. "I'd only planned as far as making a move or two and asking you out."

"Well, mission accomplished there." She nodded once and then rolled her eyes subtly. "Speaking of which, I assume this means dinner tomorrow is cancelled?"

"Raincheck, please." He gave her an apologetic wince. "Trust me, I wish we could just do what we want, but I wasn't expecting a murder."

"You've met my family." She waved it away as though he'd been foolishly optimistic. "So, do we need to cool it until this is sorted out?"

"Yes, we honestly do." He nodded and flicked his gaze over her. "There'll be a lot of interviews to be done tonight, it'll take at least another hour or two. Do you want to go put some real clothes on?"

Maiden leaned back, resting on her elbows, and crossed her legs, fully aware of what it did to her skirt.

"No. I'm happy in this," she said with a sweet smile.

David dragged his gaze from her legs up to her face and grinned before making himself stand up and head downstairs to join the others.

Maiden watched him go with a smirk that quickly faded. Apart from the frustration of having to postpone a date that had only just been made, she wasn't mistaken about some of the suspicion falling close to home.

Regardless of her unshakable confidence in Aunt Bella, the woman had to be viewed as a potential suspect, she and Gail had hated each other. Then there was Elvan, his mother had made a public scene at the climax of his wedding. It would be wrong of David not to at least consider them.

Maiden chewed at her lip as her thoughts traveled back through what she knew of the Hedgewicks. There wasn't much. She'd only just met Elvan and Bradley, she'd spoken to Gail once and hadn't even been introduced to Pierce.

Yet, she'd seen evidence of a lot of hostility between some of them. Gail and Elvan, Bradley and Elvan, Bradley and Pierce. It clearly wasn't a nice dynamic to be in the middle of, and Aunt Bella was now right in the middle of it.

Maiden pushed to her sore feet and headed for the door. It was time to finally emerge from the safety of her hiding place and check on her family. She slowly descended the beautiful staircase and heard a low hum of conversation waft up to greet her.

There were a few police officers milling around talking to some of the remaining guests. She saw a handful of the party-goers walk wearily out through the front door, presumably excused after handing over all their details.

There was no sign of her family, so she walked through the foyer and down the hallway to the left. She went far enough to peer into the ballroom and spied her parents sitting on a tufted sofa with Bella and a very distraught Elvan.

Maiden pulled a sympathetic face but stilled when she saw Officer Parker heading towards them. She could only hope the blunt young cop would use some tact with them; they'd eat her alive otherwise.

"It'd serve you right too," Maiden said under her breath and looked around for Vonny instead.

Unsurprisingly, her sister was curled up against Tony on a worn leather chaise, fast asleep with worry. Tony had draped his coat over her and watched the room quietly as he held her close. Amelia was plonked in a chair nearby and tried to look like she wasn't eavesdropping on the couple that was being interviewed on the neighboring couch.

Maiden wondered at her sister's lack of interest in the situation, but remembered that it had been a very long day and Vonny had probably never actually met Gail.

In any case, the chaise looked inviting and there was enough room for her to squeeze in. Maiden started over when she heard Bella's voice raised indignantly.

"Listen to me, you snarky little brat!" she almost shouted. "My husband lost his mother an hour ago! Don't you dare talk to him like that!"

"Ma'am—" Parker started when Bella stood and folded her arms over her chest.

"Don't you 'ma'am' me, little girl!" she said grimly. "We ain't talkin' to you tonight! There're cops everywhere, send someone else over!"

Parker looked ready to argue when Sergeant Ramirez stepped in and said something to her. She didn't object, not loud enough to be heard at least, but muttered as she turned and stalked away.

Ramirez was one of the older and more established members of the Golden Glen police department. She hadn't spoken with him much personally, but he seemed like a steady, level-headed kind of guy. He hadn't been upstairs earlier though, apparently David had meant it when he said the whole squad hadn't arrived yet.

She hadn't seen Greg yet either. She could only imagine how much he'd snigger and tease her when he found out about her and his captain. Maiden leaned against the wall, tipped her head back, and sighed. The day had been strange enough without needless complications.

"Hi, Miss Harlow."

She glanced over in time to see Officer Briggs wave and nearly collide with another officer as he tried to walk and stare at the same time. She immediately stood up straight again and smiled as neutrally as she could before glancing away.

Officer Briggs was a shy, polite person that she noticed had been nursing a crush on her for a while now. She'd always been careful not to lead him on, but he still looked her over whenever the opportunity presented itself. Thanks to her stupid dress, it certainly presented itself tonight.

"Come on, Briggs. Get moving," Greg said loudly and waved him on his way. "We don't want to be here all night."

Officer Greg Smith had been her friend since they met in kindergarten. He'd joined the police force right out of high school and was finally coming into his own as an officer. She suspected that David's presence had inspired him to take his job more seriously; he'd certainly worked harder on his fitness and attention to detail in the past few months.

"Hey, Mae." Greg grinned as he snuck over for a quick word. "You look amazing! Did they twist your arm to get you to wear that dress?"

"No, they cried until I caved," she said dryly.

"Awesome," he snorted and glanced around. "What do you make of this one? Did you find the body again?"

"Uh...no, I didn't this time," she said simply, hoping he wouldn't ask what she *had* been doing. "The victim's son found her...and I don't think Officer Parker has helped to calm him down at all."

"Typical Sarah-Jane," he muttered. "She's book smart but, when it comes to dealing with actual humans, she's heartless. Anyway, I'd better get moving, I got here late as it is. Does the captain know you're here?"

"Yes, he does," Maiden said and walked away as serenely as she could.

She was again trying to make her way towards the chaise when she saw her mother headed straight for her. She took a deep breath and braced herself. Gloria gave her a quick hug and exhaled loudly as she grasped her by the shoulders.

"Oh, my sweet angel, what a mess this night has turned into." She shook her head wearily. "If that old biddy was gonna die, it's just like her to do it here and now!"

"Mom!" Maiden stared at her and lowered her voice to a whisper. "She was killed, and I doubt she arranged it to inconvenience Elvan and Aunt Bella."

"Was she *definitely* killed?" Gloria gave her a questioning look. "It would be a heck of a lot easier if she just had another heart attack or somethin'."

"Probably true but I'm afraid I can't arrange that," she said patiently. "The police will sort it out soon enough. Everything will be okay. You must be exhausted; why don't you find an empty couch and have a nap?"

"Well, where are *you* goin'?" Gloria asked before she could get away.

"To sit down somewhere and put my feet up," she sighed, gesturing towards her garish shoes. "Is that acceptable?"

"Just one little question first, angel." Gloria wrapped an arm around Maiden's shoulders and met her clear gaze with a quiet smile. "Before, when he ordered all of us to sit downstairs and wait, did I happen to see that dishy captain smeared with a little bit of your shade?"

Maiden reluctantly met her mother's knowing gaze and pressed her lips together in an attempt to hide the betraying color. Gloria's perfectly sculpted brows were quirked provocatively and her smile was smugly pleased.

"Um..." Maiden thought quickly but this time nothing came to fruition, after far too long a pause she gave the older woman a confused look. "No one would blame you for imagining things, Mom, you've had such a long day after all."

"Of course, darlin'." Gloria gave a throaty chuckle, but then her expression grew serious and she slapped her daughter smartly on the rump. "Now the next time I tell you to wear somethin', you just hush up and wear it without a fight! You hear me?"

Maiden looked at her for a moment as words again failed her. She finally excused herself before slinking out quietly. She decided to find a seat in a different room.

Chapter Eight

Maiden wandered across the hall and into the room that sat behind the stairs. She'd heard Aunt Bella refer to it as the drawing room. It had the same vaguely stale smell that permeated the entire house. It wasn't quite mold and it wasn't exactly mustiness. It smelled like time; like the passing of countless, unoccupied years.

Snatches of conversation drifted after her as she walked further away from the ballroom, but this space was blessedly empty. She slipped inside and was pleased to see that the door on the opposite side of the room was closed at the moment. That was ideal.

As she walked inside she eyed off the nearest couch and started reaching down to slip off her shoes before she'd even reached it. But she didn't get far before she felt someone looking at her.

She glanced back over her shoulder to see Bradley in the doorway she'd just walked through. She stood up straight again, immediately wary. Abandoning any thoughts of relaxing, she turned to him with a coolly inquiring look.

"Can I talk to you for a minute, honey?" he asked very warmly.

"Only if you leave that door open," she said seriously. "And don't call me 'honey'."

"All right, all right." He held up his hands in surrender and left the door slightly ajar.

She watched him approach and noticed that he seemed even more furtive and weaselly than usual. He stood in front of her and clasped his hands together earnestly.

"I wonder if I might ask you for a teeny little favor?" He winced but still smiled. "For the sake of the whole family. We are, sort of, family now."

"What do you want?" she asked rather than debate how much any of them could be considered to be related.

"Well...you see, I was sort of on my own when poor, poor Granny died." He pulled a saddened face. "I'd stepped outside for a breath of fresh air, but no one necessarily saw that. So, I was wonderin' if you could help me out with a tiny little harmless fib?"

"You want me to lie to give you an alibi?" she asked incredulously and stepped back a bit. "Absolutely not!"

"Oh, come on now!" His expression turned pleading. "I swear to you, darlin', I didn't do a thing wrong. It'll break Daddy's heart if I end up lookin' suspicious. He knows I'd never harm that sweet lady, I adored her! You don't have to say anything, just keep quiet when I talk to the police. Please."

"No," she said firmly. "You're better off telling the truth from the start; the police will find out anyway."

"Oh, they will not." He waved it away easily. "A sweet and honest little girl like you? They won't even question it. Now listen, I stepped outside to catch my breath, that's all. I just don't have anyone to vouch for me."

"Including me," she said. "I'm not lying for you."

"Now look, lovely girl," he gave her a charming smile that could've sold a bottle of snake oil, "I know you don't want to hurt my daddy or your Auntie Bella. Just play along and keep your sweet little mouth shut. Trust me, it's better this way."

"I said no!" She glared at him. "And if you call me a little girl again I'll go to the cops right now and tell them that you asked me to lie for you."

Before he could respond the door opened wide and David walked through it. He took in the scene with an unreadable expression. Maiden shifted uncomfortably and shrugged away Bradley's awkward attempt to put his arm around her. David's eyes narrowed slightly.

"Mr. Hedgewick," David said as he pulled out a notebook and flipped it open. "I'll speak to you now. Have a seat."

"I'm happy standin'." Bradley puffed out his chest. "If it's all the same to you."

"I really don't care." His tone reflected the truth of the statement. "Where were you between 9:30 and 10 pm this evening?"

"I was with Miss Harlow here," he said boldly and flicked her a warning look.

David stilled and slowly raised his eyes to the smug man. Bradley folded his arms over his chest with a smile.

"You're saying you were with Miss Maiden Harlow at the time of your grandmother's murder?" he asked and held up a hand in her direction when she started to speak. "I'm asking Mr. Hedgewick."

"That's right, Captain." Bradley smirked and wrinkled his nose at Maiden. "You just let me tell you all about it."

"Please do." David held his notebook and pen at the ready.

"Well, it was a fine night, lots of family and friends around. Everybody was in a happy, festive mood," he said with a sly smile. "A lot of little nooks to sneak off into in this big old house...I suppose I lost my head a bit. You can't hardly blame me with such a sweet girl."

"'I lost my head'," David repeated as he wrote it down and underlined it, he then met Bradley's pleased gaze and exhaled slowly. "Did you get along well with your grandmother?"

"With Granny?" Bradley affected a startled expression. "Of course! She was like a second mama to me! I can't tell you how deeply hurt I am to lose her like this. It's just awful!"

David remained coolly expressionless as he watched Bradley stare down at his shoes and pretend to wipe away a tear. Maiden wasn't sure whether to scream in anger at his appalling attempt to force her to vouch for him or laugh because he could hardly have incriminated himself more.

"I saw you arguing with another guest earlier," David murmured. "What was that about?"

"Arguin'? Oh no, Captain McAlister, you wouldn't have seen a fight," he said in a gentle voice. "I wouldn't even swat a fly, I truly wouldn't. I *may* have had a bit of a discussion with my cousin; he's a hot-headed sort of guy. Decent though, deep down."

"What were you 'discussing'?" He cut through the twaddle to keep on topic.

"I'm afraid that's personal, sir," Bradley said solemnly. "I'm sorry, but it's not for me to say. It's my cousin's issue."

"I've already spoken to Pierce Hedgewick. He said you asked to borrow money," David informed him. "But he refused because you haven't paid him what you still owe from the last time."

"What!" Bradley's face contorted with anger, his harmless good ol' boy persona quickly forgotten. "That lyin' snake! Don't you believe a word he tells you, Captain! He's a liar and always was!"

"But he's 'decent deep down', according to you." David quirked a brow.

"I was tryin' to help him," Bradley grumbled. "A consideration he's too selfish to return, obviously."

"He was considerate enough to give me a real answer," David said coolly. "You might give that some thought and see if you can't help *yourself*. You're in a worse situation than he is, after all."

"What's that supposed to mean?" Bradley growled.

"Where were you between 9:30 and 10 pm this evening?" he repeated.

"I was with Miss Harlow, I said!" He flung his hand in her direction. "She'll vouch for me!"

Maiden set her teeth and shook her head grimly, not that anyone was looking at her. She just rested her hands on her hips and watched the spectacle unfold.

"All right. We're going to try this again, and if you don't tell me the truth, I'll arrest you right now. Got that?" David closed his notebook and slid it back into his pocket without shifting his icy gaze from Bradley. "Where were you when your grandmother was murdered?"

"I won't be treated like this!" Bradley blustered and edged past him towards the door. "I own more lawyers than you do pairs of shoes!"

"According to your cousin you can't afford any of them now." He smiled faintly. "If you can't account for your whereabouts after lying about them, I'll take you into custody. One more chance to own up, I know you weren't with Miss Harlow."

"How do you *know* that?" Bradley hissed with an angry sneer.

David pulled his handkerchief from his pocket and showed him the lipstick that stained it.

"Because the lady in question was with *me*."

Bradley paled as he stared at the red lipstick stains, he then turned a similar shade as he shifted an angry glare to Maiden. She met his furious gaze with a look of aloof disdain; she hoped she did anyway, snooty looks weren't her specialty by any stretch of the imagination.

"She didn't mention that, for some reason," he muttered through clenched teeth.

"She isn't obliged to tell you her personal business." David stepped to the side enough to block him from glowering at her. "But you are obliged to tell me yours. I think we'll continue this discussion at the police station, however."

"You can't actually intend to arrest me?" Bradley's manner was a bit calmer now that he saw no point in playing the rascally country bumpkin. "My family has been through more than enough for one day."

"You can come quietly and save them needless distress," David said, completely unmoved, and glanced towards the door. "Briggs! Parker! I've got a passenger for you."

A tightlipped and furious Bradley was quickly handcuffed and escorted out. Maiden followed and watched from the doorway, peering past David's shoulder, as Bradley was led past a few gawking stragglers. She noticed Bradley exchange a hateful look with his cousin as he was led past him. She made a mental note to ask Aunt Bella if she knew the details of their fractious relationship.

Maiden was leaning against the doorjamb when David rounded on her. She blinked up at him and backed into the room again as he stalked towards her. He stood before her and folded his arms over his chest. She knew she needed to ignore how good he looked in his suit, but the partly-open shirt and glimpse of dark chest hair was working against her.

"What was that all about?" he asked quietly.

"That was Bradley being a sleaze." She pulled a face and, reminding herself of the seriousness of the situation, managed not to flick any more of his buttons open. "Are you staring at me like that to try and intimidate me?"

"No," he exhaled slowly. "I'm trying to get an honest answer while also trying not to look down your dress."

"You're a gentleman," she giggled at his unexpected candor and kept her big mouth shut regarding her own struggles.

"Yeah, I really am...unfortunately," he said dryly and slid his dark eyes back to the doorway when Sergeant Ramirez and Greg appeared and gave the room an assessing look.

"Everything all right in here, sir?" Ramirez asked. "I see you've made an arrest."

"Yeah, the groom's son at that." David rolled his eyes and nodded to Maiden. "He tried to alibi himself by claiming he was off mauling Miss Harlow."

Oh yeah! A real gentleman, Maiden seethed internally, she knew that complaining out loud would only make things more embarrassing. Even now the two officers glanced at her and then exchanged a quietly amused look.

Maiden decided that she was sick of being thrown about like an anecdote for other people's convenience or amusement. She stared out the doorway past the politely stoic cops.

"Yes, that was a bit awkward," she said to David without looking at him. "It's just as well it was *you* doing the mauling, isn't it, Captain? At least you know he was lying."

A heavy, but very brief, silence descended. Ramirez looked like he'd swallowed his mustache. Greg made a small choking sound as his startled laughter almost escaped, he turned and quickly walked away. As the more senior officer, Ramirez dredged up enough sobriety to actually speak.

"I'll go and check on the remaining guests, Captain," he wheezed and only let go of a small chuckle as he vanished down the hall.

The room felt very empty. Maiden was a bit embarrassed, but it was definitely worth it this time. She slowly turned to David with a coquettish look; he was staring at her.

"That was kind of fun." She grinned at him. "I can see why you keep doing it."

"You were a bit more blatant than I was!" he pointed out in a quietly incredulous voice.

"They're detectives, Captain McAlister. They probably figured out even your cryptic innuendo." She was trying not to laugh as she saw a hint of color in his cheeks. "But never mind that. The most important thing is that you don't take any of this as flirtation. Flirtation isn't allowed right now."

"Oh, you are *brutal*, Harlow," he shut his eyes and whispered with a rueful smile. "I really had better get back to work."

Yeah. And that's what you get for telling other people my business, she smiled to herself as he walked out without another word.

Maiden promptly gave up on any hope of resting. A murder had taken place and it involved her family, again. She knew David wouldn't want her getting involved, especially if there was the risk of a conflict of interest, but she saw no harm in gathering a little information. She was in the case to some extent regardless.

Even so, she wasn't game to be too obvious with David actually floating around in the vicinity. She went to the door on the opposite side of the room and quietly opened it. A quick look around revealed that the hallway was empty, and that the lounge across from her was not.

Only sparing a brief thought for the fact that one house had no less than two bars in it, she walked carefully closer to the slender brunette that was perched on a high-backed stool nursing a very full glass of champagne.

Maiden sat on the stool next to hers and smiled nicely when she glanced over. The lady looked a little startled to see her but quickly recovered and inclined her head. A moment of uncomfortable silence passed. Maiden was about to attempt some causal conversation starter when the other lady spoke up.

"You're one of Bella's nieces, right?" she asked quietly.

"Yeah, I'm Maiden," she replied.

"Marti Drake," she inclined her head by way of introduction and smiled a little wider as she looked her over. "I like your dress. Mom and I were talking about it earlier."

"Oh, thank you. I know it's a bit much." Maiden shifted awkwardly. "It wasn't my choice, believe me."

"I think it's pretty." Marti said kindly. "Don't let other people put you down; it's just their opinion against yours. I wear whatever I like."

Easy to say when you're wearing a tasteful evening gown, Maiden thought wryly as she considered the mocha-brown silk dress that Marti wore with effortless grace.

"So you and, your mother, is it?" Maiden lifted her dark brows inquiringly. "Are you friends of Aunt Bella's?"

"I don't really know her too well, to be honest." Marti admitted. "We're, um...*acquainted* with the Hedgewicks."

"That's nice," Maiden said neutrally and saw the lady beside her shift a little.

"Not really," Marti murmured dryly and took a long sip of her champagne. She glanced at Maiden and then frowned at herself. "Sorry, would you like a drink?"

She'd gestured towards a tray of glasses surrounding a half-empty champagne bottle in front of her. Maiden didn't particularly want another but she wanted to keep Marti feeling comfortable and, hopefully, chatty.

"Sure, why not?" Maiden said and reached for a glass. Her eyes widened a fraction when Marti filled it almost to the top. "Thanks."

Marti smiled distractedly and went back to her own drink. She looked quietly unhappy. Maiden turned her glass idly without drinking from it and tried to decide the best way to proceed.

"I noticed earlier that you seemed to know Pierce," she said as mildly as she could, "and...Bradley."

Marti shut her eyes and bowed her head a fraction before topping up her glass. She took another long sip and gave a shaky nod.

"Yeah, I know them both," she said softly. "Bradley and I were dating...until recently."

"Really?" Maiden couldn't help the hint of disbelief in her voice as she asked that. She quickly scrambled to play it down a little. "That's interesting. It was good of you to still come to Elvan's wedding...things must have ended amicably?"

"Not even close, honey," Marti said flatly and shot her a grim look. "Bradley Hedgewick is the biggest turd that was ever squeezed out of Florida, that's for certain."

"That's really, um...really gross." Maiden finished the observation under her breath before facing the other woman with a kindly expression. "I'm so sorry if things went badly. Are you okay?"

"Yeah, I'm great. Except for the fact that he's a pig, and he acted like a stupid, selfish pig," Marti said angrily as she set her glass down and folded her arms over her chest. "If he didn't want to marry me, fine, whatever. I don't need a guy that doesn't really want me. But he should've told me privately and left it!"

"*Marry?*" Maiden knew it was impolite to gawk while asking that sort of question but the reaction was too heartfelt to suppress. "You were engaged to Bradley?"

"Unofficially, yes." Marti scrunched up her nose and shook her head in disgust. "That's what he called it anyway. It was a good excuse to get as cozy as he wanted without having to buy me a ring."

"He probably couldn't afford one," Maiden mused aloud.

"Yeah, how's that for irony?" Marti only swayed a little as she turned to her and propped her chin in her hand. "That creep was after money because he didn't have any of his own, and then he made big show of breaking up with me in front of a room full of our friends. Can you believe that?!"

"I'm sorry, but I'm really confused now." Maiden shook her head helplessly. "I kind of already got the impression that Bradley's a jerk, but what was ironic about the situation?"

"That's where Gail comes in," Marti muttered.

"Marti!"

They both turned quickly when a sharp voice cracked through the air like a whip. The older woman Maiden had seen earlier was standing in the doorway glaring at her daughter.

Marti glanced back at her and then at Maiden before lowering her gaze to the bar. Maiden knew she needed to make an effort to keep things civil. She turned to the striking newcomer and smiled as she sauntered over.

"Hello," Maiden said politely. "Mrs. Drake, right? My name is Maiden Harlow, it's nice to meet you."

"Yes, I'll just bet it is," the lady grumbled and stood closer but not quite between them. "As I understand it, Gail was murdered tonight, we really don't need to be speaking ill of the dead."

"Are you suggesting that you can think of something nice to say about her instead?" Maiden asked dryly. It was a tactic, not a particularly nice one, but she was hoping to keep the ladies talking. A little common ground might help.

The effect was immediate. Both Marti and her mother quickly looked away to hide their smug amusement. Maiden wasn't sure what the history was, but she was confident that both of these women hated Gail.

Marti's mother turned to Maiden with begrudging interest. Maiden returned the silent appraisal. The lady was probably in her mid-fifties, she wore a tailored cream pantsuit that showed off a very nice figure and her dark hair was perfectly styled in bold, rolling curls. The streak of silver at her temple bespoke experience and strength, it was surprisingly sexy and a little intimidating.

"I'm Sylvia Drake," she held out her hand and gave Maiden's a firm shake. "You can call me Sylvia."

"Thank you," Maiden had a feeling that she had just been granted an honor that not everyone received. "Hey, please don't be upset with Marti about having a little vent. It's been such a strange day, and we're all a bit off kilter."

"To put it mildly," Sylvia scoffed and eyed her a tad warily. "I'll be honest with you, this has been a very rough year for us and our business. We don't need our personal disgraces dredged up yet again, all right?"

"I totally understand," Maiden raised her hands soothingly. "My family runs a business too. Nothing on the same scale as yours I suspect, but I know how much a scandal can hurt."

"You don't know what a scandal is, Maiden," Sylvia gave a humorless laugh. "Do you know what it's like to have your whole legacy pulled out from under you out of spite?"

"No," Maiden admitted with a tilt of her head. "Do *you* know what it's like to have a heartless killer choose your family establishment to settle their scores in?"

"You're kidding me." Sylvia quirked a brow.

"Sadly, no," Maiden replied. "If you get bored later try looking up the 'Harlow House Killings', you might also find the story under 'Hotel of Death'."

Sylvia fought a smirk but lost the battle. She gave a conceding nod and slid her daughter a worried look.

"You all right, cupcake?" she asked gently.

"Yeah, fantastic." Marti smiled benignly. "Gail's finally dead. I only wish she'd taken Bradley with her."

"You're drunk," Sylvia said under her breath but gave her daughter a look of loyal understanding. "Just be careful what you say."

"I'm not drunk," Marti said sharply. "I'm stuck here in this creepy old house with a dead body upstairs and police crawling everywhere! The fact that Bradley's here just makes an awful situation worse, am I supposed to pretend not to notice that?!"

"Marti, please!" Sylvia gave an exasperated sigh and nodded towards Maiden.

"Oh, Mom, leave it," Marti grumbled. "You honestly think Bella hasn't told her the whole stupid story already?"

"Actually she hasn't," Maiden spoke up quickly, hoping to quell any burgeoning arguments. "I'm really not trying to pry. To be honest, I'm more interested in Bradley."

Maiden rolled her eyes at herself after that unfortunate statement tumbled out. Marti and Sylvia both pinned her with incredulous glares.

"No! That's not what I meant!" she hurried to explain. "I have a, kind of, boyfriend already. No, I'm curious about Bradley's angle because he asked me to lie and give him an alibi."

The women gawped at her for a heartbeat and then eased closer. Slowly and eerily closer.

"Did he?" Marti whispered, her gaze was fixed on Maiden and a smile curled her lips. "That must mean he has no one to account for him...and that he might've been somewhere he shouldn't have been."

"Maybe upstairs with Gail," Sylvia suggested, looking deeply pleased by the idea. "Did you tell the police about it?"

"Yes, I did," Maiden nodded and tried not to be too creeped out by the sinister glee that lit Sylvia's eyes.

"Good, that's very good. You did the right thing," Sylvia nodded and slid her gaze away as she quickly became lost in thought.

"Yeah, I try to do the right thing as much as I can," Maiden cleared her throat and waited until the lady looked at her again. "You don't seem surprised by the thought of Bradley being involved in Gail's death."

"It wouldn't surprise me at all!" Sylvia said a little too quickly. "They're both terrible people. He won't miss her, I guarantee you that. He always complained about Gail. Didn't he, Marti?"

"Yes, he didn't have many nice things to say about her." Marti nodded. "He always called her a cranky old tightwad. She liked to make him beg for everything he got, he hated her for that...that's probably why he did it."

"Well, we don't know that he did," Maiden pointed out as mildly as she could.

"Who else would have?!" Sylvia demanded with a dismissive wave.

"Did anyone else dislike Gail?" Maiden asked delicately. *Besides you two?*

"Everyone hated Gail," she leaned forward despite not lowering her voice. "*Everyone*! She ruined people for fun and it finally caught up with her. The only wonder is that it took this long!"

"Okay," Maiden said under her breath as she struggled to hide any reaction to the hatred that was roiling in Sylvia's intent gaze. "I honestly didn't know her at all, I only met her once and she was a bit, um, rude."

"Where Gail's concerned, we don't call it rude, we call it *normal*," Sylvia informed her.

"That's unfortunate," Maiden wet her lips and tried again. "Anyone else you can think of that hated her? Specifically?"

"I'm sure Bella would've," she said mildly. "Old Gail was obviously set against her relationship with Elvan. And I doubt that tacky fake heart attack would have been her first attempt to spoil things."

"It wouldn't have been the last either," Marti said with grim certainty, "if she weren't dead."

"We can only speculate about that now, but Aunt Bella has witnesses to vouch for her at the time of the murder," Maiden said even as her stomach lurched at the women's calmly voiced sentiments. "Obviously Bradley doesn't. You two have someone though, don't you?"

She took care to look innocently worried as she asked that question. They'd just admitted to strong motives, she wondered if their alibis were as robust.

"We were in the dining room all evening," Sylvia said quickly and firmly. "There were lots of other people there, we have plenty of friends that will swear to that."

Marti frowned so briefly that Maiden almost didn't catch it. An instant later the lady smiled at her and gave a confident nod. Maiden returned the smile faintly and picked up her glass.

"Good, that's a relief." She took a sip of her drink in an attempt to appear nonchalant. "In any case, Bradley just got arrested."

"*What?!*"

The shrieks of girlish delight that met that announcement were jarring. Maiden nearly spilled her drink and Marti *did* fumble hers to the floor. Sylvia chortled merrily as she patted her daughter's arm and picked up her glass, fortunately the carpet absorbed enough impact to keep it intact.

"He was actually arrested?" Marti's dark eyes were wide and hopeful. "For murder?!"

"Well, for lying about his whereabouts and refusing to explain it," Maiden corrected with a shrug.

"Still," Marti held up a finger before Maiden had finished speaking. "It sounds pretty incriminating if he refuses to say where he was when a murder took place...I wonder if he needed to get his hands on his inheritance sooner than anyone realized."

"Is he expected to inherit a lot?" Maiden dredged up her most innocent look.

"His family has *millions*," Marti said frankly. "And he and Pierce are the only children. He'll inherit big time. He'll probably blow through it all in a few months too."

Maiden was about to reply to that when she almost sensed something stolid and responsible filling the doorway. They all turned to find Sergeant Ramirez watching them placidly. Marti sucked in a deep breath, probably worried about how long the moustachioed cop had been standing there.

Maiden, who was fairly used to police and investigations by now, smiled at him and slid to her feet, wincing as her stilettos touched the floor.

"Hello ladies, I need to take your statements and get your contact details, then you'll be free to go for tonight." Ramirez said mildly but his eyes twinkled a little when he glanced at Maiden. "You can go though, Miss Harlow. Your whereabouts have been established."

Maiden shut her eyes briefly but felt a begrudging smile slip free. She glanced at Marti and Sylvia and said goodnight before walking bravely to the door.

"Thank you, Sergeant," she murmured and slipped back into the hallway.

CHAPTER NINE

Maiden had lingered just past the door long enough to hear Ramirez begin asking the Drakes for their names and addresses. Not wanting to get caught listening in, she soon made her way to the foyer.

No one was there now. The ribbons and flowers on the banister of the grand staircase were looking a bit tattered from the sudden increase in traffic it would have seen. She felt a chill chase over her as it occurred to her that they may have removed Gail's body already. She certainly hoped so. As far as she knew, her family was still staying there overnight and she'd rather not sleep next door to a corpse.

The old house was steadily emptying as guests finished their interviews and were excused. She heard snatches of conversations drifting down the hallways. A moment later a weary-looking couple walked past her with a slight nod before leaving. Maiden could sympathize, she was getting pretty tired too, but she couldn't rest yet.

She walked down the hall to the left of the stairs and back into the much quieter ballroom. She smiled sadly when she spotted Aunt Bella. The lady looked rather uncomfortable in her tremendous gown but she was still doing her best to comfort a quietly sobbing Elvan.

Maiden walked over and sat beside her on the worn but stylish settee. She glanced covertly at Elvan, who was dabbing at his eyes with a handkerchief even as more tears welled up to replace the ones he'd just wiped away.

"I'm sorry about this, Aunt Bella," Maiden said softly. "What a terrible end to your day...are you both okay?"

Bella shrugged as calmly as if they were dealing with a flat tire but caught herself and looked swiftly at Elvan. Fortunately, he was staring down at the floor and missed her lack of decent response.

"Well, it's been horrible, of course." Bella shook her head at the terrible shame of it all. "Not only Gail but Bradley too...just awful."

"Yeah," Maiden said quietly and then cleared her throat and nodded across the room. "Can we talk for a minute?"

"Of course, baby." She smiled at her and then patted Elvan's shoulder. "I'll be right back, sugar."

Maiden led the way to a deserted couch in an empty corner and waited while Bella ambled after her. Bella's massive, flouncy skirts were creased and wrinkled as they swished around her. She finally hitched them up to her knees as she grew annoyed over wrestling with them. A moment later she sat heavily beside Maiden and leaned back with a weary sigh.

"Is Elvan okay?" Maiden asked discreetly as she glanced in the tearful man's direction.

"Apart from havin' his witch of a mother killed at his weddin' and his awful son arrested for it." Bella replied. "What more could you ask for at a party?"

"Touché." Maiden smiled. "You don't exactly sound heartbroken."

"No, sweet baby, I suppose I don't," Bella replied.

"All right, let's leave sentiment aside, shall we?" she murmured and then gave her aunt a more serious look. "Apparently Bradley had an argument with his cousin earlier, did you see any of it?"

"Oh, with Pierce?" she mused as she reached under her voluminous skirt and pulled a flask from somewhere. "Bit of a scamp that boy, but he's still way better than Bradley. I don't believe they're close, so they might've been fightin', I didn't see it though."

"Is it true that Bradley owes him money?" Maiden asked quietly.

"Ooo! I hadn't heard that!" Bella's pale eyes lit up and her deeply rouged cheeks somehow darkened as she took a swig. "It wouldn't surprise me. Bradley was forever askin' Elvan for 'an advance on his allowance'. That was comin' to an end straight after the weddin', I can promise you that! Not that it'll be a problem now. Imagine killin' his own grandmother, shameful."

"We don't know that he did it," Maiden reminded her but then pulled a face. "Bradley was on an allowance? At his age? I thought he was a doctor or something?"

"No, baby girl," Bella chortled. "He supposedly went to veterinary school but took a "hiatus". Washed out and never bothered to try again is more like it!"

"How long ago was that?" Maiden stroked her jaw thoughtfully.

"About three years," she smirked. "He's a spoiled brat that just wants to sponge off daddy. I hope it was him that did it, it'll save throwin' him out."

"Aunt Bella!" Maiden gave her a startled look. "What a thing to say!"

"What?" Bella batted a double row of false eyelashes. "You have to be practical, honeypot. And don't frown like that, you'll make wrinkles."

"You obviously don't like Bradley even a little." Maiden obligingly cleared her scowling forehead.

"What's there to like?" Bella scoffed. "He spends most of his time with his equally spoiled mother and only visits Elvan when he wants somethin'."

"His mother?" Maiden blinked at her. "I didn't realize she was still alive."

"And chiseling." Bella rolled her eyes and took another swallow from her flask. "She and Elvan married years ago; she cheated on him with his brother and that was that."

"That's terrible!" Maiden gasped, starting to understand why so little of Elvan's family had been present for the ceremony.

"She certainly is." Bella nodded. "I only met her once. Saggy old bit of mutton. She's got a smile like a rattlesnake and is just as personable. In any case, she and Bradley can find a way to support themselves from now on. Elvan's got other priorities."

"Yeah, I guess," Maiden mumbled as she absorbed everything Bella had just told her. "Is Pierce still here?"

"No, I think he left a little while ago," Bella said. "Why?"

"He might know why Bradley disappeared outside at the time of Gail's murder." She chewed at her lower lip.

"No, he won't, because Bradley wasn't outside," Bella scoffed. "He was upstairs doin' the murderin'!"

***

It was nearly 1 am when the police finally left. The body had been removed and all the guests had been allowed to go, only family remained. The other guest rooms had been carefully searched but nothing of interest had turned up. The family was allowed to stay the night as originally planned, except that one of the rooms was now sealed off as a crime scene, so Maiden and Vonny were compelled to share.

The others had already gone upstairs, only Maiden lingered. She tried to ignore Greg's smirking look as he paused beside her on his way out the front door.

"'Does the Captain know you're here?'" he repeated his earlier question wryly and arched a pale brow at her. "Hell yeah, he does!"

Maiden gave him a quietly patient look and then punched him in the shoulder without comment.

"See you tomorrow, Mae," he said slyly as he walked on to his car.

Maiden pulled a face and rubbed her arms against the cool night air. Her teasing insistence on staying in her bridesmaid's dress had backfired at this point. It was getting colder by the minute and she was wearing half a dress.

David walked out last, giving the foyer an assessing look as he came and stood beside her near the door. He glanced over as the Greg's car vanished into the night. He turned to her with a faint smile.

"Everything to do with the crime scene is blocked off and locked up. And we've posted a guard on the door," he assured her. "We'll be back tomorrow morning."

"Okay, thanks for letting us stay tonight," she replied quietly and then smiled. "And thanks for coming. I hope you enjoyed the wedding."

"All things considered," he gave her a warm look, "it's still the best time I've ever had at one of these turkey-circuses."

"You've been talking to Dad," she laughed and hugged herself against the cool evening air. "Do you think...will this be a straight-forward case?"

"No such thing, Harlow," he sighed and edged closer. "I'll do my best, let's just say I'm extra motivated this time."

"Good. Get some sleep, McAlister," she murmured, matching his more formal address. "I hate waiting."

"Ah, demanding results already?" He smiled faintly. "I know how you feel, trust me, this isn't how I saw the evening unfolding."

"How did you see it unfolding?" she looked up at him through her thick lashes.

"You promised not to flirt." He grinned at her.

"No I didn't. I never have," she said as she grasped his tie where it hung loose around his neck.

She pulled it free and slid it around her own throat. David instantly smiled and started to draw closer until he stopped himself.

"What are you doing?" he asked.

"Collecting an IOU," she murmured.

"That's my best tie, you know," he said mildly.

"Good, I don't want your rubbish," she sniffed and grasped either end of the silky accessory. "You can have it back when the case is solved."

"Challenge accepted," he chuckled and stepped reluctantly away. "Goodnight, Maiden."

"Goodnight, David."

Chapter Ten

The room was quiet and softly lit. David heard a door close and turned to see Maiden walking towards him, she was still in that sexy little red dress. He didn't hesitate or question anything this time, he walked straight towards her and pulled her against him the instant she was within reach.

"Hey, baby," he whispered as he folded her close.

She felt so soft and perfect as she smiled up at him and nestled in. David held her as tightly as he could without hurting her. He lowered his head as she slid her fingers into his hair and kissed him; every inch of his body felt warm and alive.

He couldn't recall ever being so completely content in his life. It felt so achingly perfect; he didn't want the moment to end. His grip tightened instinctively when she pulled back a little. He buried a hand in her hair and slid the other to the small of her back, silently urging her to stay there tucked against him.

But she wriggled and finally managed to lean away enough to look at him. He smiled a little as he ran his fingertips along the smooth skin of her back. She gazed up at him with an intense look in those incredibly green eyes, wet her soft lips, and then—the alarm blared on the table beside his bed.

David's weary eyes cracked open reluctantly and scanned his surroundings. He wasn't in that oddly cool old bar and there was no sign of the gorgeous woman that had felt so vividly real in his arms. He was in his bedroom. He'd collapsed on the bed and fallen asleep even before he'd turned off the bedside lamp.

He glanced down to find that he was clutching his spare pillow tightly to his chest. He rubbed his eyes with one hand and reached over to switch off his alarm with the other. The resulting silence was deafening. For a moment he laid on his back and stared up at the ceiling.

"Damn it," he sighed and ran a hand over his face.

The dream was more of a tease this time around, since he'd finally had a taste of the reality. His mind dragged him back, entirely willingly, to his kiss with Maiden. He shut his eyes and wished he was still holding her.

Stop it, David. Get to work, he told himself sternly. He tossed the disappointing pillow aside and sat up. A cursory glance around the room confirmed that it was still dark outside and his best suit was lying crumpled on the floor where he'd left it. It didn't matter.

It was 6 am, he was exhausted and he had another murder case on his hands. It was going to be a big day. He was also going to come face-to-face with Maiden again, something he both longed for and dreaded.

Can I actually call her 'Maiden' now, or should I stick with 'Harlow' until the case is done? Or maybe go back to 'Miss Harlow', keep it professional. How do I have three forms of address for this one woman? He shook his head and threw the blankets back.

"I'll wait and see what she calls me," he said quietly to the empty room and immediately scowled. "No, I'll set the tone because I'm the cop conducting the case. I'm being an idiot and I need to get up and get to work right now."

Sufficiently chided, he stood up and walked over to the window, pushing back the curtains just enough to look out at his street. It was dimly lit by the streetlights, all of the other houses were still dark and quiet.

He liked the street he lived on. The houses were big enough and well kept, there were lots of trees and the yards were clean and tidy. People here seemed to really care about where they lived and it showed in how they looked after it. It was nothing like his old apartment in Stanton.

Dirty alleyways, loud music blaring all night from some unknown neighbor, trash in every gutter. None of it had really bothered him at the time, but he doubted he could go back to that kind of life now. He liked Golden Glen; he felt at home in his quaint neighborhood.

As far as he'd seen he was the only single guy on the block, the rest were young families and retired couples. It was peaceful. The neighbors all waved when they saw him and he waved back. It was nice.

I wonder if Maiden would like living on my street, he wondered to himself before he could help it, he immediately pulled the curtains shut again. *Brilliant, way to keep your head in the game. And you're officially thinking of her as Maiden now. Murder case, McAlister, murder case.*

He steered his thoughts back to Gail Hedgewick. She'd looked so determined and assured when he'd spoken to her before dinner. The next time he saw her she was dead.

Elvan had stood tearfully beside him as he checked the body and barely managed to explain that he'd stopped in to say goodnight and saw her in bed with a pillow pressed over her face. He'd thrown it across the room and tried to wake her but she never responded.

When David checked her he was struck by how undisturbed everything looked. Gail's expression had been serene, no sign of distress or fear, no indication of a struggle. The blankets were barely disturbed and her body was still slightly warm.

Doc Jenkin's full report along with the results of the lab tests would be available soon. That might shed more light on what had happened to her. All they knew at the moment was that the lady died of suffocation probably shortly before 10 pm. He'd have to gather more information from the people that had come and gone around her before he could be sure though.

There was no shortage of suspects either. It hadn't taken much detective work to realize that Gail Hedgewick hadn't been loved by many. He'd heard enough background grumbling after her heart attack bluff to feel confident that no one had been fooled, or impressed.

The most obvious suspects were the family, of course. Those that in all likelihood had a lot to gain. That meant Elvan, Bradley, Pierce and now Bella. Things had the potential to get very messy. He took a deep breath and tried not to think about how devastated Maiden would be if he ended up having to arrest someone she loved.

It was going to be a long day and he needed to be at his best. He wasn't though, and he knew it. He was exhausted and already fighting an internal battle to direct his focus. David shook his head at himself and flicked on the overhead light, giving his eyes a moment to adjust.

He walked over and picked up his suit coat and debated whether to put it away or get it cleaned; he knew he should probably get it cleaned. His eyes strayed to the handkerchief that was peeking out of the top pocket, he smiled faintly and pulled it out.

Maiden's cherry-red lipstick had simultaneously ruined a perfectly good handkerchief and turned it into his single most favorite object in the entire house. Knowing full well that he was being pathetic, he laid it carefully on his bedside table.

He turned back to his jacket and allowed himself a moment to picture it around Maiden's shoulders again. He frowned uncertainly at a few flecks of glitter on the lining, they winked and shimmered in the dim light.

Was she even wearing anything with glitter on it? Do sexy women leave some kind of pixie dust behind? He looked closer and caught a whiff of her perfume. *Right. No. Doesn't need cleaning, not for a while yet. Now put it away, take a shower, drink coffee, stop being stupid.*

***

Gloria had woken up early, thanks to Alfie's insistence on getting back to the inn even though the sun had barely risen. She couldn't complain too much, he'd put up with a lot of her family dramas lately and, frankly, she'd rather he was out of the way before David got there anyway.

She was thoroughly pleased with her efforts to get the handsome policeman to stop trifling with her daughter's feelings. She was confident that he wasn't deliberately toying with Maiden, she'd have steered her sweet baby as far from him as possible if she thought that was the case. No, he was too shy and too hesitant for his own good, that's all.

The dress they'd carefully selected for the girls had worked perfectly. She couldn't wait to tell Bella all about it. Common decency dictated a tactful approach, however. She wasn't honestly sorry that Gail was gone, she'd been a mean and spiteful person. Gloria just hoped that David and Maiden would solve the murder quickly so they could all move on.

She'd found Bella alone in the kitchen and started getting things ready for the inevitable parade of police officers that were due to arrive any time now. After they'd filled a few carafes with coffee and arranged several dozen pastries on a large tray, Gloria and Bella walked into the spacious downstairs lounge.

The room was bright and welcoming, despite sharing the air of casual neglect that permeated the entire mansion. Situated down the hall from the kitchen, it was warmly lit by a bank of large windows which looked out at a moldering gazebo that was overrun with ivy. The sleepy old structure was something out of a fairytale. Gloria smiled as she imagined a sleeping princess waiting inside.

She and Bella were talking quietly, by their standards, about the untimely loss of Bella's contentious mother-in-law.

"It's an awful tragedy, naturally," Bella said with an appropriate amount of drama. "And poor Elvan is terribly upset."

"Where is he anyway?" Gloria asked as she led the way into the room.

"Upstairs, fast asleep. He was absolutely beside himself last night so I gave him one of my sleepin' pills. He'll probably be out for another hour or two," Bella grumbled dryly. "Happy honeymoon to me."

Gloria tittered and started to say something rather naughty in reply but they both stilled and smiled sweetly when they saw a familiar, and rather unwelcome, young woman already there. Gloria recognized the tightly wound curls and sour expression instantly.

Officer Parker had made a fast and terrible impression on just about the entire family in the short time she'd been in Golden Glen. Even if Maiden hadn't quietly mentioned that the officer hadn't been very nice to her, Parker would have betrayed her cranky nature all on her own last night. She'd walked right up to Bella and Elvan and started asking some very rude and personal questions about how much they were expecting to inherit now that Gail was gone.

And Officer Parker didn't look ready to try and improve things at all as she perched at the empty bar and frowned down at a clipboard as she scribbled away. She glanced up at them as they approached.

"Good morning, ladies," she said impassively.

"Officer Parker, aren't you an early birdie," Gloria said lightly as she came closer and set the tray on the bar. "Have some coffee with us."

"No, thank you, I'm fine," she replied coolly and went back to whatever she was writing.

Gloria and Bella exchanged a mockingly snooty look before smirking at each other. Gloria ignored the younger woman's reply and set a cup of steaming hot coffee under her nose before adding a side plate with a slice of cherry strudel perched on a crisp white napkin.

"There you go, sweetheart. Have at it," she said nicely and poured a cup for herself and Bella.

"I said I'm fine." Parker gave the pastry a dubious look. "I don't eat stuff like that."

"You don't eat pastries?" Bella gave her a look. "No wonder you're so cranky! Eat up, babydoll, and don't be so strict with yourself. After all, men don't mind a little something to get their hands around."

***

Sarah-Jane glanced up in time to see Bella squeezing the air suggestively. She certainly wasn't about to engage in such a theoretical and ridiculous debate. She turned quietly back to her notes with a scowl.

She really wasn't in the mood to fraternize, and certainly not with murder suspects. It had only been a few short hours since Captain McAlister made his preference for Miss Harlow crystal clear. Despite numerous attempts to catch his eye, Sarah-Jane had to accept that he simply wasn't interested in her.

It was a humiliating rebuff and everyone in the station knew about it. Deep down, she admitted to herself that Captain McAlister had never tried to lead her on. He treated her like every other officer in the station. He'd never once responded to her flirting or even offered her a hint of encouragement. Not even once.

It wasn't as though she were in love with the guy, but he was incredibly hot. He was also smart and steady and a really good cop. She admired him, but he wanted Maiden Harlow.

Nancy and Greg had tactfully warned her repeatedly when they'd noticed her interest in him and her instant dislike of the other woman.

Don't mess with Miss Harlow again, Officer Parker, remember the flack you caught the last time. That's what they'd told her. *The captain has a thing for Maiden, he won't put up with anyone being nasty to her; don't even think about it.*

She'd been too determined and too interested in the captain to listen to reason. When she really wanted something, she went after it. Her mother had taught her to never give up and never let anyone else tell her what her limits were; she had to find those things out for herself. But that was a moot point in this situation.

It was unreasonable and she realized that. She didn't know Maiden Harlow from a bar of soap, but she hated her. The first time she swaggered into the station like something out of a magazine and politely asked to see the captain, Sarah-Jane had immediately hated her.

I'm a loser and everybody knows it, she thought sadly. *I wish I'd never come to this pokey little town.* She didn't realize that her unhappiness showed in her expression until the big blonde lady rested a hand on her shoulder.

"Oh, what's the matter, baby?" Gloria frowned gently when she saw her downcast expression.

"Nothing…" she said in a fragile little voice and fiddled with her pen. She was quickly realizing that she was more disappointed and embarrassed than she'd thought. Her cheeks felt warm and her heart started thudding loudly against her ribs. "I'm okay."

"Except for—" Bella trailed her hand through the air, prompting Sarah-Jane to fill in the gap.

"I'm ugly and frumpy and no one likes me." She couldn't believe she'd said it out loud. She clamped her mouth shut and felt her cheeks redden further. "No! I'm fine! I'm a police officer and I'm good at what I do! It doesn't matter; *everything's fine!*"

She saw the two women exchange an uncertain look. Bella's thickly painted lips formed an O as understanding settled over her. She nodded subtly to her blonde cohort and rested a hand on Sarah-Jane's other shoulder, and then apparently forgot what subtlety was.

"Sweetie-pie, tell Bella the truth now, were you lustin' after that gorgeous captain yourself?" she asked frankly.

Sarah-Jane's eyes rounded in horror and her mouth fell open. Gloria rolled her eyes at the revelation, but quickly found her store of southern charm.

"Now, listen darlin'," she said kindly but firmly, "don't you blame yourself for that one. What's happenin' between him and little Maiden has been brewin' for months, long before you got to town."

"Out of your control completely," Bella asserted and gave her frizzy hair an affectionate pat. "And you're not ugly. You're real pretty, and you'd be surprised what you have to work with if you tried a little harder…a lot harder."

"I am *not* lusting after anyone!" Sarah-Jane's voice cracked a little as she finally found the nerve to speak. "Certainly not Captain McAlister! He's my superior officer; that sort of conduct isn't acceptable! He doesn't even notice me. No one does!"

"Mm-hm," Bella murmured patiently as she pushed the plate with the pastry closer to her. "Settle down and eat that...I'm thinkin'."

Sarah-Jane felt too exposed and humiliated to argue; she picked up the pastry and bit into it. The sweet cherry flavor filled her mouth and she resisted a ridiculous urge to cry. Romance never worked out for her, not ever.

Even as she sank into the ill-timed sulk she knew she was overreacting. But seeing Maiden dressed like some kind of modern-day bombshell and knowing that she'd been cozied up with the captain—it was so disappointing.

The whole station knew about them by now and, since Sarah-Jane had never tried to be subtle about her own interests, they all knew that she'd never had a shot.

She'd started work early that morning and heard Greg and Nancy talking about it. Not about the murder that happened a few hours before, no, about the captain and Maiden. They'd both clammed up when they saw her walk in, which was even more embarrassing, but no one else bothered with even that much subtlety.

There was no shortage of whispers and jokes about how great Maiden had looked last night and how long it had taken Captain McAlister to finally give in and make a move. She'd quickly volunteered to be one of the first on scene at the manor, and no one questioned it.

Sarah-Jane was so lost in sadness and self-pity that it took her too long to realize she was being circled and sized up. By the time she raised her tawny eyes to the two older women they had just nodded to each other as though agreeing to a plan. She swallowed hard and took a bracing sip of the coffee they'd served her.

"Uh, look, I don't usually talk like that. I'm sorry, I'm just a little out of sorts today. Overtired maybe." She strove to recover some dignity. "Please don't tell anyone what I said, I didn't really mean it."

"Don't you worry about that, honey. Talk is only talk." Bella waved her concerns away as she pulled gently at one of her springy curls. "You got more important things to sort out. What do you think, Glory?"

"Lot to be done," Gloria sighed and shook her head. "It'd make quite a difference, though. And it's not like we got anyplace else to be at the moment."

"What's your name, honeypot?" Bella asked as she grasped her shoulders and turned her to face them.

"Sarah-Jane," she said cautiously.

"That's so precious!" Bella said happily but then her expression turned serious. "Do you ever wear mascara?"

"She doesn't," Gloria answered for her, despite having only seen her three or four times. "Not even a hint of lipstick...oh gosh, Belle, look at the eyebrows. What's happenin' to people these days?"

"Don't you be unkind, Gloria. Maybe she didn't have a mama to teach her these things, we don't know, do we?" Bella whispered despite standing a foot away from the subject of their discussion. "Go grab me my purse."

"What's happening?" Sarah-Jane frowned uneasily and leaned back as Bella rummaged around her voluminous leather bag and produced a pair of tweezers.

"Now don't you worry, sugar. Aunt Bella's here to help." She smiled sweetly before a look of frightening intensity overtook her features. She held the tweezers poised in an expert grip and moved in for the kill. "Don't move."

***

Vonny walked downstairs and across the foyer. She'd left Maiden lying in bed pretending to still be asleep. As much as she wanted to hear about her sister's rumored run in with a certain handsome cop, she knew that Mae wasn't ready to talk about it yet.

Their mother would spill everything she knew however, and she'd also be a virtual font of coffee and doughnuts. The promise of baked goods and gossip made the choice to give her little sister a moment's peace an easy one.

Her thoughts wandered briefly to Gail Hedgewick's murder. She hoped it wouldn't turn into a big thing, but she knew it probably would. At least she could be certain that Tony was safe this time, she'd been glued to his side all evening.

She hoped Aunt Bella had someone to vouch for her the whole time. If Gail had tried to ruin *her* wedding, Von knew she'd have screamed the old bat's head off. Aunt Bella had handled it pretty gracefully, considering.

Who'd kill a cranky old lady? Yeah, she was mean, but she was almost 90. Why not just leave her alone? And why do it at a wedding reception? Von tried to reason on it but it was just a tangle of nonsense to her; she briefly wondered how Maiden managed to figure stuff like that out.

"Ow! That hurts!"

Officer Parker's irate voice stopped Vonny in her tracks as she neared one of the numerous doors. She poked her head inside a partly refurbished lounge and blinked at what she saw.

Officer Parker was sitting on one of the old barstools, arms crossed and mouth pressed grimly shut while Gloria and Bella circled like vultures ready to peck the flesh from her bones.

Vonny had met the surly officer a month ago, after the horrific train-wreck that was her high school reunion. She honestly didn't like her, but that was only because Maiden told her how nasty the chick had been.

But something must have changed if her mom and aunt were primping her like a show pony. She knew the women wouldn't tolerate any rudeness to her or Maiden.

Gloria was digging through a pile of makeup that had likely all been stuffed in Bella's purse, while Bella herself deftly tweezed Parker's sulky visage. Vonny debated about whether she wanted to get involved, but curiosity won and she stepped inside.

"What the heck are you doing?" Vonny asked as she approached and braced her hands on her hips. "Is Officer Parker being held against her will?"

"Hush up," Bella said without looking up from her task. "I'm trying to lighten up Sarah-Jane's eyebrows, they're thick as hedges."

"Oh...good," Vonny said as she sauntered over to the bar. "Get that mole on her neck while you're at it."

"Ooh! How'd I miss that?" Bella's eyes lit up as she tore the offending hair out without waiting for the girl to lose courage.

"Ow! Hey!" Sarah-Jane didn't dare move but her eyes darted angrily to Vonny. "I don't need an audience, this is bad enough as it is."

"You should be used to this at your age." Gloria clicked her tongue. "Unless—are you an orphan, sweetheart?"

"No, I am not," Sarah-Jane said tartly. "Mom doesn't wear makeup either; she says it's a waste of time."

Gloria and Bella's horrified gasps resounded throughout the large room. They stared at her with their mouths agape, unable to grasp what she'd just uttered.

"Wow! It takes a lot to hush these two up." Vonny laughed and grabbed a chocolate doughnut from the tray.

"I've never heard of anything so irresponsible. To say a thing like that to your own daughter," Bella breathed and shut her eyes briefly. "The sheer neglect!"

"A lot of women don't wear makeup." Sarah-Jane couldn't help smiling at the women's dramatics. "Or pluck their eyebrows."

"A lot of women are homely as a dog's butt and don't have to be!" Bella retorted sharply. "Now sit still, honey, I'm nearly done."

***

Half an hour later Bella had liberated every extraneous hair from the younger lady's face and Gloria had applied a deft layer of cosmetics to her virgin skin. A handful of hairpins made a bit of progress in taming her wildly curling hair, but they warned her emphatically that she needed to seek professional help to get it under control.

The pair then stood back and admired their handiwork with pleased smiles. Vonny glanced up from her phone and gave an approving nod.

"Not bad, Officer Hottie." She gave her a nudge with her elbow. "Go take a look."

Sarah-Jane only hesitated for a moment before turning to look at her reflection in one of the massive mirrors that hung from the wall beside them. Her breath caught and she gazed in surprise at the woman that stared back at her.

She pushed to her feet and walked tentatively closer, unable to believe she was seeing herself. Her features looked so feminine; it was her only softer somehow. The ladies had reshaped her eyebrows, they were still full but they looked lush and inquisitive rather than the untamed forest she'd always kind of wanted to clean up but typically ignored.

Her eyes looked large and mysterious thanks to a medley of eyeshadow she knew she'd never be able to recreate and a thick rimming of black eyeliner. She turned her face to the side and marveled at the sight of cheekbones; she'd never understood the point of wearing blush until now.

"Well then, gorgeous," Bella sounded thoroughly pleased with herself, "what do you think about that?"

"I...I don't know what to say," Sarah-Jane said slowly, still unable to look away. "I'm really not the 'girly' type. It does feel kinda good, though."

"You're still you, Officer Parker." Vonny gave her a sympathetic smile. "It's okay to dress yourself up a bit if you want to; it doesn't take anything away from what you can do."

"It enhances it!" Gloria said happily.

They all turned to the doorway when they heard footsteps. Greg appeared and Sarah-Jane held her breath and turned to the others anxiously. Without missing a beat, Bella scooped up her makeup cases and shoved them back into her purse and Vonny sipped her coffee casually.

"What's going on?" he asked as he walked inside.

"Interviewin' and such." Gloria shrugged innocently and pointed to the tray. "Have a doughnut."

"Is that a cop joke?" He arched a brow even as he helped himself.

"Oh you!" Bella tittered and waved him away. "Well, I'd better see if Elvan's awake yet. I don't want him to worry if he can't find me."

Greg watched her go and then turned to Sarah-Jane and scowled uncertainly.

"Hey, Parker," Greg murmured and flicked a glance over her. "You look...nice. You get a haircut or something?"

"Sort of." She smiled mildly as she walked past.

CHAPTER ELEVEN

Upstairs, Maiden was standing by the window looking out at the sprawling driveway. She hadn't slept well, but she also wasn't ready to leave the safety of the bedroom in search of coffee yet.

Sleeping next door to a crime scene had been unnerving, despite everything being securely locked up and an officer posted on the door. Reliving her encounter with David had been far more enjoyable, but her mind kept sneaking back to what had happened to Gail.

She hadn't personally liked the woman and there was apparently no shortage of people that hated her. If Gail could be that rude and heartless to her own son, it stood to reason that she would have treated others just as bad, if not worse. Her thoughts drifted to Marti and Sylvia Drake. She didn't know the details but they certainly detested both Gail and Bradley.

She also thought about the three rings Gail had worn to the wedding along with her blatantly mournful black dress. It was weird and it had to have been significant to someone.

There was also Bradley's strange behavior and the fact that he admitted he had no alibi. He'd also argued with Pierce, possibly a few times, and he had some bitter history with Marti. Those things unto themselves didn't mean he'd killed Gail, but it was odd, all of it seemed very odd.

She wondered how Elvan was holding up. Even though she'd turned mean and had hated his fiancée, it would have still been traumatic for him to find his mother murdered. And at his own wedding reception.

Her mind flitted back to Elvan's nervous behavior. He'd told her that he'd been the victim of strange 'accidents', and now his mother was dead. What did it mean? Was he really in danger? What about Aunt Bella, was she safe now that she was part of the Hedgewick family?

Maiden stayed hidden in her room, pondering these problems, until she saw more police cars drive up. Specifically, until David arrived.

She'd used the time to take more than the usual care with her makeup. Eyeliner, lipstick, everything. She knew that the focus of everyone's attention needed to be on Gail's murder, but a lot of very significant personal things had happened to her last night; for her own personal reasons, she wanted to look nice.

She knew she'd be teased and winked at and could only hope that having a crowd of police there might keep her family a little more subdued. She peered down from the third story window and watched David climb out of his car and walk inside.

She wet her lips and felt a fluttering in her stomach. He looked incredible, handsome and authoritative, and he was walking into a room full of her relatives. Her eyes widened in horror and she hurried to the door.

She ran down the hallway but stopped near the top of the stairs and took a deep breath. She did her best to steady her nerves before descending with the grace and elegance of someone who actually belonged in a mansion.

It was completely fake, of course, she was so nervous that she half expected to twist an ankle and plummet to the ground floor in a heap. But until that happened, no one would be the wiser.

She somehow managed to reach the bottom portion of the stairs without incident and glanced around. The foyer was empty, except for David...and Greg.

Maiden felt instantly awkward and now wished she'd stayed upstairs a bit longer. It wasn't like she'd never been interested in a man before, she had, but never with the amount of tension and speculation from others that had gone along with her relationship with David.

It didn't help when Greg glanced over and gave her a knowing smile. She wasn't sure how to respond or even where to look but then David flicked a calm glance at her.

"Good morning, Harlow," he said mildly. "Did you sleep well?"

"What?" She looked at him, mentally scanning his perfectly normal question for hidden sarcasm, and then reminded herself to relax. "Yeah, I did. Thanks. You?"

"Fine, thanks." He was shuffling through the papers he was holding and didn't look up at her again.

"So did I," Greg volunteered with a smirk. "Isn't that nice? We all slept well, and after such an exciting evening, what with the murder and all."

"Why are you covered in powdered sugar?" Maiden looked him over with a tiny frown.

"Oh." Greg's amusement faded and he flicked a glance at the captain as he started brushing the incriminating dust from his crisply ironed uniform. "Your mom forced me to eat a doughnut."

"Did she force you to wear it too?" Maiden asked.

"I'll be right back," he grumbled and walked off towards the kitchen.

David finally glanced up and smiled wryly at Greg's retreat. Maiden had risked edging a tiny bit closer but her breath caught when he turned to her and swiftly closed the gap between them. He leaned close and met her gaze fully.

"Listen, today's going to be long and challenging. Don't look at me and try not to talk to me, I have to work," he whispered warmly and tapped his forefinger gently on the tip of her nose. "I barely slept and I need all the help I can get."

"I'm always eager to help, as you know." She grinned and obligingly turned and walked away.

Maiden focused on walking straight even as she was convinced that David was watching her go. It was distracting and she knew she was overthinking absolutely everything and she hadn't even had coffee yet.

Play it cool, Maiden, she attempted to bolster herself before joining the others. *It doesn't matter that every cop and his dog knows you made out with the head of the department last night. You have to act like nothing's changed. Just survive breakfast and then find a place to hide, that's all you have to do.*

With that plan solidly in mind, she followed the sounds of conversation to the spacious lounge she'd sat in the night before. She peeked inside and found complete chaos.

Her mother and Aunt Bella were talking and laughing loudly while several officers tried valiantly to get some questions answered. Vonny was sitting beside them eating a bear claw and smiling unhelpfully.

This is gonna take years! she thought irately. *Just stop being turkeys and answer their questions!* Maiden caught herself and was startled by how much she sounded like her father; she quickly buried the worrying thought. She shook her head over her entire family and ducked quietly inside, trying to stay out of sight.

"*Maiden!*"

She cringed as her mother called her name loudly across the room. She glanced over as Gloria waved happily and gestured for her to come over. With an inaudible sigh she made her way over to the bar, ignoring absolutely everyone that looked at her as she walked past.

When she was within reach, Gloria wrapped her arms around her and pulled her close, mashing her into her cleavage and dropping a kiss on the top of her head.

"How's my sweet baby?" she asked happily.

"Struggling to breathe," Maiden wheezed and was promptly released.

"Sorry, angel." Gloria patted her arm and her hair but then gave her a petulant look. "Where you been all mornin'?"

"Upstairs," she mumbled and glanced around for assistance. "Where's Dad?"

"He got up at first light and went back to check on the inn," Gloria said as she leaned her elbow against the bar. "Said somethin' about turkeys and off he went."

"Oh, well maybe I'd better go and help him." Maiden had barely got the words out when Gloria and Bella gave her a furious look.

"*You* can't go!" they both nearly shouted.

Maiden tried to look innocently confused while also trying not to die of embarrassment. The police officers fell abruptly silent and all started scribbling notes and reading their reports in an attempt to hear the entire exchange. Maiden gave her mother a silently pleading look that Vonny unfortunately noticed.

"What's up, Mae?" she asked loudly. "Don't you want to stay and help the cops this time?"

"I'm sure they don't need my help, Vonny." She gave her a warning look.

"Well *I* do!" Bella stared at her. "You wouldn't leave me here all alone? With Elvan."

"He can't be that bad; you married the guy," She frowned a little and glanced around. "Wherever he is. Anyway, if the police want me they'll call me."

She heard a few badly concealed sniggers from around the room; she felt her cheeks turn pink but refused to react in any other way. Vonny was smirking and swinging her feet like a child, a bratty little crap of a child.

"But wouldn't things be easier if you were close by?" she suggested mildly. "More opportunities to, you know, *help.*"

Maiden arched a brow at her sister and got a smug smile in return. She decided it was time to pull out the wildcard she'd been saving.

"Why worry about what I'm doing? Don't you have your own life to organize? Speaking of which, when are you and Tony getting engaged?" she asked. "Has he said anything?"

"That's all you've got?" Vonny mouthed the words and then answered louder. "We haven't discussed it. We're taking things slow."

"Yeah, *real* slow." Maiden pulled an unimpressed face. "It's just, well, something he said the other day got me wondering. Something seems to be in the air, that's all. But maybe it's just him kicking ideas around."

Maiden noticed that Gloria was paying closer attention now, and so was Bella. She cleared her throat and fired with both barrels.

"You don't want to waste too much time, though," she cautioned. "Especially since you both want kids. I'm sure Mom would love to have some grandbabies running around."

"*Grandbabies!*" Gloria whispered with widened eyes and turned to Vonny with renewed interest.

"We haven't been dating very long." Vonny sat up straighter and leaned subtly away from Bella, who was staring at her like she was made of pure gold.

"Yeah, but you've known each other for over 20 years," Maiden said easily. "You're practically there."

"Oh!" Bella squealed delightedly and grasped her niece's arm. "Vonny, you'll have cappuccino babies! They'll be gorgeous!"

"How adorable!" Maiden was shaking as she tried not to burst out laughing.

"I don't want to be rushed!" Vonny said tightly, giving her mother and aunt a warning look.

"Oh, no one's rushin' you!" Gloria and Bella both assured her in accents that had grown thicker with dreamy thoughts of beautiful, fat, caramel-toned babies.

"Now, come along, sugar." Gloria smiled as she took Vonny's hand and tugged her off her stool. "You can come back to Harlow House with me. I doubt you've called Tony today and I'm sure he'll be worried about you. What with all this murderin' goin' on."

"And Maiden stays here with me," Bella added sternly, giving her niece a look that warned against any argument.

Maiden held up her hands in surrender. She wasn't about to push Aunt Bella; she'd managed to chase Vonny off and was content with that. As her sister was dragged past she leaned closer and glared at Maiden.

"You cow!" she muttered through clenched teeth.

Maiden smiled and blew her a kiss; Von had started it and they both knew it. As she watched them go, however, she glanced back and felt herself pale. David was in the room now and standing closer than she expected as he conferred with a few of his officers.

How long have you been there? Please tell me you didn't hear the baby stuff! I don't want babies! I haven't even been on a date in nearly two years! Maiden took a deep breath and turned to Bella. The buxom southern queen was frowning at her watch and tapping her foot.

"What's wrong?" Maiden asked carefully.

"Elvan was supposed to be downstairs by now," she tsked and shook her head. "I swear sometimes he's weak as a wet noodle."

"His mom died last night!" Maiden said louder than she meant to; the chatter in the room had died down and her words echoed further than she'd expected.

Bella frowned a tad sullenly but nodded as she tucked her ample backside onto the nearest stool. David approached and deliberately focused on Bella. Maiden knew why he was ignoring her and took no offense at it.

"Mrs. Hedgewick," he said as he flicked through his notebook, "I apologize for any distress this investigation may cause you. I'm aware of the circumstances around it, of course."

"You're too sweet, Captain." Bella smiled warmly. "You just do whatever you need to do, sugar."

"Right." He smiled faintly and briefly. "Can you recall anything strange that happened yesterday? Any indication that Gail Hedgewick was in danger from anyone?"

"I was busy gettin' ready for the weddin', I barely saw her," Bella explained and then added, rather needlessly, "I typically avoided the old bat whenever possible anyway."

"So...you didn't get along well?" He gave her a watchful look. "You're not particularly sorry that she's dead?"

"No, but I'm sorry she was murdered," Bella said candidly. "Even in death she's managed to be a pain in the butt."

Maiden shut her eyes briefly and turned her back to David as she grasped her aunt's arm. She leaned a bit closer and whispered in her ear.

"Please keep in mind that you're speaking to the police," she reminded her seriously. "Do you want to call your lawyer?"

"What for? Am I under suspicion?" Bella batted her false eyelashes and still spoke in her usual loud tone.

"You probably are now!" Maiden said bluntly, abandoning her pointless attempt at subtlety.

"I said I was sorry the old sack of bones was murdered!" she protested, her accent getting thicker as her anxiety grew. "Am I supposed to lie and say I liked her? *No one* liked her, she was awful!"

"You could choose to say nothing—" Maiden stopped and looked at her resignedly. "Actually no, I don't think you can. I was told there's coffee around here somewhere."

"Over there," David informed her, pointing to several carafes that sat beside a large plate of pastries on the bar. "And don't interrupt while I'm questioning people."

Maiden shot him a furiously warning look; he visibly fought a smile and stared resolutely down at his notepad. She rolled her eyes and poured herself a cup of coffee. As he resumed his questioning, she took up the stool beside her aunt and listened closely, ready to intercede out of spite if nothing else.

"Had Mrs. Hedgewick expressed any disapproval of your marriage to her son apart from the incident during the ceremony?" he asked.

Bella's ingenuous expression darkened slightly but she merely shrugged.

"She didn't say anything to me personally."

Maiden thought back to the argument between Gail and Elvan that she'd interrupted the night before the wedding. She wasn't sure if she wanted to mention it in front of Bella, and certainly not after being told not to interrupt. She pulled a cranky face and bit into a cheese Danish with an irate little sigh. Unfortunately, her huff of breath sent a cloud of powdered sugar out in front of her.

Maiden was quietly grateful that Greg wasn't in the room after she'd teased him about making a mess with his doughnut. She looked up at David to find him glaring at her. She blinked uncertainly but then glanced down to see that the snowy sugar had gently dusted across her full bust and décolletage.

That's probably not going to help him to focus, she thought to herself as a tell-tale blush warmed her cheeks. She smirked at him as she turned her stool back around to face the bar. As she attempted to brush the powdered sugar away she decided to keep her back to everyone while she finished her coffee.

The room was silent for a moment. She tried not to grin when she heard David release a steadying breath before speaking again.

"All right, where's Mr. Hedgewick?" he asked an unusually stoic Bella.

"I'm right here, Captain McAlister."

Everyone turned to see Elvan stride determinedly into the room and station himself at Bella's side. He looked pale and weary and his eyes were still a bit red. Despite his fragile appearance, Elvan stood stoically beside his bride.

"I apologize to everyone for fallin' to pieces like that." He took Bella's hand and patted it. "I never meant to leave others to deal with my responsibilities."

"It's quite all right, Mr. Hedgewick." David kept his expression impassive. "Considering the nature of the events, there wasn't much you could have done anyway. Let's move forward, shall we? I'll ask you the same thing I asked your wife, did you notice anything out of place yesterday? Any hint of threat to your mother?"

"Not honestly, no." He shook his head. "She was in one of her bad moods, they'd been gettin' worse over the past few months, but she seemed normal. For her."

"I noticed that she was very angry as she took her seat for the ceremony," David murmured candidly. "Specifically, she appeared to be angry with you. Why was that?"

"Well..." Elvan slid a reluctant gaze to Bella. "Mama didn't like the idea of me gettin' married again. My first wife was so horrible that it put her off the idea completely."

"That's a fine thing to say behind my back!" a caustic voice sliced through the air.

With all thoughts of hiding her candied cleavage forgotten, Maiden turned fully to see the source of the disruption. A shortish woman sauntered into the room wearing a tight and startlingly fuchsia dress. Her hair was bright red and sculpted into a shiny bouffant. Her eyes were hazel, heavily painted and mean.

"What the heck are you doin' here, Ree?!" Elvan demanded angrily. "How'd you even know we were here?"

Ree. Maiden recalled Aunt Bella's ungenerous description of Elvan's ex-wife. Seeing her in the flesh, Maiden was more inclined to agree with Bella's critical assessment. She looked like trouble.

"Our son told me, obviously." Ree drawled and crossed her arms as she stood in front of them. "You think he wouldn't mention your latest bad decision?"

She flicked a distasteful look at Bella with that last remark; Maiden disliked the woman immediately. Bella, who had obviously met her before, just quirked a brow and returned the unimpressed study.

"Speakin' of bad decisions," she replied mildly, "couldn't you afford that dress in your size? I suppose it would be a lot of extra material to pay for."

Ree's lips pursed angrily, showing the deep lines that were etched around them, and her nostrils flared. David raised a hand and his voice before she could retort.

"Who are you, and who let you in here?" He gave his officers a sharp look and Greg quickly stepped forward.

"I met her in the foyer, Captain," he explained. "She says she's Ree Hedgewick, Bradley Hedgewick's mother."

"That's right." Ree smiled nastily, her version of southern was harsh and grating. "Where is Bradley?"

Bella snorted a laugh and sipped her coffee. Elvan squared his shoulders and opened his mouth but David interceded. He turned to Ree and flipped to a new page in his notebook.

"How long have you been in Golden Glen?" he asked calmly.

"I only arrived last night." She smiled as she looked him over and fingered the pearls that hung around her throat, "I heard that some sad old fool tried to have a weddin' yesterday, I just wanted to see if the rumors were true."

"What do you mean 'tried'?" David asked, holding up a hand to silence Elvan when he started to answer.

"Well, Elvan, of course!" she tittered and patted her stiffly shel-lacked hair. "Thinkin' his mama would stand by and let a disaster like Bella Fontaine barge her way into their lives."

"Are you saying you have reason to believe that Gail Hedgewick disapproved of her son's marriage?" he continued smoothly.

"Do I have reason?" she laughed. It was a jaded sound, roughened by years of cigarettes; if the nicotine stains on her fingers were any indication. "Only that Gail said he'd marry that woman over her dead body!"

The room fell uncomfortably silent again.

Ree frowned at the stony look on David's handsome face. She glanced around and started to realize that something wasn't right.

"Why are y'all here, by the way?" she asked uncertainly.

"You finally noticed that the place is full of police?" Elvan scoffed. "You were never half as bright as your hair."

"Shut up, you idiot!" she snarled and fixed her gaze on David. "Where's Gail? And where's my son?"

"Are you claiming to be unaware that Gail Hedgewick was murdered last night?" David asked coolly.

"What?" she gasped and backed up a step. "She's dead?"

"Murdered." He nodded once. "Where were you last night between 9 and 10 pm?"

"Where was I?" She pressed a hand to the bony expanse above her low neckline and shook her head a little. "I was at my hotel. Why? You don't really think—"

"Is there anyone who could vouch for your whereabouts?" he asked before she could argue. "Anyone that was with you at the time?"

"Well...no, but I didn't do nothin'." She looked startled and nervous now. "I had no reason to harm Gail."

"No reason except for you both hatin' each other for years!" Elvan said angrily. "I'd like to know when you heard mama say anything about our weddin'."

"I had a good relationship with Gail!" Ree glared at her ex-husband. "Even though you tried to poison her against me!"

"You did that yourself when you slept with my brother!" he snapped.

Maiden had paled but Bella was watching the scene with an unperturbed smirk. The officers in the room shifted subtly closer, perhaps anticipating a physical turn to the confrontation. Ree jabbed a finger in Elvan's direction and started to shout.

"You drove me to it!" she declared angrily. "You were never anything like a good husband to me!"

"This is not going to turn into a domestic dispute!" David's deep voice boomed loudly but then calmed when the bickering pair turned to him and clamped their mouths shut. "A murder has been committed."

"She probably did it!" Ree snarled and pointed at Bella. "She'd have hated Gail for stoppin' the weddin'!"

"Who told you she stopped the wedding?" David eyed the angry woman curiously.

"She did." Ree glowered at him. "Gail told me she'd never let the weddin' go forward."

"When did she tell you that?" David pressed relentlessly.

"I don't know, a couple weeks ago." Ree shrugged.

"When did you last speak with Gail Hedgewick?" He turned to his notebook and started writing.

"Not since then," she said uneasily as she watched him scrawl something.

"Well, you'll be relieved to hear that the weddin' went ahead as planned." Bella smiled and held up her impressive rings as proof.

Ree stared at them and then instinctively looked down at her own hand and the slightly smaller diamond that sat there. Maiden frowned but kept quiet as Ree turned back to Bella.

"It did?" Ree looked stunned. "You mean...you're actually married?"

"Mm-hmm," Bella said as she admired the massive diamond on her finger. "Poor old Gail did try to spoil things by fakin' a heart attack but we soldiered on. Amazingly, she recovered real quick and was just fine after that."

"Until she was smothered," Maiden pointed out quietly, not that anyone was listening.

Ree looked genuinely shocked as she looked from Bella to a smugly pleased Elvan. Maiden could almost see her mind racing as she tried to absorb what she'd heard. A moment later Ree's sharp eyes narrowed furiously.

"Well, it don't matter!" she hissed. "It won't do you a bit of good! Gail told me she was changin' her will!"

That got everyone's attention. Maiden barely caught a gasp and looked at Bella. Bella slid an uncertain look to Elvan but relaxed when she saw that he wasn't perturbed in the slightest. He took a step towards his seething ex-wife and scowled grimly.

"So, you discussed wills with a frail, dementia-stricken old woman? A woman that had ordered you to never speak to her again, back when she had her wits about her," Elvan murmured suspiciously. "What's it got to do with you? You can't have been expectin' to inherit."

Ree finally seemed to realize she'd said too much, she clamped her mouth shut and folded her arms stubbornly. Maiden glanced at David but he was just watching and listening. Elvan continued happily.

"Well, I'm afraid you've wasted your time." He smiled smugly. "Mama never changed her will and, since you signed that wonderful little prenuptial agreement, it don't make a bit of difference to you anyway."

"There's the matter of our son, don't forget!" Ree rose to the bait, smiling triumphantly. "Dear Gail confided in me that she was goin' to bequeath everything to Bradley if you married that slab of mutton you never did get over."

"Don't you ever speak of Bella that way!" Elvan glowered but was smart enough to keep his temper in check. "Are you sayin' that you and Bradley thought he was goin' to inherit everything when Mama died?"

"That's right." Ree smiled viciously, completely unaware that she'd just suggested an even stronger motive for her son. "She said he was gonna be rich as a king and you'd have nothin'!"

"Just as well he's been arrested then." Bella failed to withhold a chortle.

"Arrested?" Ree's mouth fell open. "You liar! He can't have been!"

"You ought to know that already." Bella looked her over and was clearly unimpressed by what she saw. "You were probably lurkin' in the bushes all night."

"Don't you try to drag me and my boy into your mess, you piece of trash!" Ree growled.

"I said leave her alone!" Elvan stepped between them and regarded Ree with a look of disdain. "Honestly, Ree, if you'd been anywhere near as good a woman, your filthy betrayal would have hurt me more. As it is, I was glad to be rid of you! Now you listen and listen good, Mama never changed her will. She and I discussed it a week ago and agreed that Bradley wasn't capable of handlin' that much money. The suggestion that he'd only turn it all over to *you* was all the persuasion she needed to dismiss the idea."

"That ain't true!" Ree grated. "Gail hated you! She told me so!"

"Wrong again." He smiled a cool and superior smile. "It looks like you sent your little angel of death too soon. He killed Mama without botherin' to make sure he was really in line to inherit."

"How dare you!" Ree shrieked in outrage and launched herself at Elvan.

Not one to be upstaged, Bella quickly entered the fray and a lot of shouting and hair-pulling ensued. Maiden stared in startled dismay as several police officers labored to break up the brawl.

Elvan, his face scratched and clothes rumpled, turned to David with a thunderous expression.

"I want that woman arrested!" he demanded, pointing a stout finger at Ree. "She's unhinged and just tried to kill me!"

"You miserable worm!" Ree snarled. "Turnin' on your own son!"

"Who you just admitted was tryin' to cheat his own father of his inheritance." Bella rolled her eyes. "I'd call you devious but you're too blasted dumb to manage it. 'Clumsy wannabe gold-digger' is a better description."

"Don't talk to me about gold-diggin'!" Ree stomped her foot. "If you'd known Elvan was rich you'd have married him back in high school! Now that you're old and desperate you'll settle for him? Nothin' at all to do with his money?!"

"You're the one that got lost on the way to your bedroom!" Bella laughed derisively. "I'm not about to be shamed by a tramp that turned her back on her husband and baby to run after some gigolo. Enjoy your night in jail, sweetie, you'll probably meet a lot of other nice prostitutes."

Maiden's mouth fell open and she turned to David in horror. She caught him just barely hiding his amusement before his face became a stony, unreadable mask. He approached and stood between them all; Maiden wasn't at all confident that the feisty women wouldn't climb over him to reach each other again.

"We will *all* go to the station and have a talk," he said loudly and motioned to his officers. "If warranted, charges will be filed."

"What?" Bella's penciled brows reached for the sky. "But I'm no criminal!"

"I was referring to Ms. Hedgewick's attack on your husband," he explained patiently.

"It's *Mrs.* Hedgewick!" Ree snapped.

"You're no 'Mrs.' of mine anymore, thank heaven!" Elvan barked back. "Can we all hush up and let these people do their jobs?"

"Fine, but I'm not walkin' in there alone." Bella looked horrified and glanced around anxiously. Maiden felt her heart sink and tried to edge subtly behind Greg, but she wasn't quick enough. "Maiden! Thank goodness! C'mon, baby, let's go."

"I'm sure that won't be allowed, Aunt Bella." Maiden slid David a wide-eyed look even as Bella waved her over.

"Its fine under the circumstances," he said, apparently missing the unspoken plea. "Since your aunt isn't under arrest."

Maiden kept quiet but her eyes betrayed all the annoyance she wanted him to see. He blinked at her as Bella and Elvan bustled around them and slipped out the door towards the foyer.

"Oh." He visibly realized that she'd been trying to get out of it, not ask to go along. "I'm sorry…well, you're sort of a witness anyway, so…"

"Oh yeah? You want to discuss my alibi?" she asked acerbically as she walked past, throwing him an irate look over her shoulder. "Maybe have me describe my movements at the time of the murder?"

"At some point, yes." He failed to suppress his grin, particularly as a chorus of muffled laughter rippled through the handful of officers that were still in the room. "Probably not today, though."

Chapter Twelve

Maiden drove Bella and Elvan in her car as he seemed too annoyed and shaken up to take the wheel. It didn't take nearly long enough to reach the station; Maiden wasn't looking forward to it and would have been fine with a much lengthier journey.

Elvan and Bella spent the time muttering to each other about Ree's temerity and Bradley's hateful and greedy betrayal. Maiden half-listened but she was already on edge and didn't want to get angry on top of it. It wasn't as if she could do much about Elvan's unkind family anyway. And yet, she could see herself getting steadily more involved in the whole mess.

Maiden marveled at the strange situation she now found herself in. Normally she was trying to get deeper into the case, but this time she was being dragged in practically kicking and screaming.

It wasn't that she wasn't interested, she had to be, it affected her family tremendously. But to have to actually walk into the police station, the absolute center of the rumors about her and David, she dreaded the inevitable winking and nudging.

She parked the car and took her time to follow as Bella and Elvan charged inside with purpose. The front door had fallen shut behind them by the time Maiden reached it. For a brief, impetuous moment she toyed with the idea of sneaking back to her car and going home. She knew it wouldn't work though, Aunt Bella would smell the rebellious thoughts and would flag her down before she'd made it out of the parking lot.

Maiden smiled at her own nonsense and walked into the station with resignation. She spied Nancy behind the desk. Nancy had always been professional, and surely her obvious fondness for Captain McAlister would—no. No, it didn't make a stinking bit of difference.

As soon as Nancy saw her, a slow, knowing smirk appeared. Maiden glanced away smoothly to avoid eye contact.

"Good morning, Miss Harlow," Nancy said with a little more fondness and welcome than usual. "They're all in the Captain's office."

"I can wait out here. That would probably be more appropriate." Maiden tried to sound casual and ignored Nancy's puzzled look. "I'm happy to wait out here."

"I think they're waiting for you, Miss Harlow," Nancy said politely as she gestured down the hall.

"Oh, I see. Great. Thanks," Maiden murmured and didn't budge. Nancy noticed and lifted her brows inquiringly.

"*Maiden*!" Bella's powerful voice echoed loudly through the corridor an instant later. "Get your sweet little tush in here!"

Maiden cringed and headed down the hall with Nancy's quickly muffled amusement ringing in her ears. The door to David's office was ajar; she pushed it slowly open.

Maiden peered inside with all the cool serenity of someone waiting to be struck by a deadly cobra. She decided she was happy enough to stay hovering in the doorway.

Maiden glanced at David; he was sitting at his desk looking at some notes while Greg and Sergeant Ramirez were skulking about in the background. Bella and Elvan were sitting in front of the desk.

Maiden tried to linger near the door but then Bella spotted her. She knew in her heart that the older woman would never let her off that easy.

"Maiden," she patted the chair to her left, "come sit by me, baby."

"Yeah." She smiled weakly and glanced around for any possible excuse, she spied the coffee maker. "Just getting some coffee."

"I'll get it for you, Mae," Greg said helpfully. "You can go sit down."

"Thanks," she said with a touch of surrender and dutifully took up her seat.

She was painfully aware of the extra people in the room. She didn't believe for a second they were there to learn more about the case. She'd turned up to answer questions and give statements more often than most and never had an audience until now.

Silently wondering why David would tolerate the presence of the nosy officers, Maiden accepted the coffee cup Greg brought her and leaned back in her chair, willing herself to be invisible.

"All right, let's go back a bit," David began, his gaze still on his computer. He clicked a few buttons and then glanced at Bella, looking only briefly startled when he saw Greg and Officer Ramirez hovering. "Um...what were your exact actions leading up to the moment you learned Gail Hedgewick was dead?"

"I was sayin' goodbye to a few dozen people, that takes time. I was in the foyer surrounded by friends for ages." Bella folded her thick arms over her impressive bosom. "Thirty or more people would've seen me and Elvan both. I hardly think I need remind you that it was our weddin', folks knew we were there."

"No one is accusing you of anything, Mrs. Hedgewick," David assured her. "It's standard procedure to ask everyone where they were and who they were with."

"I suppose it must be," Bella allowed with a dainty sniff. "But this is all new to me. I'm not used to pokin' my nose into other people's business."

Maiden let out an involuntary snort and put a hand to her mouth. Bella turned slowly to her with a highly arched brow. Maiden gave her an innocent smile and pointed to her coffee, making some vague reference to it being too hot. Bella smiled faintly and waggled a finger at her but let it drop.

"Mr. Hedgewick?" David pressed on. "Where were you and did anyone see you?"

"Well, I went to see Mama at about 8:30. Agnes was sittin' with her, that's her regular nurse." Elvan ran a hand over his thinning hair as he thought. "Then I was downstairs for a while, I checked in the kitchen to make sure everything was being packed up and the caterers didn't have any questions...then I sat with Bella and we talked to a few friends. I don't know quite what time it was when Agnes left for the night. I saw her come down the stairs, so I walked her to the door and thanked her for lookin' after Mama so well.

"We certainly weren't goin' to send Mama away after the heart scare, so Agnes was fine to leave for the night. Then I talked to a few more people and eventually wandered upstairs to look in on her before retirin' for the evenin'." He took Bella's hand when he made the last comment and shut his eyes before he continued shakily. "She was just lyin' there with that awful pillow over her face...I threw it off her and tried to wake her, but she was gone. She looked so peaceful and still...I should've never let her be left alone!"

No one spoke for a moment while he shook with silent tears. Bella wrapped her arm around his shoulders and laid her head against his. Maiden let out an inaudible sigh and reflected on the selfishness of the situation. Not only the horrible act of killing a helpless old woman but choosing her son's wedding reception to do it.

David waited a moment before clearing his throat and folding his hands neatly on the desk. Everyone looked over to him.

"I'm sorry, but I have to ask this," he said solemnly. "Can you give me the names of the people you spoke to before you went upstairs and found your mother?"

"Oh really!" Bella looked aghast. David shrugged but kept his gaze trained on Elvan.

"I understand, of course." He took a shaky breath and rubbed his reddened eyes. "I-I can't think of their names. I talked to so many people last night, it's just a blur."

"Now, honey, lots of people will have seen you!" Bella said comfortingly and then turned to her niece. "Maiden, you're an observant little angel, you would've seen him, right?"

Maiden's eyes widened and she kept her gaze fixed on her coffee. She heard tell-tale shuffling from the officers behind her; she didn't dare look at David.

"I...no, I'm sorry," she said weakly. "I, um, didn't happen to notice where Elvan was. I'm sorry."

"Oh, you must've done!" Bella scowled. "You got a brain like a damn camera! Think harder!"

"I wasn't around, Aunt Bella." Maiden slid her a warning look. "I wasn't claiming to have forgotten anything."

"Well, where the heck were you then?" she exclaimed in exasperated disbelief. "What could you have been up to at that time of night?"

"I was doing other things," Maiden said through her teeth. "Just drop it!"

Bella blinked at her and then glanced at David who was staring down at his notes with a hand raised to his forehead, obscuring his face. That, along with the other officers in the room that were strug-gling not to laugh, made it clear that there was quite a tale to be heard there.

"I seem to be missin' some pertinent details. We'll talk later," Bella murmured. It could've been a promise or a threat but was said with a pleased smile either way.

It took what Maiden considered an embarrassingly long time before David tried to speak again. She set her coffee on the desk and folded her arms stubbornly. The captain didn't raise his eyes to look at anyone and appeared to be talking to his desk.

"We'll leave it there for now, I'll speak with Ree Hedgewick and let you know if I need anything further from you," he spoke steadily enough. "Stay in town, I'll have more questions. I'll be in touch."

"And will you be touchin' all of us?" Bella asked with an ingenuous expression. "Or just Maiden?"

"Oh, that is *it!*" Maiden yelled angrily as she shot to her feet and pointed to her aunt. "You can walk home!"

She stormed past the officers who were nearly doubled over and threw the door open. She flicked a glance at David to find him col-lapsed rather uselessly over his desk; she muttered angrily all the way down the corridor. It was only a few seconds before she heard the rapid clicking of Bella's high heels close behind her.

"What have I done now, baby?" Her tone was innocent and a bit more southern than usual. "How can I help sayin' the wrong thing when *you don't tell me nothin'?*"

Maiden threw her a scathing look that was met with a bright, toothy smile. She shook her head and faced forward. The looks and giggles were bad enough, but having Aunt Bella joke outright about the ticklish situation was too much.

She charged past a wide-eyed and interested Nancy, deliberately said nothing, and headed straight for the door.

By the time she'd reached the car, Bella and Elvan were jogging to catch up. She gave them both a warning look, despite Elvan having nothing to do with any of it, and reluctantly waited for them. She held up a finger and stared her aunt down.

"You say *nothing* on the ride back," she ordered grimly. "Got that?"

"Scout's honor, baby." Bella grinned happily and gave a little salute.

Maiden climbed in and started the car without a word. Bella was thoroughly amused and Elvan looked quietly tickled but they still got in quickly before she could change her mind and drive off without them.

Bella even kept her promise. She didn't utter a word, but she did hum 'Here Comes the Bride' until Maiden cranked the radio to drown her out.

Chapter Thirteen

Maiden drove them back to Riley Manor without a word. She parked out front, well away from the handful of police cars. Bella and Elvan obligingly took their time walking in, giving her plenty of time to get inside first.

She was quietly pleased by their tact and went straight upstairs to the room she'd stayed in last night. While she was still a bit embarrassed, she also had her own agenda brewing and it didn't include the newlyweds.

She shut herself inside and quickly gathered up her things. She hadn't packed much, it was always the plan to stay the one night and then head home.

Vonny had already packed up; she and Gloria would've cleared out completely before leaving them to deal with the police earlier. Maiden chewed at her bottom lip as she thought back to that encounter, and the rest of the events of the morning.

She was letting herself be goaded, she could see that. The tension between her and David had come to a head but now it was stuck there. That was a big part of what was getting to her. Sure, the teasing was embarrassing, but she realized that she was taking it too seriously. They weren't teenagers.

Maiden nodded approvingly at her logic and looked around to make sure she hadn't forgotten anything. She then eased towards the door and listened carefully. It was another five minutes before she heard Aunt Bella twittering away as she and Elvan marched past on their way to the stairs.

She heard her name mentioned and enough of the conversation to know that they were opting to give her some space and come home when she was ready. Maiden smiled faintly, that suited her plans perfectly.

Shifting stealthily to the window, Maiden watched until they loaded their suitcases into Elvan's shiny Mercedes and drove away. She waited until they turned out through the massive old gate and then scampered to the door and crept out into the hallway.

The house was quiet, but there had to be cops around somewhere, she'd seen the squad cars parked outside after all. She slung her bag over her shoulder and edged slowly towards Gail's room.

She looked long and hard at the closed door as she drew closer. A part of her contemplated checking if the door was unlocked and taking a quick peek inside, but the rest of her knew it would be a terrible idea.

Maiden sternly reminded herself that David and his team knew what they were doing. What was she hoping to achieve that a team of trained detectives couldn't?

It was fine, he was a good cop and she trusted him...but she still wanted to take a look. Just one quick look.

Don't do it, Maiden, she warned internally even as her fingers itched to give the doorknob a twist. She had no right to butt in now, she hadn't even seen anything of Gail after her outburst during the ceremony. She had found Gail dismally rude and made the choice to avoid her.

But Aunt Bella's a suspect, she reminded herself. *You can't stand back and do nothing. What if she's arrested? How could you live with yourself if you didn't even try to help her?*

While she engaged in the internal debate, the doorknob rattled from the other side a moment before the door swung open. She jumped slightly and quickly backed up as she found herself facing an equally startled Officer Briggs. For a heartbeat or two they just looked at each other in silence.

"Good morning, Miss Harlow. I thought I heard someone out here," he finally mumbled and glanced away.

"Hi, Officer Briggs," she said nicely, aware that he too would have heard about her and his captain by now.

"Um...are you," he wet his lips, "leaving now?"

"I was, yeah." She shifted and readjusted the strap of her bag on her shoulder. "Is that okay?"

"Yes, of course it is. You were just kind of close by the door." He met her eyes very briefly.

"It's sort of on the way to the stairs," she pointed out politely, hoping he'd buy it.

He looked dubious but didn't question her. She'd had a feeling he wouldn't. Maiden was struck by an odd pang of guilt; she knew he'd had a crush on her and was probably really disappointed.

She also knew she didn't owe him anything, they'd only spoken a handful of times and she'd never encouraged him. But he was so shy and awkward around her. It was sweet, but it had never been enough to make her fake an interest that wasn't there.

"Well," she said mildly. "I'd better get going."

She stepped back a bit more but they both looked over when they heard someone coming up the stairs. David stepped into the hallway and took in the scene. He smiled almost imperceptibly when he looked at Maiden but his expression was more sedate when he turned to Briggs.

"Everything all right, Briggs?" he asked calmly as he approached.

"Yes, sir," he replied impassively. "Miss Harlow said she was just leaving."

David gave her a teasing smile. Maiden didn't return the warm expression, partly because she was still annoyed with him for not getting her out of that farce of an interview, but mostly because she was very conscious of Briggs standing there staring down at his shoes. It made her stomach hurt a little; she slid her gaze away.

"You can go and help Smith search the kitchen," David told Briggs.

The man nodded and walked away without another word. Maiden watched him go until he disappeared downstairs. She was too preoccupied to notice that David was studying her until she glanced back and saw him frowning uncertainly.

"What?" she asked innocently, hoping he wasn't going to lecture her about hanging around the crime scene.

"Are you mad at me?" he asked quietly.

What?! She stared at him. *I was until you asked me that!*

"No," she said slowly. "Not exactly."

"What does that mean?" he shook his head and studied her watchfully.

"I don't really know," she admitted with a shrug. "You made me go to the station with Aunt Bella and then you let half your team stand around to enjoy the show. But the fact that you might actually care if I'm mad at you makes me slightly less mad. So, I guess that's what 'not exactly' means."

David rubbed his hands over his face, failing to hide his amusement entirely.

"Getting a bit angrier with you now, though." She glared at him.

"I didn't *make* you go! And I didn't know you were going to lose it like that," he protested even as he struggled not to laugh. "I felt terrible, I swear."

"Yeah, you look pretty choked up," she said dryly and folded her arms over her chest. "I can't ever set foot in that station again, I hope you're pleased with yourself."

"You have to go again!" He was still laughing. "You were great!"

She pinned him with the highly-arched-left-eyebrow look she'd learned from Aunt Bella. It worked; he met her gaze and quickly reined himself in. He glanced down the hall to make sure they were alone before turning to her again.

"I promise I didn't ask for anyone to observe the interview," he assured her as he stepped a bit closer. "I didn't even realize they were there until your aunt started talking."

"You still didn't say anything." She rolled her eyes.

"Making an issue of it would've been awkward too," he said. "At least it was only Smith and Ramirez."

"I don't know about Sergeant Ramirez, but Greg happens to have a big fat mouth, Captain," she informed him sardonically. "Your whole team has heard the story by now, I guarantee you that."

"Well, what if they do? It doesn't really change anything. Look, it was never going to be easy to keep this professional," he sighed and held her gaze a touch earnestly. "I thought it might help to have more people in the room with us, so I left it."

"Oh really?" she asked. "And do you feel like it helped?"

"Not as much as I'd hoped," he admitted as his good humor quickly re-emerged. "It was embarrassing for me too, incidentally. And I couldn't walk out like you did."

Maiden studied him for a moment, her quiet annoyance clearly didn't worry him, he was still smiling warmly at her. She draped her hands on her hips.

"Are you at least sorry that you left me with no option but to go?" she asked.

"Oh, Harlow." He folded his arms loosely and edged a little closer still. "Don't ask me questions you already know the answer to."

"Why are you being a jerk?" she smiled begrudgingly.

"Because I *really* want to kiss you, but I can't." He grinned at her. "I have to keep my mouth busy somehow. So, had you managed to sneak into the crime scene or did Briggs stop you?"

"Is that the crime scene?" she asked ingenuously as she pointed towards the open door. "How interesting. Did you remember to look under the bed?"

"Brat," he said under his breath as he turned and took a few steps into the room. He glanced over his shoulder. "You stay in the doorway, got it?"

"Yes, Captain," she said dutifully.

The instant she was on the threshold she ran her gaze eagerly over the room. The heavy damask curtains had been pushed back, filling the space with bright light. The layout of the room was similar to the one she'd stayed in next door.

To the right of the door was a plush, queen-sized bed covered in thick quilts. These were still disturbed from where Gail's body had been removed. She gave the exposed sheets a cursory glance but they looked clean and unmarked, just rumpled.

On the left wall was a long, highly polished oak wardrobe. It matched a petite writing desk that was tucked on the other side of the bed. The large window directly across from her was bright and looked to have been recently cleaned. The view beyond was seemingly endless miles of trees that were just starting to show the kiss of autumn.

It was beautiful and very tranquil. Her gaze slid back to the bed. It again struck her as cruel to kill Gail there and then; there must have been other opportunities. Was she killed at her son's wedding out of spite?

She noticed that David was poking through the wardrobe. Despite her earlier teasing, she really did want to look under the bed. He was blocked by the large door as he searched deeper into the cupboard. She set her bag aside silently and dropped to her knees.

The floor was reasonably clean, there was some dust and a few larger bits of fluff here and there. The gaps between the old wooden floorboards betrayed their age, they were wide and irregular.

She remembered the floors of the attic in Harlow House before they'd renovated the space into luxury suites. The boards were similar to these aged planks. When they'd first started to clean up the area in earnest, they'd found a few interesting things hidden in the gaps.

Hoping to find something even more significant under Gail's bed, she peered closer. She scanned the area until something caught her attention, something that just barely peeked out from one of the cracks. It looked almost like a bit of plastic. She started to ease closer when a large shadow fell over her.

"Do you know what 'stay in the doorway' means?" David asked grimly.

Maiden sat back immediately and tried to look innocent despite having no legitimate reason to be crawling around on the floor.

"I fell over?" she offered.

"Not funny, Harlow." He folded his arms.

"Don't let it worry you, I'm fine." She stood and brushed her hands clean. "And there's something stuck between the floorboards under the bed."

"You can't just go around—"

"Pointing out possible clues when I see them?" she interrupted smoothly. "Sorry, I didn't mean to be so helpful."

David shut his eyes briefly and then knelt by the bed. He'd been grumbling under his breath but fell silent when he saw what she was talking about. He drew a small case out of his pocket and cracked it open.

Maiden eased closer and peered over his shoulder as he pulled out a set of long tweezers. He knelt down and carefully extracted the object from between the worn boards. As they both studied it for a moment, she quickly realized that it was half of an empty capsule. Something that would have contained medicine, or drugs.

It was interesting, but Gail hadn't been poisoned. It could have been lost by the room's previous guests but she somehow doubted it. She glanced at David's face, he looked focused but neither confused nor surprised.

Of course he had a good poker face, he was a detective, that was a given. But she had a feeling that this made sense to him; he almost smiled and his breathing was very calm. He said nothing as he pulled a small plastic bag from his little case and dropped the empty shell inside. He looked at her briefly and stilled when he found her studying him so closely.

"What are you doing?" he asked as he stood.

"Learning things." She smiled faintly.

"About what?" He eyed her warily.

"Was Gail drugged before she died?" She watched him ruthlessly.

"How did you get that from my expression?!" He stared at her.

She smiled at him and shrugged as she turned to the door and scooped up her bag.

"I should go," she sighed. "Officer Briggs will probably notice that it's taken me ten minutes to get downstairs."

"Wait." David's deep voice stopped her in her tracks, he was beside her a few seconds later. "Has someone told you about how Gail Hedgewick died?"

"Not beyond what you've said in front of me. She was suffocated with a pillow." She frowned at him.

"Then how did you..." He stopped and just looked at her.

"Deductive reasoning, David." She dropped the formality for one clandestine moment. "You think you invented it?"

"No," he conceded. "It seems like a bit of a jump though."

"Not really." Maiden shook her head. "Elvan said she looked peaceful when he found her, no one heard anything even though the party was winding down and the room is close to the stairs. You're holding part of a capsule that used to have something inside it and you weren't surprised to see it. It just made me wonder if she'd been knocked out before she was killed."

"Still a jump." He pulled a face.

"But I'm right, aren't I?" She smiled and turned to go. "Talk to you later, Captain."

"Right," he said dryly and reached out long enough to tap her on the shoulder. "You packed everything, didn't you? Like, *everything*?"

"Yeah, I think so." She gave him a questioning look.

"You've got that dress?" He leaned against the doorjamb and smiled down at her. "It's yours, isn't it? You own it?"

"I...yes." Her lungs felt a tiny bit tighter as she met his deeply brown eyes.

"Just checking," he said softly and stroked the back of his finger down her cheek. "Drive safe, Harlow."

***

Maiden managed the trek to her car despite her wobbly knees and headed back to the inn. As she drove through town she waved to a few people she knew and let her mind wander through what she'd gleaned so far.

Gail had been drugged and then killed. Her former daughter-in-law had breezed into town expecting the wedding to have been stopped and all Gail's money bequeathed to Bradley.

Maiden frowned; that couldn't be right. Ree said that Gail threatened to change her will if Elvan married against her wishes. So, if Gail *had* successfully halted the wedding, why would she still disinherit Elvan? Why was Ree expecting that her will had already been changed?

She also wondered how much Bradley knew about the situation. He claimed he'd been outside for a while on a cool night by himself and right at the time of the murder. It was flimsy.

If he'd had a fight with his cousin and wanted to get away for a few minutes there were plenty of options in the manor. That's what she'd done when she'd had enough of the constant chatter and ogling, she found an empty room and hid.

Maybe he was just close to the front door and needed a quick escape. He could have been telling the truth. But, the fact that he tried so hard to force her to cover for him sat badly. To ask at all was suspicious enough, yet almost understandable under the circumstances, but to force it that boldly suggested that he was very nervous about where he'd actually been.

She didn't know how close Bradley and Ree were, it was too soon to say whether he knew about any supposed changes to Gail's will. It was extremely likely, but she couldn't assume it, that could be disastrous if she was wrong.

Elvan had mentioned a feeling of being followed from time to time, and then there were the so-called accidents. She needed to find out when that had all started. It also occurred to her that she hadn't mentioned it to David. Maiden shook her head at herself. This infatuated haze she went into when she saw him really wasn't helpful in the middle of a murder case.

She smiled and waved at Mrs. Beals as she drove past the small organic market where they tried to source most of their fruit and vegetables. Mrs. Beals had owned the business for as long as Maiden had known her. The lady's long, silvery-gray ponytail made her think of the stripe at Sylvia Drake's temple.

Both Sylvia and Marti had been elated to learn of Bradley's arrest. Maiden wished that Sylvia hadn't interrupted her conversation with Marti when she did, she wanted to know what they really had against the Hedgewicks.

Breakups could be painful, sometimes downright nasty, but they were a little too pleased about it all. Gail's death and Bradley being suspected for it, they were genuinely glad and that seemed harsh, unless they had a good reason to hate them both.

By the time she parked her car in her usual spot beside the inn, she'd decided that her next step would be to gather information from the sources that were right under her nose: Bella and Elvan.

She walked into the foyer, dismissed the thought that it felt tiny and quaint after being in Riley Manor, and approached her mother at the front desk.

"Hey, angel." Gloria slid her a smarmy smile. "You took a while. How's David?"

"Presumably he's fine. Hopefully he's working hard." She withheld a sigh and hurried to continue before Gloria started asking for details. "Did Aunt Bella and Elvan come back here?"

"Of course, where else would they go?" Gloria sniffed, perhaps still smarting from Bella's decision to have her wedding elsewhere. "They're stayin' in Bella's suite until this mess is sorted out."

"Good, I need to talk to them," she said as she set her bag behind the desk and hurried to the stairs.

"Why?" Gloria called after her. "What's happened?"

"Love you, Mom," she replied without stopping.

She made her way to the third floor and the luxury attic suites. She went straight to the door of what her mother called the Romance and Glamor Suite; it was the favored choice for newlyweds.

A twinge of awkwardness struck her as she raised her hand to knock. Aunt Bella and Elvan were technically on their honeymoon, despite the circumstances. She hesitated, but then recalled Aunt Bella's embarrassing behavior at the police station. With a childish smile Maiden raised her hand again and knocked quite loudly.

It was a minute or two before she heard giggling and then Aunt Bella's distinctive tread heading towards the door. It swung open a minute later and Bella stood beaming at her.

"Maiden baby!" she said happily. "I knew you couldn't stay mad at me."

"You're absolutely right, but that's not why I'm here," Maiden informed her. "I need to ask you a few things."

"Come on in." She stepped back and beckoned her inside.

Maiden glanced around at the elegant furnishings. It wasn't as grand in scale as the rooms in Riley Manor, but it was certainly in better condition. The entire suite, in fact, looked like something from a glamorous old Hollywood movie.

The furniture followed an art deco style, complete with sunbursts and chevrons in the décor, curved leather couches, and an extravagantly impractical mirrored coffee table.

She saw Elvan sitting on one of the couches reading a newspaper, she wondered if that's what he was doing before she knocked. She cleared her throat uncomfortably and turned to Bella with renewed purpose.

"So, we should talk about what happened at the wedding." Maiden noticed how Aunt Bella's eyes lit up and realized she was hoping for spicy details about her and David, she hurried to clarify. "To Gail."

"Oh." Bella's enthusiasm shriveled. "Well, you'll solve all that for us, won't you?"

"Me?" Maiden blinked at her.

"Mm-hm." Bella nodded. "You helped Tony, and your daddy. You'll help your Aunt Bella and Uncle Elvan too, right?"

"That might be difficult...considering." Maiden chewed at her lip.

"*Surely* that gorgeous captain of yours won't mind you floatin' around him a little bit more," Bella teased.

"It's kind of the opposite, actually. I think I distract him," Maiden said quietly, ignored Bella's pleased chuckle, and considered the matter a bit more. "But you being involved might give me the chance to legitimately look things over a bit."

She had an ulterior motive, of course, since she and David had to put any change in their relationship on hold until the case was solved. But she was determined to keep her aunt out of trouble too.

"We should discuss the suspects," Maiden said pensively.

"Ooo, this is excitin'!" Bella grinned and urged her to come and sit down. "Elvan, honey, we need your help."

"Certainly, sweetheart." He smiled as she settled close beside him, he then glanced over and appeared to notice their visitor for the first time. "Oh hello, honey. You feelin' better?"

"Yeah, thanks," she murmured as she sat in one of the chairs she knew her mother had spent far too much money on. "We were talking about the wedding and...your mom. Are you okay to discuss it a little?"

"I suppose so," he sighed and rubbed his eyes. "It isn't as though I've been able to think of too much else, except my Bella, of course."

"Okay, good. Well, let's look at the list of known suspects," Maiden began carefully, she needed to be tactful. "For a start we have Bradley, you two, Pierce and now Ree."

"I suppose in all fairness, we have to be included." Elvan nodded. "But it is interestin' that Ree turned up when she did. I don't like that she was hoverin' around in the background tryin' to get at Mama."

"Yeah, if we believe what we see, it looks like she was trying to get Gail to leave her money to Bradley so she could get it through him." Maiden mused, watching his expression closely. "I can't help wondering how Bradley feels about his mother. Do you think he was happy to have her scheming along with him? Assuming that's what they've been doing."

"I rather doubt she did anything on her own," Elvan replied simply.

"I agree, to be honest." Maiden nodded. "And she admitted to having a motive. But why commit the murder at the wedding? Especially if Gail hadn't changed her will yet...you're *sure* she hadn't changed anything?"

"No. She did threaten to, a couple of times, when she wasn't gettin' her way." Elvan stroked his well-trimmed beard. "But she hated Ree enough to stop short of actually givin' her everything via Bradley. He never could say no to Ree and I don't think he'll start any time soon. This little horror show is proof of that."

"You really think he could've done it?" Maiden asked.

"I..." He frowned down at his hands. "I'm preparin' myself for that to be the case. As much as I wish I could never imagine him harmin' someone for personal gain, I'm sure he would if he had enough reason. It's a lot of money, Maiden, a lot."

She considered that carefully. She had no idea how vast the Hedgewick fortune actually was, but it was obviously considerable. Gail's threats to change her will must have had some weight; surely no one would tolerate her behavior if there wasn't a pot of gold at the end of the rainbow.

"Did Bradley know that Gail took a sedative at night?" she asked.

"Yeah, she'd been takin' one every night for a while now. Insomnia, she said," Elvan shrugged. "Agnes always stirred it into a hot drink for her. Bradley would've known, or certainly could've asked what kind of meds she was takin'. He visited her a lot in the last few months, more than he ever did before."

"Okay. So, you mentioned the other night that you'd noticed some strange things happening," Maiden began as discreetly as she could, glancing briefly at Bella before fixing her gaze on Elvan. "How long has that been going on?"

"Um," he also slid his eyes anxiously to his now-scowling wife, "a month, maybe two. Thereabouts."

"What things are we talkin' about?" Bella arched her left brow. "And why ain't I heard about it before now?"

"I need information, Aunt Bella," Maiden told her mildly. "Please don't scare anyone out of talking."

"It ain't so bad, sugar," Elvan grasped Bella's hand and patted it reassuringly. "Maiden noticed me acting a bit nervous and I just told her why, that's all."

"Feel free to tell *both* of us," Bella said.

"I just had a funny feelin' a couple of times, like maybe someone was followin' me, or at least watchin'," he sounded subdued. "And there were a couple of little accidents that probably weren't nothin'. I reckon I let my imagination run away with me."

"Was it Bradley?" Bella blurted the question Maiden was trying to broach more tactfully.

"Oh, I don't think so!" Elvan said quickly and shook his head. "I don't think he'd do a thing against me..."

"Except try to steal all your money," Bella reminded him, pulling her hand away and folding her arms over her chest, "and possibly murder your mother. Other than those two little quibbles, he's a veritable prince!"

"You mentioned that Bradley had been upstairs when that flowerpot nearly hit you," Maiden cut in. "Was he around for any of the other mishaps?"

"Well..." Elvan's reluctance was obvious. "He-he might've been visitin' the day I nearly slipped on the stairs. Come to think of it, he was at the house when that fire started in my office too...but he helped put that out. He was real worried about me."

Maiden and Bella exchanged a startled look and then turned back to Elvan, he looked a bit flustered now.

"Have you told Captain McAlister about any of that?" Maiden asked.

"No, I haven't," Elvan admitted. "I sort of fell to pieces after what happened to Mama. You ladies have been there for the only discussions I've had with him."

"It might be worth mentioning," Maiden managed not to scowl or throw a cushion at him when he pulled a face and glanced away. "You have to think of keeping Aunt Bella safe, after all."

That got his attention. Elvan sat a bit straighter and glanced at Bella. He smiled gently the instant their eyes met and nodded.

"You're right, darlin'," he said solemnly. "I was thinkin' of Bradley, but I can't really do that anymore."

Bella looked slightly mollified by that sentiment, she stopped scowling at least. Maiden decided to mention it to David as well, she didn't fully trust Elvan not to lose his nerve when it came to the push.

It was possible that Bradley had been scheming to get his hands on the family fortune for some time. She'd observed firsthand that there was friction between the father and son. But Bradley also wasn't the only one that stood to inherit. Her thoughts went to the cousin she had yet to meet, Pierce Hedgewick.

"Elvan," she began tactfully, "forgive me for asking, but who all inherits now that Gail is...gone?"

"Oh, gosh." Elvan sighed and ran a hand over his beard again. "Well, to be honest, I get nearly everything. By extension, so does Bella. But Bradley *was* goin' to get some money, in trust, and then Pierce gets a nice legacy as well."

"Is his money also in trust?" Maiden asked.

"No, honey," Elvan said dryly. "Pierce knows how to handle his money far better than Bradley ever did. He helped put the family's manufacturin' business back on track after it was, um, strugglin'. He's smart, young Pierce, I'm very proud of him."

There was enough subtle emphasis put on the word *him* to suggest that he wasn't as pleased with his son. Maiden decided that she needed to meet Pierce Hedgewick, she wanted to know more about the business struggles Elvan alluded to. It was possible that the inheritance of a grandson was motive enough for murder.

Chapter Fourteen

David returned to the police station after his foray at Riley Manor. He walked past the heavy steel doors until he reached the seldom used third holding cell.

Golden Glen, despite the recent spate of killings, wasn't exactly a hotbed of crime and disorder. In the handful of months that David had been heading up the police station he hadn't seen more than two of the cells occupied at a time.

Today was actually no exception, but he had opted to leave a bit of space between Bradley Hedgewick and his mother. He had limited experience with southern women of a certain age but he'd quickly noted that their voices were powerful, and they carried.

With the safety of an empty room between the pair, David walked through the sturdy door and ran an assessing eye over Ree Hedgewick. She was sitting heavily on the narrow cot at the back of the room chewing nervously at her nails.

Her sharp, beady eyes locked on him and she quickly stacked her hands in her lap. Her feet shuffled and her knees bounced despite her efforts to look cool and collected. David smiled faintly and shut the door behind him.

"Feeling a bit calmer now?" he asked as he approached.

"I'm calm as a millpond, officer," she sniffed, doing her best to look down her nose at him.

"Good. You'll be better able to explain yourself then." He pulled his notebook and pen from his pocket. "Whenever you're ready."

"I got nothin' to say," she harumphed and folded her arms stubbornly.

"You'd really rather stay locked up?" he asked and then shrugged. "Up to you, I suppose."

"You can't keep me here forever." She sounded confident.

"I don't intend to," he replied and deliberately didn't elaborate.

He flicked back through his notes and jotted down a few incidental observations about her as he subtly watched Ree's tranquil veneer start to crack.

"Well, what *are* you gonna do?" she finally demanded loudly.

"That depends on what the investigation turns up." He didn't look up. "I already know that you checked into your hotel on Thursday evening, not last night. And if you refuse to account for your whereabouts, much like your son, I have no real choice but to consider you a suspect."

"I never hurt Gail!" she said through gritted, yellowed teeth.

"So you say," he replied and finally lifted his eyes to her. "When did you *really* last speak to Gail Hedgewick?"

"A couple of weeks ago, like I said," Ree grumbled. "I didn't touch her, she was more useful to me alive."

"How so?" He quirked a brow.

"That's my business." She turned a bit on the bed and looked away from him.

David studied her for a moment. She wore a lot of makeup in bright, almost garish shades. It emphasized the effects of what appeared to have been a hard life, or perhaps a recklessly self-indulgent one.

He wondered if she and Elvan had married out of any actual affection for each other. They certainly seemed to hate each other now. And from what he'd heard of the ceremony, when he wasn't contemplating Maiden's legs, he had the impression that Elvan fell for Bella when they were teenagers and never got over her.

"How long were you and Mr. Hedgewick married?" he asked. The unexpected question caught Ree off guard, she clasped her right hand over the ring she wore on her left.

"About two years," she muttered with noticeable bitterness.

"Not a happy marriage?" he prompted.

"No. *Obviously*." She glared at him.

"What happened?"

"For a start, he was in love with someone else!" she hissed. "Beyond that, he was a clueless clod and a cold fish at the best of times. Not exactly a girl's dream come true. Why do you think Bella didn't want him when she was young enough to do better?"

"Is that why you slept with his brother?" David asked placidly. "Spite?"

"Weakness and desperation, more like." She bristled but was clearly considering her words more carefully now. "Everyone blamed me for that mess, no one blamed Alan. That was Elvan's brother. The man got tipsy and made a pass at his own brother's horribly neglected wife! But *I'm* the one that got the blame! I was the only real victim there and nobody cared one bit!"

"What about Alan's wife?" David asked in a flat, unrevealing tone. "It was probably a bit hard on her too."

"Alice? Frigid old prissy-pants." Ree sneered. "If she'd been doin' right by him he wouldn't have come sniffin' around me, now would he?"

David could feel the approach of the ridiculous old cliche that *a man has needs, after all*. It wasn't exactly untrue, but he was quite aware that women had needs too. In any case, it was a weak excuse for ripping an entire family apart for the sake of a quick fumble. He decided to move the conversation along.

"You signed a prenuptial agreement before marrying Mr. Hedgewick?" he asked impassively.

"Unfortunately." The answer was forced out through her teeth again.

"That must have been problematic for you when everything fell apart." He let the sentence dissipate into the air and waited for her to elaborate. She quickly and visibly riled; it was clearly a sore point.

"It certainly was! That *animal* seduced me and then I was thrown out with nothin'!" she nearly shouted. "If it weren't for Bradley, I would've been left to starve!"

"So you maintained custody and lived off the child support?" he jotted another note.

"That ain't what I said!" she blustered.

"It's what you implied," he murmured. "I can read it back to you if you like. No opportunity to work and support yourself?"

"Why should I have to work?!" she demanded, stomping a foot indignantly. "I married a multi-millionaire! I shouldn't have to stand around some rotten old store servin' other people!"

"You've ceased to be married to a multi-millionaire for some years now," David pointed out. "And you willingly signed away any access to his money. Correct?"

"'Willingly'?! *Ha!*" she nearly spat. "He refused to marry me unless I signed that damn paper! And Gail wouldn't budge an inch on it! She was mean as a junkyard dog even back then! And I'll bet you Elvan wouldn't have dared ask his *precious* Bella to sign a thing like that! That's why Gail disinherited him!"

"Did she?" David ignored her furious shouting. "How do you know that?"

"Because Gail said she was gonna do it." Ree shut her eyes briefly and pulled in a steadying breath. "She was furious with him and couldn't wait to strip him of everything she could."

"Did Gail have control of the entire Hedgewick fortune?" He wasn't about to rely on Ree's knowledge of the family's legal and financial status, but he was curious to know what she believed it to be.

"Of course she did," Ree scoffed. "Everything was in her name and the whole family knows it. That's the only reason they didn't lock her in a home years ago. No one liked her."

"Including you?"

"Let's just say I softened right up when she promised to leave everything to my sweet little Bradley." Ree pursed her lips into a crooked smirk, her almost neon pink lipstick settling deeper into the grooves around her mouth.

"But are you sure that she actually did?" he asked, watching her expression closely.

"Yup." Ree gave a pleased nod. "Mark my words, officer, there's another will. And it'll turn up, don't you doubt that for a moment."

***

Bella was eager to help Maiden's investigation in any way she could. She quickly arranged a lunch meeting with Pierce for the following day.

Maiden and Bella had selected a quiet café in a discreet little side street downtown. Maiden wasn't exactly sneaking around, but she was hoping to get Pierce talking about some sensitive and very private family matters, a secluded setting would help things along.

It was a nice day but still rather cool, she dressed in her favorite jeans and one of her more flattering sweaters. Bella, who didn't know what the word underdressed even meant, wore a blue sequined blouse and tan slacks under a brown leather trench-coat. Despite the nip in the air, she'd chosen a pair of gold studded mules.

Pierce was waiting for them when they arrived. He stood and waved to get their attention. Bella smiled brightly and led the way to a secluded corner table. It wasn't lost on Maiden that Pierce seemed to be seeking privacy for their meeting as well.

She looked him over as she approached and watched Bella plant a big kiss on his cheek, she hadn't been exaggerating when she'd said she liked him a lot more than she did Bradley.

Pierce was a nice-looking man, a bit taller than his cousin, and with a far more intelligent glint in his gray-green eyes. His sandy blonde hair was long on top and slicked back, it was a sleek and sophisticated look but it emphasized the start of a receding hairline.

His tailored three-piece suit looked expensive, so did the large gold watch that glinted from beneath his cuff as he held his hand out to her. Maiden shook it with a politely friendly smile and noted his quick, assessing gaze as it took her in from head to toe.

They sat down and chitchatted a bit as they looked at the menu. Maiden had already coached Aunt Bella to discreetly draw Pierce out; it would be harder for Maiden to introduce anything too touchy considering she'd never met the man before. She could only hope that her exuberant aunt wouldn't blow it.

The food came and they ate companionably. Bella and Pierce discussed a few mutual friends in Florida and Maiden learned that Pierce actually lived in Tennessee. His business was based from there apparently.

Once they'd eaten, Bella folded her arms on the table and sighed wearily.

"What a strange weekend it's been." She propped her chin in her palm.

"I'm so sorry, Bella." Pierce gave her a sympathetic look. "To have all this happen at your weddin', it's not fair."

"Life sometimes ain't," Bella said stoically. "What about you? You holdin' up all right since losin' your grandma?"

"Yeah, I guess," he mused. "Not much choice. Oh look, she was gettin' up there in years, I knew it was comin' but I never thought it would be anything like this. Old people shouldn't be treated like they're in the way. She should've been allowed to finally have that heart attack she always lied about."

Ouch. Maiden glanced at Bella. *That joke seems a little tacky.*

If Bella took any exception to the off-hand reference to Gail's mid-ceremony stunt, she didn't show it. She actually smiled and shook her head sadly.

"Well, I won't lie and say I was ever close to Gail, she didn't want me to be," Bella said. "But I'm sorry she went the way she did. And I'm sorry it was done when it would hurt Elvan the most."

"That's true," Pierce said as though the thought hadn't occurred to him before. "It could hardly have been meaner to Uncle Elvan could it? I just wonder if Bradley did..."

"Did what?" Maiden prompted quietly; he'd trailed off and she didn't want him to wander too far.

"Oh." Pierce looked briefly uncomfortable. "It was a wicked thought, I'm sorry."

"Honeypot, now ain't the time to hide your worries." Bella reached over and patted his hand gently. "What's the matter?"

"Just that Bradley was so nasty about the weddin'." Pierce winced as he said it. "Goin' on the way he did, and then to actually tell his cow of a mother about it. It's pretty awful."

"I hadn't realized that Bradley was *that* upset about the wedding," Maiden said it almost like it was a question, hoping he'd explain the strong statement.

"I shouldn't have mentioned that in front of you ladies." Pierce shut his eyes briefly. "Look, he didn't get too personal about it, but Uncle Elvan takin' a wife cut substantially into the money he was expectin' for himself, and he's the only thing he cares about. Well, himself and Ree, sort of."

Maiden was intrigued by that frank admission and looked again at Aunt Bella to see the stirrings of anger in her crystal blue gaze. She didn't blame her, Bradley was already a sore point but to sit there and learn that he'd griped about his father marrying her would certainly stoke the fires.

Being less involved, Maiden tried to view the matter more objectively. It stood to reason that Bradley would have no particular affection for his father's new bride.

Not only had Bella been vocal about his freeloading, something that may have already had an effect on his lifestyle, but she also represented a huge cut into his future prospects. To him, Bella may have been just another person taking a piece of the family pie, and the biggest piece too.

Her attention went back to her companions when Bella rather tersely mentioned Ree turning up and shooting her mouth off in front of everyone, hoping to bask in Elvan's misery. Pierce's posture stiffened noticeably.

"I'd like to say that I can't believe she had the nerve to turn up here but, sadly, it's exactly the sort of thing she'd do," he muttered and flicked Bella a kind look. "I truly am sorry you've been put through all this, Bella."

"That old heifer don't worry me none," Bella assured him. "But I know it must've been awkward for you. Have you actually seen her?"

"Very accidentally and very briefly." He picked a bit of lint from his cuff. "She was bein' released when I stopped by to check on Bradley this mornin'. She had the good sense to avoid me."

"Ree's out of jail?" Bella gasped unhappily. "She must've found someone dumb enough to bail her out! I'd better call Elvan and warn him. I'll be right back."

Bella fished her phone out of her handbag and stalked away to find a quiet corner. When they were alone, Pierce shifted his gaze to Maiden and smiled a little more warmly. He cleared his throat and leaned subtly towards her.

"So, Maiden." He studied her face casually. "You were one of the lovely bridesmaids, as I recall."

"Oh, yes, I was." Maiden was a little thrown by the reminder, and the admiring glint in his eyes. "Such an...interesting ceremony. What did you really think of your grandmother's little episode?"

"Fake," he said with a smile. "And mean-spirited. She used to be too good for that sort of a stunt but, well, her age was catchin' up with her."

"Yeah, that's what Elvan said." Maiden eyed him curiously. "Do you really think she was getting senile?"

"I don't know if I'd go quite that far. Maybe, she was nearly 90 years old after all." He screwed up his face as he thought it over.

"Can I ask you an odd question?" She bit her lip.

"Sure." He smiled and leaned a little closer still.

"Do you know why Gail had three diamond rings on her hand at the wedding?" She asked as ingenuously as she could.

Her efforts didn't help much. His expression hardened abruptly and he stared down at his coffee. Maiden wondered at his strong reaction but could see him trying to suppress it. He cleared his throat and glanced up at her with a smile that didn't reach his eyes.

"No. I did notice them and thought it a bit too showy," he replied lightly. "But she was in a strange mood that day. I really didn't feel inclined to ask her about it."

"That's understandable." Maiden acknowledged gently, trying to keep him talking. "Were you very close to her?"

"I used to be, when I was real young. She was good to me and Mama after the divorce." He gave an acknowledging nod. "Some women could've sided with their sons regardless of the facts but she was too decent for that. Early on, anyway."

"Sorry," Maiden shook her head and gave the impression of complete ignorance, "what divorce?"

"Mama and Daddy's." He smiled faintly. "Haven't you been told about all the Hedgewick's dirty laundry? Elvan's first wife Ree took advantage of my father because she was bored. Blew both marriages apart and ruined my father's life, but that meant nothing to her of course."

Maiden noted the sheer bitterness that twisted through his words. She knew that Ree had cheated on Elvan with his brother, but she wanted to hear Pierce's take on the situation. He was still looking at her but seemed lost in angry memories, she tried to keep him talking.

"That's so terrible," she said softly. "How old were you?"

"Two," he said grimly. "Bradley was less than a year. How the miserable hag thought she could lure a man like my father in, I don't know."

"But you said that—" she began with an uncertain shake of her head when he cut in.

"She got him drunk, Maiden," Pierce said with a speaking look.

"Oh." Her eyes widened slightly. "That's horrible...You must hate her."

"I certainly don't love her," he said dryly. "Dad was devastated about it, but...Mama said she couldn't ever feel the same about him again, so they separated. I've been told he got real quiet after that, eventually stopped visitin' me, stopped lookin' after the business and then he...well, anyway."

What? she asked silently, *What did he do?*

"Oh," she said aloud. "Your poor mother, did she ever remarry?"

"No, she never got over what happened. She'd loved and trusted Dad completely," Pierce murmured into his cup. "She was still alone when she died; that was a couple of years ago."

Pierce stared sadly down at the table and she didn't have the heart to press him on it any further. She switched topics instead.

"You mentioned a business," she said with polite and innocent curiosity. "Is that the same one you still run?"

"It is." He smiled proudly and managed to lift his gaze again. "'Hedgewick's Premium Finishes'. Wood stains and varnishes, things like that. The company's been a household name for decades."

"Oh," she smiled as recognition struck, "I've seen your bottles in my dad's workshop. I didn't realize it was the same Hedgewick."

He shrugged and tried to look modest but she detected another sort of gleam in his eye now. A gleam that said he thought that he might've turned this small-town girl's head a bit. Maiden lifted her brows inquiringly.

"Are you a woodworker then?" she asked expectantly.

"Uh, no." He pulled a face at her quaint suggestion. "A bit too tame for me, I'm afraid."

She recalled Bella saying Pierce was a bit of a scamp. She was tempted to ask him what that meant in his case but was afraid it might sound like a come on. They were both distracted anyway when Bella came back to the table and sat down with a grunt.

"Well, hopefully she won't know where to find us." She rolled her eyes, clearly referring to Ree.

"As long as no one tells Bradley," Pierce said dryly.

"Are they close?" Maiden took another stab at learning something useful. "Bradley and Ree, I mean?"

"He spent most of his time with her growin' up." Pierce said.

"And it shows." Bella muttered.

"Yeah, old Brad was never one for workin' hard, or workin' at all for that matter." Pierce smirked. "He only wants to party, chase girls and live off his father's money."

"Okay," Maiden nodded, "but where does Ree fit in?"

"She lives with him." Pierce glanced up at her again.

"Really?" Maiden pulled a face. "Wouldn't that, sort of, inhibit him?"

"I don't know that he's happy about it," he said laconically. "It started off as lettin' her land there for a few months while he was off at college, but she made herself real cozy and never left. That was years ago now. To my knowledge, Ree never tried to hold down a job for very long, so she's got every reason to stay and live off Elvan, via Bradley."

"That ain't happening, honey!" Bella fisted her hands on her hips. "She can just learn to take care of herself like the rest of us! Honestly, married to him for less than two years, tore his family to shreds, and still expects a free ride for the rest of her life? I don't think so!"

"She seemed to think that Bradley would have all of Elvan's money, though." Maiden neatly side-stepped Bella's unhelpful explosion. "That's what she said, anyway."

"I wouldn't put it past her, or Bradley, to try and get Uncle Elvan out of the way," Pierce sighed. "When he first mentioned that he was courtin' Bella, Granny wasn't thrilled, but she wasn't too worked up about it either. Next thing I heard she was set against it—*dead* set."

They all fell silent at that unfortunate turn of phrase. Maiden recovered first and decided to change the subject completely.

"I met Marti Drake and her mother at the wedding," she smiled benignly. "They seemed nice. A little shocked by everything, but we all were."

"Oh," Bella's eyes darted to Pierce and she gave Maiden's knee a warning squeeze under the table. "Yeah, they are nice. Nice of them to come along to the weddin'. Anyway—"

"Quite right," Pierce cleared his throat and stood. "It's gettin' a bit late."

Bella smiled sweetly as he inclined his head politely to them both; Maiden was more circumspect.

"I must be on my way, ladies. Thank you for joinin' me." He smoothly snatched up the bill and smiled warmly at Maiden. "I hope we can all meet again before too awful long."

As he turned and walked away Maiden considered what she'd learned about him. She tried to anyway, but Bella dug her elbow into her arm and leaned closer.

"Isn't he a nice boy? Cute too." She smiled and winked. "If that gorgeous captain hadn't finally got down to business I might've been proddin' you in Pierce's direction. Speakin' of which…you never did tell me what happened between you two at the weddin'."

"Really? That's odd," Maiden said dryly. "In any case, we were interrupted when Elvan started wailing like a banshee."

"Sorry, honey." Bella slid her a commiserating pout. "I'll talk to him."

"And say what exactly?" Maiden asked. "Not to panic if he finds another corpse?"

They both laughed at the absurdity of the situation but glanced around at the handful of other patrons when they realized her voice had carried. Conscious of the curious looks they were getting, Maiden gave Bella a speaking look and nodded subtly towards the exit.

They walked outside and headed leisurely towards her car. The sun shone overhead, taking some of the icy sting out of the autumn breeze. When they were a discreet distance from the café, Maiden edged closer to her aunt.

"What happened back there when I mentioned Marti Drake?" she asked. "You and Pierce both went a bit weird."

"Oh, honeypot," Bella stopped and turned to face her. "What a thing to bring up to Pierce of all people. He'd been buzzin' around Marti for months, until Bradley swooped in and stole her away."

"What?!" Maiden's eyes widened. "Bradley actually made a play for his cousin's girlfriend?"

"I don't know if they'd officially started datin' yet," Bella said begrudgingly. "But he knew. Bradley knew exactly what he was doing and how much it would hurt Pierce. He did it anyway, the selfish toad."

"That's…a bit messy," Maiden breathed.

"Yeah, and didn't poor Marti learn her mistake the hard way," Bella shook her head and whistled. "Bradley had his fun and then dropped her like she was nothin'. And Pierce certainly wasn't gonna have her back, it was an ugly drama."

"When did this all happen?" Maiden asked as she started fitting the pieces together. She recalled Pierce escorting Marti back inside and, apparently, away from Bradley during the reception.

"I think he broke things off a couple of months ago," Bella said.

"So, why were they at the wedding?" Maiden asked a tad incredulously.

"Elvan insisted on invitin' them. He's known Sylvia for a long time and didn't have the heart to risk them feelin' snubbed," she sighed. "But to be honest, neither of us thought they'd actually come."

"I wonder why they did," Maiden said more to herself than anyone else.

They were silent for a moment and resumed walking towards the car. Bella's pale eyes shifted to Maiden more than once.

"So," she said slowly. "What's next?"

"I'm not sure yet," Maiden said pensively. "I need to think more about what exactly happened. Try to figure out precisely where everyone was through the evening. I might ask Vonny if she saw anything."

"No, I mean with the captain!" Bella gave her arm a light swat. "Has he asked you out?"

"Not exactly," she said carefully, a raincheck for dinner didn't feel like anything to brag about so she didn't mention it.

"What?" Bella scowled. "Glory told me she saw him covered in your lipstick! He ain't even asked you out after that?!"

"He wasn't 'covered'," Maiden protested with dignity and slid her a look. "And he can't really do much while he's investigating several members of my family, can he?"

"Well, what's the point of bein' beautiful if he won't let you use it against him?" She sounded exasperated. "Don't tell me he'd really mind all that much? What's the worst that could happen?"

"I'm not sure. He could maybe get taken off the case and someone else brought in," Maiden murmured.

"Hm, I don't think I'd care for that," Bella said as she considered the possibility. "I like the captain, he's a gentleman...and he has a nice butt."

Maiden grinned and kept her own sentiments to herself.

CHAPTER FIFTEEN

David walked into Harlow House and scanned the foyer. He'd brought Smith and Ramirez with him but started to wish he hadn't when he saw Vonny sitting at the front desk watching him with a smirk.

David suppressed a weary sigh as they approached. He had spent the morning dealing with a few of the out-of-town guests and then Ree Hedgewick's bail. It's not like there was nothing else to be done and he really wasn't in the mood for Vonny's somewhat childish sense of humor.

He was only there at all because Alfie had slipped out and returned home without clearance yesterday. There were only a few things he wanted to ask him but he was hopeful the eccentric man could lend a little insight.

"Good morning, Miss Harlow," he said.

"Hey, Captain." She smiled knowingly and glanced at the men behind him. "Gentleman...and Greg."

He didn't turn to see for certain but he was confident that Smith would have made some sort of mocking face in reply to her rude greeting. He didn't care, he had neither the time or the inclination to be waylaid by spats.

"I need to speak with your father." He kept his tone polite.

"Sure thing, Captain." She was still smirking obnoxiously as she glanced over to the partially open office door and called out. "Dad! Captain McAlister's back!"

From the depths of the room they could hear papers shuffling and the wheels of an office chair creaking.

"I know, he came to the wedding," Alfie scoffed loudly. "About time he started making an effort with your sister. I was starting to wonder if the fool needed glasses!"

"No, Dad," Vonny grinned and barely held back her laughter. "He's here right now."

The creaking of wheels resounded again as Alfie rolled his chair to the doorway and peered out.

"Hmm?" Alfie grunted and still didn't bother to stand as he saw David watching him with a grim frown. "Oh, you should've called, young man. Maiden's not here at the moment."

"I need to speak with *you*, Mr. Harlow," David said with as much calm and dignity as he could manage. "I have to ask you a few questions."

"That's a bit sudden! Have you even taken her out yet?" Alfie scowled deeply and pointed a finger at him. "The answer's no!"

"Oh my—" David covered his mortified exclamation by running his hands over his face, he glanced over his shoulder at his sniggering officers. "Wait outside, and keep your mouths shut."

Smith and Ramirez didn't dare to argue but Alfie spotted them before they could escape.

"Gregory!" he said sharply. "Tell your father he still has my spokeshave, I need it back if he's done with it."

"Will do, Mr. Harlow," Greg giggled as he ducked outside.

Vonny was watching the exchange with considerable enjoyment until Alfie waved her out of the room as well. She pulled a sulky face but still slipped off into the dining room.

When they were alone, a quietly smiling Alfie pushed to his feet and walked over to face him.

"How can I help you, young man?" he asked placidly as he stacked his hands atop the desk.

"How can you help me?" David repeated. "Where was this rational greeting before?"

"Fair's fair," he said. "If you think my little Maiden is going to be the only one put on the spot you're dreaming. Do you know what she goes through living with Gloria and her scheming?"

"So, you deliberately embarrassed me in front of my officers?" he asked.

"You shouldn't be embarrassed." Alfie arched a brow. "You think you could do better than my daughter?"

"No," he conceded. "But my hands are tied until this case is sorted out. It's not really fair to rub my nose in it."

"I think you're doing just fine." Alfie smiled slyly. "You got that Bradley moron out of the way. That's good, he was annoying her."

"That's not why I arrested him, Mr. Harlow," David said in his most professional tone and folded his arms.

"Didn't break your heart to do it though, did it?" Alfie chuckled.

David smiled at him, he couldn't help it, but he knew he needed to get back to the point.

"Going back to the day of the turkey-circus," he persevered. "I'd like your take on what happened."

"A lot of over-dressed twits swanned around for hours and then some cranky old broad got knocked off." He frowned faintly. "What more is there to be said?"

"Had you met Gail Hedgewick personally?" David asked tolerantly.

"Not really," Alfie admitted. "She left the rehearsal, without a speck of good grace, about fifteen minutes after she limped through the front door. She looked around, didn't say hello to anyone and demanded a private discussion with Elvan. Then at the wedding she just skulked around glowering at people."

"But she did show up at the rehearsal?" he asked curiously. "Why, if she clearly wanted nothing to do with the wedding?"

"I think she wanted to harass Elvan," Alfie said frankly. "He's a mama's boy whose mama hated him. Pretty pathetic actually. He should've told the old broad to shove it."

"It's probably not that straight-forward with that much money involved." He smiled at him.

"He should've earned his own money," Alfie said coolly. "How can you get to his age and have nothing in your own name? You can't let every cent spill into the same piggy bank; not when its reigned over by some ferocious old bat. We raised our girls to earn their money and made sure they didn't throw it away, but what they earn is theirs and always was."

"Yeah, Harlow doesn't strike me as frivolous."

"She isn't, she's clever. And she's a lady." Alfie held his gaze easily. "Remember that, Captain, or she'll show you the door. Like the others."

"The others?" David asked in a carefully unrevealing tone, he knew he was letting himself get distracted but he wanted the information.

"Mm, there were a few. None of them lasted."

"Why not?"

"You're a detective and you've seen her, figure it out," Alfie said dryly. "She's a person, not a piece of meat or a trophy. None of the over-heated idiots bothered to find that out, so off they went."

"That's really not my style, Mr. Harlow," he said mildly.

"Well, frankly, I didn't think it was," he conceded. "Or I'd have warned her away from you already. Just don't lead her on and don't waste her time."

"Thanks for the advice," David said and decided they'd pursued that topic long enough. "Did you see Elvan or Bella from 9:30 to 10 pm the night of the wedding?"

"No." He shook his head. "But I wasn't looking for them. I did notice that other guy, Pierce, looking pretty angry when he came downstairs."

"When was that?" David pulled out his notebook and pen.

"Not sure," he admitted. "It was after dinner sometime."

"Any idea where he'd come from or why?"

"I'm guessing he'd gone to talk to the old lady, no other reason he'd be upstairs…I guess there's that little nurse." Alfie rubbed his chin thoughtfully. "But she looks like she'd break if you squeezed her too hard."

"Did you notice anyone else at the wedding or the reception that seemed ill-disposed towards Gail Hedgewick?" David opted not to give his own opinion on the diminutive nurse.

"Nothing outright menacing." He shrugged. "A few of their friends expressed some disgust at the way she interrupted the wedding. No one seemed too surprised by it either. I didn't get the impression that the old broad was well liked in general."

"Yes, I picked up on that too." David admitted. "Anything else?"

"There was a young woman that got into a bit of a dust up with that Bradley idiot," Alfie murmured and narrowed his eyes thoughtfully. "I'd slipped out to use the bathroom and saw Bradley and Pierce talking, fighting actually. Then this young lady walked near them and Bradley started sniping at her."

"What do you mean exactly?" David drew his brows together, this was the first he'd heard of another woman being involved with the Hedgewick clan. "Who was she?"

"I'm not sure. She was sort of slim, she had quite long brown hair. Very pretty," Alfie mused and then shook his head. "And that idiot started calling her a social climber, or maybe it was a homewrecker...I can't remember. Anyway, she looked ready to punch his lights out until Pierce stepped in and led her away."

"Is that all you know about it?" he asked a tad suspiciously, perhaps because he was talking to a Harlow and knew they could be wily.

"Yes, and that's more than I wanted to know," Alfie scoffed. "A bunch of idiots injecting needless drama into someone else's party. Just plain rude, really."

"Right. Well, as usual, Mr. Harlow," David said wryly, "you've been fascinating to talk to."

"Glad to oblige." He inclined his head with a smile. "Incidentally, if you find some excuse or other to lock up Bella for a while, I could do with the peace and quiet."

***

When they got back to the inn, Maiden left Bella to be alone with her new husband and went in search of her sister. She found Vonny in the family apartment sitting on the floor in front of the sofa with a ball of yarn and two perplexed kittens.

Maiden watched for a moment as Vonny seemed to be trying to teach Rowdy to balance on the ball like a Russian circus bear. The tan and white cat was more interested in biting the yarn than standing on it and took a few impressive tumbles. Finally, Ruffian got tired of being a spectator and lunged, claws bared, into the fray.

A lot of hissing, swatting and yowling erupted before the kittens ran a few furious laps around the couch and then tore off towards Vonny's room. Maiden watched them go and then turned to Vonny with an inquiring shake of her head.

"I'm trying to teach them some tricks, but they distract easily," she said. "How goes the sleuthing?"

"I don't know that I'm doing any 'sleuthing'." Maiden demurred.

"Yeah, yeah, blah blah blah." Von rolled her eyes.

"All right, it's going slowly," she conceded. "Try and be helpful. What do you remember from the wedding? Did you see anything weird?"

"I saw Tony doing the hustle with Mom." She shuddered delicately.

"So much for grandkids," Maiden laughed.

"Shut up, little cow," Von sniggered and then looked more pensive as she actually considered the question. "I saw Aunt Bella several times through the evening, she looked like a giant snowball, she was hard to miss. Elvan came and went a bit but he was usually nearby whenever I saw her."

"What about Bradley?" she asked. "Notice anything weird about how he acted?"

"I'm not sure, he's kinda weird in general," Von admitted. "I didn't like the way he looked at you, or me for that matter, so I kept a distance. But I did see him go outside around 9:30."

"Alone?"

"I didn't see anyone with him," she said carefully. "That doesn't mean he wasn't meeting someone though."

"Maybe Ree?" Maiden suggested.

"Maybe." Von nodded. "Aunt Bella told me about her bursting in yesterday. Was she really that awful?"

"She thought her ex-husband's wedding had been ruined and hurried in the next day to gloat over it," Maiden shook her head in wonder. "She's not exactly a sweetheart. She also essentially admitted that she and Bradley were trying to squeeze Elvan out of Gail's will."

"Whoa!" Vonny's pale blue eyes widened. "Dirty little secrets. Did Elvan know about that?"

"It's hard to say," Maiden admitted. "And Pierce, the cousin, claimed not to know what they were up to but it didn't surprise him to hear about it."

"But his inheritance was safe, right?" Von quirked a brow.

"I have no idea," she sighed. "But Ree only mentioned going after Elvan's money. Pierce seems to think they were using Aunt Bella to make Gail hate Elvan, convincing her that she was a gold-digger."

"Thanks pot, just how black is that kettle?" Von scowled.

"Yeah, pretty much," Maiden gave a humorless laugh. "Maybe Gail figured that Ree could spot her own kind. But, however it came about, she really didn't like Aunt Bella."

"So, where is Gail's will?" Von asked.

"With a lawyer probably." Maiden tilted her head to the side as she sank into thought. "I'd like to know if anything actually was changed. Elvan says no, but I still wonder."

"Don't people read books or watch movies?" Vonny hugged herself. "You should never *threaten* to change your will, it just makes people kill you before you get the chance. You should change it and then offer to change it back if people do what you want."

"Logical, in a manipulative sort of way," she said.

"Well, if you're going to do it anyway, at least be smart about it!" Vonny frowned. "What else have you learned?"

"Pierce Hedgewick hates Ree, not too sure he doesn't hate Bradley as well," she mused as she sat across from her. "But he didn't seem to specifically mind Gail."

"Could be an act," Von suggested as she rolled the yarn ball towards Maiden.

"True." She nodded as she caught the ball and rolled it back even faster. "I'd definitely be suspicious of him if Ree was the victim."

"Okay, so what else?" She rolled the yarn again.

"He said Gail was losing her marbles, Elvan did too." Maiden grabbed the ball and tossed it this time. "I'm not so sure though. I only talked to her once but she seemed pretty sharp."

"Why would they lie though?" Von threw it back.

"I don't know why, or if they even did." She shrugged and let the yarn arc higher this time.

"So, is Captain McCutie a good kisser?" Vonny smirked as she took her turn.

"Yes," Maiden murmured and whipped the yarn in a bit harder.

"But you both have to back off until the case is solved?" She matched her sister's speed.

"Yes." The yarn came faster again.

"Is that why you're cranky?" A snigger and another high lob.

"Yup." Maiden's eyes narrowed as she tossed the ball at her sister's face.

Vonny barely caught it when two fuzzy missiles launched straight at her. The kittens darted in out of nowhere and pounced with a chorus of terrifyingly squeaky roars. Von let out a startled shriek and fell backwards onto the floor, still foolishly clutching the coveted yarn, the kittens swarmed in with no trace of pity.

"Ow!" Vonny scowled and pulled her hand away from Rowdy. "No biting, you little turd!"

Maiden was laughing too hard to even try to come up with an excuse for not helping her.

Chapter Sixteen

David sat at his desk looking over his notes. They'd interviewed everyone on the guest list at this point and hadn't learned of anyone among the guests that admitted to any specific complaint against Gail. But only the most nervous people that were probably afraid of incriminating themselves had anything nice to say about her.

He'd also been quietly relieved when he'd been able to find people that could vouch for Bella's whereabouts all day and evening.

Not that he'd have let himself be swayed otherwise, and he didn't believe that Maiden would ever expect him to hide the truth. He was still glad that he didn't have any immediate cause to pursue the possibility of Bella being the killer.

She still could've been involved, though. His more professional side reminded him. *You can't dismiss such a strong motive completely. Even if it would hurt Maiden, she'd understand.*

He hoped she would at least, but he'd deal with that if he had to. He had more critical things to focus on than hypothetical conflicts.

The timing, according to the medical report and corroborating evidence, placed Gail Hedgewick's death around 9:45 to 10 pm. She was probably killed soon after he found Maiden in the bar. He refused to let his mind wander down that path yet again and stuck to the facts.

There were no signs of a struggle and the victim had a high dose of sedative in her system. They'd already confirmed that Gail had been prescribed a regular sedative.

It was possible that the killer either knew she was in the habit of taking the drug or it simply made their task easier when they found her unconscious. Realistically, they only had to press the pillow over her face and walk away. It would've taken them seconds, they might have been out of the room before she died, it could have been almost anyone.

He thought back to the brief conversation he'd had with Gail when he went to check on her before dinner. She'd appeared calm and composed, not someone who had any idea they would die in a few hours' time. She'd also said something about having a lot to do the next day. But she never made it to the next day.

There was also the unknown woman that Alfie had mentioned, he needed to find out who she was too. She might not be connected to Gail but, if Bradley verbally attacked her, there could be a connection. He'd have to find out.

He glanced at the clock on the wall. He'd sent for the nurse, the friendly young woman who had been sitting with Gail that evening. She'd left the reception before the murder but, when he'd sent Ramirez to conduct a preliminary interview, she'd also admitted to preparing and giving Gail the sedative.

A few minutes later he saw a shadow through the heavily frosted glass on his door. A light knock followed.

"Come in," he said as he turned to his laptop and brought up a fresh page.

Agnes Gray opened the door and peered inside. She was quite petite in stature, her wrists and hands were very fine, almost bird-like. He remembered Alfie's comments about her being too fragile to squeeze and suppressed a smile.

She walked inside and sat very delicately on a chair in front of his desk, he was tempted to peer over and see if her feet still reached the floor but refrained.

"Thank you for coming, Miss Gray," he said as he started typing out a few details.

"Oh, no trouble at all, Captain McAlister." Her southern accent was very subtle, just a hint of something in the background of her soft voice. "I'm more than happy to help however I can."

He smiled politely and noticed the way she watched him. It wasn't overtly flirtatious but there was an interest there, he couldn't be fully sure what it was yet.

"Your full name, for the record?" he asked, poised to start typing.

"Agnes Lillian Gray," she replied dutifully. "26 years old, 5 years a nurse. Single."

He glanced up briefly and found her still watching him. She set her purse aside and began unbuttoning her coat. He looked away again and started typing.

"How long did you work for Gail Hedgewick?" he asked in his most disinterested cop tone.

"Two years," she told him.

"Exclusively?"

"Yes, she insisted on having my full devotion," Agnes said wryly.

"Is that unusual?" He gave her a curious look.

"Not amongst clients that can afford that level of service," she replied.

"I see," he said as he noted that. "Did you get along well with her?"

"Yes, mostly." She pulled a face. "Mrs. Hedgewick could be...challenging, but nothing I haven't encountered before."

"Challenging in what way?" he murmured.

"Well, she was from a very different generation." The look on Agnes' face made it clear that she wished she'd kept her mouth shut. "People from her walk of life sometimes view private nurses as servants, not caregivers. Like I said, nothing new, and I was well paid, so it didn't bother me."

I doubt it would've slipped out if it really didn't bother you. David mused to himself.

"What were your typical duties when caring for Mrs. Hedgewick?" he asked as he turned to face her.

"What's that got to do with anything?" She frowned slightly.

"Any reason why you don't want to answer the question?" he asked.

"I didn't say I didn't want to." She sat a little more stiffly. "I just don't see what it's got to do with her death."

"Then it's very fortunate that you don't need to figure that out," he said. "You realize that you were quite likely the last one to see Mrs. Hedgewick alive? Apart from her killer, that is. You also brought her the sedative that left her helpless in bed."

Agnes stared at him with widened eyes. She was now clutching her coat closed over her chest as if warding off a painful chill. David gave her a moment to process her situation and then repeated his previous question.

"I-I looked after all her physical needs." Agnes swallowed hard as she made an obvious effort to gather her thoughts. "She was usually able to shower herself and that sort of thing, but she was declining, it was only a matter of time before I'd have had to do all those sorts of things for her too. But I sat with her for hours, brought her things when she asked for them, fixed meals if the cook wasn't there, and I made sure she took all her medications on time."

"Including the sedative?" he asked.

"Yes sir," she replied meekly.

"Did she take it every night?"

"For the last couple of months she did, yes." Agnes nodded. "One capsule every night at 9 o'clock."

"Was that safe?" He started typing again. "Wasn't that risking dependency?"

"I didn't prescribe it, sir." Agnes shrugged and shook her head. "I suspect that her doctor took into account that she was 89, it's not like it was gonna take years off her, was it?"

"No, a pillow did that," David said grimly.

"Oh Captain, honestly! I'm sorry!" Agnes paled and stared at him, horrified. "I wasn't trying to sound unkind! I just meant, well, what harm was there in making her nights a little more comfortable?"

"Under the circumstances, it possibly did exactly that," he acknowledged. "Did you have to do anything else for her?"

"Like what?" She frowned at him.

"You mentioned being treated like a servant," he reminded her. "But you only listed your duties as having to cook an occasional meal and hand her some pills. That's not exactly slavery. What else was there?"

Agnes blushed angrily at his obvious skepticism and folded her arms over her chest. David waited for her to get over her annoyance and answer the question.

"She made me clean up after her, a *lot*," she finally muttered. "For one little old lady she made a huge mess. She was sloppy and careless and that didn't bother her in the slightest. She just snapped her fingers and told me to clean everything up. That wasn't in my job description but I couldn't risk being replaced, so I just did it."

"That's all?" He held her gaze sternly.

"Yes, that's all!" she huffed. "What did you expect? I wasn't swinging from a scaffold to wash windows!"

"Good for you." He smiled again. "Who all came to see Mrs. Hedgewick the evening of her death?"

"All the Hedgewick men came by at some point to look in on her," Agnes grumbled and flicked him another, much less friendly look. "And *you* of course."

"I've already checked my alibi, but thanks for the tip-off." He gave her an exaggerated wink and her icy façade cracked slightly.

"Honestly," she chuckled and shook her head.

"Were you in the room when Pierce Hedgewick visited her?" David asked.

"No, they asked me to step outside." She cleared her throat discreetly. "I think they quarreled, to be honest."

"Any idea what about?" he asked impassively.

"I didn't hear anything distinctly but Pierce looked really angry when he left." Agnes tapped her finger on her chin thoughtfully. "It was probably about money, Gail liked to hold the family fortune over their heads and make them jump for it."

"Sounds charming," he said dryly.

"Yeah, she was a sweet little lamb," Agnes scoffed.

"What about Bradley?" He quirked a brow. "Did they argue?"

"Oh no, Captain," Agnes shook her head. "Bradley and Gail got along great, they were about the only members of the family that did, to be honest."

"Were you in the room when they spoke?"

"I was, sir. Bradley rarely asked me to leave," she shrugged. "When he came to visit Gail, it was genuinely to visit. He wasn't just after money."

"Are you sure about that?" David's eyes narrowed minutely.

"According to what I always heard," she said.

"Interesting. So, what did they talk about?"

"The wedding. Gail was quite annoyed over it, as you saw for yourself," Agnes sighed. "Bradley tried to calm her down a bit but she wasn't in the mood to play nice, so he said goodnight and left."

"What do you think of Elvan and Bella's marriage?" he asked.

"That it's none of my business, sir," she replied primly.

"Hmm. No one else came by that night?" he pressed. "You're certain?"

"Not while I was there." She shook her head. "But I left at 9 o'clock, right after I gave Mrs. Hedgewick her warm milk, she preferred her sedative dissolved in a drink. Mr. Hedgewick met me on the stairs and told me that I could leave it with her and go."

"Which Mr. Hedgewick was that?"

"Bradley." She smiled placidly.

***

Maiden drove to the police station and parked. She then sat in her car for a long moment while she considered how best to proceed. She wanted to tell David what she'd learned from Pierce but she didn't want him to think that she was running her own investigation; especially since she was.

She hadn't decided yet if she was going to bring up Marti Drake. Ramirez had already spoken to her and Sylvia, but it just seemed unlikely that the women would air their grievances to a cop. In any case, she did want to mention Pierce's hatred of Ree and, most likely, Bradley. There was also his reaction to the rings that Gail had been wearing.

She could always approach it from a neutral angle, saying she and Bella had had lunch with her new nephew and he happened to tell them a few things related to the case. It wouldn't be unusual under the circumstances, of course they'd all be discussing the murder. It would be strange if they didn't.

It sounded plausible enough and it meant she got to see David again and potentially away from the amused stares of his staff. Maiden nodded, satisfied with her plan and climbed out of the car.

As she locked the door and turned to head into the station, she saw a young woman coming out. It was Gail's nurse, the one she'd caught eavesdropping. They'd officially met at the wedding when she came downstairs to fix a plate of food for Gail.

"Miss Gray?" She smiled politely as she approached. "Maiden Harlow, I'm Bella's niece."

"Ah yes, of course." Agnes' expression was guarded and her eyes a tad cool. "How are you, Miss Harlow?"

"Okay I guess, in shock about Mrs. Hedgewick, like everyone else." She put on her most sincerely worried expression. "How are *you* though? You must find this particularly hard, you would've spent so much time with Gail."

"Well, yes that's true, thank you." Agnes looked a little surprised by the show of concern. "Sadly, when one works with the very elderly and frail, one grows accustomed to losing the poor dears eventually."

"It must be so difficult, though." Maiden shook her head sadly. "Especially when it wasn't...natural causes. Were the police kind to you?"

"Mostly." She pulled a face. "They can't help it, of course, it's their job to be suspicious."

"But they can't be suspicious of you?" Maiden did her best to sound scandalized. "You'd already left, hadn't you?"

"I certainly had." Agnes nodded firmly. "I wonder though, would she still be alive if I'd stayed until the normal time?"

"Oh? How late did you usually work?" Maiden asked.

"10 o'clock, most nights." She shrugged. "Although, I guess that's done now."

"Oh, of course. It's a double blow for you, isn't it?" Maiden tsked. "What will you do next?"

"I don't know yet. I haven't thought too far ahead, this all came about so fast." She glanced away and suddenly seemed more circumspect. "I might take a little time off, get my head around everything that's happened and then, well, I might just see where fortune leads me."

Fortune, eh? Maiden found that a curious choice of words. She looked the other lady over consideringly as new suspicions started to sprout up.

Agnes Gray didn't look like the flashy, fortune-hunting type. She was pretty, but it was in a very genteel and understated way. There was no mistaking the mercenary gleam in her eyes though. She'd worked for a very wealthy family for some time, she might be harboring some ambitious hopes.

"I wonder if Mr. Hedgewick could find you a new position?" Maiden offered in a deliberately ingenuous tone. She was rewarded by a brief and knowing smirk that was quickly tucked away again.

"That's possible, maybe," Agnes said casually. "I might just have to talk to him about it. Once everything settles down."

Maiden was hoping she'd elaborate, at least enough to tell her which Mr. Hedgewick they were talking about. She decided to test the waters.

"Maybe Pierce would have a role for you?" she suggested. "In his company. Assuming you'd be willing to quit nursing and move to Tennessee."

"I'd be quite happy to quit nursing," Agnes allowed, but her eyes didn't light up at the mention of a job. "But I don't know that I'm the secretarial sort."

Interesting. Maiden suppressed a smile of her own as they closed in on the target.

"Well, Elvan's going to be caught up with his new marriage for a while." Maiden stroked her chin thoughtfully. "Do you think Bradley's in a position to do anything for you?"

There it was. The flash of pleasure in the depths of Agnes' soft eyes. Maybe she wasn't aware that Bradley's prospects were limited, or maybe she was aware that they were better than anyone else realized.

"I really don't know, I suppose anything's possible," Agnes said cagily and shifted a little. "Really, *all* the Hedgewick men have been quite kind to me. I expect that something will work out."

Maiden managed not to frown at that broad statement. Agnes glanced at her car and rattled her keys a little, likely preparing to end the discussion and leave. Maiden spoke up quickly.

"One more thing, Miss Gray, I'm sure *you'd* know better than anyone." Maiden felt a bit petty resorting to flattery but did it anyway. "Did you feel that Gail was slipping mentally?"

"What do you mean?" She gave her an uncertain look.

"A few people have mentioned a suspicion that Gail's mental faculties weren't what they used to be," she said tactfully. "You must've known her better than most, what do you think?"

"I think..." Agnes pursed her lips thoughtfully and considered her answer carefully. "I think that anyone who didn't know Gail quite well might mistake her behavior as meaning more than it did."

"How so?" Maiden shook her head a little.

"Gail was mean," Agnes said frankly. "A lot of people didn't realize just how mean she could be."

"It sounds like *you* knew." She gave her an empathetic smile.

"Oh heavens, yes." Agnes rolled her eyes and whistled. "She used to make the biggest mess, deliberately, and used to giggle like a child while she watched me clean it up. She'd tip bottles of juice off her side table, smash plates full of food on the floor if she didn't like what she'd been served. Once she even threw a bottle of mouthwash at me because it was cinnamon flavored instead of peppermint."

"Are you sure that's not senility?" Maiden gave a weak laugh.

"Oh no, that was just Gail," Agnes said with a confident nod. "Nasty as could be, but she was still sharp. Which means that anything she might've chosen to do or change or sign, even right up to the end, was perfectly legal and binding. And I'd swear to that in court. Now I'd better be on my way. See you later, sweetie."

Maiden didn't even try to phrase a reply as Agnes smiled smugly and sauntered past. The dainty little woman had claws and she'd just given her a glimpse of them. She watched until Agnes climbed into a blue car with the sticker from a local rental company in the window and drove off. It was the same car she'd seen outside the manor the night of the rehearsal.

As Maiden turned and headed into the station, she considered what Agnes had revealed. While she didn't admit to any personal aspirations, not outright at least, she certainly seemed to have her toe in the water.

It was possible that she was eyeing off Bradley and whatever money she thought he might possess. Would she have killed Gail to make sure he got it?

Maybe Gail really had discussed changing her will; Agnes could have easily overheard it and started plotting. Even if Gail had ultimately changed her mind, Agnes might've heard the first conversation but not the last one.

Maiden chewed pensively at her lip as she pushed through the station door. She looked up and exhaled quietly when she saw Greg and Nancy standing at the desk talking. They glanced over at her and fell conspicuously silent. Maiden ignored it and walked up to the desk exactly like she'd always done before.

"Hey, how's it going?" she asked nicely.

"Hi, Mae." Greg smiled knowingly.

"How can I help you, Miss Harlow?" Nancy's tone was polite.

"Would you ask Captain McAlister if he has a moment?" She strove for a dignified expression. "Please?"

"Seriously?" Greg snickered before he could help himself.

"Is he here or not?" she asked with forced patience.

"He is, Miss Harlow." Nancy's eyes were mirthful. "He's not expecting you?"

"Have I said anything to make you think he's expecting me?" Her tone matched her grimly serious expression.

Nancy pressed her lips together and slid her gaze away as she reached for the phone. Maiden sighed softly and shook her head, but she glanced over to her left when she heard footsteps approaching.

***

Officer Sarah-Jane Parker walked towards the small group with her head held high and her chin lifted to a confident, defiant angle. Her eyes settled on Maiden with more than a hint of challenge in their tawny depths.

She felt like a new woman, a woman that was invincibly self-assured, a woman that didn't stand shyly in the corner while others lapped up all the attention. She controlled her own destiny; she wasn't intimidated by anyone.

You may have won the captain over, honey, she thought stubbornly as her eyes ignored the others and focused squarely on Maiden, *but you didn't break me. I'm still here and I am not threatened by you!*

She stood before her and arched her new, perfectly sculpted brows, daring her to say anything to challenge her revitalized and confident self. Maiden looked at her and blinked in surprise. Sarah-Jane smiled triumphantly.

She'd bought brand new makeup, she'd also had to spend far more time learning how to use it than she'd ever expected to but it was worth it. Even the money she'd shelled out on going to a salon downtown and getting her first professional haircut and style, the expensive products she'd already forgotten how to use, it was all worth it to see the stunned look on Maiden Harlow's face.

But then a genuine and happy smile graced that frustratingly pretty face. Maiden's eyes widened with delight as she reached over and actually touched her slightly less-frizzy hair; she looked so pleased.

"Oh wow, Officer Parker!" Maiden didn't struggle or choke on a single word. "You look fantastic!"

Sarah-Jane's victorious expression faltered. She hadn't expected good grace, certainly not a compliment that hadn't been wrenched unwillingly from her rival's spiteful and crestfallen heart. She pulled in a deep breath and let it out slowly.

"And...you're nicer than me too," she muttered as she studied Maiden darkly through half-lowered lids. "It's getting gradually harder to keep hating your stupid guts."

Beside her Greg snorted with laughter and slapped his palm down on the desk. Maiden just stared at them and stepped away slightly.

"That's...good, I guess," she murmured and turned to Nancy when she hung up the phone.

"Incredibly enough, the captain said he can spare you a moment or two, Miss Harlow." She gestured towards the hallway with a flourish. "Last door on the right, in case you've forgotten."

"You guys are getting really weird," Maiden informed them as she turned and walked down the hall.

CHAPTER SEVENTEEN

David stayed deliberately shielded behind his desk. He had no idea why Maiden was there but he knew that time would feel like it had stopped until she left. But time never stopped, and there was a murderer on the loose.

He'd been typing up his notes from his brief interview with Agnes Gray. He glanced at the screen and quickly closed the file.

There was no chance of keeping Maiden out of the case entirely, but he didn't want to risk her getting in any deeper than necessary. Not only was it potentially awkward with members of her family under suspicion, but he needed space so he could function.

He'd been struggling to keep his mind off her in quiet moments, and sometimes even in busy moments when his mind unwillingly drifted to the other ways he'd rather be spending his time. Every time he gave himself a break he inevitably spent most of it looking through the few pictures he'd taken of her at the reception when she wasn't looking.

His favorite was a shot of her with her knee resting on a barstool, glancing up at someone across the room while she reached down to adjust her shoe. The cleverly inquisitive expression combined with an unintentionally sexy pose was quintessentially Harlow.

No one fully understood his struggle, he barely understood it himself. Nancy had been so smug when she called and asked if he'd see Miss

Harlow. He knew they all thought it was silly to pretend nothing had happened, but that's not what he was doing. It wasn't about whether or not something had happened, it was making it known that nothing was *happening*. Not until the case was done, after that they could all laugh and smirk as much as they wanted.

When less than a minute passed and she still hadn't walked in he looked at the door and frowned. He started drumming his fingers but a few seconds later he saw her silhouette behind the glass and then heard the knock on the door.

"Come in," he said and braced himself.

The knob rattled and then turned as Maiden opened the door and slipped inside. He took a deep breath and looked her over.

She was wearing those jeans, the really snug ones that were faded in all the right places. Her slouchy sweater was dark green, the cowl-neck collar fell loose enough to expose her decolletage and the long sleeves reached halfway down her fingers. Her big eyes locked onto him and a slow smile curved her lips; he felt his stomach drop to his knees.

He marveled at how things had changed so quickly. A week ago, sure, he thought about her. They'd flirted and teased each other for months, he wasn't immune to that, he didn't want to be, but one day had changed everything. He hadn't felt this ridiculously distracted by a woman in a long time, maybe never; she was special.

He'd finally let go of everything that had been holding him back, but he still couldn't be with her. Mentally and emotionally he'd progressed to the next step and he knew he couldn't go back now. It was a problem.

"Hi," she said quietly, still standing by the door.

David smiled nicely and let his gaze slide over her. Today seemed more difficult than yesterday when they'd been surrounded by others.

Maybe because they were alone in his office with its dim lights and air of privacy.

It's too dark, he thought absently as he forced his eyes to her face. *It's like a nightclub in here. Except for the beige walls, filing cabinets and the forty-year-old furniture. I could always act like a genius and open the shades a little wider. I swear this woman has turned me into a massive idiot and I haven't even taken her out yet...I am in so much trouble.*

***

Maiden tried not to fidget but it wasn't easy. David still hadn't actually said anything but he was staring at her like she was edible. The strain of having to maintain a polite distance was getting old fast.

"How's everything going?" she asked, hoping she wasn't betraying her impatience.

"Slower than I'd like," he said grimly and fiddled with his pen. "How are you?"

"Fine, I guess." She shrugged weakly, not wanting to be the one to admit that they were frustrated and lonely. "You?"

"Yeah, okay," he murmured. "What brings you here?"

Maiden stared at him; she couldn't remember. It had seemed so relevant and important until she saw him sitting at his desk with his sleeves pushed up to his elbows. She could hardly tell him she came to gawk at his muscular forearms. They were nice though, strong and dusted with dark hair.

Stop it, Maiden! she chided herself. *He's going to think you're an idiot if you keep acting like one! You came here for a reason, figure out what it was and get on with it. Oh, he's talking. Pay attention, it might be important.*

"Sorry?" she asked.

"I said I'm trying to make some headway." He shut his eyes and then gave her a tolerant look. "I was working on something when you showed up...can I help you?"

"Oh." She pulled a face and felt some of the wistful longing that was rendering her useless start to dissipate. "I didn't realize I was annoying you. Sorry."

"Please don't," he said tightly.

"Don't what?" She frowned.

"Just *don't*." He gave her a look. "I'm struggling, all right? There are a dozen other things I'd like to be doing, none of them police related, but there's nothing I can do about it right now and that's incredibly difficult to accept. Particularly when I'm looking right at you."

"Are you angry with me?" She shook her head uncertainly.

He dropped his face into his hands and let his shoulders sag for the briefest moment before looking back at her with an irate expression.

"No, I'm not angry!" he almost growled.

"You know what 'angry' means, right?" A corner of her mouth tilted upwards. "Are you okay?"

"No, I'm not okay, Maiden." His deep voice was intense and frustrated and gave her goosebumps. "Do you know how hard it is to focus on work thanks to you?"

"Thanks to *me?*" she demanded. "You could've made a move on me a month ago!"

"I realize that," he said through his teeth. "You want to ask me how much that helps right now?"

"Well, don't take it out on me." She rested a hand on her hip. "Waiting was your brilliant idea."

"You said it first," he reminded her.

"Only after you whined about things 'getting complicated'," she mocked his deeper voice.

David's eyes widened incredulously. He stood and took a step towards her before stopping and clenching his hands at his sides.

"Don't push me, Harlow." He eyed her sternly. "Do you really want to sneak around behind everyone's back and then watch me pretend to do the right thing and give this case impartial attention?"

"Yeah, I think I could live with that!" she admitted grumpily before she could stop herself. Her breath caught and she quickly looked away as she strove for something less desperate and undignified to say. "And by that I mean, no. I certainly don't want you to do anything you'd regret."

"*Harlow*, I'm not going to lie to you," he warned soberly in the face of that feeble agreement. "I'm really not sure how much I can expect of myself right now; I'm not made of stone."

"Neither am I, Captain." She was secretly appalled by how sulky she sounded.

"Oh, don't pout, honestly!" He looked away with a pained laugh. "And stop staring at me like that!"

"I'm not staring." She folded her arms.

"Yes you are and it's killing me, *please* stop." He rubbed his face with his hands.

"Fine," she said tolerantly and leaned back against the wall. "Let's just get through this, how can I help?"

David resumed his seat and shuffled through his papers, his eyes strayed to her more than once. She gave him a cranky look and he fought a smile as he obligingly went back to his notes.

She sighed loudly as he shuffled some more. This was taking way too long; she'd go crazy at this rate. She came and sat in the chair directly in front of him and drummed her fingers on the wooden arms.

"So, Ree admitted that she'd been in contact with Gail Hedgewick some time before the wedding," she prompted. "And that suggests that Bradley knew about the plan to disinherit Elvan. He was probably in on it."

"Yes, but according to Elvan, the plot wasn't necessarily all that secret and he'd already talked Gail out of it." David rubbed his forehead. "So, who's lying?"

"Maybe no one, maybe all of them." Maiden shut her eyes briefly. "What did Ree have to say for herself?"

"A lot of bluster and self-pity," he murmured.

"Did she mention another will?"

"Conflict of interest, Harlow." He slid her a warning look.

"That means yes," she surmised and pressed on before he could complain. "Who stands to benefit the most from Gail's death?"

"Potentially Elvan." David was tapping the end of his pen against his lip as she tipped her head back and stared up at the ceiling. "Assuming he's still Gail's principal heir. If that's the case then, by extension, Bella also benefits because she's now his wife."

"Aunt Bella has her own money, she doesn't need his." Maiden waved it away.

"Does she have *that* kind of money?" David asked frankly. "The Hedgewick's are loaded, to put it delicately."

"I haven't actually asked Aunt Bella how loaded she is, sorry," Maiden chuckled. "But I suspect that Bradley was hedging his bets, he didn't know if Gail would disinherit his father or not, so he didn't let on that he knew what Ree was up to."

"Possibly, but Bradley also might not have known about the scheme." David paused as she slid one hand behind her head and crossed her legs, posing rather daintily. "You're not being...fair. Or impartial."

"Ree acted surprised that Gail was dead," Maiden pressed on. "But she was genuinely shocked that Elvan had actually married Aunt Bella...I wonder when she *really* last spoke with Gail. What did they tell each other? Maybe Gail was playing games with everyone."

"Speaking of playing games," he muttered. "Are you sitting like that on purpose?"

She grinned up at the ceiling. "I am, quite honestly."

"Maiden, knock it off." His smile was in his voice but it became muffled as he buried his face in his hands again. "This isn't helping."

"I guess not," she said softly and sat up again.

"So, why did you actually come here today?" he asked. "Was it just to mess with my head?"

"No, that wasn't the only reason," she mused and thought more carefully. "Oh! Yes, that's it. Pierce Hedgewick."

"What about him?" David chewed at the end of his pen.

"He hates Ree, she broke up his parent's marriage. I think he probably hates Bradley too. And he gave the impression that Ree is using Bradley to sponge off Elvan," she explained.

"So?" He shrugged, he didn't look surprised or impressed by any of it.

"'So'?" she repeated incredulously. "Well, does Pierce inherit much? Would he have the same prospects if Bradley edged out Elvan? Would he be forced to deal with Ree more often? Did he try to get Gail to disinherit Elvan in favor of *him*? Come on, this is gonna take forever!"

"Thanks, the added pressure helps a lot." He rubbed his eyes.

"Please, David," she said earnestly. "You won't even talk to me about it?"

"Do you promise not to flirt?" He gave her a stoney look.

"No!" she scoffed. "And neither do you, so just deal with it. You think this is any easier for me?"

"Great, thanks for your cooperation," he smiled faintly, obviously flattered despite losing the argument.

"Did you notice that Gail was wearing three engagement rings at the wedding?" she quickly forged ahead.

"Yes, and *was* wearing is the key point." He gave her a look. "They were gone when I checked on the body."

"What?" Maiden's eyes widened. "That's so weird."

"Yes and no." He tilted his head slightly to either side. "If the diamonds were real, she could have been wearing tens of thousands of dollars on her hand. If someone was willing to actually murder her, theft probably wouldn't have troubled them. But the fact that she was wearing three engagement rings in the first place was definitely weird."

"So, you're assuming that the murderer is also the one that took them?" she asked carefully.

"It's certainly possible." He smiled at her subtle reasoning. "But I didn't say that, no."

"Pierce seemed...upset about the rings," she said as casually as she could.

"Yeah, he did." He nodded and she looked over at him sharply.

"How did you know that?" she asked.

"I saw him at the wedding when he first realized she was wearing them," he replied, his eyes narrowed a fraction. "How did *you* know about it?"

Maiden sighed to herself and smiled a little as she held his chocolate-brown gaze. *You're really cute when you go all grumpy like you're about to. Just as well.*

"I asked him about it when Aunt Bella and I had lunch with him today," she admitted.

"Why?" he asked tightly.

"Be more specific," she said, knowing it would annoy him but not sure exactly how much she wanted to volunteer yet.

"You had lunch with this guy?" he demanded irately and shut his eyes when she started laughing. "That's not what I meant. Why were you asking him about the case?"

"What else would we be discussing right after his grandmother's murder?" she asked. "Which happened at my aunt's wedding. My aunt who was also there with us, please keep in mind."

"I wasn't being jealous." He rolled his eyes. "I don't want you investigating on your own."

"Why?" she exhaled loudly.

"Be more specific." He smiled faintly at her; she laughed again.

"I took advantage of a fine opportunity to casually glean a bit of information, which I brought straight to you," she said calmly. "How is that 'investigating on my own' and what exactly is your problem with it?"

David slid his gaze away and was quiet for a moment. Maiden wasn't entirely sure that he'd be any more accepting of her input now but she felt that she'd raised a reasonable point. He evidently agreed; he gave a conceding nod at no one in particular and turned back to her.

"What did he say about the rings?" he asked as though there'd been no disruption to the conversation.

"He looked very angry about it when I brought it up, but then he acted like he didn't know anything about them," she explained. "Does Pierce happen to have an alibi?"

"Kind of," he said. "But it's the same 'lots of people saw me through the evening' alibi that most of the others have."

"Great...Have you actually seen Gail's will?" she tried again, hoping he'd tell her.

"Not yet," he conceded. "Her lawyer's been contacted, he'll be here tomorrow. Obviously there's a lot of red tape and protocols in place."

"So, you don't know yet who the main beneficiaries are?" She lifted her dark brows a fraction.

David just looked down at the papers on his desk. Maiden's eyes widened and her heart started pounding; he did know.

"So...Pierce isn't the main beneficiary," she deduced.

"How do you know that?" He gave her a look.

"Because you aren't overly interested in Pierce, you don't think he has a strong enough motive," she said, holding his gaze as she tried to follow his reasoning. "You also haven't mentioned Agnes, but probably because you don't think *I've* thought of her yet."

"Amazing," he said dryly. "What am I thinking now?"

"You're wondering what my favorite flowers are." She rubbed her temples as though trying to focus her thoughts. "Roses, by the way, pink ones."

He smirked at her and tried to redirect the discussion.

"At the wedding, while you were still downstairs," he quickly added, "did you see Bradley or Elvan slip upstairs at any point?"

"Yes," she said as she thought it over. "I saw Bradley go up around 8 o'clock. Elvan...not really sure. I wasn't that interested, to be honest. Then around 9:30, maybe 9:40, I'd had enough of the whole reception and went upstairs to escape. I didn't see any of them after that."

"Had you been trying to escape me too?" he asked mildly but his eyes were watchful.

"No," she conceded, "but you weren't exactly giving me any reason to stick around."

"Excuse me?" he demanded with a frown.

"You never tried to talk to me, never asked me to dance." She shrugged a shoulder. "What was I supposed to think?"

"Did you really want to dance with me right *then*?" He gave her a speaking look. "With your entire family smiling and speculating?"

She slid her gaze away. She still smiled but it was quiet, so was her tone. "Kind of. Yeah."

"Oh...I'm sorry," he said softly.

"It's okay. You made up for it later." She shook off the mild regret and quickly changed the subject. "Did Bradley ever tell you where he really was when Gail was killed?"

"Just that he went outside for a while." He rubbed the back of his neck. "He said the argument with his cousin upset him and he didn't want to spoil the reception, so he took himself outside to cool down."

"How long does he claim he was out there?" she asked skeptically. "It was pretty chilly that night."

"Twenty minutes or so," he mumbled as he studied her face and then let his eyes wander lower. "It's not impossible."

"Please stop looking at me like that," she said. All the warm feelings were flooding back in like waves on the seashore.

"Sorry," he whispered and dragged his gaze away.

David pushed to his feet and walked to the window. He grabbed the cords on the shades and pulled one end until more sunlight flooded in. He stayed there with his back to her and cleared his throat.

"What else do you remember?"

"I remember absolutely everything, you know that," she said seriously. She'd quickly sunk back into the emotional mire and didn't really want to claw her way out again. "The way your cologne smells slightly different on your skin than it does on your clothes. Your hands, they're big and warm and a little calloused."

"Are my hands rough?" he turned enough to see her but then looked down at his palms.

"Yeah, don't change it." She closed her eyes gently and trailed her own hand slowly down her throat. "I like it. And I like how your breath comes out in a ragged little gasp when you get excited."

He was quiet for a long moment, so long that she opened her eyes and looked over at him. The intensity in his gaze told her she'd pushed too far. He still didn't say anything but he gave the cords he was holding a sharp tug, shutting the blinds completely.

Uh-oh. You just had to say what you were thinking, didn't you? she scolded herself. She sat up properly and took a deep breath.

"I'm sorry," she said more solemnly and glanced around, preparing to quickly leave. "I shouldn't have come here. I'll just call you if I remember anything else. I'm so sorry, David."

She pushed to her feet and headed for the door, but before she'd reached it she felt his hand on her arm. He pulled her back to face him and moved closer until she was gently pressed between him and the wall. She looked up at him and felt her heart beat harder in her chest. She heard that ragged little breath and bit her lip to hide a smile.

He was staring at her but seemed to be fighting to try and stop himself as well. He managed to take his hands off her and planted them flat against the wall on either side of her head but he still leaned in close. While he waged his internal war, her gaze wandered.

She looked at his shirt pocket and smiled faintly when she spied the notebook he kept there. It always struck her as cute that, despite the digital gadgets that were available, he used a pad of paper and a pen. She was still smiling as she shifted her gaze to the tie that always hung loose around his neck.

Silently hoping his eyes were closed so he wouldn't catch her doing it, she picked up the longest end and held it to her nose, inhaling the scent of his cologne.

He sighed shakily and she felt the backs of his fingers stroke her cheek. She wet her lips and risked looking up at him, there was a fondness in his eyes that she hadn't noticed before, affection maybe.

"So..." he spoke quietly even as he attempted to get back to safer ground. "What do we know so far?"

"Aunt Bella has an alibi, so do Mom and Dad, Vonny and...me, of course," her voice dropped to a whisper as he braced his forearm against the wall beside her head and edged closer. "We can't be sure about Elvan or Pierce. No one saw Ree or...I can't remember his name...Bradley."

David grinned and spread his other palm flat on the wall beside her shoulder, pinning her in place. She breathed in the scent of his skin and felt bold enough to lay her hands against his chest. He shut his eyes and rested his cheek against her temple.

"They all had a motive," he grasped her shoulder and gently kneaded her warm flesh through her heavy sweater, "and they all potentially knew the victim's habits well enough to make use of her usual sedative."

"Yeah, they probably all did." Maiden slid her hands around his narrow waist. "Did Elvan tell you about his close calls and feelings of being watched yet?"

"What?" his scowl was in his voice as he leaned back enough to look at her. "No! What's that about?"

"He said he's had a few suspicious accidents and some uneasy feelings for the last month or so," she said as she stared at the buttons on his shirt straining against his well-muscled chest. "Apparently Bradley was always visiting when it happened."

"How long have you known about that?" he demanded with a hint of exasperation.

"Long enough that you'll be annoyed about it," she admitted and pulled him a little closer. "Do you think getting angry with me now will help distract you?"

"Damn I hope so," he said seriously. "Why didn't you tell me about that sooner? You've had opportunities since the wedding."

"Because every time I see you I start thinking about your big calloused hands on my back...and your chest hair," she murmured candidly as she stared at the dark shadows that peeked out from his unbuttoned collar, "which I also really like. Not that I can do anything about it."

"Maiden! Come on," he almost pleaded as he leaned in close and buried his face against her throat. "You're making the most painful task of my life even more difficult."

"I'm sorry," she blatantly lied and hugged him tighter.

"Be professional, McAlister," he muttered to himself under his breath. "You've been a cop for over a decade, you can do this. Step back."

Maiden felt herself smiling at his incredibly flattering struggle. She wasn't helping him very much but she was secretly okay with that. She knew she was being weak, but since they were getting looks and winks anyway, maybe another kiss or two wouldn't really hurt anything?

He let out a slow breath and touched a kiss to the side of her throat as he slid an arm around her and pulled her firmly against him. She nestled closer and relished a precious moment of feeling him hold her.

"Maiden," he said at last.

"Yes, David?" Her voice was soft and breathy, she doubted that helped and did indeed feel his hold tighten. But she stilled and sobered when he spoke again.

"I need you to walk away," he said seriously even as he ran his other hand gently over her hair. "I'm sorry, I can't do it."

"Really?" She blinked at that stoic request.

"Yeah." His voice was low and unsteady. "As soon as you can, please."

"Okay." She felt her knees grow weak and hoped they were up for the task. "Um...can you let go of me then?"

"No." He shook slightly as he laughed at himself and pressed another kiss to her throat. "I can't, that's the problem. You really might have to kick me or something."

Maiden started laughing and, after a dangerous moment of burying her amusement in his chest, managed to twist and pull until she wriggled free. She stepped away and took a moment to lean forward with her hands braced on her knees as she tried to catch her breath.

Between her amusement and the same feelings that were plaguing him, it took a moment. She finally stood up straight and looked at him. He was leaning his back against the wall with his arms tightly folded to keep them in check, just watching her with a fond smile.

"So," she gave him a look of innocent inquiry, "no kiss goodbye then?"

"Get out." He grinned broadly and pointed at the door.

"Fine," she sniggered and had just cracked the door open when something else occurred to her, "Oh, one more thing, Agnes has some kind of agenda going. I caught her eavesdropping on Gail and Elvan at the rehearsal. And when I met her as she was leaving here she hinted at a changed will. See you later, handsome."

With a mischievous smile she reached over and grasped the end of his tie, whipping it free. As she stuffed it in her back pocket, she winked and blew him a kiss before slipping out into the safety of the hallway.

Chapter Eighteen

David gave himself a few minutes to calm down and gather his thoughts before heading to the holding cells to attempt to talk to Bradley Hedgewick again. Bradley had stayed tight-lipped and hostile since his arrest, he'd also turned his nose up at every opportunity he'd been offered to call the legion of lawyers he claimed to have waiting in the wings.

David walked into the room and looked him over critically. The man had grown increasingly edgy the longer he sat alone in the small, sterile cell. His cousin Pierce, despite their apparent animosity, had brought him a change of clothes when he visited him that morning. After a careful search, he'd been allowed to have the garments and change out of his rented tux.

Bradley now sat quietly on the bed in corduroy slacks and a salmon pink argyle cardigan, the contrast with his bloodshot eyes, messy hair and unshaven jaw was pronounced. He looked like a washed-up former child star that had just slept off a bender.

"Good afternoon," David said as he came and stood on the other side of the bars. "Feeling any chattier today?"

"Not 'til I talk to my lawyer," he said tersely.

"As you've been told, you're welcome to call one anytime." David shrugged. "Or the courts can supply one."

"Yeah, that'd work out great for me, wouldn't it?" Bradley sneered. "Send in one of your hired goons to 'help' me. I don't think so!"

"Up to you," he said and folded his arms loosely. "The night of your grandmother's death, you told her nurse that she could leave early. Why?"

"Who told you that load of nonsense?" Bradley glared at him.

"Are you denying it?" David arched a brow.

"Maybe...I'm not sure at the moment." It was obviously true. "I got a lot on my mind."

"What can you tell me about Agnes Gray?" he murmured.

"Her?" Bradley frowned and then shrugged. "Nothin' much. She was Granny's nurse for a couple of years."

"No other interest there?" David smiled faintly.

"No, Captain," Bradley smirked. "She's got no family, no money and she's built like a twelve-year-old. Not my type."

David quietly jotted down that rather heartlessly insulting summation. He found it interesting in light of Agnes' defense of Bradley during her interview and Harlow's suggestion that the nurse had designs on him. He decided to leave it there for the moment.

"Were you expecting to inherit a lot of money from your grandmother?" David asked.

"Now see here!" Bradley shot to his feet and shook a finger at him. "I don't like that kind of insinuation!"

"Your grandmother was nearly 90 and extremely wealthy, Mr. Hedgewick," he reminded him in the same even tone. "It's perfectly natural to give it some thought."

"Yeah, well, I still didn't," Bradley said stubbornly. "I loved Granny and wanted her to live forever."

"What about your father?" he continued. "Do you get along well with him?"

"Of course I do, I get along well with everybody!" Bradley groused.

"Not quite." David smiled faintly. "He kept you on a pretty short leash, financially speaking. Did you ever argue about that?"

"Whether or not I ever argue with my father is none of your business!" Bradley said through his teeth.

"When exactly did your mother get into town?" he droned on undaunted. "Did you confer with her outside Riley Manor the night of the murder?"

"I had no idea Mama was here at all," Bradley said after a long pause. "She didn't tell me she was comin' and she ain't been here to see me."

"You're claiming that you didn't know your mother was here until I just mentioned it?" David sounded as skeptical as he was.

"That's...yes. That's right." Bradley finally answered.

"But she lives with you, doesn't she?" he asked, despite knowing it was true.

"Only temporarily," Bradley bristled. "She's between jobs at the moment, I could hardly turn her out with no place to go, not like—"

"Like your father did?" David supplied when Bradley stopped himself abruptly.

"No, not at all." He shook his head. "My family has a complicated past, Captain McAlister, but I love all of them. I'm only tryin' to keep the peace. That's all I can do."

"Do you blame your father for divorcing your mother?" he asked.

"I-I was a baby at the time." Bradley wet his dry, cracked lips. "I don't remember what actually happened. And everybody tells a story to suit themselves, don't they?"

"So, which story do you believe?"

"I reckon there's usually a bit of truth on both sides," he finally admitted.

"Did your mother struggle after the breakdown of her marriage?"

"Yes, she surely did, they made certain of that," Bradley said tightly. "'They'?"

"Daddy and Granny," he supplied. "They made sure her name was worse than worthless all through the state. She always said she wonders that they ruined her so completely and then complained that she couldn't support herself."

"And now *you're* supporting her, using the term loosely." He managed to keep most of the cynical amusement out of his voice. "That must be frustrating when you aren't exactly established in your own right."

"And how do you know what I do or don't have?" Bradley looked down his nose at him.

"Because *I* have talked to your lawyer." He smiled benignly. "Had you ever brought up any financial concerns to your grandmother? Was she sympathetic at all?"

"Sympathetic?" Bradley's eyes rounded and he smirked acerbically. "Granny? No, Captain, she wasn't the sympathetic type."

"You knew of the rumors that she threatened to change her will?" It was more of a thinly veiled accusation than a question.

"She was always threatenin' to do that." He rolled his eyes. "Of course, Daddy just might've been a little bit more worried about it this time around."

"Why is that?"

"Well, he had his precious Bella to consider, didn't he?" Bradley's eyes took on an icy glint as he spoke of a woman he clearly hated. "He was in love with her since before he married my mama. How's that for a start to a marriage? He couldn't get the woman he wanted so he settled for the nearest alternative."

"Ouch," David said.

"To put it mildly," he grumbled. "Anyway, if *dear* Ms. Fontaine knew that Daddy might lose all his money, well, she'd be gone fast as lightnin' now wouldn't she?"

"Would she?"

"Oh come on, Captain," Bradley sniggered. "Why else would she be back after all these years?"

"How did your mother react when she found out that Elvan had found Bella again and was planning to marry her?" He shifted the attention back to Ree, curious to see how far Bradley would go to protect her.

"She was hurt, I think," he said solemnly. "Very hurt."

"Not angry?"

"Oh, that too." He waved it away.

"Even after all these years?"

"Mama's an emotional woman." Bradley ran a hand through his dirty hair. "She feels things for a long time."

"Things like hate?" David folded his arms loosely. "Resentment?"

"Things like love and disappointment!" Bradley snarled.

"How does Pierce Hedgewick get along with Ree?" David decided to poke the bear a little more.

"He doesn't." Bradley's expression grew guarded. "They hate each other."

"Why?"

"Pierce seems to think that Mama deliberately ruined his father," he scoffed. "And Mama resents him for helpin' to poison the rest of the family against her."

"Is it true that Ree Hedgewick got her brother-in-law drunk and took advantage of him?" His eyes locked on Bradley, he saw the angry red flush that mottled his face. "And that the fallout from that attack ruined his marriage and eventually led him to commit suicide?"

"'Attack'?" Bradley scowled. "That's a bit much, isn't it?"

"When one person deliberately renders another incapable of refusing sexual advances," he said grimly, "what would you call it?"

"It wasn't her fault!" He raised his voice furiously. "They were both drinkin'! Why should she get all the blame?"

"She didn't, though, did she?" David pointed out. "Alan Hedgewick's wife divorced him and he lost custody of Pierce. His business almost folded and then he put a gun to his head. Correct?"

David watched Bradley curl his hands into fists. He'd leaned on a few points that really couldn't be proven one way or the other now, but Bradley was clearly on his mother's side, despite his earlier claims of impartiality. That was all David was really looking to establish at the moment.

"I'm done with this conversation," Bradley muttered. "But you listen to this, Captain. My cousin may act like the wounded little orphan, but he's not so innocent and helpless as that. And he wasn't exactly in Granny's good graces either, her death didn't hurt him one little bit. In fact, it might've saved him from losin' everything."

***

Maiden returned to Harlow House, stashed David's tie in her underwear drawer next to the other one, and went in search of Aunt Bella. She went straight to their impressive suite, it was the largest of their luxury rooms and the most expensive to rent. She wasn't honestly sure if Bella and Elvan were paying guests or not, she didn't care either.

"Aunt Bella?" she said loudly as she knocked on the door. "Are you there? It's important!"

She heard rapid steps trundling towards the door; a second later Bella whipped it open and stared at her with widened eyes.

"What's happenin', baby?" she asked breathlessly. "Did he propose?"

"What?" Maiden gasped and then scowled. "No! As I mentioned *two hours ago*, not even been on a date yet!"

"Oh fine," she sighed. "What's all the fuss about then?"

"I need to talk to you." Maiden grasped her arm. "Is Elvan here?"

"No, he said he was going out to run some errands." She glanced briefly heavenward. "But I reckon he's gone to see Bradley. Come on in."

Maiden followed her to the elegant leather couches and perched beside her.

"Aunt Bella." Maiden turned to face her fully. "Had you ever heard anything about Gail threatening to change her will before? I mean, did you know she was supposedly threatening that well before the wedding?"

"No, Elvan never discussed it with me, but I wasn't surprised." Bella murmured. "When nasty people with money get old and realize that they never endeared themselves to their family any other way, well, they play the only card they have. They threaten to cut off the money supply unless they get what they want. Gail was a nasty piece of work and her family didn't like her, what else would she do?"

"But you aren't worried about it?" Maiden pressed as tactfully as she could. "Are you confident that she didn't already change the will?"

"Babydoll, it don't really matter. I didn't marry Elvan for his money," she said. "But Elvan swore that she didn't change anything and he would certainly know. Gail acted like every penny was earned by her personally but that ain't ever the case. Elvan and Pierce own parts of the businesses and the Hedgewick estate in their own right. Granted, she had the biggest piece of the pie, but so it is."

"Is that what Elvan told you?" she asked delicately.

"Mm-hmm." Bella nodded.

Maiden just looked at her as she sank into thought. She wasn't sure if she believed that Gail's threats weren't genuinely serious. It was possible, especially if senility was setting in, but this was the first Maiden had heard of other members of the family having any authority over the estate. Elvan hadn't used that argument when he was talking to Ree, and it seemed like that would've been the time to bring it up. If it was true.

"In any case, I've never *needed* Elvan's money," Bella continued placidly. "But I do like his house in Florida, it's real classy, I'm lookin' forward to livin' there."

"I'm sure it's incredible." Maiden smiled quietly, hoping that it wouldn't all end up pulled out from under the happy new couple.

"Oh!" Bella's eyes lit up. "You'll have to come visit us! Bring that gorgeous captain of yours and stay for a few weeks, you'll love it!"

"Sounds great," Maiden said quietly. "We'll see what happens. So...when is the will going to be read? Officially?"

"Already done." Bella nodded once. "The lawyer called us yesterday."

"What?" Maiden's eyes widened. "You already know what the will says? I thought they got everyone into a big room and read out who gets what."

"That's only in the movies, baby," Bella tittered. "Why drag everyone together just to tell some they got everything and others that they get nothin'?"

"Well..." Maiden started to apologize for being nosy but then remembered who she was talking to. "Did Elvan inherit everything?"

"Mostly," she confirmed. "The houses, the largest percentage of the businesses, most of the money. Pierce got a nice little fortune too, and so he should. I'm plannin' to ask Elvan to give the boy more shares of Hedgewick Finishes, his daddy set up most of it anyway."

"That's kind of you. Um," she pushed through to what really interested her as soon as politeness allowed, "what about Bradley?"

"He gets sweet diddly-crap!" Bella chortled. "Old Gail must've been mad at that fool when she wrote that will! He only gets what Elvan 'deems fair and appropriate', which is gonna be nothin' but a kick up the backside!"

"Whoa," Maiden breathed as she let that sink in. "Does Bradley know that yet?"

"Only if Elvan tells him today," she said with little concern in her voice. "If not, the lawyer will inform him personally when he flies in tomorrow."

"Which means Ree might not know yet either," Maiden said quietly.

Bella smirked and shrugged a shoulder.

"I wonder if Agnes knows..."

"Who?" Bella looked confused.

"Gail's nurse," Maiden said.

"What's she got to do with it?" She shook her head, making her long earrings dance.

"Oh, just the way she was talking when I bumped into her today." Maiden stroked her finger along her jaw thoughtfully. "I got the impression that she has some hopes of greener pastures, and she said that Gail was lucid enough to have 'changed things' and have it be legally binding."

"Ooh! That crafty little sneak!" Bella pursed her lips and smiled at the same time. "So that was how Bradley and Ree kept up the pressure on Gail! They must've had that little hussy feeding her all sorts of rubbish about Elvan and me."

"Possibly, but we don't really know that for sure," Maiden pointed out, although the thought had already occurred to her. "And I doubt any of them would admit it anyway. But Pierce did say that Gail wasn't as upset by Elvan wanting to marry you at first."

"That's right!" Bella tucked her feet up under her and snuggled down into the couch. "He said it got steadily worse as time went by, and what a coincidence that Gail was spendin' hours a day with Bradley's girlfriend! They must've all been hopin' she'd turn Elvan away completely so they could get everything. Talk about greedy!"

"Maybe." Maiden chewed at her lower lip. "I guess we'll see but, either way, Bradley's going to be understandably upset."

"Serves him right," Bella sniffed. "He goes through life causin' trouble and using people to suit himself. He deserves to be the one that's miserable for a change."

Maiden visited a little longer before heading back to her room and closing herself inside. She knew she ought to tell David what she'd learned but she didn't dare set foot in the station again today. Not only had she barely escaped in one piece the last time, but it was fairly safe to assume that Nancy would've noticed David's necktie hanging out of her back pocket when she left.

No, she needed to help figure this mess out and it was too distracting to be around the gorgeous captain. She took a deep breath and called him instead.

"Hey, Harlow." David sounded normal, or at least calm. "What's up?"

"I just spoke with Aunt Bella," she murmured. "She and Elvan know what Gail's will says already."

"That's not surprising really," he said. "What did she say about it?"

"Not a lot, it's what she was expecting. I mean it's what Elvan told her would happen." She silently kicked herself, hoping she hadn't made her aunt sound suspicious again. "But they also know that Bradley's been essentially disinherited."

David said nothing.

"Does Bradley know that?" she asked, not certain if he would tell her.

"I...doubt it," he finally admitted, she could hear his footsteps in the background and then the sound of a door closing, she wondered if he was in his office. "No one's been to see him and he hasn't asked to speak to a lawyer."

"Really?" She asked, surprised by both bits of information. "So, Elvan didn't go to see him?"

"No, not so far."

"Interesting," she mused. "That explains why Ree is laying low and also why Agnes was acting so pleased. They don't know they lost yet. Assuming they're plotting together."

"Possible." He was silent for another moment, when he next spoke she could hear the warm smile in his voice. "What are you wearing?"

"A spangly yellow jumpsuit and platform sneakers," she said in a sultry voice.

"Sexy," he chuckled and then sighed. "I'd better go, I shouldn't have said your name when I answered the phone."

"The situation may be frustrating," she said wryly, "but at least it's also stupid."

"That's my girl," he laughed but then seemed to catch what he'd said, she could almost hear him blushing over the phone. "I mean...I gotta go."

"Yeah, you'd better, you've caught my foot-in-mouth." She grinned. "Talk to you later."

She ended the call, leaving David to feel ridiculous in peace. Her thoughts shifted to Bradley and Ree, what would they do when they found out that it was all over?

Any scheming and conniving had not only failed, but it had been exposed. Far from being an instant millionaire, Bradley probably wouldn't even have his allowance anymore. From their point of view it was a complete disaster.

Agnes had looked so smug though, too smug. She acted as if she *knew* there was another will, but if the lawyer had confirmed that the previous version was still in effect, she must have been wrong. Unless...unless there was another will and it hadn't been found yet.

They would just have to wait and see what Bradley and Ree tried to cook up next.

Chapter Nineteen

D avid dropped his phone on the desk and shook his head at himself as he settled into his chair. He wasn't trying to play hard to get but he didn't need to start making embarrassing blunders every time he and Maiden talked. Almost mauling her to death in his office was quite enough for one day.

'*That's my girl*'. He smirked at himself as he turned to his computer. *Smooth, David. Why don't you go buy her a ring while you're at it? At least buy her coffee first, idiot.*

He was waiting for his next appointment to turn up and was grateful to have something productive to focus on. He heard a knock on the door and glanced up.

"Come in," he said steadily.

Pierce Hedgewick opened the door and walked towards him. He quietly took up a seat when David gestured towards the row of chairs in front of the desk. The man was tall and elegantly dressed. David flicked an assessing gaze over his slick hair, pristine suit and highly polished shoes.

David had run a few checks on him already; he came up relatively clean. There was a single drunk and disorderly charge from his college days, nothing overtly sinister though.

Apart from that, he was the CEO of Hedgewick Finishes and had appeared in the society pages of his local papers more than a few times.

He was rumored to have been romantically linked to five heiresses over the past three years.

"Thank you for your time, Mr. Hedgewick," David said impassively.

"No trouble at all, Captain," Pierce said politely as he stacked his hands neatly in his lap.

David noticed his expensive watch and then his manicure. He then glanced down at his own hands and recalled that Maiden said she liked his callouses, he hid a smile and sat a bit straighter in his chair.

"I have a few more questions about the night of your grandmother's murder." David said as he typed out a couple of words.

"I kinda figured that much," Pierce said dryly. "What's on your mind?"

"You visited your grandmother during the course of the evening," he murmured. "What time was that?"

"8:30, maybe quarter to 9." He shrugged. "It was after dinner but before Agnes left."

"And how did the discussion go?"

"Well, since you called me back in just to ask me about it, I have to assume that you already know." Pierce sighed but didn't look anxious. "It went badly."

"Did you argue?" David asked.

"Yes, we did." He nodded. "She was a mean old thing when she wanted to be."

"What was the argument about?"

"Would you believe she was threatenin' to change her will?" Pierce smiled ironically and met David's steely gaze with no trouble. "My daddy built up Hedgewick Finishes from a pokey little country store into somethin' bigger and far more extensive. After he nearly ruined it and then died, I built it up into somethin' even better again. It had nothin' to do with Granny, she never lifted a finger to build that business. But everything is part of the family trust."

"Which she ruled with an iron fist?" David asked.

"Pretty much," he said quietly. "Oh it's not like I have nothin' of my own, I'm not Bradley, but she owned the majority of shares in the company. She liked knowin' she could step in and take charge any time she wanted to."

"So what was the threat?" David quirked a brow.

"She wasn't happy that the weddin' went forward despite her efforts. She was gettin' a bit worked up about it." Pierce slid his gaze away. "Started sayin' some nasty things about Uncle Elvan to turn me against him."

"What did she say?"

"That he deliberately crippled Daddy's business after the *incident* with Ree." His eyes were cold and shadowed. "And that he hounded him until he couldn't deal with the guilt anymore."

"She accused Elvan of driving your father to commit suicide?" David asked carefully, Pierce nodded. "Did you believe it?"

"No, I got upset at the thought of it, but Uncle Elvan isn't like that. He's the only real decent member of the family." He let out a slow, angry breath. "Of course he has his flaws, but Granny used to defend him. All the time I was growin' up she told me that he was the one that was most hurt, him and my Mama, of course. Suddenly she doesn't like his choice of wife so she turns around and tells me it was all a lie."

"What did you say?"

"That she was a bitter old woman who was makin' up stories," he said glumly. "I called her a hateful old husk of what she used to be. She was, but that really didn't need to be the last thing I said to her."

"That's not a threat though," David pointed out. "What did she say about the will?"

"She smiled and laughed sayin' how funny it would be if she left all her shares of my company to Bradley." His hands clenched into fists. "Then he'd either sponge off all my hard work, or drive the business into the ground."

"Sounds harsh." David gave a humorless smile and a shake of his head. "Did you threaten her after that?"

"Yes...I did." Pierce finally admitted. "I told her that if she tried to change anything now, especially to leave everything to Bradley, Uncle Elvan and I would have her locked away in a dementia ward where she could live out her days talkin' to the roses in the wallpaper. Ain't I a sweetheart of a grandson?"

"Seems to run in the family," he replied dryly. "Then what happened?"

"I bid her a pleasant night and the sweetest of dreams and headed back downstairs." Pierce laughed ruefully. "Then Bradley walks up and asks me to have a conversation with him. Considering that I'd just been fantasizin' about spikin' his coffee with varnish, I wasn't in the mood to loan him more money. I therefore declined the invitation."

"I saw you having that argument a little while later," David reminded him.

"Yeah, he graciously gave me time to cool off before tryin' again," Pierce said with a hollow laugh.

"How did you feel about your uncle's marriage?" he asked.

"I was all for it," Pierce said easily. "I love Uncle Elvan and I really do like Bella, she's good for him and bad for Bradley. Perfect match."

"You were observed helping a young woman after Bradley allegedly verbally attacked her," he glanced up to gauge his reaction. "What was that about?"

Pierce was silent for a moment. David could see him struggle to submerge a burst of anger and possibly pain.

"That would have been Marti Drake," he replied at last. "She and I were…friends at one point, but then Bradley decided he was interested in her. That's entirely their business."

"Then why the public insults?" David pressed. "I'm told it got rather heated."

"Their relationship didn't last. They never do with Bradley, but she didn't know that." Pierce smiled weakly. "In any case, Bradley thought he might endear himself into my bank account if he tried to push all the blame onto her. That went over as well as you'd expect with Miss Drake. I escorted her out of harm's way and tried not to speak with either of them for the rest of the night."

"Very gallant," David murmured.

"An approximation thereof," Pierce rolled his eyes. "I just didn't want a scene at Uncle Elvan's weddin'. He deserved better than that."

"Tell me about the rings," David said without warning.

"What rings?" His eyes narrowed a fraction.

"The ones Gail wore through the wedding," David said. "She wore three very substantial diamond rings all day, but when I saw her body after the murder, they were gone."

"Why would I know anything about her odd choices in jewelry?" he asked grimly.

"Because I was sitting behind you both during the ceremony and I saw the look on your face," David replied. "You know what they are, or at least what they were. Any theories about where they got to and why?"

"Sorry, Captain." Pierce smiled tightly. "I can't help you there. Although you might want to ask Miss Gray. She spent more time with Granny than anyone else."

***

The following day Maiden and Ruffian were reading the newspaper. Ruffian mostly tried to slap the pages down with his tiny paws whenever Maiden made them crinkle. She glanced up discreetly when she heard Gloria and Bella whispering to each other in the kitchen.

"When did he leave?" Gloria asked softly.

"An hour ago." Bella shook her head and sighed. "I should've gone with him, I told him so but he was afraid that it would be too much for me."

Too much for Aunt Bella? Maiden pulled a face; she doubted that, whatever it was. She strained to hear as her mother kept whispering; she had no idea the woman was capable of that much stealth.

"They're just gonna try and chisel more money out of him!" Gloria hissed.

"They can try all they like," Bella grumbled. "Elvan's sworn to me that he won't give in again, not to that cow or her pathetic excuse for a son."

At that point Maiden abandoned the paper to Ruffy's nefarious clutches. She stood and strolled towards the older women casually. They both looked tense and anxious.

"What's up?" Maiden asked as she rested a hand on Bella's arm.

"Oh, this and that." Gloria gave her sister a worried look.

"Is Elvan going to see Bradley?" Maiden asked gently. "Is he going to tell him that he gets nothing in Gail's will?"

"Angel!" Gloria's mouth fell open. "Did I raise you to be so nosy?"

"Yes. Yes, you did," Maiden replied easily and without looking away from Bella.

"It's all right, Gloria. I'm okay, and she might as well know about it." Bella waved a placating hand. "Mr. Edmonds, he's the family's lawyer, arrives today. Elvan's gone to escort him to the police station so he can inform Bradley of the particulars of Gail's will."

"So, that's definitely Gail's last will?" Maiden knew she kept harping on it, but she didn't trust that Bradley and Ree would give up easily. "Agnes seemed pretty confident that there was a new one."

"Nothing that she took to her lawyer." Bella shrugged. "And they'll have a heck of a fight on their hands if they bring out a fake."

"That doesn't mean they won't try," Maiden said pensively. "Not with that much money at stake."

Bella gave a conceding nod but didn't look too concerned. Maiden was impressed by how well her aunt was handling the situation, of course she hadn't seen and heard as much as Maiden had. She decided to let the subject drop for the moment; there was nothing to be gained by stressing her out further.

Another hour passed, Gloria and Bella sat at the table eating, cackling and complaining about in-laws in general. Maiden was lying on the couch listening as she waited for Elvan to get back and tell them how the meeting with Bradley and the lawyer went.

Ruffian was sprawled across her stomach, twitching occasionally as he chased something in his sleep. Maiden patted him absently when he startled himself awake and slapped her with a paw. He immediately started gnawing on her thumb, she pulled a face and nudged him just enough to send him rolling onto the cushion beside her.

The sound of the door opening sent the young cat scampering curiously towards it. Maiden laid perfectly still and listened as Bella spoke first.

"Elvan, sweetie!" Her voice was filled with gentle worry. "You look upset, how'd it go?"

Maiden slowly peered up over the back of the couch and studied her new uncle critically. Aunt Bella was right, he was flustered and shaky.

"Not great, but I didn't expect otherwise." Elvan sat heavily in the chair that Bella led him to. "Bradley didn't take it well at all...I never did see him so angry."

"What'd he say?" Gloria's eyes were wide and curious.

"Oh, he screamed and bashed his fists against the bars." Elvan rubbed his eyes. "He kept swearin' that Mama had told him she was leavin' him everything. But Mr. Edmonds pointed out that she didn't update the will. So, anything she *allegedly* said means nothin'. Whether she'd planned to do anything or not is moot and holds no legal weight."

Maiden was quickly on her feet and stealthily approaching. She slid into a chair as unobtrusively as possible and watched Elvan's face closely. He looked pale and dazed.

"How did Bradley respond to that?" Maiden asked.

"He turned red as a beet. He glared at me like he wanted to kill me with his bare hands." Elvan exhaled shakily. "Then he started throwin' accusations around. Me, Pierce, even Mr. Edmonds—and he wasn't even in the state! Said we'd tricked Mama so she couldn't carry out her real wishes. Honestly, I don't know where he got the idea that he'd get everything...she left him *nothin'!* Even the money he was supposed to have in trust was left to my discretion. She didn't guarantee him a single thing."

"Did you know that before you saw the will?" Maiden kept her eyes large and ingenuous.

"I did. Mama made that will a few years ago, after Bradley dropped out of veterinary school. She was furious with him for that." He nodded his thanks when Gloria handed him a cup of coffee. "I wouldn't have left him with nothin', but if I just handed him a load of cash he and Ree would spend it in a few months and he'd be back askin' for more. I'd always planned to let him keep the house and car I let him use, maybe some investments for the future. But now...well, now I think I have to be done with him entirely."

They were all respectfully silent after that somber and doubtless painful admission. Maiden was looking between Elvan and her aunt. Bella was smiling gently at him as she slid her hand over his, Elvan glanced at her and his eyes instantly softened.

They were so obviously in love that Maiden felt intrusive watching the wordless exchange. She lowered her gaze to her hands.

Gloria broke the silence gracefully when she stood long enough to bring a platter of cookies to the table and set it in front of the them. Bella smiled at her sister and snaffled a chocolate chip cookie from the edge of the plate. Elvan took a deep breath and a snickerdoodle.

"I did my best to calm the boy down," he shook his head helplessly. "I pointed out that Mama was past the point mentally where she would have been able to make such drastic changes without a legal challenge. Mr. Edmonds backed me up on that."

"Not much comfort to a guy who's convinced he'd almost got his hands on a fortune," Maiden said aloud before she could stop herself.

"That's true, darlin'. He gnashed his teeth and swore black and blue that she was smart as a whip and sharp as could be." Elvan tsked. "Never mind that he's the one who said she was losing her marbles when she took his summerhouse away after he dropped out of college. Oh, didn't he go on about that 'senile old biddy'!"

"Do you think he could've actually harmed her though?" Maiden frowned uncertainly. "Especially if she hadn't changed her will yet?"

"Well...I wouldn't have thought so until I found out what he'd been schemin' with Ree. I never thought he'd turn on me that much, but Ree certainly would and he was raised mostly by her." He sighed and shook his head. "I shouldn't have allowed it I guess, but it's hard when the child says he wants to live with his mama. Was I supposed to force him? Hell, I guess I should've."

"But the will—" Maiden prompted.

"Honey," he gave her a tolerant look, "trust me, if Ms. Ree was the brains behind this scheme, it's a wonder the twit didn't accidently murder himself. They thought she'd already changed the will. You were there when she waltzed in thinkin' she owned the place."

Maiden had to concede that point at least. She fell silent as the older ones tried to steer the conversation in a more positive direction. They were discussing what Elvan and Bella would do once they were free to leave. There was talk of a honeymoon cruise or maybe a scenic tour of the Swiss Alps but Maiden wasn't listening.

She was thinking about Bradley, Ree and Agnes. Was it that simple? Could the whole solution to Gail's murder come down to two or even three greedy schemers that were too inept to get the plan right?

It was possible; it was ideal actually. It would mean the case was as good as closed, Aunt Bella was safe and she was achingly close to being in David's arms again.

No. It's not that easy. she told herself. *Something's wrong here somewhere.*

It occurred to Maiden that, whether he had successfully inherited the Hedgewick fortune or not, there wasn't enough evidence against Bradley. He had no one to vouch for him at the time of the murder and lied about it; that made him very suspicious but it didn't make him guilty.

She suspected that the main reason he was still in jail was because no one had paid his bail. David said he hadn't sent for a lawyer, doubtless because he couldn't afford one. Ree would only have the money she sponged off Bradley, which wouldn't have been much and was probably nothing now that she'd had to bail herself out.

She wasn't sure what Agnes' angle would be now that the cold hard facts of the will were known, but it would doubtless cool any passion she'd felt towards a man like Bradley. She knew that was ungenerous, but any guy that had tried that hard to see down her dress all through his father's wedding reception was hardly a prized catch for the woman sitting upstairs looking after his grandmother.

"Hey, Elvan," Maiden asked slowly. "Was Agnes staying with Gail?"

"Yes." He nodded. "It made more sense to have her under the same roof. Mama wasn't strong enough to live alone."

"Where exactly was that?"

Chapter Twenty

Maiden parked her dark green sedan across the street and down a bit from the Golden Oaks hotel. She rarely visited the competition and she'd already seen more of this particular specimen than she'd ever wanted to.

She did her best to banish the memory of having nearly been violently killed in one of the modern, well-appointed suites not all that long ago. Whatever else could be said about the place, it was one of the nicest and most expensive hotels in Golden Glen, which made it a natural choice for Gail Hedgewick.

Maiden waited, slumped down in the driver's seat with a scarf wrapped around her neck and pulled up to cover the lower half of her face. She held a fashion magazine as casually as she could while she watched the front doors. She sat for over an hour as guests came and went.

Every patron she saw strut out into the autumnal sunshine was well-dressed and obviously wealthy. Except for one tiny middle-class sparrow who finally emerged through the high, sparkling-clean glass doors.

Maiden noted that Agnes had taken a bit of extra effort with her appearance today. Apart from shedding her temporarily irrelevant uniform, she'd applied a lot of makeup and her smartly bobbed hair was shiny and perfect. Her clothes looked decent but nothing fancy, they weren't a far cry from the selections Maiden had in her own wardrobe. Nice enough and definitely affordable.

Maiden admired the lady's cute little pink dress. It was flouncy and flirty were it peeked out from behind her long black swing coat. Both garments barely brushed her knees and were cut loose enough to showcase her delicate, rather waifish build.

Agnes dashed across the road and slid into her blue rental car. A moment later it came to life with an anemic purr and pulled out into the attractively tree-lined street.

Maiden had never tailed anyone before but this seemed like the ideal time to learn the skill. She did her best to stay back far enough to avoid being spotted while not so far back that she lost sight of her quarry. It wasn't easy and she didn't flatter herself that she was particularly good at it.

She still managed to keep tabs on Agnes as she wove through town and finally parked in front of another expensive hotel. Maiden glanced up at the stolid and formidable Hendrick Apartments.

With apartments that came complete with laundry facilities and full kitchens, it catered to people that liked their privacy and a completely self-contained environment. Surrounded by parks and a few walking trails, Hendricks was far enough away from the center of town to afford peace and quiet. And anonymity.

Maiden parked a few spots back and watched Agnes saunter over with a particular swagger in her step. She walked through the outer door and up to the grid of call buttons on the wall.

Maiden leaned forward for a better view as Agnes pressed one of the buttons and started talking. Maiden watched as the lady made a face at whatever she heard in reply but she just folded her arms and waited.

A few minutes later, Agnes glanced over her shoulder and smiled. Maiden felt her breath catch and her eyes widen when she and Pierce walked outside together. She hadn't thought that they'd be particularly acquainted, but she supposed he would have met her every time he visited his grandmother.

But Pierce didn't look very pleased to see the young nurse, even though Agnes was chatting away happily and hadn't stopped smiling since he joined her.

As the pair walked to an adjoining park, Maiden found herself wondering why Pierce chose this hotel rather than one of the other options that were closer to town and the rest of his family. She then recalled that she'd met the rest of his family; it started to make more sense.

This meeting with Agnes threw a different and potentially dangerous light on things, however. Maiden hid behind her magazine again as she watched them settle on a bench, fairly close to each other, and fall into a more intent discussion.

Agnes was still smiling and shaking her head innocently as she looked at him through her false eyelashes. She touched a hand to her chest and then to his as she shook her head earnestly.

Pierce was watching her with a coolly indifferent expression. Whatever Agnes was saying to him didn't appear to capture his interest. They spoke a bit longer but Pierce's demeanor never softened.

Finally, he shook his head and laughed at whatever she'd said. It became obvious that she hadn't been regaling him with her best knock-knock jokes as Agnes got to her feet with an irate expression. She pointed a finger at Pierce and said something through gritted teeth. Pierce merely shrugged and waved her on her way.

Maiden stared and sank deeper into her scarf as Agnes stalked angrily back to her car and climbed inside. She slammed the door so loudly that Maiden jumped at the resounding bang. She slid her gaze back to Pierce as Agnes started her car and drove off.

Pierce watched until the car disappear around a corner. A faint, coldly amused smile passed over his features as he stood and strolled calmly back to his hotel.

Once he'd slipped back inside, Maiden took a deep breath and forced herself to relax a bit. She wasn't sure what exactly she'd just seen, but she was sure that it was significant.

Could she have misjudged Agnes' interest in Bradley? Was it possible that the nurse had actually been plotting with Pierce? If so, what was Pierce's angle and why did they seem to be at odds now?

Maiden shook her head slightly and lowered her gaze to her magazine only to see that it was upside down.

"Oh, you idiot!" she muttered to herself and threw it into the passenger footwell.

She was about to start her car and head off herself when her phone rang. She fished it out of her pocket and looked at Aunt Bella's name on the display.

"Hey, Aunt Bella," she said quietly as she peered watchfully at the door of Pierce's hotel. "Everything okay?"

"Yes, baby," Bella said brightly. "Listen, Elvan and I are going to have dinner in town and then head over to the house he and Bradley had been stayin' in. You wanna come eat with us and then go sniff around for clues?"

"You make me sound like a bloodhound," she said dryly. "Yes, I'd love to come."

***

After dinner, Maiden drove with Bella and Elvan to his rental. Situated only a few streets away from Harlow House, it was a handsome and well-kept colonial style home that was far larger than two bachelors likely needed for a weekend.

They parked in front of the house and Maiden forced herself to abandon the luxurious embrace of Elvan's car. They walked up the front path, alongside the well-groomed lawn. Maiden quietly admired the stately exterior of the old house while Elvan pulled out his key and unlocked the door.

Elvan gestured for the ladies to walk in first. Maiden led the way, scanning the entryway as she stepped inside. She found herself in a large living area and quickly noted a long hallway on the back wall that led into the inner reaches of the house. The front room was decorated in many shades of cream and there was a lot of spindly, antique furniture. It was very nice; exactly the sort of genteel 'bachelor pad' that a southern gentleman like Elvan would choose.

Maiden was vaguely aware of Bella and Elvan following her inside and locking the door behind them. Her mind had quickly shifted back to her purpose in coming—clues.

She wasn't sure what she could expect to find there, but she was hoping for something that might further any of her brewing suspicions. Any evidence of a connection between Bradley and Agnes would be helpful, or any sign that Ree had been in the house at some point.

Maiden left Elvan and Bella to sit and chat in the living room while she headed down the hallway and started peering around. She wasn't sure which room was Bradley's, but it didn't overly matter, she planned to look in all of them as long as she had the opportunity.

She walked past the kitchen and peered inside. It was more modern than the rest of the house but that was a common casualty for older homes. People wanted charm but also crisp and clean practicality. Her eyes flitted over the shiny white cupboards and stone countertops and on to a door at the back of the room. From what she'd seen of the layout from the outside, she guessed that it opened out into the garage.

Doubting that Bradley or his potential cohorts did much of their own cooking, she decided not to start in the kitchen. She continued down the hallway and was about to open the next door when she heard a scuffling from across the hall.

Maiden froze and slowly turned to look at the opposite door. She waited a moment until she heard it again, the unmistakable sound of footsteps and the creak of a floorboard or two. Her heart thumped loudly as she crept closer and listened carefully. She heard what sounded like a drawer opening.

A moment later she heard Aunt Bella's distinctive tread coming down the hallway. Maiden glanced over sharply to see both her and Elvan drawing closer. She held up a hand to stop them and then quickly put a finger to her lips.

They stopped and Elvan shook his head in silent question. Maiden pointed at the door and mouthed the words: *Someone's in there!*

Bella's eyes narrowed, she tiptoed closer and reached for the doorknob. Maiden, conscious of the potential to gain information provided they didn't blunder in like a herd of elephants grasped her by the wrist. They needed to learn who was there and why, not just chase them off.

When Bella and Elvan obligingly hesitated, she wrapped her fingers around the doorknob herself and gave it a careful twist. She opened it a crack and peered inside.

The room was dark except for the small flashlight that the intruder was holding as they looked down into a drawer. Maiden took a steadying breath and slid her hand in far enough to flick on the lights.

The stranger looked up sharply and immediately ran for the open window that had doubtless been their entry point. Whoever it was, they wore a knitted ski mask and a bulky jacket with a hood. They also moved fast as they slid out the window and ran off.

Maiden hurried over and peered out into the darkness. She saw a flash of movement as someone ducked between the neighboring houses and dashed out of sight. She quickly dismissed any thought of following; she knew she wouldn't be able to catch the person and she was quite curious about what they'd been looking at.

"What's goin' on?!" Bella demanded as she and Elvan got tired of waiting and burst into the room.

"Someone was snooping around in here," Maiden said as she eased closer to the large dresser that the stranger had been fiddling with.

It was a tall chest with eight chunky drawers sitting in rows of two. A few of them were ajar, most notably the top left. Maiden eased closer and peeked inside. She held her breath but did her best not to react in any other way.

"We'd probably better not touch anything and call the police," she said as she turned her back to the heavy piece of furniture.

"You're right," Elvan nodded. "Maybe you could call the captain for us?"

"I'll do that right now," Maiden nodded as she pulled out her phone. "Maybe wait in the living room, I'll be right out."

Bella took Elvan's hand and they both stepped out of the room. Maiden gave them a moment to get down the hall and then called David.

"Hey, what's up?" there was a smile in his voice and she noticed he didn't greet her by name this time.

If only this were that sort of call, she sighed inwardly.

"Um, we're at Elvan's rental house," she whispered and peered out into the hallway to ensure no one had snuck back to listen in. "I caught an intruder in one of the bedrooms."

"What?" All trace of good humor in his tone was instantly gone. "Are you all right?"

"Yeah, they ran out pretty quick," she assured him as she snuck back to the half-open drawer. "It's weird though, I don't think they were here to take anything, I think they left something that they wanted to be found."

"And what's that?" he asked.

"A will."

***

David mobilized quickly and was soon at Elvan's rental house with Smith and Parker in tow. He knocked and announced their arrival even as he walked through the unlocked front door. He scanned the interior and noticed that Maiden was sitting safely with Elvan and Bella in the stodgy parlor.

He'd already seen the house. They'd searched Bradley's room soon after his arrest and found nothing of particular note. He was curious where Maiden found this so-called will. Maiden stood as soon as she saw them and nodded towards the hallway.

"It's just through here," she said, sliding Bella and Elvan a watchful look before locking her eyes with his.

David frowned faintly until he realized why she looked uneasy.

You haven't told them you saw a will, you didn't know what they'd do so you didn't tell them. You came straight to me...I need to buy you some pink roses, woman. He stared at her for a second. Maiden, apparently reading his mind at will, gave him a sort of wincing shrug and turned to lead the way.

David pushed aside a lot of thoughts that were remarkably unhelpful at the moment and followed, gesturing for Smith and Parker to do likewise. He smiled faintly when, as he'd suspected, Maiden went straight to Bradley's bedroom and turned to him.

"I saw the person in here," she said quietly and waited for him to walk past.

David stepped into the room and looked it over. The place wasn't trashed but it appeared lightly rifled. Or like someone had tried to make it *look* rifled. The main object that had been disturbed was a large oak dresser.

David knew for a fact that his officers had already searched it. They certainly hadn't come across a will during their sweep, but he knew he was about to now. David glanced back at Smith.

"Gloves," he said and turned to Bella and Elvan where they stood hovering behind Parker. "Did anyone touch anything?"

"No sir," Elvan shook his head. "And I never went in that room before today, it was Bradley's."

David saw Maiden look at him sharply when that was confirmed, he gave her a subtle wink and simply nodded in reply to Elvan. David accepted the gloves from Smith and pulled them on as he walked over to the dresser.

"Right, let's hear it," he murmured as he turned to Maiden and suppressed a pleased smile. "What exactly happened?"

"We came here so Elvan could pick up a few things that he and Bradley left behind," she rubbed her arms and looked at the top left drawer. "I heard someone in here and turned on the light. They ran out through the window."

"Good thing they didn't panic and attack you," he tried to keep the cautionary chiding as inoffensive as possible.

"Glad you think so," she replied dryly.

"Could you describe this person?" he asked.

"They had a mask and a big bulky coat on," she sighed.

"All right, let's see what they were up to." He opened the drawer wide.

The drawer was empty except for a couple of sweaters, a few pairs of socks and a slim stack of papers. David pulled out the stack and set it on top of the dresser. He frowned faintly and pensively as he started reading through it. Maiden had crept closer and now stood on tiptoe beside him. He stilled and his whole body tensed when he felt her brush against his bicep.

"That had better be your arm, Harlow," he whispered warningly, even as he caught a teasing whiff of her perfume.

Maiden frowned uncertainly but then glanced down to where an entirely different part of her anatomy was pressed against him. She grinned mischievously and took a meager little half-step to her right. He forced his gaze onto the document in front of him and did his best not to smile back.

By then Bella and Elvan had slipped a few steps inside; he was grateful for the interruption.

"What's that?" Bella asked cautiously.

"According to this, it's the last will and testament of Abigail Lenore Hedgewick." David replied.

"Is it?!" Maiden made a pathetic effort to sound startled. David shut his eyes for a moment and glanced at the opposite wall.

"Oh really?" Elvan quirked a dubious brow and held his hand out for the papers. "May I have a look?"

"You can't handle evidence, sorry," David shook his head, "but you can take a quick look at it here."

Elvan gave an appreciative nod and stood at his other side. David turned through the pages while Elvan and Maiden looked on. The will was written by hand and emphatically left absolutely everything to Bradley. Not only was there no provision made for any other family member, but there was a specific declaration that nothing was to be given to Elvan or Pierce. It was signed in Gail Hedgewick's name.

David took a moment to study the flowery, distinctly feminine signature and then glanced at the words above it.

"Do you recognize this handwriting?" he asked.

"It's been a while since I've seen it, but it honestly looks like Ree's," Elvan sighed. "That stack of hate sounds like her too. That woman makes me sick...poor Mama."

"Anyone know where Ree is at the moment?" Maiden asked quietly.

"She's laid pretty low since she bailed herself out," David said as he tidied the pages. "But wherever she is now, we'll find her."

CHAPTER TWENTY-ONE

Maiden, Bella and Elvan got back to the inn later than expected. Bella led the way straight to her sister and proceeded to tell her the whole story. Gloria was suitably horrified and disgusted with the endless font of scoundrels and thieving liars that kept spewing out into the world.

The ensuing discussion was loud and lengthy. Maiden, Vonny and Alfie sat quietly in the living room petting kittens while the southern contingent vented their outrage. Maiden excused herself and went to bed at the first opportunity.

She got up extra early the next morning and slipped downstairs unnoticed. She had work to do and didn't need to be waylaid with questions. She'd already lain awake for ages thinking about what had happened.

Confronting an intruder was unsettling. David's subtle warning hadn't gone unnoticed, and she was glad she hadn't been alone. But in this case, she didn't believe she was the one that had been at risk.

The more she'd thought about it, the more certain Maiden felt that it was Agnes she'd seen sneak out of Bradley's window. The quick glimpse she'd gotten suggested that it was most likely her or Marti Drake, and Marti certainly wouldn't be trying to help Bradley inherit anything.

She crept through the foyer and past the front desk. No one was up and around yet, everything was still and silent. She slipped out through the office door, pausing just long enough to grab her jacket and her favorite scarf, and climbed into her car. It was a cold gray morning, a glance at the sky told her rain was imminent.

Maiden drove across town to the Golden Oaks hotel, parked across the street, and waited. She was curious to know what Agnes' next move would be now that she'd rather clumsily planted an alternate will. Maiden shook her head as she thought it over.

She was certainly no legal expert, but it seemed like a crudely hand-written will stuffed in a random drawer wouldn't easily overturn an official document that had been lodged with an actual lawyer. But what if it could? What if they confirmed Gail's signature and it was enough to tie everything up in court for years?

Maiden pushed those worries aside, fretting and imagining the worst wouldn't help anyone. She hunkered down into her jacket, there was a definite nip in the air today and she hadn't thought to bring coffee with her.

It didn't matter, she didn't expect to wait for long. If it had been Agnes that placed that will, she'd be anxious to find out if her efforts had paid off. She'd also taken a huge risk; for all she knew Elvan might have found the will and just destroyed it. She'd have to make sure, she was in too deep to leave it alone now.

Half an hour later, Maiden's patience was rewarded. She saw Agnes, wearing a familiar big black coat over jeans and a sweater, come dashing out of the hotel lobby. Maiden distantly wondered who was paying for her stay. Surely Gail hadn't booked in for anything after the wedding, and it wasn't likely that Agnes could afford to stay there herself. Gail wouldn't have paid her *that* well. Maiden suspected that Gail's credit card was still working, or that Agnes planned to be long gone before the hotel tried to charge it.

Maiden was distracted when Agnes got in her car and headed off down the street. She slid her perfectly unremarkable sedan out into the morning traffic and followed. She was convinced that Agnes was meeting an accomplice, and she really believed that it would be Ree.

This time, Agnes headed for the park across from the police station. That struck Maiden as being pretty gutsy, but Agnes was shaping up to be more brazenly devious than she'd initially considered.

Agnes parked her car under some big shade trees and stepped out as casually as someone who was there for a morning stroll. Maiden pulled in a fair distance away and watched her make her way towards the benches near the heart of the well-manicured park.

Maiden tried to look casual as she climbed out of her own car. She wrapped her forest green scarf around her throat and the lower half of her face, the soft knitted wool was warm and, more importantly, concealing. She doubted Ree would have taken enough notice of her to recognize her now, but Agnes would. She needed to be careful.

She spied a cluster of trees and strolled towards it. By the time she'd ducked behind the gloriously fat trunk of a very old elm, a stiff breeze had started to blow. Maiden glanced up at the sky to find it growing even more foreboding. She could only hope that the autumn rains would hold off long enough for Agnes to get on with whatever she was doing.

Agnes sat gingerly on a nearby bench. She too looked up at the sky as she shivered at the sudden drop in temperature. The small woman tucked down into her coat and tapped her foot impatiently.

Maiden watched her look off to the right and sit a bit straighter. She followed her gaze and nearly shouted *Ah ha!* when she saw Ree Hedgewick approaching. Fortunately, she managed to keep her mouth shut as a scowling Ree sauntered closer and sat beside Agnes on the bench. Both women looked tense and irate.

"You shouldn't be callin' me," Ree said tightly.

"I wouldn't have had to if you'd given me updates like you were supposed to," Agnes shot back before pulling in a calming breath. "But it's done and we've got more work to do, so let's get on with it."

"I don't take orders from you, missy!" Ree snarled, her bright coral lipstick emphasizing her disdain. "Watch how you talk to me."

"Hold on there, honey," Agnes glared back. "I'm in this as deep as Bradley is and definitely deeper than *you*! I will not be left out now that it's all coming together, and I won't be threatened either, is that understood?"

"Is it what?!" Ree spluttered in startled anger.

As Maiden quietly observed she couldn't help thinking that neither woman would make for the nicest in-law, she also doubted that it would ever actually be a problem for them. She didn't know what Agnes was expecting from Bradley, but she doubted the woman would ever be his wife.

"Don't get snarky with me, Ms. Ree," Agnes clearly wasn't afraid to show her claws today. "I've taken all the risk and done all the dirty work to get this mess back on track. All *you've* done is make it worse! What were you thinking by barging in and telling Elvan everything?!"

"I don't explain myself to little snips like you," Ree said grimly. "Don't you try to upstage me. Bradley will always side with his mama, and don't you forget it!"

"I seriously doubt that Bradley is too impressed at the moment," Agnes muttered. "Not since his *mama* blabbed the whole plan to Elvan! You just had to go in and gloat, didn't you? You didn't even know if you'd won yet! Well, thanks to you, it's all or nothing now, literally. And, frankly, I doubt you're smart enough to steer it home from here without me."

Maiden pressed her lips together at that scathing remark. She chanced a look at Ree and wasn't surprised to see that she was growing increasingly angry. Perhaps more chillingly, Ree didn't argue this time. She looked Agnes over and folded her arms.

Agnes took her silence as some sort of admission of defeat. She smiled smugly and raised her chin so she could look down at the older woman.

"Good, we understand each other at last," she said sweetly. "Now, once again, I'm the one making things happen. All we have to do now is get Bradley to tell the police about the second will. After that, we let the lawyers battle it out and wait for the money to come rolling in."

"Fine, just fine," Ree nodded tersely and got to her feet. "I'll talk to Bradley right now."

"You do that," Agnes sniffed as she also stood, "and then you send me a message and tell me how it went. I don't expect to have to chase you again, Ree."

Ree inclined her head stiffly and stalked off towards the police station. Agnes watched her for a minute and then turned and started back towards her car.

Maiden edged around the big tree, trying to stay out of sight. Agnes was halfway to her car when Maiden's phone started ringing. She gasped and struggled to pull it out of her pocket. In that moment of panic-induced awkwardness, she dropped to the ground and fumbled with the phone as if she'd never before seen such wonders.

Darn it, darn it, darn it! she grumbled as she finally remembered there were volume buttons on the side. She held her breath as she mashed the down button until the piercingly loud ring was finally silenced.

She glanced cautiously around the tree and saw Agnes climbing into her car. Maiden sighed and nearly collapsed with relief. She glanced down at her phone to see who had called and nearly blown her cover. It was David; she bit her lip and glanced over at the police station.

Ree had nearly reached the front door. Maiden wondered if she could use the missed call as an excuse to stop by. He might believe it...even if he didn't, he probably wouldn't throw her out.

***

Maiden walked into the police station just as Nancy was escorting Ree down the hallway to the left, towards the holding cells. Maiden glanced away, hoping to avoid Ree's notice on the off chance she remembered her. David was standing at the desk and smiled faintly when he saw her.

"Hey Harlow," he said. "I just tried calling you."

"Did you?" she asked ingenuously as she pulled out her phone and looked at it. "Oh, I have it on silent. Silly me. Was that Ree Hedgewick that just walked past?"

"Yes, she came to see Bradley," he quirked a brow as he glanced down the hall. "I don't think it's a coincidence that she's turned up the day after that will did."

"Yeah, that would be pretty unlikely," she agreed as she glanced around the empty lobby and took a step closer. "Have you got a minute?"

"Yes." He smiled faintly. "That's why I called you."

"Good," she forced herself to ignore the heat in his gaze and plunged straight in. "I overheard Ree and Agnes talking outside."

"What?" The warmth in his eyes abruptly cooled. "How did you happen to hear that?"

"That's not the point." She waved it away. "Ree and Agnes were arguing about who'd done what and who Bradley will side with. Then Agnes said she'd been doing all the heavy lifting and Ree got really cranky. She's here to tell Bradley to report that there's another will. Have you already told him you found it? What about...okay, you're just scowling at me now. What's the problem?"

"What's the problem?! You keep butting in!" he whispered irately. "I give you an inch and you run with it, every time!"

"You didn't give me anything." She blinked questioningly at him. "I did it without asking. And it worked; why does that bother you?"

He shut his eyes briefly, she could almost hear him counting to ten in his head. She nearly cringed when she felt a smirk curl her lips against her will, or at least her better judgement. When he opened his eyes again he wrapped his big hand around the back of her neck and pulled her gently closer.

"Do you have any idea," he whispered as he lowered his head slightly, "how much I let you get away with?"

You're letting me get away with helping you? Thanks, that sounds reasonable...it's a good thing you're hot. Maiden knew she was still smirking and it didn't bother her at all. Whether he ever admitted it or not, she'd teased out some incredibly useful information more than once.

"I guess I'm just nothing but trouble." She eased closer and slid her hand up his chest, she felt his muscles tense slightly under her touch. "While we're talking about it though, you might want to ask Agnes how she feels about Pierce."

"Why?" he asked cautiously.

"No reason in particular." She shifted closer still. "But you could mention to her that someone saw her drive to Pierce's apartment across town and have a very tense discussion with him."

"You didn't." David stared at her. "You didn't actually follow a suspect. Tell me you didn't do that."

"Is she a suspect? You don't seem to believe anything I tell you, so how was I to know?" Maiden nestled against him. "You're welcome, by the way."

"Harlow—" he began through clenched teeth.

"You're right, I don't know why you still speak to me at all," she interrupted and touched her fingertips to his jaw. "Incidentally, did you forget to shave this morning?"

"No, I was just in a hurry today," he said as he ran a hand over his stubbled jaw. "Does it look rugged?"

"It looks scratchy," she murmured, eyeing him with mild concern.

"I think I can handle it, Harlow." He smiled faintly.

"I wasn't thinking of you, to be honest." She absently touched the sensitive skin of her throat and tried not to wince at the thought of his stiff whiskers rubbing her raw.

David stilled and grinned at her when he realized what she meant.

"It gets softer as it grows out," he said.

"And much smoother when it's shaved off," she replied with a dainty shrug.

David quirked a brow at the tone of Maiden's voice, it was clearly a little too chiding for his liking. He propped an elbow casually on the high desk.

"I'm actually thinking of growing a mustache," he said a little too placidly.

Maiden eased back a step and looked him over, he kept his expression cool and confident.

"Um…" She took a moment to choose her words carefully. "That might not be the best look on you."

"Maybe. One way to find out," he said with a smile.

"I don't like mustaches," she said plainly.

"I might grow a full beard, in fact," he said as though inspiration had just struck. "A big bushy beard, something I can braid if I want to."

Maiden rested a hand on her full hip and exhaled slowly through her nose.

"That's interesting, and it's certainly none of my business what you decide to do. Actually, I was thinking I might cut my hair short." She smiled and held her hand up to her jaw line. "About to here. I think it'll look nice."

"Not funny," he said simply.

"Who said I was joking?" She lifted a shoulder serenely. "I might dye it bright orange too."

"Don't," he said with a hint of warning.

"Why not?" she asked casually. "It's my hair, I can do what I want with it. Besides, it might look great. One way to find out."

"I'll arrest you," he said seriously.

"For a haircut?" She folded her arms loosely.

"I'll come up with another reason." He waved it away without concern.

"That sounds reasonable. Or you can shave tomorrow," she said mildly and smiled warmly at him. "I wonder which option you'll choose."

He held her gaze intently and then started to smile. He glanced around to make sure they were still alone before standing close and lowering his head a bit more.

"Could we discuss this in my office?" he asked quietly, his lips just brushing against hers as he spoke. Maiden's eyes flew to his.

"Aren't you worried about what people will think?" she asked teasingly.

"I'm warming to your idea of doing what we want and then lying about it." He grinned shamelessly.

"That's not exactly what I said," she did her best not to laugh.

"Yes, it is," he countered and slid his other hand to her waist.

They'd just started to kiss when they heard a door down the hall open. David stood up straight and gently slapped her hands away before closing the perpetually undone buttons at the top of his shirt. Maiden turned away quickly but still barely muffled her laughter at his absurdly demure expression.

They both subdued their amusement just in time for Nancy to walk back in through the long hallway on the left. Her usual knowing smile had been supplanted by a look of mild caution as she glanced at David. Maiden quickly realized why when Ree came charging out after her and headed straight for the handsome cop beside her.

"Captain, thank goodness!" she breathed as she sailed up to the desk and gripped the edge tightly. "It's Bradley, he's got a couple things he needs to tell you. It's *very* important."

David didn't reply beyond quirking a brow and walking off towards the lockup area. Maiden became conveniently absorbed in readjusting her belt buckle so he couldn't give her a warning look. Once she heard the door shut behind him, she glanced up and smiled politely at Ree.

Just as she'd hoped, no sign of recognition registered on the other woman's face as she met her gaze. Maiden leaned against the desk and decided to push the boundaries a tiny bit more.

"Sounds like you're having a rough day," she said sympathetically.

"A rough life is more like it," Ree heaved a dramatic sigh. "The stories I could tell would curl anybody's hair. And this latest bit of trouble ain't any better."

"You mean your son being in jail?" she asked.

"Worse than that!" Her beady eyes narrowed. "Who robs a man's family while he's stuck in jail on false charges?!"

"Robs him?" Maiden felt her left eyebrow raise as the situation started to take on a very different angle. "That's awful, who would do that?"

"His own grandmother's nurse!" Ree said as an angry flush hit her cheeks. "Horrible little twit of a woman! She stole from her employer the night she was murdered!"

"Oh!" Maiden looked appropriately shocked. "Are you absolutely sure of that?"

"Bradley saw her do it," Ree folded her arms and nodded firmly. "Snuck down the stairs with Gail's diamond ring!"

Maiden quickly swallowed the urge to ask her which one; it didn't matter at the moment. Clearly Agnes had outlived her usefulness as far as Bradley and Ree were concerned. Ree was warming to the topic and absently fiddled with the ring on her own finger as she spoke.

"Only reason he didn't mention it before was because he felt sorry for her, he hadn't realized at the time that it might be connected to the murder."

"Didn't he?" Maiden shook her head slightly at that stupidly unbelievable claim. "Interesting. So, had this nurse ever seemed untrustworthy before?"

"Now that I think about it, yes," Ree slid closer and lowered her voice a little. "Bradley did say that this so-called Agnes was always lurkin' around Gail, and always tryin' to eavesdrop."

"Scary stuff," Maiden murmured as she recalled seeing the young nurse doing just that the night of the rehearsal. Of course, so had she. "You think she was hovering around Gail looking for a chance to rob her?"

"Absolutely," Ree scoffed. "Robbin' a helpless old woman wouldn't bother her none! I'll bet she only stuck around as long as she did because of the new will."

"A new will?" Maiden asked smoothly.

"Yup, the one Gail signed before she died," Ree said with a glint in her eye. "It was hidden away so no one knew about it."

"Then how do you know about it?"

"Um...Bradley told me," Ree said after a telling pause. "Gail promised him that she'd changed her will. She wrote it out herself and signed it, then she gave it to him for safe keepin'."

"Just before she was murdered, right?" Maiden asked and watched Ree's triumphant smile shrink. She also noticed Nancy shuffling beside her and staring down at the desk. "I did hear a rumor that someone broke into Bradley's room. Do you think they were after the will?"

"I don't doubt it," Ree huffed. "And I'll bet you it was Elvan that did it! He'll be sweatin' now that we got the *real* will!"

"But Elvan rented that house," Maiden said mildly, "he had a key. Why would he break in?"

"Maybe...to make it look suspicious?" Ree suggested.

"And then left the will there to be found?" Maiden asked. "Wouldn't he have just destroyed it and not mentioned it to anyone?"

"Well," Ree shifted her weight from one foot to the other and glanced furtively towards the front door, doubtless wishing she'd kept her mouth shut and just left. "I don't really know about that."

"Do you suppose someone else might have done it?" Maiden asked and then frowned gently in evident concern. "Maybe someone else that wanted to hurt you?"

From the corner of her eye she saw Nancy suppress a smile and stare down at a letter she wasn't possibly reading. Maiden knew she was probing more than was necessary, but it wasn't as if Ree was likely to blather all this information to David.

"Any number of people might want to hurt me," Ree rolled her eyes and pursed her lips thoughtfully. "Pierce maybe, that spoiled brat hates my guts. He won't get nothin' under the new will either. Not a blasted cent."

"So, you've seen the will?" Maiden blinked at her. "Oh wow, that's handy. Did Gail tell you about it?"

"Uh, yes," Ree stood a bit straighter. "She did, a while ago, I don't remember exactly when."

"And then she gave it to Bradley?" Maiden kept her smile friendly. "It's a shame, though, that she didn't send it to her lawyer, that would've made things easier for you."

"What do you mean?" Ree frowned.

"Well, just finding a few pieces of handwritten paper isn't a sure thing, is it?" she rested her elbow on the desk and her chin in her hand. "Not when the existing will was officially drafted, notarized and witnessed. Was the new will witnessed?"

"How would I know?" Ree grumbled, she was looking a little less cheerful now. "What difference does it make as long as it's dated after the other one?"

"But if it wasn't witnessed, how can you prove what date it was actually signed on?" Maiden kept smiling.

"Who are you exactly?" It finally occurred to her to ask. "I reckon I've seen you somewhere before."

"She's the captain's girlfriend," Nancy supplied with a placid smile, "you may have spotted her at some point."

Maiden pressed her lips together to hide her growing smile, she hoped she wasn't blushing. Ree didn't seem to notice, she had her own concerns brewing.

"How cute. I gotta go." Ree glared at Maiden and then grasped her purse tightly. She turned and stormed out without another word.

Nancy waited until the door fell shut again before glancing over at Maiden.

"You'd make a pretty handy lawyer, Miss Harlow," she suggested with a smile.

"Provided all the defendants are as cunning as she is," Maiden said dryly as she nodded towards Ree's retreating back. "I'll consider it if my reception job doesn't work out."

"Mm," Nancy mused. "You think the new will is a fake then?"

"A will that was shoved in a sock drawer after a break-in where nothing was stolen?" Maiden considered her calmly. "A handwritten, unwitnessed will claiming to strip everyone else of millions of dollars and funnel it all to the creep whose room it was conveniently found in? The same creep who suddenly decided to mention that he saw someone steal a ring from his murdered grandmother because it now occurs to him that it might be suspicious?"

Nancy said nothing but was grinning at her now. Maiden smiled faintly.

"I guess anything is possible," she said with a shrug.

Chapter Twenty-Two

"You actually saw her take the ring?" David knew he sounded skeptical but the claim Bradley just made certainly warranted it.

"I saw her walk out of Granny's room holdin' somethin' shiny," he said as he stared somberly down at his feet, "I looked closer and saw that it was one of her rings."

"You didn't confront her about it?"

"No, I didn't," he sighed wearily.

"And you're only reporting it now?" David asked.

"Yeah, I thought maybe she was desperate, and well, then I got arrested and it clean slipped my mind," he said. "Losin' Granny and then bein' blamed for it was bad enough...but Mama just told me that she saw Agnes walkin' out of a pawnshop."

"Which shop was that?" David asked impassively, despite knowing there was only one pawnshop in town.

"I don't know, she didn't say." He shook his head. "But I'm worried that another piece of Granny's legacy is gone for good now."

"Well, we'll do what we can about that." David shrugged and started to turn for the door.

"Wait a minute, Captain!" Bradley spoke up quickly. "That wasn't all I needed to tell you."

David hid a smile as he turned back to face him. Bradley looked as haggard as ever but there was a definite change in his countenance. He looked pleased, maybe even eager, despite his efforts to hide it.

David had deliberately refrained from mentioning the second will yet. He wasn't sure how much Bradley actually knew about it but he doubted he was ignorant of its existence. He was confident, however, that the intruder Maiden and her friends chased out of the rental house had planted the will.

It was being dusted for fingerprints at the moment, he'd planned to wait until he got a little more information before mentioning it. He also wanted to know if the man would betray his impatience and bring it up himself.

"There's something I hadn't mentioned up until now," Bradley wet his chapped lips and gripped the bars tightly, "I have Granny's real will."

"Really?" David lifted his brows inquiringly. "Where?"

"In my room, in the rental house," Bradley said. "If you go and search there, you'll find it."

"We already removed a document from Mr. Hedgewick's rented house," David informed him and noted the way the other man's eyes rounded. "It's with forensics and is being treated as evidence at the moment."

"What?" Bradley almost stammered. "Why would you be doin' that? Evidence of what? That's my Granny's will and my future you're proddin' at! What gave you any right to take it?"

"Bearing in mind that you just requested that I go and find it," David reminded him dryly before pressing on, "your father's rental was broken into last night and that particular room was the point of access used. I know from our previous search that the will was not there before, so it has to be treated as suspicious."

"'Suspicious'?!" Bradley exploded. "That's ridiculous!"

"Mr. Hedgewick," David murmured, "a crudely written document that seeks to overturn and essentially reverse the distribution of a considerable estate was found after an intruder was run out of your room. As yet there is nothing to attest to the legitimacy of the document and it has appeared under *very* strange circumstances. Did you honestly think it would slide through unchallenged?"

Bradley gritted his teeth and glanced away, his mind clearly racing as his former confidence wavered. He looked at David and narrowed his eyes.

"The will is real," he said.

"That's yet to be proven." He shrugged. "Who actually wrote it?"

"Granny did," he quickly answered.

"All right, the handwriting analysis will confirm that."

"The *what*?!" Bradley gaped at him. "Granny wrote it! She signed it! I-I saw her do it!"

"When?" David asked as he pulled his notebook from his pocket.

"I don't remember." Bradley said.

"You don't remember?" David asked slowly and deliberately. "Are you aware of how much the Hedgewick estate is worth?"

"Very aware." He glared at him.

"You're claiming that your Grandmother signed all of it over to you, exclusively," he paused for emphasis, "and you can't remember if she did it last week or last month? You think you were gifted many millions of dollars but you don't remember it clearly?"

"That ain't what I said," he muttered.

"Did she write and sign the will before or after you arrived in Golden Glen for your father's wedding?" David asked.

"I...um," Bradley glanced away and rubbed his head as though it hurt. "I don't feel too well at the moment, Captain. I ain't up to answering any more questions just yet."

Because you don't know what date your accomplice wrote on that will, and you didn't think to ask Ree. David kept his speculation internal but decided to stir the pot a bit more.

"Any idea why Agnes Gray might've planted the will for us to find?" he asked mildly.

Bradley's eyes flew to his and his face reddened.

"What did you say?" he asked softly.

"A witness claims they saw her rummaging in a drawer before climbing out of your bedroom window," David flicked through his notepad and pretended to read a few lines. "Then we conveniently found the supposed new will there. Any ideas about that?"

David watched as Bradley wrestled with a sharp and furious burst of anger. He gnashed his teeth together and his knuckles turned white as he tried to strangle the bars. He looked angry enough to kill someone.

"Well, Captain McAlister," he said at last as he raised coldly furious eyes to him once more, "I believe I have a theory."

***

Maiden was still waiting by the desk when David walked back into the lobby carrying a sheet of paper. He glanced at her but didn't smile; she felt a hint of apprehension as he neared.

"A word in my office, please." It sounded less inviting than the last time he asked.

She gave Nancy a look and a shrug and then turned to follow him. He waited for her to step inside before joining her and shutting the door behind him.

"What happened?" she asked as he turned to face her.

"What exactly did you overhear Ree and Agnes say to each other?" he asked rather than answer her.

"Agnes was getting a bit combative because she said she was doing all the planning and work while Ree blundered in and nearly ruined it all," Maiden said. "They snarled at each other a bit and both seemed paranoid that the other was trying to edge them out. But I think Agnes pushed too hard and now Ree and Bradley have turned on her."

"How do you know that?" he grumbled.

"I talked to Ree before she left," Maiden replied.

"Ree stood there in the lobby and told you they were turning against Agnes?" He folded his arms and scowled irately. "Were you asking her about it?"

You're genuinely angry about this. You're angry with me. Maiden felt a familiar pang of anxious discomfort rise up inside her. *You don't like me figuring things out...I need to stop coming to you when I learn things. Or at least not as often, maybe I shouldn't have tried to work with you so much. Oh, this is going to be tricky.*

"Are you listening?" He touched her shoulder. "You're just staring at me, are you okay?"

She hadn't realized that he'd still been talking, she'd been too lost in the old feelings of being sneered at and told off for trying to join in. She wasn't a kid and David wasn't a bully. Maybe that made it worse, she really cared about him and what he thought of her. This felt like chiding, it felt like rejection. He was telling her to get lost.

"I think I'd like to leave now," she finally managed in a rather quiet voice.

"Um…Right. You can if that's what you want," he said carefully as he threw the paper he'd been holding on his desk and grasped her arms gently. "But please don't walk out while you're angry with me."

"I'm not angry."

"Well, upset," he gave a conceding nod, "you're upset with me."

She held his gaze for a moment and then forced a weak smile. "No, I'm fine."

"Maiden," he pulled her closer and looked her in the eye, "I'm sorry. I promise I'll listen to you."

"No you won't." She hadn't meant to say it out loud and instantly regretted it.

She knew that would just annoy him and then they'd argue. She hated fighting so much, and she was really bad at it. He didn't get mad though; he actually chuckled.

"I said I will, so I will," he smiled and hugged her a bit closer. "Tell me what you think, I'm a captive audience."

"*You're* holding *me*," she pointed out.

"Which means I have a captive," he nodded in agreement, "and I'm your audience, so go ahead."

She held his gaze for a moment, he gave her a reassuring little squeeze and just waited.

"I believe that Agnes not only placed the will, but also forged Gail's signature," Maiden finally admitted.

"Why?" he asked after considering it for a moment.

"They would've brought it out sooner if it was legitimate," she explained, "and Gail was smart enough to know she couldn't just dash off a few notes and think it would hold up in court. They're desperate—Agnes is desperate—and they're taking a chance."

"Possibly. It's a risk either way though," he mused as he let his hand settle quite low on the small of her back. "If the will is authentic, it cements an incredibly strong motive for Bradley to have killed his grandmother. If it's fake, it's a case of massive fraud."

"Did you mention that to Bradley?" she asked as she slid her arms around his neck.

"Essentially, yes." He nodded. "I also told him that Agnes was identified as the intruder that was now throwing doubt on his newly found will. He quite happily fingered Agnes as a conniving gold-digger that mentally abused Gail for her own gain."

"In all fairness, that's probably true," she said with a humorless smile, "but he left out that he's exactly the same."

"Yes, but he was also angry enough to sign a statement accusing her of everything from theft to fraud and possibly accessory to a murderer." David nodded towards the paper he'd set on his desk.

"Yikes, he doesn't waste time." She bit her lip as she felt David's fingers wander. "Speaking of which, are you planning on heading much lower, Captain McAlister?"

"I'm not really working to a plan as such," he grinned in reply. "What did Ree have to say?"

"Way too much considering she was talking to a stranger," Maiden said wryly. "Agnes is right, she's a huge risk to their little game. Unfortunately for her, Bradley's a major mama's boy...are you going to arrest Agnes?"

"I'll certainly talk to her again." He shrugged, which dragged her a bit harder against him, a slow smile curved his lips. "Hey, Harlow."

"Hey, Captain," she replied warmly. "Is this another tease?"

"No," he said when she'd barely finished speaking, "this is blatant and unabashed weakness. You're wearing me down."

"And how exactly have I done that?" she almost laughed.

"Looking at me, walking in the room, not telling potential suspects about significant pieces of evidence," he mused. "Lots of ways, really."

He sank a hand deep into her long hair and kissed her. A blissful thirty seconds or so passed when they heard a loud pounding on the door. David tensed and slowly raised his head. He glanced at the door and then down at her, she knew she was scowling.

"Apparently my attention has never been needed so desperately before," he said with a rueful smile.

"It probably hasn't," she retorted dryly and with a meaningful look.

He did his best to hide his startled amusement and reluctantly let her go. He did his best to smooth down her hair where he'd ruffled it and then went and sat behind his desk just as the knock came again.

"Come in," he said steadily.

Maiden was silently grateful that she at least hadn't smeared him with red lipstick this time. As it was, when Sergeant Ramirez stepped in long enough to hand David some kind of report, he clearly had no trouble guessing what he'd interrupted. He barely looked at either of them before murmuring something to David and shuffling awkwardly out into the hall again.

"I hope it was important, at least," she sighed, more in hopes that he'd tell her what the report was about than out of any lingering annoyance.

"Fingerprint analysis of that will," he said distractedly as he read through it.

"Oh really?" She lifted her brows and kept her tone politely inquiring.

"Yeah," he flicked her a smiling look. "I'll see you around, Harlow."

"Charming," she grumbled under her breath and walked to the door. "Bye for now."

"You aren't slipping off to meet someone else for lunch again, are you?" he asked with a smile in his voice.

She stopped just long enough to make him wonder. "I'll see you around, Captain."

***

Maiden returned to the inn just as the rain finally started to fall. She scampered through the office door and looked back out through the little window at the darkened sky. She hung up her jacket and scarf on the rack beside the door and ran her fingers through her hair.

It had been a strange morning, to put it mildly. She was grateful that she'd thought to follow Agnes, her instincts had definitely paid off. She also knew that David wouldn't have told her about Bradley and Ree's double-cross. It was irrational to let that bug her, but it still did a little.

Obviously, she was a civilian and, particularly in this case, wasn't entitled to inside information. But she'd helped catch a lot of killers and had pointed the police in the right direction more than once. It was annoying to be blocked and shut out.

Don't be stupid, Maiden, she warned herself. *Getting annoyed at having to play by the rules isn't going to help you...work around it.* She quietly marveled that her gut instinct was no longer to be unquestioningly obedient, now she felt a persistent urge to do what she knew was right, not what fit the mold.

"Oh, I'm asking for trouble," she whispered to her reflection where it glinted back at her on the pane of glass.

"Are you okay, Maiden?" Vonny's voice floated to her through the half open door that led to the reception desk.

"Hmm? Oh, yes, fine." She walked over and stood in the doorway, sweeping her gaze around the empty foyer. "Everything okay here?"

"Who cares?" Von rolled her eyes. "Where have you been? Did you get up at midnight and sneak out?"

"Not quite that early." She gave her a wry look. "The early bird gets the worm, right?"

"Good, I was afraid you'd skipped breakfast," Von smirked. "So, what's up? You've been digging and I'm sure you turned up more than worms."

Maiden briefly related what had happened between Ree and Agnes. As well as Bradley's vindictive attack on the devious nurse.

"Whoa!" Vonny breathed. "That is a lot of awful people with their fingers in the same nasty pie! What's Agnes going to do now that the others have turned on her?"

"That's the real question, isn't it?" Maiden propped her shoulder against the doorjamb. "I don't think she'll just cut her losses and run, and I don't think she'll put up with it."

"So, you think maybe she'll turn on them and spill her guts?" Von asked.

"Possibly, but she's in it pretty deep. She actually broke in and placed the will. And I don't care what *anyone* says, I know she forged Gail's signature." Maiden's tone was a touch stubborn but she was still stinging a little. "I think she's more likely to go for extortion...or revenge."

CHAPTER TWENTY-THREE

T wenty minutes later, Maiden and Vonny were sitting together behind the desk. They'd been quietly whispering about fake wills, scorned girlfriends and greedy in-laws when Bella wandered into the foyer. They quickly fell silent and smiled innocently at her.

"Look at you sweet babies," Bella said fondly as she came and stood at the end of the desk. "The only nice part about waitin' around for a murderer to be caught is bein' with my girls while I do it."

"Thanks, Aunt Bella." Vonny smiled.

"At least you and Elvan are together," Maiden offered helpfully. "Where is he, by the way?"

"He's off to see Mr. Edmonds about that joke of a will Bradley's whipped up." She glanced heavenward. "They're gettin' ready to over-turn any challenge to Gail's *actual* will."

"Oh, okay," Maiden bit her lip and glanced briefly at Von. "Are they worried?"

"No!" Bella scoffed. "There ain't nothin' to that silly bunch of scribbles. Whoever wrote it—Ree—didn't know what they were doin'. There's absolutely nothin' to validate it; it would never hold up in court and Bradley don't have the resources to fight it that far anyway."

"You don't think he had anything better than that planned?" Vonny pulled a face.

"I think he got his signals crossed, killed Gail, and then panicked when he realized the new will hadn't happened yet," Bella said confidently. "Then he got his mother to write up that travesty and hoped we'd all be dumb enough to throw some money at him to make him go away."

Maiden considered that but really didn't agree with it. Bradley wasn't *that* stupid. Agnes wasn't either. Ree was gullible and indiscreet, true, but she hadn't been the brains behind the scheme. Maiden was increasingly certain that it had been Bradley and Agnes, but mostly Agnes.

She looked at Aunt Bella and then thought back to Marti and Sylvia Drake. There was a common thread, and she was starting to suspect that she knew what it was.

"Maiden baby?" Bella's loud voice disrupted her thoughts. "Did you hear what I said?"

"Um..."

"Marti Drake called me this mornin' and asked for your phone number," she repeated patiently.

"Mine?" Maiden frowned at her. "Did she say why?"

"Not exactly," Bella slid her gaze away. "I *might* have mentioned to some of my friends that you do a lot of detective work...she might want to talk to you about somethin' like that. Maybe."

"You did what?" Maiden asked incredulously.

"So, I said I'd give you her number and you'd call her if you had time," Bella continued smoothly as she pulled a folded-up piece of paper from her cleavage and slid it across the desk to her. "There you go, baby."

Vonny snorted her amusement as Maiden snatched up the paper and opened it.

"Busty women don't even need pockets!" she laughed and pointed at Bella's ample chest. "You have a pen in there I can borrow?"

"Sorry, honey, I'm still usin' it," Bella replied dryly.

Maiden ignored them as she stepped into the office and pulled out her phone. As much as she didn't love the idea of Aunt Bella spreading stories about her amongst her friends, there was a chance Marti had something to tell her that was relevant to the case. She quickly dialed the number and waited. Marti picked up quickly.

"Is that Maiden?" she asked.

"It, uh, yes." Maiden frowned faintly but pressed on. "Marti? Aunt Bella said you wanted to talk to me?"

"Yes, I need some advice, but I don't want to talk about it over the phone," Marti said quietly. "Will you come to my hotel and have coffee with us? We're staying at the Golden Oaks, come as soon as you can, please."

She hung up before Maiden could reply. It occurred to her that Marti was staying at the same hotel as Agnes. That could be incredibly awkward, but potentially handy.

"What's up?" Von was standing in the doorway watching her.

"Marti wants me to have coffee with her at the Golden Oaks," she murmured as she tucked her phone in her back pocket.

"Does she now?" Von arched a brow and walked to the back door, grabbing her jacket. "Let's go."

"You want to go?" Maiden stared at her. "You *never* go along for this kind of stuff."

"The Golden Oaks is where you almost got stabbed to death, right?" Vonny asked grimly.

"Yeah," Maiden felt a bit queasy at the memory.

"Well then, I think I might just make room in my packed schedule to not let you walk back in there alone," she said and gestured towards the drizzly parking lot. "After you, madam."

***

The rain had let up by the time Maiden and Vonny stepped into the terraced restaurant that stretched out beside the lobby of the Golden Oaks hotel. As they walked further inside, Maiden quickly spotted a familiar pair.

Marti and Sylvia were both seated at a table in the furthest corner. There was a carafe and a stack of dainty coffee cups sitting invitingly in the middle of the table. Making herself ignore the enticing promise of a hot drink on a cold day, Maiden ran an assessing look over the ladies.

Sylvia wore a black business suit that was both professional and strikingly feminine while Marti looked far more informal in a slinky red blouse and chocolate brown palazzo pants. They both appeared polished and poised on the surface, but Maiden could see that it wasn't genuine.

Sylvia's foot was tapping nervously and Marti was turning her coffee cup almost constantly without taking a sip. Marti spotted them first and was on her feet before they'd reached the table. She smiled and held out her hand to Maiden and then to Vonny. Sylvia was more circumspect, she eyed Vonny uneasily and then turned back to Maiden.

"I didn't realize you were bringing a friend," she said mildly enough but her eyes were watchful.

"This is my sister, Vonny," Maiden said as she gestured towards the slender brunette at her side. "She was also at the wedding and may be of some help. I'm assuming you wanted to talk about the events at the wedding?"

"To a point," Marti sighed as she resumed her seat and motioned for them to settle in as well. "There's a bit more involved though."

Sylvia shifted uncomfortably, this meeting clearly hadn't been her idea. She busied herself by offering them both a cup of coffee from the pot on the table. Maiden accepted one with a nod and then shifted her attention to Marti. The woman looked anxious, maybe even frightened.

"What's happened?" Maiden asked gently.

"The Hedgewicks, that's what," Sylvia replied before her daughter could. "They're a horrible, poisonous family."

"Mom, let me do my own talking, please," Marti shot her a cranky look. "Besides, it's not all of them. Elvan and...and Pierce are good people."

Sylvia grumbled under her breath and sank back in her chair. Marti shifted away from her a fraction and fixed her gaze on Maiden and Vonny.

"It's Bradley," she said quietly. "He contacted me and asked me to go and see him."

"You're kidding me," Maiden looked at her in sheer disbelief.

"I wish I was." She shook her head and finally took a bracing sip from her cup.

"Why would he want to see you, though?" Von, blissfully unaware of the messy history between them, asked calmly.

"Because Bradley and I used to be engaged," Marti almost whispered.

"What? *Eww!*" Vonny stared at her as if she'd been rolled in spew. "Are you stupid or something?!"

"Vonny!" Maiden said tightly and gestured towards a startled Marti.

"Oh, I'm sorry," Von gasped. She pressed a hand to her chest and winced apologetically. "That came out more audibly than I meant it to. But, seriously, yuck."

Sylvia's icy veneer finally cracked a little. She looked at Vonny and started to chuckle. Maiden felt a twinge of relief that her sister's unfiltered response hadn't ruined the discussion entirely. Sylvia waved a hand that was loaded with gold rings in Von's direction.

"She's right," the lady nodded and flicked her daughter a scowl, "I told you that you could've done better!"

"Mom, you're biased." Marti rolled her eyes as discreetly as she could.

"It doesn't matter, honey," Von said dryly as she lifted her coffee cup to her mouth, "you could have three eyes and enough back hair to pass for a rug. You could still do better."

"So, Bradley asked you to visit him in jail?" Maiden asked loudly enough to drag the conversation back on track. "That must've been an uncomfortable situation to be put in. What did you do?"

"I...I went," Marti admitted.

"You should've stayed away," Sylvia muttered. "After what those people did to us—"

Sylvia broke off mid-sentence and clamped her mouth shut. Both she and Marti looked so deeply unhappy. Maiden cleared her throat quietly and leaned forward, resting her forearms on the table.

"Okay, I don't think there's much point in beating around the bush anymore," she said gently but seriously. "Can you please tell me what you have against Bradley and Gail?"

"Bradley's an idiot and a selfish child," Sylvia again answered for Marti, "but his grandmother was even worse. He learned it from someone, didn't he?"

"That doesn't really narrow it down," Marti said and sipped her coffee. "You've forgotten about Ree."

"What do you mean?" Maiden feigned a look of uncertainty, hoping they'd volunteer a bit more. She noticed Von glance at her and was relieved when she stayed quiet.

"She's Bradley's mother, although 'smother' is more like it," Marti said before catching what she'd said. She clapped a hand to her mouth as an unfortunate laugh slipped free. "I didn't mean that! Oh, geez, what a tacky thing to say. I totally forgot that's how Gail died."

"Slip of the tongue, I'm sure," Maiden said reassuringly, although she wasn't sure she believed it in this case. "So, I take it you and Ree didn't get along?"

"Oh, I don't think she really minded me that much," Marti shrugged and stared thoughtfully down into her cup. "Even Gail was nice enough at first...but then she started getting critical and then downright nasty. I honestly think someone got in her ear and really turned her against me. But Ree was fine until she found out I wasn't as rich as she thought I was."

Maiden stilled as she heard that. The last few pieces of the puzzle clicked into place and it did not reveal a very nice picture. She wet her lips and locked her gaze on Marti.

"Do you remember seeing Gail's nurse around when you visited?" she asked.

"You mean that girl, Agnes?" Marti nodded. "Yeah, she was around. Why?"

"Someone turned Gail against Aunt Bella. Her attitude towards her apparently changed quite suddenly and it was too vicious to be a personality clash," Maiden explained. She knew she needed to handle this next part delicately but there was only so much she could do to soften the truth. "Agnes was in on a plot to drive Gail to disinherit Elvan so that Bradley would get everything...for that to be worthwhile, she needed to have Bradley."

"Are you saying that Gail's nurse was the one that badmouthed me?" Marti asked slowly, her dark eyes were frighteningly intent. "That she made Gail hate me so *she* could have Bradley instead?"

"I suspect that it's possible," Maiden held up a hand in a soothing gesture that failed completely. "Agnes spent a lot of time alone with Gail, and a lot of time running and fetching for a very wealthy family. I doubt that Gail suddenly turned against you for no reason, but I need to be sure. I'm sorry to have to ask this, but it's very important. How did Gail treat you after you left Pierce for Bradley? Could *that* have had a bearing on her change of heart?"

"No, it didn't," Marti said coolly. "She was nice to me the first few times that Bradley took me along to visit her. She knew what had happened and shrugged it off, she told me that young people change their minds all the time. That was all she ever said about it."

"Then what happened?" Maiden asked. "What went wrong?"

"I'm not sure," Marti shook her head. "I've never understood what snapped in that old woman's head, but the fallout was devastating."

"What did she do?" Von asked, her eyes wide and her cup clenched anxiously in both hands.

"My family came from money, *past tense*. We used to have money," her tone dropped noticeably lower even though they were alone in the room. "Things have been tough over the last few years, our chain of restaurants were struggling a little, but then...then Gail swooped in for the kill."

"We built our business from the ground up, and she just…" Sylvia began but fell abruptly silent as the emotions welled up.

For a moment she stared across the room at nothing in particular. She released a shaky breath and her eyes turned glassy. Beside her, Marti glanced away sombrely and rested her hand briefly on her mother's shoulder.

"She ruined us," Sylvia said softly. "We'd been struggling a bit, but a lot of our competitors were too. It was a slump, nothing we couldn't have weathered if we'd been left alone. Then one day I got a phone call; the first of many. Somehow she'd bought up all our loans, all our debts, every single thing she could get her hands on. So many of our overheads doubled overnight. There was no way we could survive."

"We did our best," Marti almost mumbled and gave her mother's shoulder a squeeze before releasing her and bracing herself up on her elbows. "But it was too much, we had to close all but two of our cafes. We own those ones outright; there was nothing that awful woman could do about those. But it's been hard, it's nothing like the money we used to earn."

"It's not just the money. So many people lost their jobs when we closed the other sites down." Sylvia ran a hand through the pale hair at her temple. "Dozens of employees, people that had bills to pay and families to feed. It was awful, we couldn't give them any notice or any sort of warning. Everything was just gone."

Maiden felt her heart sink as she watched the women relive those painful memories. Beside her Vonny had lowered her gaze to the table and let out a sad little sigh. As terrible as it was, and as badly as Maiden felt for them, she knew it was also a strong motive to kill Gail Hedgewick.

"Are you sure it was Gail that did it?" she asked tactfully.

"Yes. She made sure I knew," Sylvia slid her a look. "She liked to win and she liked to gloat. And then that idiot grandson of hers humiliated Marti just for spite."

"When everything started collapsing around us, I went to ask Bradley for some sort of help to rein his grandmother in." Marti rubbed her forehead. "He stopped answering my phone calls, but I finally found him at a party. He was standing around flirting with a group of other women. When I tried to pull him aside and ask him what was going on, he announced for all to hear that he was done with me."

"What a tool!" Vonny whispered in incredulous anger.

"Bad enough to dump me in front of an audience," Marti gritted her teeth, "but he broadcast our financial struggles at the same time! He called *me* a liar and accused me of breaking up his family and lying about having money!"

"But why would he do that?" Maiden shook her head slightly. "What did he gain from being so awful?"

"I didn't hang around to ask him that," Marti replied dryly and then lifted a shoulder. "But he would have done it to satisfy Gail. He was always scrambling to please her; he wanted her money more than anything. Once he knew how strongly she was set against our relationship, he made sure she knew it was over...As much as I hate him for how he did it, I'm actually incredibly grateful that he's out of my life."

"Yeah, I'll bet," Maiden shook her head and resisted the urge to let out a low whistle. She wanted more information but wasn't sure how to tactfully get it. Fortunately, Vonny had never been limited by such qualms.

"Sorry, but why did you ever drop Pierce for some turkey in a cowboy suit?" Von asked plainly.

Marti looked a bit teary but still chuckled weakly at that unadorned question.

"Pierce has a reputation as a bit of a playboy, so when he first started coming around I didn't think it was serious. He's had a lot of girlfriends," she sniffled. "When I started to realize that he was actually interested, I was happy about it. But he went back to Tennessee for several weeks on business, and that's when Bradley swooped in."

"Marti's too emotional and too trusting for her own good," Sylvia patted her daughter's hand gently.

"Maybe," Marti shrugged glumly. "But Bradley was persistent and convincing. He also told me a lot of lies about Pierce, which I stupidly believed. When Pierce came back, I told him that I didn't feel the same way about him anymore. I've never regretted anything so much in my life."

"Have you talked to him since?" Maiden asked.

"Briefly at the wedding reception." Marti rubbed her arms. "He was nice about it, all things considered, and he protected me from Bradley. But he made it clear that I'm a cheat and, after what happened to his mother, he promised himself he'd never end up with a cheat...and I can't really argue with him, can I?"

"Well, you were tricked," Von tried to be helpful and, thankfully, trailed off considerably as she finished the thought, "but you also shacked up with his cousin while you were still dating...it would be hard to pretend that didn't happen."

Maiden shut her eyes and made a mental note to avoid investigating with Vonny whenever possible. When she turned back to Marti she put on her sincerest-looking fake smile.

"Time will tell, I guess," she said nicely. "In light of all that, though, why did you come to the wedding? Wasn't it terribly uncomfortable for you?"

"To be perfectly honest," Marti smiled, "I came for revenge."

The resulting silence was considerable. Maiden quickly reached under the table and gave Vonny's leg a warning squeeze when she saw her start to open her mouth, she obligingly closed it again.

"I wanted to turn up and let Bradley realize what an idiot he'd been," Marti explained. "I wanted him to make a pass, any sort of pass, and then give him a taste of his own medicine by shooting him down in front of everyone."

"But it didn't work out that way?" Maiden asked, not forgetting the sight of Pierce escorting her back into the reception and away from Bradley. Marti had looked upset, not triumphant.

"No," she propped her chin in her hand, "he saw a chance to mend fences with Pierce by accusing me of deliberately coming between them. I could've killed him."

"It would've been infuriating, that's for sure," Maiden attempted a neutral tone. "But you said that Bradley asked you to see him now? What was that about?"

"That's where I need your advice," she sat up straighter and started fiddling with her cup again. "He asked me to bail him out; I laughed in his face. So, then he started talking about a will, Gail's will. He said he had a new will that she'd wanted acted on, but there was one little problem, it hadn't been signed yet."

Maiden felt her pulse kick up. It appeared that Bradley was planning to ditch Agnes even before she'd crossed swords with Ree.

"What exactly was he asking you to do?" she pressed.

"He said that if I got him out, he'd marry me and we'd share the Hedgewick fortune," Marti glanced around uneasily. "He said all we had to do was sign it in Gail's name and get *someone* to witness it."

"Who?" Maiden quirked a brow.

"Me." Marti smirked. "I told him he was an idiot and he could get lost, I wasn't about to swindle Elvan or fall for Bradley's cheap lies again."

"What did he say to that?" Maiden leaned a bit closer, so did Vonny.

"He was desperate," Marti chuckled. "Conveniently skirting past the way he'd torn into me at the reception, he started saying all sorts of nasty things about Gail and blamed her for our breakup. When I asked why he'd humiliated me in public to end it, he said Gail *forced him* to do that.

"Then he said that if I bailed him out and agreed to help him with the will, he'd marry me immediately. He said we'd find someone to do the deed and go from there. I told him what he could do with that charming offer and left."

"He was willing to marry you without even knowing if his plan would succeed?" Maiden shook her head as she asked.

"It wasn't really a risk since I now have more money than he does," Marti laughed. "It wasn't as public as I'd wanted, but at least I got to leave him as hopeless and friendless as he left me."

"More so, I'd say." Maiden rubbed her chin thoughtfully. "What advice do you want from me? You seem to have achieved what you wanted, mostly anyway."

"Do you think I should tell the police about Bradley's proposition?" she asked quietly. "I've been thinking about it ever since. I'm afraid they won't believe that I turned him down. Bradley lies, and I'm afraid that if I say anything, he'll try to drag me down with him. We have so much bad blood with Gail, and they've already questioned me about that incident with Bradley at the reception...I'm afraid to risk it, but I really don't want him to get away with the Hedgewick millions. It wouldn't be fair. What should I do?"

"Ultimately, it's up to you, but I would go to the police," Maiden said, carefully avoiding mentioning that she was dating the head of the investigation, almost. "I, um, *suspect* that Bradley and Agnes were both in on the fake will. They won't give up easily, he'll just try something else."

"Agnes." Marti's dark eyes narrowed as she whispered the now-hated name. "I don't want her to get away with anything. After she destroyed me and my family to get the man I had…no, she's not going to scamper off and become a millionaire."

"I'd wondered what made Gail turn on us so quickly," Sylvia said angrily. "All that suffering and loss, and for what? To stop Marti and Bradley getting married? Did this nurse actually think he'd marry *her* instead?"

Vonny pulled a sympathetic face and glanced over towards the sidewalk. Maiden was vaguely aware of her sister holding her breath and sitting a bit straighter but she had too much on her mind to worry about it.

"You need to go to the police," she said seriously, submerging her distracted annoyance as Von cleared her throat loudly and started nudging her. "And as soon as possible."

"Yeah, you're probably—" Marti stopped mid-sentence and sucked in an angry breath as she looked at something beyond Maiden's shoulder. "*You!*"

Maiden tensed and finally turned to her obnoxiously prodding sister, who was now glaring at her. She looked over at the lobby and her mouth dropped open. It was Agnes, and she was looking right at their table.

Marti was instantly on her feet; she rounded the table and stalked swiftly towards the unsuspecting nurse. Maiden scrambled after her along with Vonny and Sylvia. Maiden had barely reached them when Marti let loose.

"You!" Marti shouted again as she pointed at Agnes. "You sniveling, conniving, disgusting schemer! You did all this?!"

"I don't know what you're talking about," Agnes frowned and shook her head. "Kindly lower your voice and quit pointing at me like that."

"Kindness won't be entering into this discussion," Marti warned. "I know what you've been up to. You were skulking around in the background, playing games with everyone, while you looked for the cushiest spot you could find. Did you actually think Bradley would keep you after the dirty work was done? Please!"

"My relationship with Bradley is *my* business, dearie," Agnes' eyes narrowed coldly. "Butt out."

"A fine suggestion for you to make. You stuck your nose into everyone else's business hoping to chisel something for yourself! Was it necessary to hurt dozens of people?" Sylvia hissed. "It wasn't just me and my daughter. A lot of people lost their jobs and a lot of rifts formed between our friend's and Gail's."

"I didn't do anything of the sort," Agnes backed up a step. "Your business failings are hardly my fault. I was just a nurse doing my job."

"Yeah right, you did a great job of trying to dupe your employer!" Marti glared. "And you did all that damage for a guy that would never have been loyal to you?!"

"Do you *really* want to talk about loyalty, Miss Drake?" Agnes retorted with a sneer. "You're the one that jumped all over Bradley the minute Pierce left town."

"It wasn't like that," Marti curled her hands into tight fists and shut her eyes briefly. "Bradley lied to me, and you know all about lying, don't you?"

As the two women proceeded to exchange some incredibly personal insults, Von turned to Maiden with a sigh.

"So, subtlety doesn't work," she muttered. "Should I have thrown some sugar packets at you?"

"You could've said 'Hey, Agnes is here.' Or something equally inventive," Maiden whispered back. "Hissing and elbowing me isn't like morse code."

She and Vonny were quickly drawn back to the brewing exchange when the language took a steep nosedive. A few people that had been standing in the lobby quickly slipped outside or into the elevators to get out of the fray.

"If I could just interrupt," Maiden dared to step closer as Sylvia grasped her daughter's shoulders in an attempt to calm her. "Agnes, when you left the wedding reception, what did you do with the diamond ring you stole from Gail?"

"What?" Agnes gasped and clutched her coat over her chest.

"Oh yes, and was Gail already dead?" Maiden asked mildly. "Is that how you got the ring off without waking her?"

"You're making up stories, Miss Harlow," Agnes said angrily. "I will not be slandered, you hear me?"

Marti started laughing at the irony of that statement. Maiden kept her expression placid and shrugged innocently.

"I'm just repeating what Ree told me," she said.

"Ree?" Agnes arched a dubious brow. "What's she got to do with anything?"

"She told me that Bradley accused you of stealing from Gail," Maiden replied. "I saw her at the police station this morning."

"That's a lie," she said tightly.

"I'm afraid that's what she said," Maiden nodded. "The police will ask you about it anyway."

"Oh, so you were helping yourself to everything, were you?" Marti folded her arms over her chest and smirked.

"Bradley took that ring!" Agnes snapped at her. "It was Ree's engagement ring and she's got it right now! It was nothing to do with me."

"Did he meet you outside of the reception that night and give it to you for safekeeping?" Maiden asked.

Agnes gave her a sardonic look and said nothing. Maiden wasn't surprised, the lady was a little too smart to walk into such an obvious snare, she changed tack slightly.

"It doesn't matter, Bradley was talking to the police about it when I left," she said as she tucked her hands in her pockets, "and, of course, I saw you climb out of his bedroom window after you planted that fake will so..."

"I did not!" Agnes snapped. "And I'll deny it to my last breath!"

"More lies aren't going to help you," she shrugged. "I saw you climb out through Bradley's window, your fingerprints will be all over the place."

"They won't, I wore—" Agnes stopped just short of finishing the damning statement. "I was never there."

"You were, weren't you?" Marti's smile grew as she glared at the other woman. "That's that stupid will Bradley told me about, isn't it? The one he tried to get me to witness for him."

Agnes was silent for a long, wide-eyed moment as that sank in. Maiden could see her confidence falter for the briefest moment before a smug smile resurfaced.

"Lies," she said with a sniff. "All of it. Bradley would never go to you for anything."

"You idiot!" Marti laughed. "Did you actually think Bradley would settle for a nobody like you? You have no money and no connections.

Once he'd gotten you to turn Gail against Bella, he didn't need you anymore!"

"Save it, your highness. You've had a nice cushy life, you never had to work like I have, but now you want sympathy? How about a few hard truths instead?" Agnes glared at her. "Bradley loves me, all right? Just deal with it! Even when you were dating, he couldn't keep his hands off me. We've been together a long time."

"You're a disgusting little thief, and a fool," Marti raised her chin a fraction. "Bradley's already tried to get me back; you don't mean anything to him."

"Don't embarrass yourself, sweetie," Agnes sniggered, "*again*. He told me all about you and how boring you were, and how happy he was to be rid of you. Gail's tantrums were all the excuse he needed."

"I'm sure he told you all sorts of things," Marti's cheeks turned pink but she kept her tone steady. "Just like he told me that the woman he'd used to try and get over me made him feel like he was dating some hillbilly preteen. He said she had all the sultry sophistication of a boiled turnip, and she was the dumbest mistake he ever made. He didn't even bother to mention your name."

"And when did he tell you that?" she glared.

"When he begged me to come and see him in jail. And then *begged* me to take him back." Marti arched a brow. "The police can confirm that I went to see him, not that you can ask them, since you're on the run."

"Maybe we should all settle down!" Maiden said quickly as she stepped in to try and help Sylvia gently nudge the angry women apart.

Agnes was seething and looked ready to pounce on Marti. This confrontation was quickly spinning out of control and Maiden wasn't sure how to fix it. She nearly cringed when she heard Vonny's unimpressed sigh.

"I can't believe you two are dumb enough to be fighting over that creep," she said dryly. "I saw him at the wedding hitting on anything under sixty that gave him a second look. He'd be laughing his butt off if he knew he had you two about to fight to the death for him."

"Thanks, Von," Maiden gave her big sister a quelling look. "That's helpful."

"Well, where's the dignity?!" Vonny went on undaunted. "You think a guy like that, who would go to those lengths to steal his father's fortune is going to keep the witnesses around that knew he did it?"

"I wouldn't have Bradley back for any amount of money. That much money doesn't even exist!" Marti said crisply. "I told him that when he pleaded with me to marry him, he said we'd find someone and get 'hitched' that very day. I told him he could get lost. That's probably when he went back to *her*."

That last statement was rounded off with a scathing look in Agnes' direction. Agnes had turned purple; Maiden couldn't recall the last time she'd seen someone quite that angry. The petite nurse pointed at Marti with a shaky hand.

"You stay out of my way," she said in a low, menacing tone. "I got rid of you once, I'd happily do it again."

Marti lunged forward with surprising strength and grabbed Agnes by the collar, dragging her closer.

"Listen to me very carefully. Everyone that's had a hand in ruining my life is either dead or in jail. Except *you*," Marti's tone was eerily calm. "I don't like that. You'd better watch your step."

Agnes twisted free and ran back outside. Marti watched her until she ducked into her car and drove off. Sylvia whispered some soothing words as she urged her back towards the table.

When they were standing alone together, Maiden turned to Vonny with an arched brow and folded her arms over her chest. Von blinked at her and shook her head.

"What?" she asked.

"You just escalated a dangerously tense situation," Maiden was amazed that she had to explain that.

"Oh, you and your nicey-nice girl schtick." Von rolled her eyes and then gave her a look. "Sometimes you gotta say it like it is. How have you ever managed to do this without me?"

"Excuse me?" Maiden asked. "How many murders have *you* solved?"

"Ooo, aren't we fancy?" Vonny gave her a mocking look and then smirked. "So, do we try to track Agnes down or what?"

"Ladies."

They both turned sharply when they heard David's mellow greeting. He'd just walked in the front door ahead of Greg and Officer Parker. Greg gave Maiden an uncertain smile and then poked his tongue out at Vonny. Parker was watching the scene quietly and kept her expression neutral.

"Where the heck have you been?" Von grumbled at David and pointed to the side door with her thumb. "She got away."

"Who did?" he asked tolerantly as he stood in front of them and folded his arms.

"Agnes," Maiden decided it might be less perilous if she answered the questions rather than Vonny. "She and Marti Drake got into a fight and she's sort of on the run now."

"How do you know Marti Drake?" he demanded in a carefully lowered voice.

"I met her at the reception," Maiden frowned a little. "Why do you keep getting mad at me for knowing people?"

David gave her an incredulous look and then glanced at his officers. She heard him quietly instruct them to go and search Miss Gray's room. None of them spoke as Greg and Parker went to the reception desk and got the key from the receptionist after showing her what must have been a warrant.

Once they'd disappeared into an elevator, David turned to Maiden with an expectant look. She cleared her throat and shifted her weight from one foot to the other.

"I can explain everything," Maiden assured him.

"I'm sure you can," he nodded, "that's the most terrifying part."

"This isn't my fault." Maiden decided to go straight to the defensive. "Marti asked me to come and talk to her; then she realized that Agnes was most likely the one that turned Gail against her. Then Agnes turned up and she went berserk."

"She 'realized' that Agnes did it?" David eyed her with his coolest cop expression. "How exactly did she happen to just 'realize' that, Miss Harlow?"

"This isn't my fault," she tried again. "People jump to conclusions all the time, this is another one of those. So...are you going to arrest Agnes?"

"I would *love* to arrest Agnes," he said sardonically. "Unfortunately, some maniacal pixie got here first and scared her off. So, what do you think? Should I just arrest *you*, in the interests of this not being a wasted trip?"

"Oh, you'd like that, wouldn't you, Captain Hotpants?" Vonny came to her sister's defense with all the casual aplomb of a sarcastic teenager. "Drag her away in handcuffs and throw her into a big cage."

"Given the right circumstances, I certainly wouldn't hate it," David replied.

"Eww," Von pulled a face and glanced away when he took her teasing in stride. "I need to not visualize that."

"Same here." He shrugged. "I'm on duty."

"Okay, I'm out." Vonny raised her hands and quickly walked back to the table where Marti and Sylvia were sitting.

Maiden watched her go and then turned back to David with a sweet smile. He didn't return it.

"You aren't actually mad about this, are you?" she raised her eyebrows hopefully.

"Give me a second, I'm still thinking about the handcuffs." He pinched the bridge of his nose and exhaled loudly before facing her again. "You really need to stop interfering in this case, Maiden. You're stirring up a lot of trouble. You don't know that Agnes turned Gail against anyone. You don't know that she forged Gail's signature on that will. You can suspect anything you want, but you don't *know* that you're right about any of it!"

"I was invited for coffee, which is entirely legal for civilians the last time I checked," she said a bit tartly, not appreciating the warning off. "During the ensuing discussion, Marti told me that Bradley had asked her to do some very wrong things and she wasn't sure whether she should go to the police or not. I told her she should. Apparently that's *interfering*, terribly sorry."

David sighed and glanced away for a moment before turning back to face her. He visibly hid his annoyance, which did very little to placate her considering she was doing him a favor, yet again.

"What did he say to her?" he asked patiently.

"She's right over there, ask her yourself," she said coolly. "You're on your own, honey. I'd hate to cause you more trouble."

She did her best to ignore the way he smiled when she called him honey. Instead she glanced back at her sister.

"Let's go, Von," she said loudly, "we're officially in the way."

By the time Vonny had said goodbye to the Drakes and walked over to join her, the elevator door opened to reveal Officer Parker. She stepped out holding a handful of papers and walked purposefully over to her commanding officer. She glanced at Maiden and Vonny with the slightest nod of acknowledgement before turning to David.

"Captain," she said as she handed him the stack of paper. "Officer Smith is still searching Miss Gray's room but I wanted to show you this straight away. We found these in the wastebasket. Pages and pages of Gail Hedgewick's signature. Looks like a forgery job to me."

Maiden turned slowly to David, feeling her left eyebrow rise to new and wondrous heights. He was looking down at the reams of signatures with an unwilling twist to his lips.

"Good work, everyone," David murmured and slid his twinkling gaze to Maiden.

She didn't gloat, not a lot anyway, she just held his gaze without a word. She didn't need words in that perfectly satisfying moment.

David was still smiling as he pulled his loose tie from around his neck and held it out to her. Maiden inclined her head graciously as she accepted it.

"Have a lovely rest of the day, officers," she said as she sauntered to the front doors with Vonny following close behind.

"I've lost track now," Vonny whispered as she hurried to keep up, "did you win that round?"

"Yeah," Maiden replied, a tiny bit smugly, as she draped the tie around her neck, "big time."

CHAPTER TWENTY-FOUR

That night Maiden was lying in bed thinking about the day. Agnes had turned out to be way more devious than she'd thought. Chasing after someone for their wealth, or their potential wealth, wasn't a crime but to be actively involved in attempting a brazen swindle was another matter entirely.

And to separate a couple, to ruin someone's name, reputation and livelihood to try and profit off it...it was chillingly selfish. She wondered if it was Agnes' soft-spoken manner or her delicate appearance that led people to underestimate her. She was brazen, and she was mercenary.

I wonder if she's ambitious enough to kill for what she wants, Maiden thought as she stared up at the ceiling. Both Agnes and Marti had thrown around some pretty nasty threats, she wouldn't honestly want to turn her back on either woman if they were angry enough.

Agnes certainly didn't waste time and didn't balk at much. She'd been angry when Marti suggested that Bradley turned on her, but she hadn't looked heartbroken.

As Maiden thought back on what she'd observed of her visit to Pierce, she was comfortably sure that Agnes had been testing the waters. She must have found out that Bradley wasn't provided for in the existing will.

It had looked like Agnes had made a pass at Pierce, since he still inherited a fortune. But when that failed, she went to her only remaining chance to try and wriggle her way into the Hedgewick millions.

It made sense that she'd had the fake will, she would have been the first person on hand to try and get Gail's consent on it. The young nurse had as good as admitted to Ree that she'd taken it upon herself to forge Gail's signature and place the will in Bradley's room. A room he hadn't been in since his arrest, perhaps she thought that would prove that the will had been signed before Gail's death.

What Agnes hadn't considered was that the police would have searched Bradley's room after his arrest and known that the will hadn't been there previously. She also hadn't expected to be seen planting it and, perhaps due to panic and desperation, hadn't thought to witness the will. She could have signed the stupid thing herself and claimed that Gail asked her to do it.

"Clever, but sloppy," Maiden whispered aloud.

The kitten that had fallen asleep on her stomach stirred. Ruffian stretched and then rolled onto his back, within seconds his contented snoring reverberated in the quiet of the room. Maiden smiled faintly and gently rubbed his belly with her thumb.

Maiden wasn't sure how much weight that will would've ever carried in court. Aunt Bella may have been partly right when she suggested that Bradley might've used it to wring a settlement out of her and Elvan. They might well have decided that throwing some money his way would've been worth it to get rid of him. Agnes effectively ruined that though.

Her thoughts then drifted to the stolen rings. She'd been entirely sincere when she'd asked Agnes if Gail was still alive when the ring was taken. She recalled the sight of the rings on Gail's finger, they'd looked snugly tucked around a swollen, likely arthritic, knuckle. It hadn't looked like they would have slid off easily.

But Gail was still alive when Agnes left the house, that much had been established. She was alive...but was she aware? The sedative. David said that Agnes admitted to giving Gail her usual nightly sedative. But he'd also looked intrigued when she'd found that half a capsule under Gail's bed. It might well have had traces of her prescribed sedative in it.

Without stopping to talk herself out of it, she reached for her phone where it was laying on her nightstand. Ruffian shifted slightly and grumbled a little before dozing off again. She ignored the grumpy kitten and called David before her courage failed her.

She glanced at the time as it started to ring, it was almost 11 o'clock, she hoped she wasn't going to wake him.

"You're still speaking to me?" he asked teasingly; he sounded fully awake.

"I was going to ask you the same question," she replied with a smile, pleased that he didn't sound resentful or standoffish.

"I don't rattle that easily." His smile was in his voice. "What are you wearing this time? A flannel granny-nightie and fuzzy slippers?"

"Don't torment yourself with lurid fantasies, Captain McAlister," she said.

"All right, what's up?" he laughed. "Are you lonely or something?"

"Actually yes, but that's not why I called," she said candidly. "I wanted to ask you about Gail's sedative."

He was quiet, that didn't surprise her, but she pressed on anyway.

"Did you find extra sedative in Gail's system?" She chewed at her lip. "...I know you won't tell me."

"Then why did you call me and ask?" His tone was guarded.

"Because I'm awake and it's on my mind," she admitted in a small, hopefully innocent-sounding voice. "You're cute when you're annoyed with me, by the way."

"I know," he murmured and then exhaled slowly through his nose. "Look...I'll just say that there's a reason for concern."

"Okay," she said quietly, knowing she'd have to settle for that.

"Will you be able to sleep now?" he asked dryly.

"I'll try," she sighed. "David?"

"Yeah?"

"I'm wearing your necktie," she confessed with a smirk.

He was still laughing when she calmly hung up.

***

The following morning Maiden took up her seat behind the front desk. It promised to be a long morning as she waited for news so she smuggled Ruffian downstairs with her for company.

The kitten was quickly riled as he batted at the stapler that had somehow enraged him. She smiled faintly as she watched him slap at it and then run and hide behind the computer monitor. She sighed and glanced out the front windows. The sun was shining and everything looked peaceful on the street outside.

Maiden wasn't feeling terribly peaceful, however. Her mind kept drifting back to the case. The same thoughts that kept her up half the night were still dancing around in her head. Gail's death was looking less opportunistic and more like it was premeditated.

Someone had at least doubled her usual amount of sedative and then left her to die with a pillow over her face. That meant knowing about her habit of taking the drug, getting access to it and then somehow sneaking upstairs to add another dose to her drink. After that the killer would have just waited for it to take effect and then placed the pillow over her and left again.

Her gut instinct told her that Bradley was definitely plotting against his father and grandmother, but it didn't make sense that he'd kill her then. Maybe he wasn't a genius, but he'd been smart enough to slowly turn Gail against Elvan without getting caught. Although, he'd probably let Agnes do most of that.

She then recalled the conversation she'd overheard between Gail and Elvan at the wedding rehearsal, the one Agnes had tried to hear too. Gail's venom had been obvious. It also took a huge amount of gall to interrupt the ceremony the way she did. Gail had been serious, she didn't want Aunt Bella in the family.

Maiden shook her head sadly. While Gail may or may not have accepted Bradley's handwritten will, she was very likely going to punish Elvan for going against her wishes. Which meant Elvan also had motive.

Elvan was also in danger though, there'd been the possible attempts on his life. As she thought back on it now, Maiden was increasingly sure that she hadn't imagined the feeling of being watched at the rehearsal. Someone had been keeping tabs on them; it could have been Ree.

But what about Pierce? she mused to herself. She wasn't sure when he'd actually gotten into town. Pierce had managed to keep himself in the background for most of the chaos. He hadn't even been in the ceremony, he'd sat with Gail. He had also helped lead her out of the room after the fake heart attack.

He probably knew about her nightly sedative, it wouldn't have been hard to slip upstairs and empty a second capsule into Gail's drink.

And no one could deny that Pierce was far better off with the original will remaining in effect.

Maiden glanced up when she saw movement from the corner of her eye. Aunt Bella had just walked out from the dining room and was headed straight for her.

"Hey babydoll," Bella said. "Has Elvan come back yet?"

"I didn't realize he'd gone out." Maiden frowned gently at her as she pulled Ruffian out of the wastebasket he'd jumped into. "Where was he going?"

"He was supposed to be meetin' with Mr. Edmonds to update his own will," she sighed heavily. "He said what happened with Gail's was playin' on his mind, he wants to make sure I'm protected if anything happens to him."

"Oh, that's true," Maiden said. "And I guess if he gives the rest of his family no incentive to get rid of him, he'll be safer...I shouldn't have said that out loud, sorry."

Bella had propped her chin in her hands and smiled at her.

"You're practical, honeypot. I do appreciate that," she murmured. "I sure wish they'd just accept defeat and leave us alone."

"Has the new will been dismissed?" Maiden watched her carefully. "Legally and officially?"

"As good as," Bella inclined her head. "Accordin' to your gorgeous captain, the handwritin' matches Ree's, and they found a few of her fingerprints on it. Apparently there's some doubt about the signature too. Apart from that, it ain't witnessed so there's no reason to question the original will that Gail had in place."

"Bradley must be climbing the walls." Maiden noticed Bella's quiet smirk. "Has he tried to contact Elvan?"

"Mm-hmm. Some lady from the police station called to inform us that Bradley has asked his 'daddy' to come and visit him." Bella rolled her eyes. "He obviously knows that he can't win, so his next best option is to try and get back on Elvan's good side."

"After everything he's tried to do?" She gaped at her aunt. "He'd actually have the nerve to come crawling back?"

"Beats workin', in his opinion anyway." Bella shrugged. "Elvan promised that he'd stay strong for me. I don't want that rat or his mother in our lives anymore."

"I'm surprised you didn't go with him," she said honestly.

"He never wants me there when he's havin' to deal with his family," she admitted. "I haven't insisted yet, he's been through so much, but I don't intend to keep gettin' left out like this."

"Yeah, I don't blame you," Maiden said quietly and glanced at the door as if that would make Elvan walk through it sooner. "Where was he the other day, incidentally? David said he didn't go to see Bradley then."

Bella smiled a little and pointed to the impressively large ruby earrings she was wearing. Maiden gave them an admiring look and an appreciative nod.

Time ticked by. Eventually Bella brought them both a coffee from the dining room and stood near Maiden at the desk. Maiden could see that her beloved aunt was growing steadily more annoyed as the silence from Elvan stretched on.

"Still nothing?" Maiden asked tentatively.

"Nothin'," Bella muttered and glanced down at her phone. "No call, no message, nothin'."

"I'm sure he's fine." Maiden gave her hand a squeeze.

"Yeah," Bella said grimly. "But what's he doin' that he don't want me to know about?"

"What are you afraid he's doing?" Maiden knew she sounded uneasy, but she was. The fact that Bella was distrusting of his behavior already didn't bode well for their future.

"I think he's still with Bradley, and who knows what lies that evil brat is tellin' him. Especially once Elvan told him he was cut out of everything. He gave me his word he'd be strong for me, for *us*." Bella exhaled slowly. "But I think that boy has his hooks deeper into his father's heart than I realized. He's gonna be an ongoin' problem, despite what Elvan swore to me."

"Let's just wait until Elvan gets back," Maiden said soothingly. "Writing up a will takes time, especially with a big estate, I doubt it's a straightforward process to block his only child from inheriting anything. He may have his phone on silent so they can get the job done faster."

"Yeah, you're right," Bella smiled fondly at her. "Thank you, sweetie."

They both jumped when Bella's phone rang, the older woman smiled with relief as she looked at the screen.

"That's him now." She grinned at Maiden and put it to her ear. "Hey, honey. How'd you go?"

Maiden smiled faintly but a frown settled over her features when she saw the change in her aunt's countenance. Bella's whole body stiffened and her crystal blue eyes narrowed angrily.

"You did what?" she asked a little too softly. "You *paid his bail!* Are you kiddin' me?!"

Maiden's mouth fell open but she quickly closed it and turned away from her furious aunt. Elvan bailed Bradley out of jail? Even after he was clearly exposed for trying to ruin his father and his new bride and strip them of every penny? Even with the accidents that had conspicuously stopped once Bradley was incarcerated?

It was unbelievably frustrating to hear; she could only imagine Aunt Bella's feelings. She risked a glance at her and winced at the look on her face. She'd never seen her so angry.

You might be right, she thought sadly as she stared at her favorite aunt. *If Elvan's going to let him back in even after all he tried to do, Bradley really is going to be an ongoing problem for you.*

"Elvan," Bella said stiffly even as he gushed and apologized in her ear. "I'm done talkin' to you for now. You lied to me to help that snivelin' backstabber. That's how much our marriage means to you."

Maiden could hear him raise his voice as he hurried to explain himself but Bella hung up without another word. Maiden tried but couldn't suppress her look of horrified sympathy. Bella flicked a glance at her and exhaled loudly through her nose.

"I'm gonna go lie down for a while," she said and walked back towards the stairs.

"Oh Ruffy," Maiden sighed as she cuddled the kitten against her neck. "Now what do we do?"

He just purred loudly and licked her chin.

***

Hours passed and Elvan still didn't come back. Maiden finished her shift and handed over to Vonny. She stopped in the apartment long enough to plop Ruffian on the couch; he and Rowdy immediately started chasing each other around the room.

She left the kittens to play and went straight to the Romance and Glamor suite. She tried to think of what she could possibly say to help her aunt as she rapped on the door.

"Come in," Bella called out in a disinterested voice.

Maiden frowned at her downcast tone and slipped inside. She spotted her sprawled out on one of the leather couches looking down at something on her phone.

"Hey, Aunt Bella," she said nicely as she walked into the room. "How are you?"

"Not great, to be honest." She shrugged and sat up. "I know I shouldn't be sulkin' like this...but I'm really startin' to wonder if I made a mistake marryin' Elvan."

"Oh, Aunt Bella," Maiden said softly as she settled beside her on the couch. "Don't give up, you love each other, you can work this out."

"Yeah, maybe." She tossed her phone aside and propped her chin in her hand. "I'm not sure where to start though."

"Well," Maiden began slowly. She knew she could view the situation more impartially, but she also had no experience with married life; she needed to tread carefully. "It seems like Elvan trying to handle his family on his own isn't working so well...maybe if you two team up, it'll go better?"

Bella considered that quietly. After a moment she sat up straight and nodded.

"I *have* let him shut me out too much," she acknowledged slowly. "He keeps sayin' that he don't want me to get hurt, but he's not strong enough to handle them. *I* am. We need to deal with Bradley and Ree together."

Maiden smiled gently, it was good to see her calmer and more motivated. It wasn't like Aunt Bella to sit back and let other people look after things for her; she'd been making her own decisions for years and she usually knew what she was doing.

Bella smiled and sat up. She opened her mouth to speak when her phone rang. They both glanced down but stilled when they saw

Elvan's name pop up. Maiden gave her aunt a bolstering nod as the woman picked it up and put it to her ear.

"Hey, sweetie pie," Bella said quietly. "You okay?...What?! Say that again."

Bella pulled the phone away and put it on loudspeaker.

"Bradley just sent me a message," Elvan sounded frantic and out of breath. "He said that he killed Mama!"

"Oh Lordy," Bella whispered unsteadily. "Where are you now?"

"I'm headin' for the rental house," Elvan said shakily. "I'm worried about what he might do, it was the most chillin' message I've ever read!"

"All right, we'll meet you there." Bella pushed to her feet and beckoned for Maiden to follow.

"What?" Elvan gasped. "No, baby! I don't know what I'm gonna walk into, please don't go near that place!"

"I'm comin' and that's that," Bella said firmly. "We're in this together. See you soon, honey."

She hung up and hurried to the door with Maiden right behind her. They stopped only long enough for her to grab her keys; they didn't even slow down long enough to tell Vonny where they were going when she asked. They rushed through the office door and out to Maiden's car.

She threw Bella the keys and slid into the passenger seat as she whipped out her phone and called David.

"Hey, Harlow." He was smiling, she could hear it in his voice. "Is this a social call or more trouble?"

"Trouble, big trouble," she said breathlessly as Bella tore out of the parking lot. "We're on the way to meet Elvan at the rental house. He said Bradley sent a text confessing to Gail's murder!"

"Right, we're on our way," he said, instantly serious. "Harlow, don't go in that house, do you hear me? All of you stay back until we get there."

"Please hurry," she said rather than commit herself to anything. "Bye."

CHAPTER TWENTY-FIVE

Bella parked in the street in front of Elvan's rental. For a moment she and Maiden both sat and stared at the handsome, unassuming old house.

It was quiet, there were a few lights on inside and the porchlight shone brightly as the sun slowly dipped lower in the sky. It looked disturbingly normal, unnervingly peaceful; mostly because they knew that a self-confessed murderer was probably waiting inside right now.

A minute later Elvan's Mercedes pulled up behind them. Bella didn't hesitate once she saw him. She threw her door open and hurried over to meet him. They embraced tightly and whispered to each other before turning to look at the house. By then Maiden had joined them.

"The police are on their way," she said as steadily as she could. "Let's just wait here. Please."

"My boy's in there!" Elvan said shakily. "I have to help him!"

He hurried towards the house without another word and Bella took off after him. Maiden knew it was dangerous, but she couldn't abandon her aunt. She bit her lip and glanced around anxiously before following.

As they approached the front steps Maiden heard the sound of a car running. She slid her gaze to the garage and spied exhaust coming from under the large door. She grasped Elvan's arm and pointed towards the gray smoke.

Elvan's eyes widened and he cried out as he ran towards it. He pulled out his key and fumbled to unlock the door with quivering hands. When he flung it open, a thick cloud of exhaust billowed out over him. He immediately started to choke but ran inside towards the running car.

Maiden and Bella hurried after him as he opened the driver's side door and found Bradley slumped against the steering wheel. Bella edged closer but Maiden stayed put at the mouth of the garage door.

"Bradley!" Elvan shouted anxiously as he pulled him back and laid him against the seat. "Can you hear me, son! *Please,* Bradley!"

Bella clasped a hand to her mouth and her eyes glistened with tears as Elvan kept trying so desperately to awaken his son. Maiden watched Bradley's head loll around heavily as Elvan shook him. She knew they ought to stop the car but she didn't dare interrupt.

A minute later they heard sirens and saw the flashing lights as David and his team arrived. Maiden barely looked at them before returning to her stoic vigil. Elvan was sobbing at this point and hugging his son tightly.

She blinked away tears but as the police cars pulled into the driveway and shone their headlights on the area, she got a clear look at the back of Bradley's car. Her eyes widened and she felt the hairs on the back of her neck rise. She started backing out into the driveway.

"Aunt Bella!" she said loudly. "Get out of there now!"

"What?" Bella frowned. "I can't leave Elvan in here alone, honey."

"Right now!" Maiden said sharply and pointed at the trunk as David and a few other officers ran up to them.

Bella wandered over and looked at the car, she gasped loudly and scampered over to Maiden. David, Greg and Parker quickly took in the situation and got to work. Greg ran up to a gently sobbing Elvan and managed to pull him away from the car, he then reached in and turned off the ignition.

The resulting silence was deafening. Some of the neighbors had stepped out on their porches to see what was happening. Their curious whispers and Elvan's crying were oddly loud in Maiden's ears.

None of it mattered, she kept her gaze fixed on the large smear of blood on the trunk lid. Even more blood had trickled down over the bumper. Something very bad had happened. She watched and waited while David circled the car and then asked Greg to pop the trunk.

As he cautiously raised the lid, Parker shone her flashlight inside. Bella shrieked and Maiden just stared at Ree Hedgewick lying in a twisted heap inside. Her lifeless eyes stared out at them; she was drenched with blood and a large kitchen knife was still protruding from her chest.

Bella turned her back immediately but Maiden couldn't. She knew that she should, but she couldn't force herself to look away from the horrible sight.

In that instant she was back on the floor of a hotel room across town wrestling a murderer for control of an eerily similar knife. She remembered the killer's heavy breathing and sweaty hands as they tried to wrench the knife away.

Then there was blood, so much blood. None of it was Maiden's but it had trickled all over her and dried on her hands and into her clothes. It had taken days for her to stop feeling stained with that blood.

She knew this wasn't the time to let herself spiral back into the terrifying memories. She reminded herself sternly that she had fought the killer off and now they were dead. It was done; she didn't need to think about it anymore.

Maiden took a deep breath and forced her eyes to close. Her unusually sharp memory occasionally worked against her. She struggled to forget pivotal events, even when she desperately wanted to. But she'd learned a few tricks over the years to help her cope; for the most part she succeeded.

She pressed her fingertips to her forehead and pulled in a few deep breaths. She pictured herself locking the memory away and then slowly opened her eyes.

Maiden glanced immediately at David and saw that he wasn't looking her way; relief poured through her. He didn't notice her near miss with a panic attack. He was busy on the phone while also issuing orders to the other officers that had turned up and were now milling around the garage.

Maiden let out a calming breath but stilled and felt herself pale when she saw Officer Parker watching her. Despite catching herself before her mind could sink any further into the horror, she still felt embarrassed and exposed that someone had observed her struggle.

Parker didn't look annoyed, smug or even begrudgingly tolerant this time; she looked quietly curious. Maiden squared her shoulders and glanced back at the car, suddenly determined to show that she could take whatever this case threw at her.

She needed to focus on the facts, the clues, the realities. She thought about Bradley and Ree. Murder/suicide was quite a departure from the relationship they'd appeared to have. It seemed incredible that Bradley would snap like that, but he had essentially lost everything. Ree had tipped their hand more than once; had he perhaps blamed her for the way things had gone?

Maiden listened to Elvan as he struggled to speak around his grief. He shuddered and shook his head in disbelief as he told David about the message he'd received from Bradley. He then pulled out his phone and showed him. Maiden edged closer, making a point of hugging Aunt Bella's shoulders as she stole a quick look at the screen.

Daddy, I can't go on. I killed Granny, it was Mama's idea, but I did it. I can't live with myself anymore, I'm so sorry.

Maiden shook her head sadly, it was all so twisted and selfish. Gail had clearly been a tyrant but still, to not only commit murder but also try to take every penny from your own father, it was horrible. And then his mother...

She steeled herself and glanced back at Ree's body. The infamous ring still sat on her bloodied finger. She was crammed into the trunk and half wrapped in some kind of tarp. That was interesting; Maiden wondered where the woman had actually died. Her eyes slid to the house.

She stayed watchfully silent and hovered in the background while she took everything in. The next thing she knew David was standing in front of her and looking at her critically.

"Are you all right?" he asked quietly.

She shifted her eyes to his and nodded. It wasn't a lie, she wasn't exactly fine, but this was the first panicked flashback she'd had since the initial shock of fighting off a serial killer had ebbed. She was holding it together. She was okay.

David didn't look convinced but it wasn't the time or the place to pursue it. He touched the backs of his fingers fleetingly to her cheek and then glanced over at Greg and Parker.

"Doc Jenkins is on his way and we need to search the house," he told them. "One of you drive the Hedgewicks and Miss Harlow to the station and take their statements. I'll be along in a while."

"I'll go, sir," Parker said as she stepped forward and glanced at Maiden. "We'll take your car so you'll have it there when you're ready to go home."

Maiden just nodded and grasped her keys from where they were hanging out of Bella's purse. Parker smiled briefly as she smoothly snatched them away.

"I'll drive, if you don't mind," she said.

Maiden didn't argue the point; she suspected that she looked as fragile as she felt. She really didn't need to be driving if it was avoidable.

The trip to the station was quiet and tense. In the backseat, Elvan was staring out the window as tears streamed down his cheeks. Bella held his hand and laid her head on his shoulder.

Maiden couldn't think of anything to say to a man that had lost so much of his family so horribly and in such a short time. But then a heartlessly pragmatic thought flitted through her mind—everything would be so much easier with them gone.

She winced and shook her head slightly. It was a terrible thing to think so soon after seeing Ree crammed in the trunk of her son's car while he himself was collapsed behind the wheel. It actually hadn't occurred to her until now that he might still be alive.

Maiden glanced at Parker but stopped herself before blundering out the question right in front of Elvan. She clamped her mouth shut and ran her hands over her face.

"We're nearly there," Parker said quietly when she saw her shifting around.

As promised, they pulled into the parking lot of the police station a few minutes later. They walked into the station and saw Nancy standing behind the desk with a searching expression. One look at Elvan and Bella made it clear that something big had gone down.

"Hey, Nancy." Parker nodded down the hall. "Would you show the Hedgewicks to the Captain's office? I'll come and take their statements in a minute."

"Yes, of course," Nancy said as she stepped out from behind the desk; she looked towards Maiden. "And Miss Harlow?"

"I'll look after her, thanks." Was her only reply.

Nancy didn't argue but gave her a warning look before ushering the older pair politely down the corridor.

Maiden watched them go. She was feeling a little numb but at least she was calmer. She wasn't sure why Officer Parker had separated her from the others, maybe she didn't trust her not to interfere with her as she questioned them. She quietly steeled herself to be warned off.

"Are you feeling better now?" Parker asked as soon as they were alone.

"I'm fine." Maiden said a little too quickly.

"Really?" She almost smiled. "Because you were miles away back there. I know the look, I've seen it before."

"It's not nice to see a body in a trunk," Maiden said by way of explanation.

"It's not easy to see a stabbing after what you dealt with a month ago," she said plainly but nicely and quirked a full and luscious brow. "I was there too, don't forget. Have you talked to anyone about it?"

"My cat." She smiled wanly. "He says I'm coping just fine."

"Good, I was afraid you were relying on suppression alone," Parker chuckled and leaned back against the desk. "So, how'd you do that back at the scene?"

"Do what?" Maiden asked uncertainly.

"You were about to lose it," she said frankly. "But you reeled it back in. How?"

"I've learned a few tricks over the years." She shrugged and glanced down at the floor. "They don't always work but...I manage."

"Yeah, okay," she allowed. "But what do you actually do?"

"Are you being nosy or looking for suggestions?" Maiden gave her a look.

"Both," she replied.

Maiden was quietly surprised at that candid reply. She wasn't sure if the normally gruff officer was being genuine but she supposed it didn't ultimately matter.

"It might sound silly," she admitted, "but I have a big wooden cabinet in my mind. If a thought or a memory pops up and I can't shake it, I picture myself putting it in there and locking it away."

Parker just looked at her for a moment.

"And that works?"

"Most of the time," she said.

Parker smiled faintly and gave a conceding nod. "So, how do you learn to trick yourself like that?"

"It's not a trick, it's a technique." Maiden tucked her hands in her pockets. "When you grow up being hated by as many people as I was, you spend a lot of time in your own head. I know myself pretty well."

"Sounds rough."

"It was, Officer Parker."

"You can call me Sarah-Jane." She smiled again. "I know I wasn't any better to you when we met, but I really don't hate you."

"That's sweet of you," Maiden said wryly. "Okay, I will, but only if you call me Maiden."

"I was planning to," she said simply and gestured down the hall. "Shall we get a start on these statements now?"

***

Maiden sat in the corner and listened to Elvan and Bella relate their versions of events. Bella didn't have much to add, like Maiden, she'd sat quietly at Harlow House for the bulk of the day.

Elvan had spent the entire morning with his lawyer drafting and finalizing his new will. It was soon after that he gave in and responded to the message from Bradley asking him to visit.

He explained that he had felt sorry for his son and finally paid his bail, but Bella was very upset with him for it so he stayed out for a while to give her some space. Bella shut her eyes briefly at the reminder and shook her head sadly.

He went to see Pierce and then floated around town, made a few business calls and was ready to face Bella again when he received Bradley's confession message. He called Bella and headed to the house. He trailed off at that point and Sarah-Jane finished writing out her notes.

"Okay," she said mildly. "You can go for now, but don't leave town until Captain McAlister advises you to. I'll ask someone to drive you back so you can get your car."

"What about Maiden?" Bella asked warily.

"The captain will want to see her before she goes," she said simply and without apology.

After giving Bella and Elvan a bracing hug, Maiden was left to wait alone in David's office. She stood at the window and stared out at the mostly empty parking lot as a squad car pulled out to take them back to Elvan's car.

She wasn't sure how long David would be gone, he'd probably stay while his officers searched the house and possibly even check with Pierce and find out if his cousin contacted him as well.

She gazed up into the night sky, watching the stars slowly appear, as she reviewed the events of the strange day. Everything Elvan said would have to be verified, from his time spent with his lawyer to his visit with Pierce, possibly even his phone records. Not that he or Pierce were suspects at this point.

The thought of Bradley stabbing his mother to death and then treating her body so callously was unnerving. Of course, guilt over murdering his grandmother and then the frustration of having done it for nothing would weigh heavily. Especially if he really had tried to kill his father a few times too.

She wasn't sure how much time had passed when the door opened; she glanced over to see David walk inside. She'd been so preoccupied that she hadn't noticed his car pull in.

"Hey." He smiled gently as he shut the door behind him. "Thank you for waiting for me."

Maiden saw no point in mentioning that Sarah-Jane hadn't asked or offered a choice. It didn't matter, she'd have stayed regardless as long as the option was there. She turned and managed a smile as he approached.

David slid his arms around her and pulled her snugly against him. Maiden didn't hesitate, she nestled in and laid her head on his chest.

She felt his warmth and his strength and it helped her to shrug off her lingering tension. He stroked her hair for a moment before touching her cheek and prompting her to look at him.

"Are you all right?" he asked.

"Yeah." She let out a slow breath. "It's just been a weird day."

"I know, it's okay," he murmured.

"Is Bradley dead?" she almost whispered.

"Yes, he is," he said quietly. "It's going to take a while to sort it all out, but it seems straightforward. Probably."

Probably. She shut her eyes briefly and let the situation unfold in her mind.

"Does it look like Ree was murdered in the house?" she asked as she tucked back into his shirt. "Was there much blood?"

"Not a lot," he conceded. "But we did find some spattered in the kitchen."

"So, he might have killed her on that tarp she was wrapped in." It wasn't a question.

"It would explain the lack of mess." He shrugged. "You gave your statement?"

"Yeah, Sarah-Jane took it." She eased back a step and faced him. He looked guarded, she assumed that she did too.

"You're on a first name basis now?" he asked with a faint smile.

"Yes, I have that effect on people." She brushed her hair off her shoulder. "She was finally forced to admit that she doesn't despise me completely."

"Oh good," he smirked and pulled out his notepad and flicked back a few pages, "that's progress. Did you see Elvan at all before you got to the house?"

"No, he was gone before I came downstairs this morning," she shook her head, "and he didn't come back all day."

"You know he paid Bradley's bail." He glanced at her to see her reaction.

"Yeah, I was there when he called and told Aunt Bella." She pulled a face. "It didn't go over well."

"I was a bit surprised myself, to be honest," he admitted.

"How was Bradley when he left the station? Did you see him?" She chewed thoughtfully at her bottom lip.

"He was happy to be leaving," David said slowly. "He seemed...yeah, happy to be leaving."

"How was Elvan?" She locked her eyes with his.

"Quiet," he mused. "He didn't look too thrilled with what he was doing...maybe he was thinking about having to tell his wife that he'd personally let her biggest detractor out of the clink."

"'The clink'?" she finally laughed a little. "You're awesome."

"I try." He gave her a smiling look and ran a hand over his smooth jaw. "I shaved, incidentally."

"I noticed and thank you." She smiled warmly but frowned gently as her gaze drifted to his unadorned throat. "No tie today?"

"You have them all," he reminded her.

"You only own three neckties?" she asked dubiously.

"Yes. Had I anticipated you having a tie fetish I would've stocked up." He gave her a patient look and turned back to his notepad. "You could always give one back if it bothers you to see me without it."

"But they have your smell on them!" she protested before she could help it. She immediately felt like a pathetic idiot and clamped her mouth shut.

David wasn't laughing at her though. He sighed and pinched the bridge of his nose but it did nothing to hide his pleased grin. She hadn't taken him for the soppy, sentimental type, but he was clearly touched. He wouldn't look at her but was still smiling as he resumed scribbling notes.

"You're killing me, Harlow," he said under his breath.

He finished whatever he was scrawling, it could have been a drawing of a cat for all she knew, and then gestured towards the door. She didn't question the sudden retreat, it was late and he had a lot on his mind besides her minor obsession with his sexy scent.

They made their way to the foyer and found Greg and Nancy at the desk. Maiden stood before them and noticed that David kept a slight distance from her. Maiden looked at him for a minute as she let herself accept the suspicions that were still lingering.

Appearances suggested that Bradley confessed to Gail's murder and then killed Ree and himself out of guilt. It was by no means good news, but it was tidy. It was very tidy.

"Well, that's that, right?" Greg broke the heavy silence with a cheerful smile. "At least it sort of clears the way for you two, doesn't it?"

"Yes." Nancy smiled slyly. "You can finally officially be 'David and Maiden' instead of 'Captain and Harlow'."

"Mm," David grunted. "Now that everything's settled…"

"Yeah." Maiden sounded just as cautious.

Their eyes met and they stared for a long moment, quietly, pensively. Maiden folded her arms loosely and nearly sighed.

"David," she began carefully, "was there any blood on Bradley's clothes?"

"No, Maiden." A corner of his mouth curved upwards slightly. "There wasn't."

"None at all?" she pressed, he shook his head. "That seems unusual after a savage stabbing murder."

"Yeah." He still smiled at her.

"Were his fingerprints on the knife?" She lifted her brows casually.

"No fingerprints at all," he murmured.

"Find any gloves?"

"No."

"Did you ever track down Agnes?"

"Not yet."

She closed her eyes briefly and really did sigh this time. She gave David a knowing look and took a step backwards.

"Awesome," she replied mildly. "Well, I'll see you later, Captain."

"Hopefully soon, Harlow." He was still smiling at her as she walked away. "Any point in telling you not to get involved any deeper?"

"I've listened to you every other time, right?" She shrugged without slowing or looking back.

Chapter Twenty-Six

By the following morning Maiden was still feeling deeply uneasy. She had a sinking suspicion that Bradley had also been murdered, and David clearly thought so too. Her list of suspects had been shortened by two, but it was all still a muddle.

It was possible, of course, that whoever killed Bradley and Ree wasn't the same person that killed Gail. She considered the number of people that had something against Bradley and Ree. She could think of several people that could've killed him and sent that text from his phone.

Apart from the obvious possibilities of Elvan and Pierce, there was still Marti, Sylvia and Agnes to consider. Whether or not a woman could have dragged Ree into the trunk of Bradley's car was debatable, but Marti and Sylvia could probably have done it together. Or, if it was Agnes, she and Bradley could have worked together, and then maybe she turned on him.

As far as motive went, Elvan and Pierce were safe financially. Gail died before she could disinherit them. Bradley's fake will hadn't been a genuine threat, and everyone knew that *before* he'd been killed. But Pierce detested Ree and was still angry with Bradley for stealing Marti away. As for Elvan, there were the attempts on his life, and he probably didn't appreciate Bradley's plan to swindle him.

Marti and Sylvia had good reason to hate Gail and Bradley, but not necessarily Ree. She could have just gotten in the way, or she might have been sacrificed to frame Bradley.

As for Agnes, she'd been cheated and betrayed quite thoroughly. While she could hardly demand much sympathy after damaging other people's lives out of envy and greed, she'd definitely gotten slapped in the face with her own mischief.

After playing a key part in turning Gail against Elvan, lining everything up for an absolute fortune to fall into Bradley's lap, he'd turned on her as soon as she'd signed the will. Not only had he dumped her, but he tried to leave her to take the blame for it all. She'd be livid, possibly murderously so.

Maiden sighed and shook her head, it all seemed plausible. She wondered who David suspected, but he doubtless had more information to work with than she did. He'd be busy even now tracking people down and checking alibis.

It could have been any of them, but something was picking at the back of Maiden's mind. Nothing terribly specific, just a few little things that weren't sitting right.

She glanced up when she saw the front door open. She wasn't overly surprised to see Pierce walk in, but she still felt herself tense. His eyes went straight to her and he quickly approached.

She'd understand him looking shocked or even saddened, but he looked nervous, which did nothing to put her at ease.

"Good morning, Pierce," she said carefully. "Are you all right?"

"No, not really. I need to see Uncle Elvan, I tried to call him last night after I heard about Bradley. He must've had his phone off." He took a shaky breath and pressed his lips together.

"Yeah, he was in a pretty bad state," Maiden nodded and decided to be brave. "Did, um, did Bradley try to contact you yesterday?"

"No, he didn't," Pierce dabbed his forehead with a handkerchief. "He had other ideas, apparently Bradley tried asking Marti to come and visit him now that he was out."

"She told you that?" Maiden frowned.

"This mornin'," he nodded. "Right after the cops informed her of what had happened and started askin' questions. I think it scared her."

"She didn't go, did she?" Maiden felt her stomach twist.

"No! Of course not," Pierce scoffed. "She's naïve but she's not stupid. Bradley must've been desperate to try crawlin' back to her. When she told him to go away and never speak to her again, well, he might've felt that was the last straw."

Maiden didn't reply to that. She did find it interesting that Marti revealed that to Pierce, she wondered if she'd told the police as well. She doubted it. She also wondered if either Marti or Sylvia had decent alibis; she somehow doubted that too.

"Anyway, is Uncle Elvan in?" Pierce clenched his hands tightly. "I have to talk to him."

"Yes, of course," Maiden said quietly and gestured towards the stairs. "I'll, um, take you up to their suite."

Maiden led the way, very aware of the fidgety, anxious man that was following close behind. Despite telling herself not to jump to conclusions, she wasn't entirely comfortable to be the one leading him to Bella and Elvan's room.

When they reached the third floor she glanced back to see that he was still hovering quite close. Maiden cleared her throat and knocked loudly on the door. A moment later they heard footsteps and then Bella appeared before them.

"Hello, sweeties." Bella pushed the door wide and ushered them both inside. "Come on in."

She didn't particularly want to be there, but Maiden decided not to head straight back to reception. It was entirely possible that Pierce was only there to comfort his grieving uncle, but something felt wrong and she didn't want to leave Bella alone there.

Pierce didn't seem to care if she was there listening or not. He nodded his head in thanks to Bella and immediately started looking around the suite.

"Uncle Elvan?" he called out. "Are you here? Can I speak to you for a minute, please? It's important!"

Maiden stayed quietly watchful as she glanced around. She saw suitcases pulled out and sitting near the door. She knew that Aunt Bella and Elvan had gotten up early to pack their bags in expectation of being able to leave on their honeymoon at last. She could understand them being eager to get away from the horrible events that had marred the first days of their marriage and so didn't mention their optimistic haste.

She shrugged in response to Bella's questioning nod in Pierce's direction. A moment later Elvan walked out of the bedroom and smiled when he saw his nephew.

"Hey there, Pierce," he said kindly and accepted the younger man's hug. "How you holdin' up, buddy?"

"Awful." Pierce paled further as he grasped his uncle's shoulder. "I'm so sorry about Bradley."

"I know, so am I." Elvan rubbed his eyes. "We just gotta keep movin' forward...it's gonna be okay."

"Yeah, I know." Pierce took a deep breath, clearly steeling himself for something. "Uncle Elvan...I lied about a few things that night, the night of your weddin'."

Maiden's eyes widened and she and Bella exchanged a worried look. Elvan looked kind and calm, however. He smiled at Pierce and gestured for him to continue.

"I did go back upstairs to see Granny that night," he admitted quietly. "I didn't hurt her, but I did go back."

"I see," Elvan's gentle tone was soothing. "Tell me why."

"For these." He dug into his pocket and then held out his hand.

Maiden and Bella came closer and saw the other two missing rings sitting in his palm. Bella looked confused but it made sense to Maiden. If one of the rings Gail had worn had belonged to Ree, she suspected one of the others belonged to her other former daughter-in-law, Pierce's mother.

"I saw Granny flashing Mama's ring around along with hers and Ree's. It made me sick! She tricked Mama into handing it over years ago." He took a deep breath. "I took it back, it rightfully belonged to Mama, even though she's gone now."

"I agree, Pierce. You should have that ring," Elvan said kindly. "And I kinda figured it was you who took it."

Pierce just looked at him and shook his head. "But you didn't say anything."

"That's right, I didn't," Elvan said. "I thought you might've taken Alice's ring, I always wondered how Mama got it in the first place. And then I wondered if you didn't take Mama's too out of anger."

"I did. She lied to us." Pierce looked like he was trying not to get angry again. "Back when the business was strugglin', she said she'd help us out, but only if she got somethin' in return. Mama didn't have much choice so she gave her the ring; that's what Granny wanted. It was years before we found out that the money came from you, not her."

"Oh Pierce," Elvan shook his head. "I had no idea, son. I'm sorry. You keep both of those rings and we'll forget any of this ever happened."

"No. I only want Mama's," he said firmly as he dropped Gail's ring in Elvan's hand. "I shouldn't have taken this one at all...I hate to admit it, but I only took it so the old bat could get a fright when she woke up without it. Aw heck, I shouldn't have said that! I'm sorry."

"Don't worry about it, Pierce," Elvan chuckled quietly and shook his head. He tucked the ring in his pocket. "Come sit and have coffee with me. I got a few errands to run this mornin' and then we're hopin' to be on the road just after lunch. I'd like a chance to visit with you before we all head off."

As the men walked to the couches, talking quietly, Maiden couldn't help feeling like she really wanted to leave.

The whole business sat uneasily with her still and she wasn't sure how David would feel about the stolen rings. It probably wasn't a huge deal; the current rightful owner was happy to let the matter go so why should anyone else be upset about it?

Because he might be lying about only taking the rings, Maiden whispered internally. *He was there in the room with Gail after she'd been sedated, how else could he take the rings without her knowing? All he had to do was move a pillow...*

"Well, I might go back downstairs." Maiden glanced at Bella and started sidling towards the door. "Maybe you'd like to come and have coffee with me? Right now."

"Thanks, babydoll. I will in just a few minutes." Bella tapped her on the shoulder before she could get away. "Can you do me a little favor though?"

"Yeah, sure." Maiden managed a smile.

"What with the *incidents* and all, we forgot to take Elvan's tux back to the rental shop," she shook her head at herself as she walked over to a chair that had a large garment bag laying over the back. "Would you mind awfully dropping it off for me? I just got too much to do."

"Of course I don't mind." Maiden walked over and accepted the surprisingly heavy suit, "I'll take it back today."

"You're an angel." She blew her a kiss but then shook a finger at her. "Don't forget to check the pockets."

"Okay," she smiled and nodded as she slipped out again.

She made her way downstairs, still thinking about Pierce's confession. She wondered how Gail had gotten Ree's ring from her. She may have bribed her to get it, or even threatened to take Bradley away. Gail Hedgewick had probably been heartless enough for anything.

Maiden couldn't imagine seeing a woman that had been as cruelly betrayed as Pierce's mother and then actually tricking her into turning over her engagement ring. And then to wear it, and Ree's, to her son's wedding as some kind of sick protest. Maiden suspected that Gail had been trying to prove that *she* held the power in the family.

Not anymore, lady, Maiden thought sadly. *Maybe if you'd just been nicer to people. How much happier would your life have been?*

She walked behind the desk and on into the office. She laid the garment bag across the small table and glanced at the doorway to see if Aunt Bella had come downstairs yet. A part of her felt like the danger was over, but she couldn't be sure and she would just as soon Aunt Bella wasn't closed away with Pierce.

Her cautious thoughts were disrupted when the phone rang. She wandered out to the desk to answer it and ended up in a lengthy conversation. She had nearly finished a group booking for several couples when Pierce came downstairs again.

He smiled and waved to her as he headed for the front door. She waved back, subtly looked him over for blood spatters, and watched him slip outside. When the indecisive guy she was talking to was finally satisfied with the arrangements, she hung up and took a deep breath.

She went back to the office and shut the door behind her, hopeful of a peaceful moment to finish her task. She unzipped the garment bag and pushed it open as wide as she could. Her mind wandered as she started digging through the myriad of pockets. She wondered how much more Agnes knew that she hadn't admitted to before. Once she was caught, would she be more talkative now that her accomplices were dead?

Aunt Bella and Elvan seemed so confident of being able to leave soon. Of course, David wouldn't have told them about his lingering suspicions yet, he'd have to find some evidence first. Maiden pulled out a crumpled tissue from the pants pocket and dropped it in the wastebasket.

She started thinking about Elvan as she rifled through his jacket. He seemed so wishy washy about some things. He'd been angry with Ree and Bradley, he'd told her outright that he thought Bradley was in on Gail's murder...but then he bailed him out of jail.

Why would he do that if he really thought he was guilty? And he knew for a fact that Bradley had been scheming to turn Gail against him and leave him penniless. Elvan and Bradley hadn't been close, Bradley had chosen his mother at every opportunity, he didn't seem to particularly love his father.

Perhaps what struck her the most was the fact that Bradley hated Aunt Bella, and he was trying to ruin her right along with Elvan. One thing Maiden had never called into question was Elvan's love for Aunt Bella.

There's something you're not telling us, Elvan, she thought to herself as she finished with the jacket and moved on to the vest. The first pocket was empty, but as she slid her hand into the second, her fingers brushed a small, hard object.

Maiden frowned distractedly and pulled it out to look at it. Her breath caught and her eyes widened when she opened her hand and saw half of an empty capsule cupped in her palm.

Her heart pounded and her head started to spin. Panicked heat flooded her cheeks and she struggled to pull in a full breath. She set the suit on the table and grabbed her phone, quickly pulling up David's number.

"David!" she whispered the instant he answered. "It was Elvan! I just found the other half of that capsule in his tux!"

"Where are you?" he asked in a deadly serious voice.

"In the office, I think he's still in their suite." She looked anxiously at the door when she heard the knob rattle. "Oh no, that might be him."

"Harlow! Stay calm and try to get outside." He was using his cop voice, she assumed that meant he was scared too. "I'm on my way and I'm sending backup!"

She'd just hung up when the door whipped open and Elvan ran his eyes over the room, settling them on her. Maiden forced a smile and tucked the empty capsule in her own pocket as casually as she could. She saw his gaze stray to her pocket and then lock on her face, his expression was blank but his eyes were cold and watchful.

"Hi, Uncle Elvan." She tried to put him at ease with a familial greeting. "Are you done packing already?"

"Almost," he said quietly and shut the door firmly behind him. "Just a few odds and ends to tidy up."

"Cool." She swallowed and watched him closely as he stood facing her across the table. "Have you decided where you're going on your honeymoon yet?"

"We're still debatin'," he murmured as he looked down at the tux and the pockets that had been turned out, he wet his lips and turned back to her. "I'm thinkin' a tropical cruise might be in order. Very relaxin' after all we've been through."

"You have been through a lot, you and Aunt Bella." She nodded but eased back a bit as he pulled the tux towards him. "You've had a hard life, haven't you, Elvan?"

"Yes, I suppose I have." He smiled very briefly as he started checking the pockets himself. "People don't believe that since the family always had money. They don't realize that money brings as many problems as it solves."

"Like what?" She grasped at any hope of keeping him talking until David got there. He had almost checked every pocket now, she didn't have much time.

"You never know who really cares about you when you're wealthy," he explained. "That's what I love about my Bella, I've been in love with her since we were kids. People keep sayin' she only wants my money, but that ain't so."

"No," Maiden agreed with him and took a step towards the back door. "She loves you, she told me. I know you would never want to hurt her."

"No, I try my hardest not to. I've done my very best to protect her," he sighed when he reached the last pocket and found it empty, he smiled gently at her as he tossed the vest aside. "But I forgot about my tux, unfortunately."

"That's okay." Maiden waved it away. "I'm happy to take it back for you. I already promised Aunt Bella I would."

"You're a nice girl." He shook his head and glanced around as if gauging his options. "I really wish I had more choice, honey."

"There's always a choice, Elvan," she said seriously, not liking the way he was eyeing off the pair of scissors in the pencil cup near the door. "Tell me about Bradley and Ree."

"That pair? Not much to be said for them," he sniffed. "I was only about twenty when I married Ree. Bella had just broken my heart, not that she realized that, and I was a bit lost. Ree was pretty when she was younger and acted sweet. I settled for her, but I never claimed to be in love. She knew what she was walkin' into, but she wanted the money."

"That must have been difficult for you both," Maiden said as she gripped the chair in front of her tightly and slid it back, ready to defend herself however she could. "Did she really get your brother drunk?"

"Well, it's hard to prove a thing like that. They both told their own story, but it didn't really matter. I never loved Ree, and I certainly wasn't gonna keep her after that," he muttered indignantly. "And I couldn't help hatin' Alan for helpin' himself to my wife, regardless of how I felt about her. I wasn't too choked up when he died."

"Why did you kill Gail?" she found herself asking.

"Who says I did a thing like that?" He stilled and stared at her.

I did, because I'm a genius, she grumbled to herself but maintained her outward calm. She wasn't about to turn her back on him, even to run for the door, she didn't believe she could get out before he reached her. He was already stalking her, she decided she might as well get some answers.

"You had the most to lose, and everyone you hated is dead now." She shrugged. "I don't think you're an evil man, Elvan, but you've done some terrible things. Haven't you?"

Before he could answer the reception door swung open and Sarah-Jane stepped in with her gun drawn.

"Police! No one move!" she said loudly as she scanned the room.

"Look out!" Maiden shouted as Elvan grabbed her wrist and twisted the gun away.

"You stand over there with her!" Elvan ordered grimly as he pointed the gun at the scowling officer. "Hurry up!"

"Elvan, this won't work," Maiden said steadily as Sarah-Jane sidled up next to her. "I called the police already, she's not the only cop on their way here."

"No, I was just the closest," Sarah-Jane said, clearly annoyed with herself for being disarmed. "It won't be long."

"Hush up!" He scowled and stomped his foot. "I was so damn close, why'd you have to keep pokin' at it?! You and your boyfriend both, you kept diggin' and lookin' for motives. Mama was a horrible old woman, she hated everyone and we hated her back! There's your motive! Ree was a selfish hag and Bradley was her only asset, what does that tell you?! I put up with all of them for years and years! All I wanted in return was to be left in peace with my Bella. But no, even that was too much! No matter what I did or said they just wouldn't let us be happy!"

"So, you murdered them?" Maiden arched a brow.

"You look so much like Bella when you do that." He smiled sadly. "Aw dammit girl, she loves you. How am I supposed to explain this?"

"You can't explain it away, Elvan. You've killed all your scapegoats," she pointed out. "The police are on their way and they know it was you. You're better off stopping now rather than adding on more guilt."

"No!" He glowered. "I'm not gonna lose Bella again! That's why Ree had to die. I'd never planned a scrap of harm for that old wretch. But when I told her I wasn't gonna help Bradley she screamed and cried, and when I didn't budge she threatened to kill Bella! Said she'd take her away from me forever if I didn't support her in style. Oh, you should've heard her listin' demands like she was the only one in the world that mattered. The look on her face when she died...she always was the biggest fool I ever knew."

Maiden held her breath for an instant and exchanged a wary look with Sarah-Jane.

"What about Bradley?" she asked carefully. "Why kill him too?"

"Someone had to be responsible, didn't they?" he murmured.

"Your claim that someone was trying to kill you," Maiden drew her brows together pensively, "was that just another trick to incriminate Bradley?"

"Oh no, darlin'. He did try a couple of times, but he wasn't smart enough to pull it off. I knew straight away what he was up to. When that didn't work, he stepped up the pressure on Mama. That useless waste of breath tried to take the fortune he never helped to build just to chase Bella away from me!" he said with a huff. "So what's wrong with what I did? They tried to take my life away, so I took theirs. It was fair, Maiden, the fairest thing that's ever happened in my whole miserable life."

"Elvan," Maiden felt herself grow angry, "Aunt Bella would've still married you without your money. Why didn't you trust her?"

He shut his eyes for a moment, when he opened them they were glassy with unshed tears. For that moment he was the lovely, sad but kind man she'd met not all that long ago.

"They were all so sure. They all said I was worthless without the family fortune. I love her so much; I couldn't risk them bein' right. Can't you understand that?" He looked smaller and crestfallen for a moment but then he turned thoughtful and reflective. "I don't miss any of them, you know. Pierce is the only one who's worth anything. I'm glad I still have him."

Maiden could see the change coming over him, he was eerily calm now. Sarah-Jane noticed too; she took a steadying breath and edged closer.

"He's about to blow," she whispered from the corner of her mouth. "Get ready to duck for cover. I'll try to slow him down."

Before she could respond or dive under the table, the door opened again and Aunt Bella peered inside.

"Why's everyone in here? And what's all the yellin' about?" She scowled and then blinked her clear blue eyes at Elvan. "What're you doin' with a gun, sweetheart?"

Elvan's eyes widened in horror, he clearly didn't know what to do now. Maiden felt her heart start pounding again.

"Aunt Bella," she said stiffly and nodded towards her uncle-in-law. "It was Elvan. He killed his family and now he's threatening us."

"What?" Bella gave her a look and turned to Elvan. "What's goin' on, sugar?"

"Just trust me, Bella." Elvan managed to smile placidly. "I'll handle this and everything will be fine."

"Now hold on just a minute! I'm sick of you tellin' me to stay out of everything!" she said sternly, bracing her hands on her hips and walking in a bit further. "That's my favorite niece you're glarin' at, and I don't like that one bit!"

David appeared in the doorway at that point with his gun drawn. He took in the scene and obligingly held up a hand when Elvan sidled in further and pointed his gun threateningly at Maiden. Bella noticed and her expression darkened.

"Elvan," she said grimly. "Stop this right now!"

"Bella, honey," his voice was shaky, "just let me handle this, then we'll be on our way. You want to go on a cruise, sugar? I'll take you on a luxury cruise, right around the world. You-you go wait outside for me now."

"Elvan," she said seriously. "You aren't goin' to hurt my little Maiden, or that other girl. You hear me? Put that horrible gun down this minute."

"You don't understand." He swallowed hard, sweat was trickling down his face and his hand shook slightly.

"I understand that you're threatenin' my niece. She's the closest thing I have to a baby of my own, Elvan." Bella's tone was steady and unyielding as she came and stood between him and Maiden. "Don't you break my heart, you promised you'd never hurt me."

"I won't, Bella honey!" His eyes were wide and pleading. "She knows! She knows what I did! If I let her live they'll take you away from me again! I won't let that happen!"

"Elvan Hedgewick." Bella stepped closer, her eyes were locked with his. "Listen to me. I'm your wife now, through thick or thin. You put that gun down and I promise I'll help you some other way. No more violence; I don't like it."

He faltered and slowly eased the gun downward. Bella's left brow quirked as she curled her pudgy hand into a fist and drove it into his jaw. Elvan crumpled to the ground.

"Honestly!" Bella muttered as she grabbed the gun and held it away from her as if it were made of dog poop. "I swear there's not a decent man left to be had!"

"Mrs. Hedgewick," David said cordially as he stepped forward and confiscated the weapon, "nice work."

"Yeah, just dandy," she sighed as she stared down at Elvan and shook her head sadly.

Behind her Maiden finally relaxed a fraction. Sarah-Jane glanced at her and swatted her arm.

"She's awesome!" she whispered excitedly. "That was a one-punch takedown! I *trained* to do that and still split the skin over my knuckles!"

"Yeah, she's really something," Maiden said and stepped towards her aunt.

Bella was looking down as David handcuffed Elvan. She was quiet and a few tears had rolled down her cheeks. Maiden wasn't sure what to say so she just drew closer and rested a hand on her arm.

Bella glanced over and smiled faintly as she hugged her close. Maiden felt tears sting her eyes as she squeezed her in return.

"I'm so sorry, Aunt Bella," she whispered.

"Don't be sorry, honeypot. You did well," she murmured ruefully. "And I did ask you to figure it out, after all."

Greg and Officer Briggs arrived moments later and helped drag Elvan to his feet. He shook his head as he came to and was guided through the door.

"Bella honey?" he called in a panicky voice.

"I'm right here, sugar," she said numbly. "I'm comin'."

Maiden gave Bella another quick hug and dabbed at her eyes with her sleeve as she watched her aunt follow them out. She took a deep breath and glanced at David to find him watching her quietly. She met his intent gaze uncertainly.

David glanced at Sarah-Jane and held out her gun with an unimpressed look.

"Is this yours?" he asked flatly.

"Yes sir," she mumbled as she reclaimed it. "Sorry sir."

"I'm glad it didn't end differently," he said and nodded for her to go.

Sarah-Jane flicked Maiden a quick look, almost smiled, and then disappeared through the door. When they were alone, David tucked his own gun back into his shoulder holster and walked up to her.

"I don't care who sees what anymore," he said as he pulled her close and kissed her.

Maiden slid her hands up to his neck and kissed him back. She could feel his heart pounding and wondered how much of it was adrenaline and residual fear, she soon found out when he raised his head enough to speak.

"Would you *please* stop confronting lunatics?" he whispered, cupping her soft cheek in his hand.

"Good idea," she smiled wryly. "What was I thinking?"

"You terrified me," he said, resting his forehead against hers.

"I'm sorry, but it wasn't my idea. Elvan found me right after I pulled that capsule out of his tux. Oh!" she gasped as she remembered and leaned away slightly. "Wait a second!"

She dug into her pocket and pulled out the empty capsule shell. Her fingerprints would be all over it, of course, but she hadn't been expecting to find it. She dropped it in his hand with a lopsided smile.

"There you go," she sighed and rested her hand on his chest. "Are you absolutely sure you want anything more to do with my crazy family?"

"Yeah. Pretty sure." He smiled and dropped another quick kiss on her lips before grasping her hand. "Come on, Bella will need you with her. And I'm not letting you out of my sight until I can take a full breath again."

CHAPTER TWENTY-SEVEN

Maiden and David were still holding hands as they walked out into impossibly cheerful sunshine. Everything felt so unreal and disjointed; she was grateful to have the grounding sensation of being next to David.

As they started down the side walk towards his hastily parked car, Maiden raised her eyes and spotted Elvan's big, expensive Mercedes. She froze and stood staring at it.

"Are you all right?" David stilled beside her.

"David," she said softly, "did you ever track down Agnes?"

"No, not yet. She seems to have effectively vanished," he admitted. "But at least we know we don't have a killer on the loose anymore. She has to surface sometime, we'll find her."

"David," she whispered as a disturbing but absolute certainty gripped her. She let out a shaky breath and pointed at Elvan's car. "He said he had errands to run before they left..."

David followed her gaze and then looked at her questioningly; she nodded and bit her lip. With a conceding nod and a squeeze of her hand before releasing it, he motioned for her to stay put.

Maiden felt her heart thumping as she watched him approach the car and start peering in the windows. She knew in an instant that something was wrong, he frowned faintly and then glanced up at her with a quirked a brow.

"Can you find the keys for me?"

Maiden ran inside and tore up the stairs to the Romance and Glamor suite. By the time she'd found the keys and hurried back downstairs, Gloria was behind the desk.

"What's goin' on, angel?" she asked with a frown. "You look pale enough to faint."

"Elvan's the killer and almost shot me. He's been arrested, but I think there's another body in his car." She stopped long enough to quickly explain and then ran out the front door with her mother noisily following.

"What the hell do you mean he almost shot you?!" she screamed as she ran after her. "If he ain't dead yet, he's gonna be!"

Maiden didn't stop or even slow down until she reached David, who had just put his phone away. She skidded to a halt in front of him and handed him the keys. A moment later a heavily winded Gloria was right beside them. David unlocked the door and flicked them a wary look.

"You ladies should both step back," he warned.

"Yeah, we probably should." Maiden nodded. Neither of them budged.

David shook his head with a resigned sigh and opened the rear passenger door. Maiden stared at the smallish lump that was lying on the floor of the backseat with a blanket thrown over it. She knew exactly what it was, she didn't want to see it, but she couldn't look away. David peeled the blanket back enough to reveal Agnes' face. Her mouth was slightly open, so were her eyes.

Maiden reached over and gently placed a hand over her mother's mouth just as her horrified scream erupted. Gloria grabbed Maiden roughly and dragged her back a few steps, as if afraid that the corpse could somehow harm them.

"It's okay, Mom," she managed to sound steady, although internally she was anything but. "It was Elvan, he's been arrested."

Gloria wasn't listening, she was blathering away in a voice so panicked and breathy that it was practically incoherent.

Maiden was trying to settle her down despite still dealing with the strain of having almost been shot; she didn't have a lot to give at the moment. She closed her eyes and felt her knees go a bit wobbly but then David was there. He stepped closer and hugged them both tightly.

"Gloria," his deep voice was serene and soothing, Maiden was again reminded that he dealt with crises for a living, "calm down. There's no danger anymore. I know it's awful, but we've got him, he's being locked up right now. Your family is safe, I promise."

It took a few minutes but Gloria gradually pulled in a few deep breaths and her body grew less rigid. She leaned back and managed a weak smile.

"Thank you, honey. I'm sorry I panicked," she said quietly and stroked Maiden's hair before taking a step back and looking at the car again. "What...what happens now?"

"I've called it in, someone will be here any time," David kept hugging Maiden, who hadn't moved, and looked over his shoulder when they heard sirens. "We need to get to the station. You can come too if you want to, Gloria. Bella's on her own at the moment."

Gloria gasped and hurried towards David's car as Sergeant Ramirez arrived, the lights on his car flashing ominously.

***

David drove Maiden and a still-unsettled Gloria to the police station. Gloria had let loose a barrage of questions for the entire drive. By the time they reached the station, she'd had heard enough to render even her speechless with shock.

David held the door open for the ladies but then charged ahead down the long hallway to the left of the foyer. Maiden and Gloria followed close behind.

Elvan had been locked into the first holding cell, ironically the same one Bradley had occupied for days. Bella was standing close by. She was stoic and subdued, but Gloria swooped in the instant she saw her and held her hand as they stood before the cold, sparse cell.

Maiden stepped quietly off to the side and observed, there was simply nothing she could say in that horribly stark moment. It was surreal to see the lovely, gentle man standing behind bars with a disturbingly calm expression on his face.

She glanced over at David as he whispered something to Greg. The younger officer nodded solemnly and flicked Maiden a brief, worried look before going to a nearby table and sitting down behind a small laptop. She assumed he'd been told to record whatever was about to be said.

David glanced at her and lifted his brows sadly. She offered a helpless, accepting shrug and shook her head. It wasn't his fault and there was nothing he could do about any of it. David gave her a quick wink and then turned back to his task.

She followed his gaze and took a slow, deep breath. Aunt Bella was standing near the barred door watching Elvan. He was now sitting on the cramped little bed staring at the floor, rocking slightly back and forth. Gloria stepped away discreetly and came to stand beside Maiden.

"Tell me about your mother's murder." David appeared completely poised and detached.

"Go on, honey," Bella said gently when Elvan hesitated. "And tell the truth."

"Well, I'd been plannin' it for weeks, I knew she'd been serious about changing her will this time. Bradley and Ree had really worked her over good," he sighed. "I had to stop her, and I really wanted it to happen at the weddin'. It was poetic, you see, it was a triumph. I wanted her to know before she died that I'd defied her and married the woman I loved."

"How did you do it?" David asked as Greg typed away in the background.

"I pocketed one of her sedatives when me and Bradley went to check on her that day we arrived in town," he explained with a small smile. "Then I just snuck upstairs after Agnes had prepared her warm milk. I got her distracted and stirred the extra dose in before handin' her the cup myself. She thought she was invincible."

"Why did you call it murder?" David quirked a brow. "Why not try to make it look like she died of an accident?"

Maiden briefly wondered why he asked that question before realizing how it connected to the other killings. Elvan exhaled slowly and stared off into space.

"Well, I must admit that I knew what Bradley had been up to. It was bad enough that he was lazy and useless, but to actually attack me? Try and take everything from me? No, he had to go. Besides, Bella didn't like him." He waved it away as though it were nothing. "I hadn't really thought about killin' him at first, I'd have been satisfied with leavin' him to rot in jail for the rest of his life. But then Ree turned up and started causin' trouble again...I truly enjoyed killin' her."

Bella looked chilled to the bone, she was staring at Elvan like he'd grown another head right before her eyes. Maiden could only imagine her horror as she realized what she'd married, what sort of monster had been sleeping beside her at night.

"Tell me about Ree," David said simply, his arms were folded and he refused to look away from Elvan.

"After she threatened Bella, I told her to meet me at the rental to talk about Bradley. I had everything all set up and waitin' for her." He smiled faintly. "She waltzed right in, spoutin' demands and sneerin' at me like I was helpless to do anything except what she wanted. The fool didn't even notice she was standin' on a tarp until she saw the knife in my hand."

He glanced at Bella when a tiny gasp escaped her lips. Elvan gazed adoringly at her and she made an obvious effort not to recoil.

"I made sure it was quick, honey," he assured her.

David, unmoved by the attempt to be soothing and doubtless aware of the distress being felt by the women in the room, cleared his throat loudly. Elvan turned back to him and waited.

"Then what?" David's tone had cooled slightly.

"I put her in Bradley's car, changed my clothes, and went and bailed him out of jail." He slid Bella a look but David stepped closer and he obligingly continued. "He thanked me *once* as I escorted him home, but he spent most of the time bellyachin' about his lot in life and how unfair everything had always been. That didn't worry me none. I just fed him half a bottle of his favorite whiskey to celebrate his freedom and then it was into the car for a nice long nap."

Maiden could feel her mother's shiver as they listened to Elvan's chillingly calm recounting. She wasn't immune personally, but it wasn't her first brush with coldly calculating murderers. She took Gloria's clammy hand and gave it a squeeze.

"And Agnes?" David pressed. Bella stiffened and looked sharply at David and then at Elvan.

"Did you kill her too?" she barely managed to ask.

"Aw, that ain't even really a crime," Elvan rolled his eyes and sat back a little. "She started all this mess! She wanted Bradley to get the money so she could get at it; she's the one that hounded Mama until she lost what was left of her mind. Honestly, if I'd known what she was up to sooner, I'd have killed her ages ago. Maybe none of this would've had to happen. I did the world a favor gettin' rid of all of 'em."

"What happened?" David sounded deeply unimpressed.

"Bradley told me that turnin' Mama against me and Bella had been her idea. I didn't believe him at first but then he mentioned that she'd done it to Marti too." Elvan shrugged. "I couldn't let that slide, too many people died because of her mischief. So, I told her to meet me to discuss a settlement to repay her for helpin' the family. It wasn't hard to choke the life out of a little thing like her."

"But why, honey?" Bella looked aghast. "Why keep killin'? She couldn't of done nothin' to us now."

Elvan looked at her with the calmest, most charming smile Maiden had ever seen. "Because she deserved to die, sugar."

David ended the discussion there. He discreetly approached Bella and asked if she wanted a few minutes alone with her husband. When she stoically agreed, he cleared the room.

Gloria staggered numbly down the hallway with David and Maiden on either side of her. They were all uncomfortably quiet.

"Are you all right, Gloria?" David broke the silence as he guided her to the lobby.

"I will be, thanks, baby." She patted his arm and let out a shaky breath. "I can't believe this...Bella's got the crappiest taste in men of anyone I've ever known!"

"That's not entirely fair in this instance." David slid her a wry look.

"Having a whacko for a brother-in-law ain't real fair either," she replied tartly.

"At least you've got Alfie." He managed not to laugh when he said it but still got a swat on the arm.

They'd barely entered the lobby when Pierce burst through the door looking frantic. He stared at them and shook his head incredulously.

"I just got a phone call from this station that I simply do not believe! Are you serious?!" He looked absolutely horrified. "*Uncle Elvan?*"

"I'm sorry, Mr. Hedgewick." David said solemnly. "But it's true; he's admitted to everything."

"That's my whole blasted family either dead or in prison!" He rubbed his face with his hands. "I couldn't stand most of them, but they were mine."

"You still have Aunt Bella," Maiden pointed out gently and his eyes widened.

"Oh lord! Poor Bella!" He shook his head anxiously. "Is she all right? He didn't hurt her?"

"She's fine, all things considered. She could probably use some help at the moment though," David said and glanced at Nancy who was at her usual perch behind the desk. "Take Mr. Hedgewick through to see his aunt and uncle, please."

Nancy nodded as she stepped out and escorted Pierce to the holding cells. Gloria watched them go and shook her head. She then pulled out her phone and headed towards the door.

"I'd better call Alfie and Vonny real quick," she said shakily. "They'll have no idea what's goin' on. I'll see you outside, angel."

Maiden nodded and then shifted her gaze to David as Gloria disappeared through the front door. He was watching her quietly. She shook her head a little and sighed.

"Well, it wasn't the resolution I was hoping for," she said. "But still..."

"Yeah." He nodded once. "At least it's done."

"So, what happens now?" She bit her lip.

"Bella needs to call their lawyer back, he'll probably lean heavily on an insanity plea. Which looks pretty legitimate in this case." David glanced briefly heavenward. "And for me and the team, it's a lot of tedious behind the scenes work to piece everything together."

"Of course," she nodded. "It's all such a mess."

He took a step closer to her and lifted his brows sadly. "I'm sorry that all this has happened to your family, Maiden. I wish—"

They both fell silent and turned when they heard a heavy door open and close. A moment later Pierce and Bella came shuffling back down the hallway. Bella's crystal blue eyes were reddened and Pierce discreetly dabbed away a few tears of his own as they stepped into the lobby.

"Well..." Pierce still sounded shaken but looked at Bella and stood a bit straighter. "Come on, ladies, I'll take you home. We'll call Mr. Edmonds and try to sort everything out."

"Thanks, honey," Bella whispered and let him lead her to the door. "Come on, Maiden baby, let's go."

"Yeah, I'm coming," Maiden murmured but lingered when they walked outside, she glanced back at David but didn't really know what to say.

He seemed to be having the same trouble. The case was essentially wrapped, as far as it affected them at least, but it still seemed a bit complicated. When he still didn't say anything, she decided to give him a bit of space to get his head around everything that had just happened.

"I'd better go," she said quietly. "I'll see you around."

"Are you serious?" he demanded with slightly widened eyes. "You'll 'see me around'? That's all I get?"

"Well?" She gave a helpless little laugh. "You weren't speaking up. Do I have to do everything?"

"Cute," he said dryly but grinned at the same time; he let his gaze drift over her face. "So, can I call you?"

"I guess so," she said warmly as he closed the distance between them and kissed her.

"I hope Bella's okay," he whispered as he kissed her one more time. "I'll talk to you soon."

David winked at her as he stepped away and started walking towards his office. She watched him go for a full second or two and then felt her impatience rear its head again.

"When?" she called after him.

"Give me half an hour?" He glanced back at her and lifted his brows a fraction. "An hour at the most?"

"I'll clear my calendar." She smiled.

CHAPTER TWENTY-EIGHT

Two hours later, the ladies were all sitting around the Harlow's kitchen table. Vonny had met them at the door as soon as they'd walked through it and now they were all enjoying an early, but entirely appropriate, glass of wine. Maiden studied Aunt Bella as she took a sip; her heart squeezed painfully as she looked at the older woman's forlorn expression.

"You spoke with Mr. Edmonds?" she prompted gently.

"Yeah, he was shocked as anything." Bella said glumly. "He's workin' on it all right now, consultin' with some criminal-legal colleague. I still can't believe it, just this mornin' I was packin' for our honeymoon...damn crazy fools."

They were solemnly quiet for a few minutes. Ruffian was asleep in Maiden's arms and Rowdy was gnawing on Vonny's sleeve. Bella and Gloria were staring down at the table, both lost in thought. Until Vonny broke the silence.

"You still get his money, right?" she asked with an anxious frown.

"Yvonne Louise Harlow!" Gloria said angrily. "His body ain't even cold yet!"

"He's not dead, Mom!" Maiden pointed out in a dismayed whisper.

Gloria and Vonny both sank into their chairs and stayed resolutely silent. No one dared to look at Bella until she started making a few muffled, choking noises.

The tacky blunders were enough to start Bella chuckling, before long she was laughing heartily, they all were. The sheer horror and heartbreak of the situation spilled over in a slightly tasteless explosion of hysterical laughter.

"Oh, good heavens!" Bella finally sighed as she pulled a tissue from her cleavage and wiped at her eyes. "Girls, whatever am I gonna do with you?"

"You stay here with us, honey, that's what you do." Gloria patted her hand gently. "For as long as you need to."

"Thanks, Glory." She rested her chin in her hand. "We'll see what happens and where Elvan ends up."

"Hopefully he can go someplace where he can get some...help." As soon as she said it, Maiden wished she hadn't.

"Yeah, that's somethin' to put on the 'thank you' cards." Bella rolled her eyes and mimicked writing into the air. "Kind regards from the groom in his spacious room at the local nut house. Thanks for the lovely chafin' dish."

"Why don't you let me write the cards for you," Maiden offered dryly. "Where's Pierce by the way?"

"Back at his hotel, I think," she murmured. "He's got to head back to Tennessee soon; he's got a business to run. I think he needs some space anyway. He lost a lot more family than I did, after all."

They talked a bit more and Bella stayed long enough to finish her wine before excusing herself to go and lay down. Vonny took the opportunity to slip off to her own room to call Tony, keenly aware that he and Amelia knew nothing about the latest news.

Once they were alone, Gloria glanced at her youngest daughter hopefully.

"So," she bounced in her seat, "have you spoken with David yet?"

"Yes." Maiden nodded. "We're going out next Saturday."

"Finally!" Gloria laughed happily and clapped her hands. "Well done, baby!"

Maiden smiled a little shyly, her thoughts lingered on David and her smile grew.

He'd be busy for several days sorting through the details of the case, even with a confession there would be a lot of loose ends and unanswered questions. That was okay. They'd been flirting and keeping each other guessing for months, she could wait another week. Not that she planned to leave him alone entirely until then.

***

David sighed heavily as he walked back into his office and shut the door firmly behind him. He'd just spent another exhausting hour trying to get some lucid information from Elvan.

The man had declined noticeably, both mentally and physically, in the few days since his guilt came to light. He seemed to understand that what he did was wrong but was also strangely comfortable with it. David had finally had enough and left him to consult with his bemused lawyer.

He glanced at his desk and arched a brow when he saw a small white gift bag tied with a narrow red ribbon. There was no card.

Curious, he sat down in his chair and looked the bag over for a moment before untying the dainty bow. He peered into it and found two of his ties folded and tucked neatly inside.

He smiled as he pulled them out and set them aside, noting that his blue silk tie, the one Maiden took after the reception, was conspicuously missing. At the bottom of the bag was a small box with a note sitting on top.

He pulled them both out and opened the carefully folded sheet of paper.

I'm afraid I can't return your best tie just yet, I still need it, so I've replaced it. At least this one matches your handkerchief.

Maiden

David was grinning as he opened the box. Nestled inside was a pristine white necktie. Right on the wide, blade-shaped tip was Maiden's perfect lip print in cherry red. He ran a hand over his face and then rubbed the back of his neck.

"What are you doing to me, woman?" he asked softly under his breath as he touched a finger to the silky fabric.

Saturday suddenly felt much too far away.

JOIN THE FUN!

Sign up to my mailing list to get your **free** copy of Blood and Money – A Maiden Harlow Mystery Prequel! It's a fun and twisty mini-mystery that's only available to subscribers!

My newsletters are geared towards book news, writing insights and sneak peeks of new content. If you're interested in hearing from me now and again as well as the **free** eBook, just head to my website, **https://camillesharpbooks.com**, where you can sign up!

THANK YOU!

Thank you for reading Maiden of Honor! This was an exciting book to write for various reasons. I do love the drama of a wedding, and the complicated issues of the Hedgewick clan lent itself easily to murder!

I hope you enjoyed the mystery, the growth in Maiden and David's relationship and the time spent in Riley Manor. It's a very special old house that was fun to wander through as I wrote this story.

If you did enjoy the book, it would be so helpful if you left a review. Publishing is a tough business and it's easy for indie authors like myself to get overlooked. Your reviews make a difference, and they're much appreciated.

If you feel inclined, here's a link that will take you right to the review page: http://www.amazon.com/review/create-review?&asin=B0DB SVQCHN. I appreciate your time, and I hope you had fun joining Maiden on her latest adventure.

Warm regards,

Camille

ALSO BY CAMILLE SHARP

<u>The Maiden Harlow Cozy Mysteries</u>

Murder Checks Inn

A Fair Chance of Murder

Pretty Little Princesses

Maiden of Honor

Treasure Hunt

<u>Coming soon!</u>

Deathly Cold

Faraway Kingdoms

ABOUT CAMILLE SHARP

I've been writing for as long as I can remember, but my serious storytelling began in my teens. I dabble in mystery, fantasy and speculative fiction.

I write from many perspectives – heroine, hero, side characters and sometimes even villains. I like to write about heroines that are smart, sexy and basically kind. All the things I want to be if I ever decide to grow up.

While I weave romance into most of my books, I love to explore other relationships as well. Friendships and the various bonds within families are deeply important and I draw on my personal history for a lot of it.

I firmly believe that books are vital, that our imaginations need to be protected and cultivated, and that boredom has the potential to breed creativity.

One of the most useful lessons I've learned along the way is that if you're in a situation where you can't really conquer or surrender, stories give you the option to **escape**. Even if only for a few hours. I hope I can help transport you someplace you'd like to be.

Camille

www.ingramcontent.com/pod-product-compliance
Lightning Source LLC
Chambersburg PA
CBHW050613170726
48283CB00001B/234